WHO DARES DEFY CONAN?

One of the bandits stood. His beard was forked, stiffened to point forward and dyed bright red. "Things are not as they were, Conan. You were caught like a fool, and such a one cannot be our leader." He gestured to the man next to him, who stood slowly, never letting his eyes leave Conan's. "Arghun is our leader now. He's twice the man you are, northern savage!"

"Aye," said the other man, a burly brute dressed in blood-stained leathers, his face a mass of scars. "I lead now." His hand rested on the hilt of a short, curved sword.

"Is that so?" Conan said quietly.

Arghun began to draw his sword, but before it cleared the scabbard, the Cimmerian, quick as a tiger, leapt across the fire and buried his dagger in the man's groin. With a vicious twist, he turned the curved edge upward and ripped up until the blade stopped at Arghun's breastbone. Arghun screamed once, then fell, spilling entrails.

Kasim was stunned by the sudden, savage violence. The Cimmerian jumped upon him, wrapping his massive hands around the man's neck, and wrenching them in different directions. There was a popping sound. Suddenly the forked, red beard was pointing straight back over the man's spine.

Conan dropped the man, faced the rest of the bandits and said, "Is everyone satisfied?"

Conan Adventures by Tor Books

Conan the Invincible by Robert Jordan
Conan the Defender by Robert Jordan
Conan the Unconquered by Robert Jordan
Conan the Triumphant by Robert Jordan
Conan the Magnificent by Robert Jordan
Conan the Victorious by Robert Jordan
Conan the Destroyer by Robert Jordan
Conan the Valorous by John Maddox Roberts
Conan the Fearless by Steve Perry
Conan the Renegade by Leonard Carpenter
Conan the Raider by Leonard Carpenter
Conan the Champion by John Maddox Roberts
Conan the Defiant by Steve Perry
Conan the Warlord by Leonard Carpenter
Conan the Marauder by John Maddox Roberts
Conan the Valiant by Roland Green
Conan the Hero by Leonard Carpenter
Conan the Bold by John Maddox Roberts
Conan the Indomitable by Steve Perry
Conan the Free Lance by Steve Perry
Conan the Great by Leonard Carpenter
Conan the Guardian by Roland Green
Conan the Formidable by Steve Perry
Conan the Outcast by Leonard Carpenter
Conan the Relentless by Roland Green
Conan the Rogue by John Maddox Roberts
Conan the Savage by Leonard Carpenter
Conan of the Red Brotherhood by Leonard Carpenter
Conan and the Gods of the Mountain by Roland Green
Conan and the Treasure of Python by John Maddox Roberts
Conan, Scourge of the Bloody Coast by Leonard Carpenter
Conan and the Manhunters by John Maddox Roberts
Conan at the Demon's Gate by Roland Green
Conan the Gladiator by Leonard Carpenter
Conan and the Amazon by John Maddox Roberts
Conan and the Mists of Doom by Roland Green
Conan the Hunter by Sean A. Moore
Conan and the Emerald Lotus by John Hocking
Conan and the Shaman's Curse by Sean A. Moore
Conan at the Demon's Gate by Roland Greene
Conan and the Grim Grey God by Sean A. Moore

AND THE MANHUNTERS

BY

JOHN MADDOX ROBERTS

A TOM DOHERTY ASSOCIATES BOOK
NEW YORK

CONAN AND THE MANHUNTERS

Cover art by Ken Kelly
Maps by Chazaud

A Tor Book
Published by Tom Doherty Associates, Inc.
175 Fifth Avenue
New York, N.Y. 10010

ISBN: 0-812-52489-6

First edition: October 1994

Printed in the United States of America

0 9 8 7 6 5 4 3 2

To Kendric Madog Mygatt
His parents Kenneth and Marlenn
and brother Zachary
with Love from Granddad.

WESTERN SEA
VANAHEIM
ASGARD
CIMMERIA
PICTISH WILDERNESS
BORDER KINGDOM
BOSSONIAN MARCHES
GUNDERLAND
TAURAN
Velitrium
Galparan
Tanasul
NEMEDIA
AQUILONIA
Numalia
Belverus
Black R.
Thunder R.
BOSSONIA
Shirki R.
Tarantia
Shamar
Tyborg R.
Ianthe
OPHIR
Alimane R.
Kordava
ZINGARA
Red R.
Khorshemish
KOTH
RABIRIAN MTS.
Khorotas R.
ARGOS
BARACHA ISLES
Eruk
SHEM
Messantia
Asgalun
River Styx
Khemi
Luxur
STYGIA
SIPTAH'S ISLE
Sukhmet
KUSH
DARFAR
Xuthal
BLACK
Zarkheba R.
Xuchotl
CHAZAUD

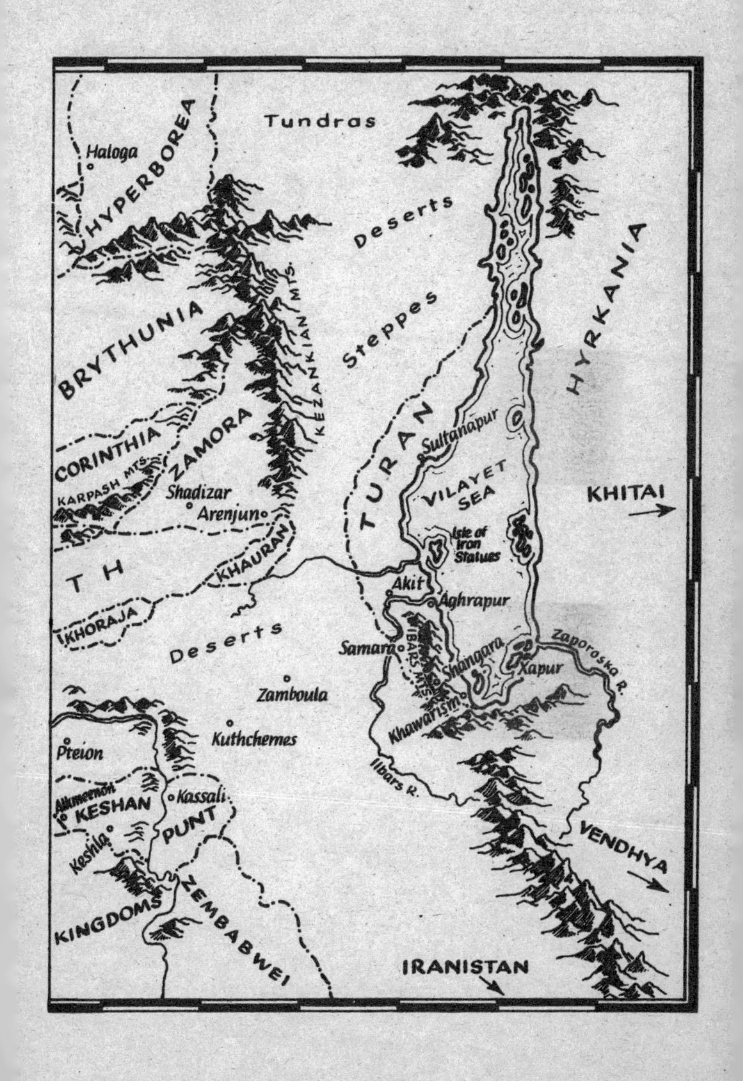

Tundras
Haloga
HYPERBOREA
Deserts
KEZANKIAN MTS.
Steppes
BRYTHUNIA
HYRKANIA
CORINTHIA
ZAMORA
TURAN
Sultanapur
KARPASH MTS.
VILAYET SEA
Shadizar
Arenjun
KHITAI
Isle of Iron Statues
KHAURAN
Akit
Aghrapur
KHORAJA
Deserts
Zaporoska R.
Samara
ILBARS MTS.
Shangara
Xapur
Zamboula
Khawarism
Kuthchemes
Pteion
Ilbars R.
Kassali
KESHAN
PUNT
VENDHYA
Keshla
KINGDOMS
ZEMBABWEI
IRANISTAN

One

The sensations were familiar: the blazing pain in his head, the raging thirst, the itchy irritation of rotten straw beneath his back, the pervasive stench. At least being able to sense all these things, however unpleasant, meant that he was alive. It was not the first time the Cimmerian had awakened in a dungeon. Of course, there were certain dungeons where being alive was not an advantage.

By straining the muscles in his face, he managed to wrench his gummy eyelids open and felt a certain relief when they parted. He knew there was a judge in this province whose favorite punishment was to order a felon's eyelids sewn shut. Through his blurred vision, he could make out stone walls, stone ceiling, and morning light slanting in through the close-set bars of a tiny window high on one wall. He longed to get to that window and breathe some fresh air.

This longing compelled him, slowly and carefully, to sit up. The back of his head, glued by dried blood, parted reluctantly from the floor, and as it came free, a handful of straw remained plastered to his black mane. He heard a clink of metal as he moved and looked down at his scarred hands and heavily muscled arms. Manacles had been fastened around his thick, swordsman's wrists, the dingy brown iron secured by shiny new rivets. Similar fetters confined his legs. A quick touch told him that another ring encircled his corded neck. All the rings were attached by chains to staples buried deep in the stone floor and walls.

Clearly, he had impressed someone as a dangerous man. That made sense, because he, Conan of Cimmeria, was the most dangerous man he knew. He managed to stand, but he found that there was no chance of reaching the window. Standing, he could move no more than a stride in any direction. As the blood began to flow freely through his veins, he became fully aware and tried to remember what had brought him to this pass.

The face of a woman swam into his consciousness. Minna? No, Minata. He had come into the town the night before to visit her, as had become his custom. He had ridden in from the hills to the south, swathed in a hooded desert robe. There was a price on his head throughout this kingdom. He had intended to clear out months ago, to ride south into Iranistan, but he stayed on because of the woman. Even in his pain and predicament, the memory of her huge gray eyes and raven hair, her ripely lissome body, still stirred him.

He had passed the gate guard with a small bribe, such as was customary in this land when a traveler wished to pass through the foot-gate after sunset. He had made his way through the mazelike huddle of tenements in the Foreigners' Quarter, climbed a rickety stair and rapped upon the door of Minata the Zamoran. She was a "priestess" in the ill-famed Temple of Ishtar. He cared not what she did with her days so long as she saved her nights for him.

The door had opened and the woman had stood before him, beautiful as ever in the candlelight, her body scarcely veiled by a robe of Vendhyan gauze. But on her lips was no welcome for him. As he stepped within the room, he saw her eyes widen with dread.

"Conan, I . . ." His memory of the night ended with those words. Whoever had struck him from behind had had a strong arm and a thorough knowledge of his craft, because Conan knew that he must have lost consciousness instantly.

So Minata had sold him. He would settle things with her, if he ever got loose from these chains and these walls. He cursed himself for a fool. He knew better than to trust any woman, especially where such a reward was involved. And yet, knowing that, it was something he often did, usually to his regret.

"Jailer!" he shouted, his voice raspy from his dry throat. He rattled his chains and took the opportunity to try their strength, his muscles standing in chiseled relief as he strained at the restraining rings. They were old and rusty, but they were sound. He would not get loose through his strength alone.

A man shuffled back along a narrow corridor and came to the barred door. "What do you want, barbarian?" He was a fat lout with patchy, graying hair and a mouth full of brown teeth.

"Water," Conan bellowed.

"Why?"

"Because I thirst, you fool!"

"What is that to me? You will die soon and it will be a waste of water." He turned and walked away with a jingle of the keys fastened to his belt by a stout ring.

Conan could not argue with such logic, but he raged anyway, his fury doubled by the fact that he could do absolutely nothing, not even move. Then he was distracted by a voice close by.

"Be easy, man. The wretch will bring you food and water presently. You are not to die just yet. The viceroy is saving you for a special occasion."

The voice came from a wall to Conan's right. By squinting,

he could just make out a face regarding him through a small, square hole in the wall. "Who are you?" Conan grunted.

"Osman the Shangaran, here through a shameful miscarriage of justice." A lopsided grin gave irony to the words.

In spite of himself, Conan grinned back. "I'll wager you're even more worthy of this place than I."

"The judge thought so," Osman sighed. "And all because his wife's jewels somehow appeared in my pouch when I was arrested."

"And why were you arrested?" Conan asked, wanting some amusement.

"Some fellows accused me of using loaded dice in a friendly game!" His eyes went wide with wounded innocence. "I offered them my dagger in amends, but in their clumsiness, they managed to fall against the blade and were injured. A mere misunderstanding, followed by an accident."

"And how did you explain the presence of the jewels?"

"What could be simpler? Clearly, a baleful wizard wished to do me harm and placed them there through his black arts."

"Was that the best you could do?" the Cimmerian asked. "You deserve to hang for being such a poor liar."

"I feel pity for judges," Osman said. "They hear the same excuses over and over again. I hoped, by affording this one some amusement, to mitigate his wrath, especially since he suspects I gained access to his wife's belongings in a manner that casts doubt upon her virtue."

"Enough of this," Conan said, giving his bonds a final tug. "What was this you said about me being saved for a special occasion?"

"Ah, that! Know then that Torgut Khan, the viceroy, is preparing a great festival to celebrate the dedication of the new Temple of Ahriman. Besides the usual feasting and revelry, there is to be a mass execution of prisoners to clear out the jails and start the new year with a clean slate. He has been saving felons for months and has brought in a famous torturer from Aghrapur. You are to be the centerpiece."

"I see. And when is this great occasion to be celebrated?"

"In a fortnight. So you see, the jailer must bring you water soon. He dares not risk harm to Torgut Khan's prize exhibit!"

The chamber was fitfully illuminated by candles set in sconces of bronze wrought in the shapes of serpents or of flowering vines. Two men sat with a small table between them. In the center of the table was a pitcher of wine and before each man was a cup of hammered silver.

"I do not like this plan," said the elder of the two. He was a portly, heavy-featured man in clothes of the finest silk. "It is too complicated. It leaves much to chance."

"It leaves nothing to chance," said the other. On his body was a cuirass of etched steel and on his head was a spired helmet. Its veil of fine, silvered steel-mesh framed a harsh, hawk-featured face. His drooping black mustache framed a mouth that was no more than a tight, straight line. "I know men and I know gold, and I know what one will do to get the other. Leave me to my work and we will bag the lot."

"There will be trouble," mused Torgut Khan, "and bloodshed."

"Worthless blood," snorted the other.

"Be that as it may, it will mar my festival. I wish to make it especially magnificent, an occasion that will be remembered forever."

"And so it shall be," said the armored man impatiently. He took a drink to calm himself. One hand caressed the ivory hilt of his long, curved sword. The nicked, age-yellowed grip showed many years of hard use. "Think of it," he went on. "After a brief excitement, no more than an entertaining break in the ceremonies, you will be able to put the lot of them upon the scaffold even now being erected before the new temple and have them all put to death as imaginatively as that torturer—whom you have brought in at such great personal expense—can devise."

Torgut Khan's eyes glittered. "It would be a fitting cap to the festivities."

"You see? And I need hardly tell you how pleased his majesty will be that you have suppressed brigandage so skillfully."

Torgut Khan nodded tentatively, then decisively. He slapped the table with his open palm. "Let it be so, then. You have my leave to carry out your plan."

The man rose from the table and saluted, clasping a fist to his steel-sheathed breast. "At once, Excellency."

"And, Sagobal?" the viceroy said as his minion was about to leave.

The man turned, his hand on the latch. "Excellency?"

"Do not fail, else you forfeit your own head." The viceroy's murky gaze was torpid but menacing, like that of a fat, lazy dragon who yet had power and a poisoned breath.

Sagobal inclined his head. "Yes, Excellency."

He left the chamber and shut the door behind him. Only then did he let his face express his feelings. The guardsmen he passed stared rigidly ahead, anxious to avoid the notice of their commander. He was dangerous in the best of moods, and when he was like this, he could be deadly. Wine on a man's breath, a speck of rust on a spear-point, even a dangling bootlace at such a time, were sufficient provocation for him to draw that ivory-hilted sword and sweep a man's head from his shoulders so swiftly that he was wiping the blood from his blade before onlookers realized he had set hand to hilt.

Sagobal was furious that the man he had served so loyally and well treated him with disdain. It was ever the same. The viceroy was always a royal cousin or an influential nobleman and came to his powerful and lucrative office through family connections. Whether he was an able administrator had no bearing on the matter. By contrast, Sagobal, a fine soldier, would never be more than a captain of the provincial guard. That was because he was the mere second son of a minor landowner and had earned his rank through skill, courage and a life of hard soldiering.

No more, by Set! No more! he thought as he strode toward

his quarters. *I'll not serve another fat, perfumed courtier who bought his rank with gold and flattery!*

Two men sat upon a bench outside the door to Sagobal's quarters and at his approach, they rose and bowed. "Come with me," he said peremptorily. He passed within and they followed.

Inside, he doffed his helm and set it carefully upon a stand atop his arms chest. His black hair lay sleekly against his skull. He turned to glare at the two men. They were nondescript, wearing the clothes of ordinary townsmen, but they possessed skills of which he had need.

"Here is what you must do," he said.

By the third day of his captivity, the Cimmerian thought he would go mad. There were others imprisoned in the dungeon, but only the man in the next cell, Osman, could he see and hear. At least the fellow was an amusing companion, with an endless store of tales and scurrilous gossip, mostly concerning the officials of Turan. Also their wives, about whom he seemed to know more than was healthy for a man who valued his neck.

"Enough," Conan said after a particularly unedifying tale about the former viceroy and how he had punished his unfaithful wife. "We have to find a way out of this place, else we'll grace the temple dedication, and I've little taste for that."

"You have been saying that for three days," Osman pointed out, "yet your chains bind you as tightly as ever."

"You are such a fount of cleverness I was hoping you had come up with an idea."

"What about your band of brigands?" Osman asked. "Might they not come hither and rescue you?"

"Them!" Conan barked a laugh. "The only thing that will tempt them here is to see me killed on the scaffold."

"I thought you roving robbers were a band of brothers," Osman said in mock reproach.

"Aye, the same as the cutpurses and assassins of the cities," Conan said. "They valued me for my strong swordarm and my skill at raiding. Once you are separated from such men, though, they do not pine for you."

"How tragic," Osman said.

Conan sat on the floor and tried to come up with some stratagem that would allow him to escape. Every thought was foiled by the simplicity of the arrangements. The bonds were too strong for him to break and they were too short to let him get close to the walls, window or door of the cell. The keeper never got near enough to seize. By simple neglect, he was kept secure.

He was roused from his brooding by the sound of voices outside. He knew that the cell window opened onto ground level on a small, paved square. The sun shone through it in the morning but by mid-afternoon, it lay in shade, and people sometimes stood there to escape the heat of the day. He could make out the shape of a pair of feet wearing military boots.

"No wine!" said one man. "What sort of festival is it to be if we cannot even drink?"

"Not until the treasure is secured upon the third day, by Set!" said the other. "Only then can we soldiers stand down from alert and take part. To disobey is death."

"If Sagobal promises death, he will deliver, by Asura! But what treasure is this? I have heard of none such."

"Keep your voice down," said the other. "I stood watch at the treasury yesterday and I heard the clerks speaking of it. All the tax revenues of the province, they said, are to be concentrated in the vault beneath the new temple. At another time, it might attract attention on the road, but with all the wagons coming to the festival, no one will notice. Until every last coin is in the vault and Torgut Khan has put the royal seal on it, not a drop of wine for us!"

Presently the men wandered off and Conan was left to his brooding.

"Heard you that, Cimmerian?" Osman hissed.

"I heard, much good does it do me now."

Osman's voice grew cunning, insinuating. "Such treasure might tempt your robber band, might it not?"

"Surely. What of that? They could accomplish nothing against the whole garrison, which is sure to be on alert."

"But you are a clever raider," Osman said, again insinuatingly. "Surely you could find a way to purloin it."

"You chatter idly," Conan said. "My band is in the hills. I am here, and likely to stay here until the festival, at which time I will have things on my mind other than treasure."

"Suppose I were able to get you out of here?" Osman asked.

Conan hissed. "You have a plan?"

"Perhaps, perhaps. Of course, I would require certain assurances from you."

"Assurances?" Conan echoed, infuriated. "Talk sense, man!"

"What I say makes perfect sense to me. I want a share of the treasure."

"Are you not getting a little ahead of yourself?" the Cimmerian said. "You, too, are a prisoner."

"Not for long. If I help you escape, will you come take the treasure and give me a double share?"

Conan decided to humor the man. "Aye. A double share for you if you can get me out of here. Now, how do you plan to do this?"

"There is a way. I am not chained like you. It would be no great difficulty for me to overpower the stupid jailer and get his keys. But to get out of here, I would have to get through the guardroom atop the stairs. This prospect has given me some pause."

"And what is your solution?"

"You are a great warrior. If I get you loose, can you fight our way out through the guardroom?"

"Aye. There remains the little problem of these chains," the Cimmerian said, rattling them significantly.

"That is the one difficulty. Atop the landing, before the guardroom, there rests an anvil used in fastening and breaking the fetters worn by dangerous prisoners such as yourself. If I can get it down here, with a hammer and a chisel, can you carve off your iron jewelry?"

"By Crom!" Conan said, feeling a stirring of hope. "If you can get that anvil down here, with the hammer and chisel, I will have this iron off faster than a Zamoran harlot gets out of her clothes!" Then, suspiciously: "I can see little of you, but you do not strike me as a powerful man. Can you get this anvil down the stairs before anyone misses the jailer?"

"Well," Osman said, grinning crookedly, "we shall find out, shall we not?"

That night Osman set up a groaning. After an hour of it, the jailer came to investigate.

"What ails you?" he called, shuffling along the dank floor.

"A thousand demons have invaded my belly!" Osman cried. "It is the poisoned food you have brought me! Get me to a leech, else I shall die and you will take my place on the scaffold, rogue!" He vented another prolonged groan.

"It is not as bad as all that," grumbled the jailer. He came to the door of Conan's cell and raised his torch. Conan feigned sleep, making sure that his fetters were visible from the door. Satisfied that the Cimmerian was secure, the jailer went back to Osman's cell. There was a rattle of a key in a lock, the sounds of shuffling and low, grumbling talk, then of a blow and a sharp cry, then of another blow.

"I am free, Conan!" Osman said.

"No you are not. You are still down here with me. Get me out of these irons and I will make you free."

Osman came to the door with the key ring and worked his way through the keys until he found the right one. The door swung wide. "I go to fetch the anvil now," he said.

"Less talk and more action," Conan advised. "Hurry!"

The thief dashed off and Conan heard the patter of his feet skipping up the stairs. Then there was a scraping, grinding noise, then a groan. It seemed to go on forever, the groaning and the scraping, with frequent clanks of heavy steel against stone. The Cimmerian was in an agony of impatience until the thief appeared again in his cell doorway, staggering with the weight of the anvil cradled in his arms. He all but collapsed at Conan's feet.

Conan grasped the anvil in his powerful hands and righted it. "Quick, man, the hammer and chisel!"

"Think you," Osman gasped, "this anvil was such a trifling burden that I could bear the other tools in my free hand?"

Conan yanked him to his feet. "Run fetch them ere I wring your neck!"

Osman staggered off, gasping and wheezing. A few minutes later he returned with a short-handled sledge in one hand, a notched chisel in the other. "I trust you know how to use these?"

"My father was a blacksmith," Conan said, snatching them away from the thief. "I learned the hammer before I learned the sword."

Kneeling, he set one foot on the anvil and placed the chisel against a link of the leg-chain next to the ring. With a single explosive blow of the hammer, he hewed through the resisting iron. The sound rang through the dungeon like the tolling of a great bell.

"They'll hear that above," Osman said fretfully. "Hurry!"

"Do I look like I am wasting time?" Conan demanded. He repeated the action with his other ankle ring. Bending forward as far as he could, he sheared through the chain that bound his neck ring, leaving a few spans of chain dangling. Then he laid his left wrist on the anvil and positioned the chisel. "Hold this chisel," he ordered.

Osman took it gingerly. "You will not miss and strike my—"

Conan did not bother to reassure him, but pounded the top of the chisel, breaking the chain. With a curse, Osman dropped the chisel and shook his stinging hands. Now Conan took the hammer in his left hand.

"Again!" he ordered.

Osman picked up the chisel doubtfully. "Can you hammer with your left hand? Surely you might miss." Then they heard stirrings and voices from above. "Mitra help me," Osman said, positioning the chisel and shutting his eyes tightly. With a brutal sweep of the hammer, the last chain was severed.

The Cimmerian laughed as he sprang up. "Free!"

"Free?" Osman said frantically. "We are in a dungeon and the guards are coming!"

Conan took the hammer in one hand and the chisel in the other. "Then we had best be going!" He charged out through the door of his cell, Osman close behind him.

Up the stairs they went, to meet a pair of astonished guardsmen coming down. The guard in front aimed a sword-blow at Conan's head, but the Cimmerian batted the blade aside with the chisel and in the next instant, brained the man, his hammer crunching the metal of the stout helmet as if it had been parchment. Before the man could fall, Conan shoved him back up the stair to catch the other guard across the legs. The man threw his legs wide to retain his balance and as he did, the Cimmerian rammed the chisel through his breastbone, where it spit his heart and buried its blunt edge deep into the spine beneath.

As the man fell, Conan snatched his sword, then bounded over both bodies and into the guardroom beyond. There, three other guardsmen were scrambling into their harness and snatching up weapons. One began to raise a shout, but the sword in the Cimmerian's hand swept across his gullet, ending the cry in mid-syllable. Another tried to run out the guardroom's exit door, but Conan hurled the massive hammer and smashed the back of the man's skull like an eggshell.

The last guard managed to get a shield on his arm and began to raise an ax. Conan's first blow sheared away the shield and much of his arm. The second cleft his skull. Abruptly, the guardroom was silent.

"Five men!" Osman said with awe. "Five men slain in the space of a few breaths!"

"You were of cursed little help," Conan said, availing himself of the best weapons to be had in the room. None of the helmets or clothing were of a size for him, so he had to remain content with his loincloth and a full panoply of weapons, together with their supporting harness.

"But you were doing so well!" Osman protested. "What had I to contribute?"

"A horse, for one thing. Get outside, find us two mounts quickly and bring them here."

"By myself?"

"Aye, by yourself. Look at me!" The near-naked barbarian's giant frame was scratched and bruised, his hair matted and his overall appearance not at all improved by his stay in the dungeon. "I could not get five paces from the door ere some townsman raised the alarm. Nobody will mistake these iron bands for jewelry. Go steal us some horses, and be quick about it!"

The small man dashed out the door and Conan waited, fretting and expecting at any second the harness-jingle of guardsmen running to avenge their slain companions. Then he heard the clatter of two horses approaching at the gallop. His perfectly attuned hearing told him that one was ridden, the other not. Seconds later, Osman reined up before the door, astride a splendid charger and leading another. Both mounts wore cavalry saddles.

"Quick, mount up!" Osman cried. "There are two troopers back at the inn who are very angry with me and coming this way!" His urging was unnecessary. Before the third word was out of his mouth, the Cimmerian was in the saddle, his heels digging into his horse's flanks. With a whoop, Osman galloped after.

"Look at this one, Captain," said a guardsman. The second body was dragged from the dungeon, and the others gaped.

"By Mitra!" said another. "Is that a chisel buried in his chest? Thrust clean through the brisket, by Set!" He set a foot against the corpse, grasped the protruding shank of the tool and pulled. It would not come free. "Set take it!" the man said admiringly. "It's buried in his backbone! What arm could strike such a blow?"

"Conan's, fool," said the first speaker. "The brigand leader is as strong as men say."

Sagobal examined the body and saw that it was true. "Five guards slain?" he queried.

"Aye, and the jailer," said the first speaker. "That one has a broken neck."

Sagobal pointed at four men in succession. "You four take over guarding this place. The rest, haul the bodies away for burial. I shall report to Torgut Khan."

"Do we not pursue, Captain?" asked the first speaker.

"Nay, they have too great a lead and we are stretched too thin with the preparations for the festival. Doubtless we shall see them anon."

The men did his bidding, mystified that the easily enraged Captain Sagobal was taking the incident so philosophically. Shrugging, they did their duties as soldiers without asking questions.

For his own part, Sagobal went to report to Torgut Khan that his prize exhibit had escaped after wreaking slaughter among the guards. His iron-trap mouth bent almost into a smile of satisfaction that all was going according to plan.

Two

It is not far now," Conan said.

"I hope you are right," Osman said, wincing at the pain in his backside. The easy life of a city thief had left him unprepared for the rigors of a hard ride.

The landscape through which they rode was barren and sere, not much of an improvement upon the desert to the south. The place was dominated by vast boulders instead of rolling dunes, and the only vegetation was scrubby brush. The trails between the boulders and cliffs wound in labyrinthine fashion, and nowhere could a man see farther than a few score paces. It was ideal bandit country.

Conan glanced at an overhanging crag of stone. "The scum have grown lax in my absence," he said. "There should be a sentry on yon spur of rock. A man can lie there on his belly like a lizard and see all the approaches."

They rode another few minutes, entering a narrow defile so deep that the clear blue sky was no more than a ribbon overhead, constrained between beetling cliffs. Abruptly, the path opened up and they were in a small canyon with a bubbling spring in its center. The spring ran into a pool with no visible overflow. There was a tang of smoke in the air. A score of men sat around a fire and started to their feet when the two intruders rode into the canyon.

They were a mixed lot: Turanian, Iranistani, and men of a half-dozen desert peoples who ranged the wastelands south of Koth and Turan. They had the predatory look common to outlaws everywhere: gaunt, scarred, many of them branded by the public executioner. More than one had had a hand lopped off for thievery. They regarded the newcomers with uncertainty, except for two men who squatted by the fire and did not rise. These two looked at them with open resentment and hostility.

"Ho, villains!" called the Cimmerian. "This is a poor welcome for your old companion, returned from the dead!" He dismounted and swaggered to the fire. "I know, I know. You are so overcome with joy that you do not know how to put it into words." He stared around at them, but they would not meet his lion gaze. Conan inhaled mightily through flared nostrils.

"I smell dinner cooking, by Set! I've not had real man's food in too long!" He swaggered over to the fire and the others drew back to give him room. A pair of plump, young gazelles roasted over the coals, giving off a savory aroma. The two ill-favored men glared at him over the carcasses. The Cimmerian grinned at them as he drew his dagger and sliced off a generous strip of smoking flesh.

"Arghun, how good to see your sour face again. And I see your toady Kasim is by your side, as always." He tore off a mouthful of flesh with strong, white teeth, chewed for a few moments and swallowed. "I might almost think that you did not rejoice to see me alive."

One of the men stood. His beard was forked, stiffened to point forward and dyed bright red. "Things are not as they were, Conan. You were caught like a fool, and such a one cannot be our leader." He gestured to the man next to him, who stood slowly, never letting his eyes leave Conan's. "Arghun is our leader now. He is twice the man you are, northern savage!"

"Aye," said the other man, a burly brute dressed in blood-stained leathers, his face a mass of scars. "If you want to run with us, you follow as an ordinary member of the band. I lead now." His jaw thrust forth truculently and his hand rested on the hilt of a short, curved sword.

"Is that so?" Conan said, his tone quiet and deadly. "I have been enjoying the viceroy's hospitality, no more. It changes nothing."

"If you think that," Arghun said, "then you are a dead man!" He began to draw his sword, but before it cleared the scabbard, the Cimmerian, quick as a tiger, leapt across the fire and buried his dagger in the man's groin. With a vicious twist, he turned the curved edge upward and ripped up until the blade stopped at Arghun's breastbone. Arghun screamed once, then fell, spilling entrails, across the fire.

Kasim, stunned by the sudden, savage violence, turned to run, but he got no more than a single pace before the Cimmerian sprang upon him, wrapping his massive hands around the man's neck and wrenching them in opposite directions. There was a popping sound and suddenly Kasim's forked red beard was pointing straight back over his spine. His eyes bulged with disbelief, his last view in the mortal world the sight of Conan's face grinning into his own.

Conan raised the flopping corpse and hurled it into the water, where it struck with a mighty splash. Then he went to Arghun's scorching body and wrenched his dagger from the cleft breastbone, wiping its blade on the filthy leathers, staining them yet further. He carved himself another strip of flesh and began to eat.

"Is everyone satisfied?" he growled around the mouthful of gazelle.

"It is good to see you again!" shouted a one-eyed Turanian named Ubo.

"Aye! We all hoped you would come back to us, Conan!" said another, and everyone agreed that this was so.

A desert man waded into the pond and dragged out the body of the unfortunate Kasim. "Shame on you, Conan!" the man scolded. "It is a great sacrilege to defile running water." He wrung out the hem of his brown-and-black-striped robe.

"I'll warrant he made it no sweeter, Auda," Conan said. "But the men provoked me and I lost my temper. Men, this is my friend, Osman. It was his doing that got me out of the dungeon, so he is one of us now."

The men welcomed Osman, but they eyed him with calculation. He walked to Conan's side. "I knew that would happen, after seeing you in action once before. But it puzzles me that they dared defy you, knowing the sort of man you are."

"Huh!" Conan snorted, chewing on a rib. He looked around and said in a low voice: "These dogs? They have the minds of beasts. You have to prove yourself to them every day. Before long, they will have forgotten these two and another of them will think himself my better. Then it will be to do all over again. As you saw, it is best to deal with them quickly and decisively, before defiance spreads."

"I understand," Osman said. He carved off some gazelle and chewed on it, relishing the rich smoky taste. "What now?"

"We plan," Conan said, "and you will help."

"Of course," Osman assured him. "I want only to aid you, as I already have. I will be your right hand." He grinned ingratiatingly.

The Cimmerian stared at him over the near-stripped thigh bone. "I already have a right arm," he reminded Osman.

Sagobal went over his preparations with satisfaction. His own men were well drilled, and the men he had sent for should be arriving soon. He went into the new Temple of Ahriman through its processional door, carved in the likeness of a huge demon's head, the gaping mouth forming its entrance.

The iron spikes of its heavy portcullis formed a set of grotesque fangs for the demon's upper jaw.

New though it was, the interior of the place was oppressive. The only light was provided by small, round windows high in the clerestory. The windows were of scarlet glass, so that the light poured down like sheets of blood. In two rows from entrance to altar stood pillars supporting the roof. The pillars were carved in the form of naked, chained women who were being crushed by the weight they bore on their shoulders, their beautiful, tormented faces twisted with pain.

Sagobal walked between them until he reached the altar. It was in the form of a great nest of writhing snakes, carved with wonderful skill in a style far older than that of the female pillars. In fact, it was of workmanship so ancient that no man in the city, however learned, knew of its provenance. Hard man though he was, the sight of the sinister altar sent a shudder through Sagobal.

For centuries, the site of the new temple had been a pile of rubble. Though it lay on the town square, flanked by fine buildings, no one had ever sought to clear the site and build upon it. There was a vague, ancient legend in the town that any who sought to do so would suffer for his presumption.

Then, two years before, a strange priest had appeared in the city, coincident with Torgut Khan's assumption of the viceroyship. The priest's name was Tragthan, and he appeared in the viceroy's court one day, asking for an audience. Tragthan announced that he was a brother in the ancient Order of Ahriman, and he had come to rebuild the Order's derelict temple.

Torgut Khan had at first been indifferent, but Tragthan proclaimed that the Brotherhood would willingly undertake all expenses. Torgut Khan told him that in such a case, he would have no objection, but there were certain matters of deeds and licensing to be attended to, and these might be facilitated if the priest were to make a contribution toward the renovation of the district treasury, which Torgut Khan had been charged with rebuilding.

Sagobal knew that at a later, private audience, Tragthan had told Torgut Khan that the deep crypt beneath the temple site would serve well as a treasury, and the temple itself would be so strongly built as to be impervious to attack. Torgut Khan saw immediately that this would be to his advantage. He could now pocket the royal monies already advanced for the building of the treasury, together with those already extorted for the same putative project. Sagobal had seen the letters Torgut Khan had sent to the king, claiming that this money had been donated toward building the new temple, thus securing for the crown a treasury at far less expense than projected.

As he pondered these things, Sagobal studied the repellent altar. When the rubble of centuries was cleared away, the altar was uncovered. At first, the workmen fled the disturbing object and refused to go back, despite threats from the priest and the viceroy. In the end, they used convicts to complete the job of uncovering the altar, then wrapping it in heavy cloths so that the workmen would not have to see it as they went about their labors.

As Tragthan promised, a large crypt lay beneath the floor of the temple, unaffected by the passage of centuries. The new temple rose with unusual speed, for the priest seemed to have limitless funds for hiring the best craftsmen and artists, although some of them looked with distaste upon the drawings and plans Tragthan supplied for their guidance. More than one of them, after too much wine in one of the town's many taverns, said that the parchment upon which they were drawn was made of human skin. But Tragthan's generous recompense always eased their sensibilities.

Slowly, Sagobal walked around the horrid altar. Impossibly, the light from all the windows seemed to converge upon it. How, he wondered, could light shine in such a fashion through windows set in different walls? Had the priest set angled mirrors on the roof, to direct the sun's rays in from each direction? He preferred to believe that it was something so easily explained. One serpent-head in the great tangle shone in the red light with especial luridness, as if it were made of a different substance. Unlike the others, its features were a combination of the ophidian and the human. Sagobal reached to touch it.

"Touch not the altar of Ahriman!"

Sagobal whirled and half-drew his blade. Then he slammed it back into its sheath. He prided himself upon his keen hearing, but the priest had come up behind him without sound.

"I did but admire your altar, priest," he said, with poor grace.

"Forgive my abruptness. This is one of the most venerable and sacred relics of my cult. It is to be touched only by consecrated hands." The priest was tall, his form hidden by a rust-colored robe, his features all but concealed by its deep cowl, revealing only a skeletal face and strangely luminous eyes.

"I want to take another look at the crypt," Sagobal said. "The day approaches swiftly."

"Very well. If you will come with me . . ." The priest took a key from within his robe as he led the way to a short stair that went beneath the dais upon which the altar squatted in malevolence. At the bottom of the stair was a pair of heavy bronze doors, richly worked with scenes from the myth-cycle of Ahriman, God of Darkness, and his endless struggle with Ormazd, God of Light. By the doors a candle burned in a sconce, and Sagobal took the taper as Tragthan unlocked and swung wide the portals.

Beyond the bronze doors was another stair, hewn, as was the whole passage, from the solid stone in unthinkable antiquity. The crude marks of the workmen's tools were still plain upon the walls and ceiling. Sagobal knew that this was a particularly hard stone, and he knew also that the greenish stains left in the rough gouges meant that the tools had been made of soft copper. The builders must have had an inhuman lack of concern for the passing of time, for the formation of the passage and the crypt beneath had undoubtedly consumed centuries. It would have meant decades for men with tools of iron.

The long descent terminated in a vast, echoing chamber hewn from the same living stone. The chamber was so large that the light of the single candle was swallowed by the gloom. Sagobal walked to a wall and began to pace along it, turning at right angles each time the wall met another. These walls were better finished than those of the passage, and they were carved with a maze of geometric designs that drew and twisted the vision until he had to look away, sickened.

Sagobal realized that he had not yet returned to his starting-place even though he had taken more than four of the right-angled turns. That was not possible. He decided he must have been distracted by the puzzling designs on the walls and walked right past his starting-place. Like the strange light in the temple, it was easier not to think about it. Whatever the explanation, the crypt seemed sufficiently large.

"It will do," he said. "The passage and stair seem to be the only means of exit."

"The only means any ordinary man could use," Tragthan said, obliquely.

"As long as it will keep treasure in and men out," Sagobal said brusquely. "Let's get out of here. This gloom oppresses me."

They climbed the stair, and Sagobal avoided looking at the crudely hewn walls. Everything about the place was steeped in ancient evil, even the new structure above.

"Will there be . . . irregularity in the coming festival?" the priest asked.

"What mean you?" Sagobal said.

"I mean that my Brotherhood offered the use of the crypt of Ahriman for the viceroy's treasury. If it is to be used for some nefarious purpose—" he paused significantly "—that could be unfortunate."

"Why should that be?" Sagobal asked impatiently. "Is your god not a being of evil and darkness? Does he not thrive on the misdeeds of men and rejoice in bloodshed?"

"He does, indeed. But his priests do not relish surprises."

"If you are easily surprised, Tragthan, you should find some gentler god to serve. Good day to you." They emerged from the crypt and Sagobal strode briskly between the caryatids, toward the clean light spilling in through the doorway.

"I shall see you again at the festival," Tragthan said gloomily.

Sagobal felt intensely relieved as he walked out of the temple, and he cursed the day Torgut Khan agreed to its rebuilding. Still, it might serve his own purposes. The bright sunlight washed over the plaza, cleansing it of the ancient, inhuman evil that radiated from the temple. Sagobal breathed deep of the clean air and scanned the busy, crowded scene. To the usual throng of hawkers and travelers had been added the temporary booths of vendors drawn by the upcoming festival, the mountebanks who performed for the gawkers, the cutpurses, gamblers and whores who preyed on all alike. In this remote end of southern Turan, a dozen tongues were spoken by folk from Hyrkania, Vendhya, Iranistan and the nameless sheikhdoms and principalities of the nearby deserts. Many caravans passed through this town of Shahpur, rounding the southern tip of the Vilayet, coming through the passes of the great southern range, faring across the desert from Koth, Punt and Zembabwei.

Then Sagobal saw the sort of evil he preferred, the sort untouched by gods, priests and magic—the sort provided by men. Through the Arch of Good Fortune, whence the Samara Road emptied into the plaza, a file of horsemen came riding. They made no uproar and their horses ambled along at a walking pace, but all gave them room. These, Sagobal knew, had to be the men he awaited. Smoothing his long mustaches with a gold-ringed finger, he walked down the temple steps to meet them.

Sagobal was one of the best-known figures in the town, and feared above all others. Though he walked without a guard, people parted before him like fishing-smacks before the prow of a warship. The lead rider espied him and raised his hand for a halt. Sagobal saw about a score of riders behind the man; they appeared to be a hard-bitten lot.

The guard commander stopped before the leader's mount and said nothing for a full minute. The man was a huge brute, with a battered, blue-eyed face. From beneath the edge of his steel cap, graying blond hair hung to his bulky shoulders. He wore neither tunic nor shirt, but went bare-chested, displaying a powerful, scarred torso. His forearms were wrapped with leather straps, plated on the outsides with iron. The back of each hand was protected by an iron plate with spikes over the knuckles, but the harness left the fingers bare. A belt of thick leather five inches wide, studded with bronze nails, supported a heavy knife in a fur sheath and a curved, wide-bladed sword.

"You would be Sagobal?" the man said.

"I would be," Sagobal affirmed, continuing to stare the man down.

"I am Berytus of Aquilonia. You sent for me." His voice was a deep rumble, almost without inflection.

"So I did. Your men may take your mounts to the guard stables. One of my guards will lead them. Then have them report back here. As for you, come to my quarters."

Berytus dismounted and handed his reins to a Kothian even larger than himself. The Kothian's face was black-bearded to his tiny dark eyes, and his dense black hair hung almost to his elbows. He grunted something to the others and they sat back, waiting.

Sagobal walked to his headquarters in the military wing of the viceregal palace. He instructed a guard to take Berytus's men to the stables and find them housing in the royal barracks, and told another to send food for himself and his guest. The men obeyed with swift, silent efficiency.

Inside, Sagobal doffed his steel-veiled helmet and sat at his table, gesturing for Berytus to take the chair opposite his. The Aquilonian sank into the chair and Sagobal poured wine for both of them into goblets of hammered silver. As his guest drank, Sagobal made a quick assessment of the man. He had the look of a pit-fighter. It was not a trade that commonly attracted men of intelligence, but this one had built a certain reputation in other sorts of work. Besides his wide belt, he wore fur-topped boots and a clout of deerskin. Thus were displayed his many scars, of which the man was clearly proud.

"The military governor of Sultanapur has written me saying that you gave him good service," Sagobal began.

"Aye." Berytus leaned back and hooked his thumbs in his belt. "There was a band of crackbrained revolutionaries holding out in the hills north of there. It took us three months to locate all their hideouts and discover which peasants were hiding and supporting them. Once we had them located, we set about driving them back down into the lowlands. First we burned out all the peasants who helped them, then we destroyed their hideouts and caches of supplies. When they got together to fight us, we drove them down to where the governor's men could catch them. The governor hanged the lot."

"You seem to understand your work," Sagobal commended.

"I understand many kinds of work. I was a pit-fighter, but the king shut down all the fighting-pits. I took to slave-raiding in Argos and Shem. Then I began leading my band in catching runaway slaves. That was lucrative, for masters will pay far more for the return of a trained slave than for a new-caught barbarian. Now we serve local governors and magistrates, hunting down bandits and insurrectionists who are too difficult for the regular troops to find."

"That is just what I need. Ah, here is our repast." Sagobal held his silence while the two of them dealt with the food set before them. When the Aquilonian was gnawing on the last rib, he continued.

"Of late I have been plagued by a band of robbers. They have infested the hills roundabout for years, preying mostly on caravans, but a while back they began to strike the local towns, taking the hoards of wealthy merchants, even appropriating royal treasuries and payrolls. Not haphazard attacks, mind you, but skilled, well-planned raids."

"New leadership?" Berytus asked.

"Correct. Have you ever heard of a man called Conan of Cimmeria?"

Berytus's brutish face registered surprise. "Aye, by reputation. He's a thief and a mercenary. I've run into word of him in a score of places, but never this far east. What brings him to these parts?"

"Who knows what leads the steps of such a man? Whatever it was, he fared hither and began to plague my days. I trapped him once, and would have hanged him forthwith, but my master, the Viceroy Torgut Khan, wanted to make the hanging the centerpiece of his upcoming festival, so the brute was locked in the dungeon. He broke out, slaying five of my men in the process."

Berytus grunted. "Aye, you lock up a man like that one at your peril. I have known many such, and they should be killed at first opportunity."

"I know that well. Anyway, I wish to bag the lot of them all at once. My men are adequate, and if it were just the ordinary bandits, my troops would be enough. But this Cimmerian is another matter. It is to deal with him that I have summoned you. If all goes according to plan, you can handle it with a few minutes' work, dangerous but brief, without wasting months chasing around through the hills."

"Things often do not go according to plan, in my experience," Berytus said.

"If that is the case," Sagobal said grimly, "you will have a long, hard task ahead of you, and you may wish you had never accepted the proposal."

In the small courtyard outside Sagobal's quarters, Berytus's men were lined up for inspection, although in this attitude, they looked utterly unlike regular soldiers assembled for the same purpose. They were rough and polyglot, of differing races, and there was nothing uniform about them save an attitude of brutal deadliness. At one end of the line was the hulking Kothian, and Berytus led Sagobal to this one first.

"This is Urdos of Koth. He is my second in command. He

speaks little, but his actions are sufficiently eloquent." The brute saluted with a heavy ax, which was as light in his massive paw as a willow wand.

The next man's black beard and hair were similar but he was shorter, though almost as broad. In his hand was a thick-limbed, recurved bow. "Barca the Shemite," Berytus said, "a master of the bow."

Beside Barca stood a thin, dark-brown man with narrow features, his hair bound up in a greasy turban. His only visible weapon was a slender spear. "Ambula of Punt. He can track the signs left by a shadow on bare rock." Ambula smiled, revealing yellow teeth filed to points.

"Bahdur the Hyrkanian," Berytus said, standing before a squat, yellow-complexioned man who carried a bow and cased arrows at his belt. He wore armor of lacquered bamboo laced with colored leather. "Another fine archer, and he can track almost as well as Ambula."

So they went down the line, and each man was as exotic as the last. Each was stamped with the unmistakable look of villainy, but all looked eminently qualified for their task. They were manhunters and killers, and Sagobal knew well that one did not hire delicate scholars for such work. They were cruel, merciless and efficient.

"Very good," Sagobal said. "For the next few days they are to stay out of sight. Even in Shahpur, a lot such as this may excite comment, and I doubt not the bandits we are after have their spies in the city."

"This evening we will ride out as we came in," Berytus said. "In the late watches, have your guards on the gate to let us back in. We will return here unseen."

"Excellent," Sagobal said approvingly.

"My men will not like being cooped up in barracks," Berytus said. "They had a long ride hither and were looking forward to a carouse."

"They will be well supplied with food and wine," Sagobal said. "I will even find some women for them. Bag Conan and his band for me, and I'll reward them with the carouse of their lives."

That night another strange group assembled in the ancient city of Shahpur. The priest Tragthan stood in the long nave of the new temple, his hands thrust into the wide sleeves of his robe. He was utterly still, waiting. The unearthly red light still streamed bloodily through the glass windows, although the crescent moon above cast only the dimmest of rays. He did not move when a figure robed like himself appeared in the grotesque doorway.

The newcomer walked on silent feet into the red glow, then pushed his cowl back, revealing a gaunt face and a hairless head covered with strangely mottled skin. Slowly, he turned his head, surveying the imposing interior.

"Splendid," said the newcomer, a slight hiss in his voice. "It is just as it was in ancient times!"

"Greeting, Master Shosq," Tragthan said. "It is not quite as it was in the great days, but it shall be. Whence came you?"

"From the land of Khitai, which is so changeless that save for the suppression of Ahriman's temples, all is much as it was in ages past."

Even as the faint echoes of these words faded, two more figures entered. The backthrust cowls of their russet robes displayed faces similar to that of Shosq's. The face of one was turned a grotesque purple by the reddish light. That of the other was paler, but the flesh was covered with tiny, close-set bumps, as if he suffered from some disfiguring disease.

"Greetings, Brothers," Tragthan and Shosq said in unison.

"Brother Nikas," Tragthan said, "long has it been since we last beheld you. Whence came you?"

"From an island in the Western Sea, a fragment of lost Atlantis," said the purple-visaged man. In ordinary light, his skin would have been faintly blue. "I made my way to the nearest coast, in what men now call the Pictish Wilderness, as primitive now as in olden time."

"And you, Brother Umos?" Tragthan inquired.

"From Belverus, in Nemedia," said the man with knobbed skin. "Her Temple of Ahriman is not even a pile of rubble now. A great crude fortress rises atop the site." He laughed—a sinister, hissing sound. "The tower that now stands above the altar is known as the Tower of Lost Hope, for in every siege since the building of the fort, all the defenders of that tower have been slain."

Tragthan directed his eyes toward the doorway. "How many others will join us this night?"

"There will be no others," said Nikas.

"None?" Tragthan turned to face the purple-visaged man. "What of Brothers Khinat, and Spor, and the great Learned One Jasup, and Master Relk, and a score of others?"

"Gone," said Nikas. "Their temples and sanctuaries lay in what is now Stygia, and in the lands that have since been under the rule of Stygia: Koth and Shem, Kush, Darfar and others. The ancient enmity between Ahriman and Set caused the Stygians to hunt down even the ruins of our temples and grind them to dust and lay them and all their adherents under the most baleful of curses."

"Set!" hissed the others.

"He is a jealous god," Nikas said. "The priest-kings of Stygia have grown powerful in his service, and they will allow no hint of a rival."

"Then it is to be we four," Tragthan said. He raised a hand and the portcullis slid down like a great jaw shutting. Then the bronze doors swung silently shut. "Even so, it is not the first time that the worship of our dread Lord has been resurrected by a core as small as this, or even smaller."

"There are Temples of Ahriman in many lands," Nikas said, "but in these our Lord is worshipped in debased form, as a mere adjunct to the cult of Ormazd."

"Ormazd!" the others hissed.

"Aye, the bright god is a great favorite in many lands, and as such, he must have a rival, so that he may ritually defeat him in the thoughtless ceremonies of the common herd. Our great and terrible Ahriman has been reduced to a figure in a puppet-play!"

"This we shall rectify," said Tragthan. "Here, in this unimportant town of Shahpur, which was once mighty Elkar of the Waves when the Vilayet was a vast inland sea, we shall reestablish the great cult of our Lord. Here alone have the foundations of one of his true temples survived intact. Here alone has his altar lain perfect through the passage of aeons."

"Many times has this temple been rebuilt," intoned Shosq. "Always, when our Lord has bestirred himself, have the surviving Brothers converged here to bring him once again into the world."

"Before Elkar," said Umos, "it was Zhagg of the Black Desert, when Atlantis was a chain of smoking volcanoes, their sides not yet clothed in green. Even before that, it was a place with a name none in our present form can pronounce. Always, our Lord Ahriman has had the center of his worship here."

"Come," said Tragthan. "There is much to do. Tonight The Moon enters the House of the Lion, and we must begin."

The priests walked the length of the nave until they stood surrounding the altar of Ahriman. As The Moon entered the House of the Lion, they began to chant. Their voices were low, and they made sounds not intended for the human palate and tongue. Before the sun rose, the altar began to glow with an unearthly phosphorescence.

Three

Conan, Osman and Auda, the desert nomad, lay on their bellies studying the royal road that led into Shahpur. It bore a heavy traffic this day: much foot traffic, the lumbering carts of farmers, a few palanquins borne upon the shoulders of stalwart slaves and carrying wealthy men and women, the colorful wagons of traveling entertainers, coffles of slaves chained neck to neck and driven to market by brutal-faced men dressed in leather and steel. For these travelers, though, the men on the hilltop had little regard. But they did not have to wait long for a sight to draw their greedy eyes.

"Ay!" said Auda excitedly. "Here comes another!"

"Keep your voice down," Osman urged.

The three had lain thus since before sunup, on the sandy soil beneath a clump of brush, a dun-colored blanket covering them so that they blended from view into the terrain. Only the keenest-eyed could have seen them from the road, and then only if their attention were drawn by sound or movement. The three outlaws ignored the scorching sun overhead as they ignored the biting insects. Capture could mean death.

"Listen to the squealing of those wheels," Osman whispered. "I can hear them already."

Conan said nothing, but his blue eyes blazed at the sight. A four-wheeled wagon lurched around a bend, the groaning of its axles matched only by the jingle and clatter set up by the weapons of its escort of heavily armed riders. The wagon was not large, but its slow progress and the sound of its wheels indicated great weight, as the heavy escort indicated great value.

"The third one since sunrise!" Auda said, fighting hard against his enthusiasm. "By Mitra, but this is tempting! With just a few of the men, we could ride down there, slay those useless hirelings and be away with the treasure."

"I want no little part of this treasure," Conan said. "I want it all." With predatory eyes they watched the escorted wagon as it made its leisurely way up the road and finally disappeared through the open gates of the city. The battlements of Shahpur were draped with bright cloth and flowers. Its tall, slender towers were hung with long, colorful banners proclaiming the great festival. The gilded domes crowning the towers gleamed brilliantly in the sunlight.

"How will we move it?" Auda asked. "If that one wagon is so overloaded, many such must be even more so."

"He is right," said Osman glumly. "Best we take just the lightest, most valuable things, such as we can escape with quickly."

"I want it all!" Conan insisted. It was not merely the wealth he craved. He wanted revenge. To rob the king of the whole district's revenues would bring about Torgut Khan's utter disgrace. He had conceived a burning hatred for the man. "Come, we've seen enough."

The men crawled backward like reptiles until they were well below the crest of the hill. Then they rose and trekked to a small gully where they had picketed their horses and remounted. This small range of hills to the south of the city lacked springs or other sources of water, so it was uncultivated. Even the shepherds grazed their flocks among these hills for but a few weeks after the brief rainy season. Thus, for men who did not wish to be seen, the terrain formed a natural approach route to the town.

The bandits had shifted their camp to a spot a bare four miles south of the city. Such propinquity was not without risk, but they would make their strike soon and they needed to be near their prey. Besides this, the concentration of the guards in the city made the location somewhat safer. There had been no roving patrols in days.

The new hideout was an old caravanserai, abandoned a hundred or more years ago when certain wells in the deep desert between Turan and Punt had dried up, forcing caravaneers to forgo a route employed for centuries. The serai still had a low confining wall, but its inn had no roof save such temporary shelter as occasional occupants saw fit to improvise from branches and palm fronds. It had a good well, accessible with a rope and a hide bucket.

The three men rode into the enclosure, dismounted and unsaddled their horses. The rest of the bandits were in the old inn, which at least gave shelter from the wind.

"Gather round, you lazy rogues," said Conan, striding through the doorway. "We have some plotting to do."

The men grinned wolfishly as they learned of the heavy-laden carts entering the city. They looked sorely vexed when the problem of the great weight was presented.

"We are not pirates," said one-eyed Ubo. "We cannot load this treasure on a ship and sail away."

"We could easily round up wagons in the city," said another. "But then we would have to travel by road, and would be readily caught by cavalry."

"If we had many, many camels," said Auda, "we could disappear into the desert, where men on horseback could not follow."

Conan considered that. "It would take a long time to load so many beasts, and half our number would have to tend them, and could not fight. We'll need every man's sword on that day."

"We cannot fly it out," Osman said.

There was a long silence, then: "Well, there is Volvolicus."

"Be still, Osman," said Ubo.

"Who is Volvolicus?" Conan demanded.

"No one you want to deal with," Ubo assured him.

"Let me be the judge of that. Speak, Osman."

The smaller man cleared his throat. "Well, he is a man who lives in the desert no more than half a day's ride from here. He is a wizard, they say, and able to do many wondrous things."

"I want nothing to do with wizards!" Ubo said heatedly.

"Stay, my friend," Conan cautioned. "Osman, why do you mention this mage?"

"In truth, I have heard that he is learned in the art of moving great burdens, such as huge stones and masses of earth. Might he not sell us a spell that can move this great mass of gold, at least beyond easy pursuit, where we may divide it and carry it off at our leisure?"

"I do not like wizards either," Conan said, unstoppering a wineskin and upending it over his mouth.

"It is not necessary to like this thaumaturge," Osman pointed out, "merely to do business with him. Auda, can you guide us to him?"

"Aye, the way is not hard."

"Do not seek him out," Ubo urged.

"Wherefore?" Osman asked.

The Turanian had the look of one who feared his very words endangered him. "He traffics with demons!"

"What wizard does not?" Osman snorted. "We do not propose to sell ourselves to him, but rather to purchase some trifling services. Wizards stay alive by keeping their demons under a tight rein. Perhaps he can whistle us up some demons with strong backs or wings or whatever to fetch our treasure to a safe spot. What say you, Conan?"

The Cimmerian glowered. "I like it not." He brooded a

while longer. "But I see no other way. Let us go and find this Volvolicus."

Osman clapped his hands and rubbed his palms together. "Done, then! Who goes?"

"A moment," said Chamik, a potbellied Corinthian. "If this can be done, where should the treasure be transported?"

"Our old hideout near the desert will be good enough," Conan said. "It has three fine escape routes, plenty of water, and it is hard to find if one knows not the path. We can round up many camels, divide up the loot, and each man can take his share where he will. Best to make up several small caravans and take different roads."

"Break up the band?" said Ubo.

"Why not?" Osman cried. "Are we a family, that must stay together? Nay, we are a pack of rogues looking for easy wealth! With such a haul, each man of us may go someplace where he is not wanted for a hanging and set himself up as a rich lord, or spend it all on women, drink and gambling if it so suit him!"

"Aye," Chamik said. "My tribe knows nothing of my life here. I can go home and be a wealthy horse-breeder."

"I was once in wicked Shadizar, in Zamora," Ubo said, "and I liked the place. P'raps I'll set up there as a banker and be respectable. That way, a man may be a robber and the judges kiss his hand for it."

All hooted in derision at the thought of the one-eyed Turanian turning respectable. Each man babbled his dreams of quick, unearned wealth.

"What of you, Conan?" Osman asked.

"I've a yen to see Iranistan," the Cimmerian said. "I may fare thither."

"And what will you do with your share?" Osman pressed.

Conan shrugged. "Live fully and carouse for a while, scout out the land. With much gold, I can recruit and pay my own mercenary band."

Ubo looked at him as if he were demented. "You mean to *pay* your rogues?"

"That is how it is done," Conan said. "Mercenaries expect to be paid. But with a stout band, they can earn their captain many times their keep. They can enhance their pay with loot, and when the war is over, no one will seek to hang them for it."

Chamik shrugged. "You have been a soldier, Conan. We are all just simple bandits here. Spend your share how you will."

"Conan, you must seek out this magician," Osman said. "And Auda must be the guide. Who else goes?" The rest all found something else to absorb their attention. "Well, I am no coward! I'll go with our captain."

"So you shall," Conan said, lurching to his feet. "As for the rest of you lazy louts, you can make yourselves busy as well. Go steal us all the camels you can find and take them to our old hideout. And none of you think to shirk the fighting by staying with the beasts—they'll not stray far from the water and grass. As soon as that is done, we all meet back here. The great festival commences in five days, with the dedication of this new temple. Auda, Osman, let us be off!" As always, having determined upon a course of action, the Cimmerian did not waste time.

The three mounted and rode south, into the desert, with Auda in the lead. The scrubby hills gave way to rolling, stony land where the brushy clumps grew ever farther apart. Toward evening, Auda led them to a tiny water hole and they gave their horses drink, then continued. The sun dipped below the western mountain range, the sky turned vivid violet and the first stars appeared. Then they were riding beneath a bowl of deepest black, the stars in their countless millions forming ethereal veils and hard, bright points of brilliance overhead. In time, the moon rose, casting a ghostly luminescence that to desert-trained eyes was almost as good as sunlight.

All around them was silence. Nighttime was when the creatures of the desert left their dens to hunt, feed and mate, but they did these things quietly, for the most part. To make a sound was to reveal their location to enemies. Likewise, the men rode in near silence, keeping to the softer ground where their horses' hooves made little sound, their weapons and harness wrapped in cloth or leather to give forth no betraying clink, speaking little, and then only in whispers.

Auda rode to the crest of a sandy ridge and held up a hand as he halted. The other two drew even with him and reined their mounts. Below the ridge was a tiny oasis, its long pool surrounded by date palms. A small, low-roofed house stood at one end of the pool. Their horses nickered and grew restless, stimulated by the scent of fresh water.

Even as they watched, an eerie purple light flooded from the windows and door of the house. The light changed color, first to a brilliant blue, then to aquamarine. Abruptly, it shifted to orange, then to a bloody red, before fading back to darkness.

Osman cleared his throat. "It seems to me that the wizard might deem us unmannerly, calling upon him so late at night. Perhaps in the morning, when the sun is high . . . ?"

"Aye!" Auda said fervently, if a little shakily. "Among the desert folk, it is deemed a great discourtesy to come upon strangers out of the darkness. Such greetings are often answered with a shower of arrows."

" 'Twas only light," Conan said, his voice offhand despite the crawling of his scalp. "But perhaps it were best not to disturb—"

"Come with me." The woman's voice made them all jump, curse and snatch at steel. The horses reared and plunged, until they were fought under control.

"Set take it, woman!" Conan said when his mount was quiet again. "Why did you not let us know you were there? We might have swept off your head from pure surprise!"

She released a tinkling laugh. "Slain me? You have yet to see me!"

"Yet we long to," Osman said, a slight quaver in his words, "for surely you are as beautiful as your voice."

Conan looked around them, chagrined. He prided himself

upon his great skills in the wild places, yet this girl (for she sounded very young) had approached within sword's reach unseen. And, he thought, he *still* did not see her!

"Show yourself!" the Cimmerian demanded.

"It is you who trespass here," she said. "But I will do as you say." A shape detached itself from a great stone and they saw the outline of a woman, as graceful and delicate as a desert gazelle. Conan could not understand how he had missed seeing her, but he knew that in the uncertain light of the moon, a man's eyes notice movement before shape and do not register color at all. Often he himself had escaped searchers passing nearby in the moonlight, simply by holding absolutely still. Doubtless the wench had done something of the sort.

"Gracious lady," Auda said, bowing low from the saddle, touching his breast and lips, "we come seeking——"

"You seek the great mage Volvolicus," she said, interrupting. "He is aware of this, and sent me up here an hour ago to bring you to him."

"How knew he we were coming?" Osman demanded.

"But he is a wizard," said Auda, as if speaking to a simpleton.

"Let us go," Conan ordered. "Lead on, girl." Despite his apprehension at approaching the mage, Conan had to admire the woman who walked so gracefully before them, her bare feet soundless on the sand, her rounded hips swaying liquidly beneath a robe so sheer that the light of the moon seemed to pass through it, revealing a small but ripe figure. A woman walking the boulevards of a well-policed city in broad daylight could not have been more nonchalant.

They dismounted by the long pool and let their horses drink. Conan noted that the pool was lined with cut stone, and that the water tumbled musically into one end from a stone artfully carved in the likeness of a grotesque face. There was no visible outlet.

"Shall we unsaddle?" Osman asked.

"Nay," said the Cimmerian. "Our leave-taking may be in haste. Keep them saddled until we know for certain."

Again the woman laughed lightly. "Come. Volvolicus awaits you." She led them to the doorway from which now only natural lamplight shone. Hands on hilts, they ducked beneath the low lintel and passed within.

Inside, the house was illuminated only by a smokeless fire that burned upon a small hearth. The light sufficed to reveal scrolls of many sorts upon shelves lining the walls. From the rafters hung peculiar instruments of metal, crystal, wood and glass. Arcane objects of diverse sorts lay upon the long table that was the main room's principal item of furniture. Large, strangely faceted pieces of crystal stood mounted upon pedestals of ivory, gold or intricately carven wood. Some of these crystals seemed to glow faintly.

"Welcome to my house," said a man who sat at the far end of the table, little more than a man-shape shrouded in shadow.

Conan gripped his hilt fitfully, his nerves set on edge by the sorcerous trappings, and Auda muttered native counterspells under his breath, but Osman answered smoothly.

"Peace upon this house, venerable Volvolicus, mystic of the desert. We are travelers who seek your storied wisdom in aid of a certain enterprise close to our hearts."

"We will speak of this after you have taken refreshment. Layla, attend our guests." In this he followed the custom of the desert, where it was deemed a great discourtesy to inquire of a stranger's business before the requirements of hospitality had been met. He gestured to a carpet near the hearth, furnished with large cushions. The three men bowed respectfully and seated themselves thereon.

The woman padded into a room closed off by an arras and emerged moments later with a broad tray laden with seed cakes, thin-sliced cheese, dates, figs, and a steaming pot of heated wine diluted with water and fragrant with herbs. Three cups were neatly arranged around the pot. Conan wondered how the mage had known that he was to receive three guests. But then, one versed in the magickal arts might be expected to have such abilities. The Cimmerian was hesitant about partaking, but Auda and Osman quickly took a ritual sip of wine and a bite of the food. By the ancient law of hospitality, for a man to attack one who had accepted hospitality within his camp or beneath his roof was to incur the wrath of the gods. Whether the mage had respect for such laws remained to be seen, but Conan went ahead and refreshed himself from the tray. To give offense at this juncture would be utmost folly.

Volvolicus said nothing, nor did he stir from his seat while the three men emptied the pot and the tray. At last they replaced their cups upended, acknowledging their satisfaction, and the woman removed the tray. At last the sorcerer rose from his seat and strode into the circle of light before the hearth.

He was a tall man, exceedingly spare of build as was so often the case with wizards, many of whom practiced severe austerities to purify themselves and strengthen their powers, sacrificing the flesh for the sake of mind and spirit. His hair was brown, confined by a thin silver fillet and falling almost to his shoulders. His narrow face was dominated by very large, intensely black eyes in which gleamed an eerie light.

"And now, my friends, what would you have of Volvolicus?" His voice was deep and resonant, as if it should have issued from a much larger chest. He was clad in a plain robe of rough brown cloth, girded with a knotted leather cord. He sank to a cross-legged seat upon one of the thick cushions.

"Our ears have delighted in tales of your puissance, revered Volvolicus," Osman began. "Far has your fame spread, and great are the—"

"We hear you can lift heavy weights," Conan broke in rudely. "Is it true?"

The wizard looked faintly amused. "The mountebanks who

perform feats of strength at the fairs pride themselves upon hoisting heavy weights. I am none such."

"Wise Volvolicus," Osman said, glaring at the Cimmerian, "what we had in mind was a bit worthier of your talents than lifting a bullock upon your shoulders for the delectation of the mob. Nay, this is to be a glorious feat: to enter the city of Shahpur and remove therefrom a ponderous great weight of metal, such as no ordinary man, nor even a multitude, could raise in a single burden."

"I see," mused the wizard. "Could it be that this weighty cargo will consist of gold?"

"Some substantial part of it will be silver," Osman said, "and precious gems are a definite likelihood."

To their surprise, the wizard laughed heartily. "I have been approached for my aid in many projects, but this is the first time thieves have sought my assistance in escaping with their loot!"

"Sir, you wound us," Osman said, his face and voice radiating false innocence. "We are students and seekers after virtue. Torgut Khan and his master, the king of Turan, are evil men. The loss of this treasure, and the humiliation they must endure thereby, may go far toward purging their souls of wickedness and bestowing upon them a sheen of righteousness when they must appear for judgment before the throne of Mitra."

"A virtuous undertaking, indeed," said Volvolicus, nodding and stroking his beard. "And the nature of this treasure?"

"It will be the year's revenues for this entire district," Conan said. "At the time of the festival, all will be concentrated in the city, gathered from a half-score of small treasuries."

"Truly? This is an odd practice."

"And such an opportunity may never come again!" said Osman. "Please, great Volvolicus, we implore you to help us in this feat, which is far beyond the power of ordinary mortals. In no other fashion may we get away with our treasure and be safe from pursuit."

"Can you raise such a weight?" Conan asked. "And bear it to our lair in the desert, where we may divide it and each man go his way with his share?"

"I doubt it not." The mage took from within his robe a palm-sized slab of thin crystal, and his long, thin fingers swept over its surface in an arcane rhythm. "Let me see—this is a rich province, albeit Shahpur is in the poorest part of it. In years past, the principal towns have returned fifty thousand dinars to the royal treasury, the lesser towns half that, and the villages a few hundred each. Plus, there are the caravan duties and the customs dues from the Vilayet ports." His fingers danced for a while, then he studied the result. "I believe we are considering something in excess of one and a half tons of precious metal, plus whatever stones are included, and of course, the weight of the strong boxes in which they are stored, a total of over two tons."

"You understand our problem, then?" Osman asked, his face rapt with contemplation of such unbelievable wealth.

"You have a problem, indeed," the wizard affirmed. "Alas, I may not help you."

"Wherefore not?" Conan demanded. "Is the weight too great for you?"

"By no means," replied Volvolicus. "I am Turanian by birth, but I spent many years in Stygia, learning the arts of *Khelkhet-Pteth*, which is the raising of giant stones. The Stygians of old developed this art beyond all others, for they built monuments of a size never seen before or since, employing stones of unrivaled magnitude. I last exercised the art some ten years ago, when the priests of Ashtoreth required my aid in lifting a magnificent new statue of their goddess upon its pedestal, a distance of more than fifty vertical feet. The statue weighed more than thirty tons."

"Then raising a mere two tons should be as the play of children to you, great mage," wheedled Osman.

"Not exactly," Volvolicus amended. "The density and compressed mass of metal, especially gold and silver, render the spells far more complex. The difference between metal and stone is greater than the mere disparity of weights."

"But this is your art, Volvolicus," Osman said. "Surely you are the master of such things."

"And," the wizard went on relentlessly, "this burden must be transported not only vertically, but for a great distance horizontally, flying, as it were, like an eagle of the desert. That would be most difficult."

"A splendid challenge, fabled Volvolicus," Osman prodded. "Surely this lies not beyond your puissance?"

"It does not, though it would tax my powers to the utmost."

"Then you will do it?" Conan asked.

"Nay."

"Wherefore not?" the Cimmerian exploded.

"Because I have no wish to. What have I to gain, removing myself from important labors to take part in this frivolous adventure?"

"Frivolous?" Osman said, aghast. "A ton and a half of precious metal is not frivolous!" He calmed himself with an effort. "Forgive my outburst. Perhaps we approached this wrongly. We are willing to reward you most generously. A double share of the gold and silver for your help." Conan and Auda nodded agreement.

"But I have no need of gold or silver. Worldly wealth is nothing to one such as I."

"With what did the priests of Ashtoreth pay you?" Conan asked.

"With an ancient and precious manuscript, a tract upon the properties of the dragon's-eye crystal writ three thousand years ago by the wizard Baalkar of Shem. Such things as this are valued by the masters of my art."

"But think of the glory!" Osman urged. "It will be a feat unheard of and will make you renowned in the great world!"

At this the wizard laughed once again. "My friend, for me

to take part in this escapade would render me a laughingstock among my peers! For the wizard Volvolicus to play the part of the thief would make my name a jest."

"I do not understand," said Auda. "You mean to say that sorcerers think that plunder is dishonorable?" He shook his head in disbelief. "Surely only judges, merchants and dirt-grubbing farmers think thus!"

"Oh, we are not as ordinary men," said the mage. "Many a wizard takes pride and delight in purloining the spells, grimoires, instruments and suchlike from other members of the fraternity, and may even gain honor thereby, but to stoop to something as petty as robbery from ordinary mortals is deemed unworthy. I must decline."

"But I must have that treasure!" Conan barked. "Like you, I care not for the gold. But it must be mine!"

For the first time, the wizard gave the Cimmerian a searching look. "A bandit who cares not for gold? This is a marvel indeed. What is your nation, warrior? I have never seen a man of your sort."

"I am a Cimmerian, a man of the far north."

"Yes, there is something of the Atlantean about you. It has been written that the last remnants of the Atlantean race dwell in the rocky fastnesses of Cimmeria."

"I know nothing of that, but it does not surprise me that you have never seen a Cimmerian. Few of my kin travel far from home, and none save I have ever visited Turan."

"So, Cimmerian, how is it that you lust for the treasure, yet care not for the gold and silver?"

"It is a matter of honor," Conan said. "I want to see Torgut Khan and his dog, Sagobal, crushed and humbled. I could slay either of them or both, but for such men, disgrace is a fate far worse. Torgut Khan has boasted to the king that he is worthy to guard all the treasure of the district. Were I to snatch it from beneath his pig's snout, he would have to send his own head to the king! And Sagobal, who thinks he can keep me from the treasure, if he escape the headsman, can aspire no higher than the rank of common trooper for the rest of his life!"

"These men must have wronged you marvelously to have inspired such enmity," Volvolicus observed.

"Aye, they did that," Conan answered. "They tricked me by suborning a woman I favored. Then they bound me in a dungeon—chained hand, foot and neck like a contemptible beast—from whence they condemned me to death upon the scaffold!" The Cimmerian burned with rage.

"Annoying to you perhaps, but many would consider these to be the actions of men concerned with the public weal. A thief who does not want such treatment would do well to avoid capture."

Conan was unmoved. "It was not enough to kill me, but they must make a mockery of my execution. I was to be tortured and flayed as part of a celebration Torgut Khan has declared to the dedication of his new Temple of Ahriman. A clean death I can look upon without fear. Death by torture I can endure. But to be made a spectacle, for cowards and common city folk to laugh and jeer at, *that* I cannot endure. They must pay for their insolence and arrogance!"

The wizard seemed not to have heard the last part. His expression sharpened, became more intense. A hand shot out and grasped the Cimmerian's thick wrist. The cold, inhumanly strong grip repelled Conan, but he did not draw back.

"Did I hear you say 'Temple of Ahriman'?" the mage demanded.

"You heard me aright."

"Can it be that you have not heard of this?" Osman said. "You, who knew that three men were to visit you this night? For two years, the rebuilding of the temple has been spoken of up and down the Vilayet coast and far into the desert. So grandiose a project has not been seen in southern Turan in a generation."

"My home exists, as it were, an island removed from the

times and turmoils surrounding. My guardian-spells warned me of your approach when you were within an hour's ride, but I take little interest in things that might upset my studies. Surely, it is the priests of Ormazd who erect this temple, honoring their god's adversary?"

"Nay," said Osman. "This temple is no part of the Ormazd cult, and the priests of that god only spit and will say nothing when asked about it. It is a vast, ugly building with a door like the gaping maw of a huge, hellish beast. Workmen had to be tempted with high wages to take part in the work, and some of them picked up their tools and departed in the middle of the night, forfeiting their pay rather than continue."

"Aye, that I do not doubt if this temple is what I fear." The wizard spoke in a near-whisper, so that the others had to lean forward, straining to hear his words. He released Conan's wrist and the Cimmerian rubbed the indented finger marks, which burned with cold fire.

"It is the crypt of this temple that is to serve as the new treasury," Conan remarked.

"Say you so?" Volvolicus murmured. "This puts matters in a different light."

Osman pounced eagerly upon the mage's words. "Mean you that you will help us?" he asked.

"It seems that I must."

His three guests looked at each other in surprise, wondering what had brought about the sudden change of heart.

"Good," Conan said succinctly.

"Tonight I must make preparations. Tomorrow at dawn, I shall ride with you. I must see this temple and this city. Layla will prepare quarters for you. There is a vacant room in the back of this house. You will find it most comfortable."

Conan rose. "With your leave, I will sleep beneath the stars. My recent stay in the dungeon has made me long for the open air."

"I am a city dweller," said Osman, "and I shall avail myself of our host's hospitality."

"As shall I," Auda said.

"Then," said Volvolicus, rising, "if you will give me leave, I shall retire to my meditations. Sleep safely in this house." He looked at Conan. "The desert night is not without dangers, but you seem to be a man equal to most challenges."

Conan uncoiled himself to his great height and nodded. "I have yet to be slain by man or beast. The sand does not blow tonight and the stars are a fair ceiling. Good night to you."

He exited the house, and his companions followed to unsaddle their mounts and collect their gear.

"What think you, Conan?" asked Osman in a low voice as he loosened a girth. "He does not seem as forbidding as one would expect a great mage to be."

"Aye," said Auda, "but what of his sudden change? One minute he was too good to go raiding with us, the next he was all too ready. What means this?"

"The man is playing his own game," said Conan, "but if he can accomplish what we require, I'll not demand an explanation from him. It sounds to me as if some enmity lies between him and these priests of Ahriman. Perhaps he wishes to do them an ill turn. He may do so with my good wishes, for I've no love for priests. If he can get the treasure out of that city for us, the rest is his own business."

"Aye, aye," said the others. Laden with gear, they trooped back to the wizard's house, leaving their hobbled horses to munch at the grass that grew in abundance in the little oasis.

Conan took his blanket roll and walked around the pool to find a place whereupon to lie down. His recent experience in the dungeon was only a part of the reason he had declined the mage's offer. He detested wizardry, and the house was steeped in it. He knew he would sleep better beneath the stars.

Between two palms heavily laden with dates, he found a

spot where the grass lay thick over springy turf. There he unrolled his blankets and took off his sword-belt, leaving his hilts close to hand at need. A half-moon was rising, its silver beams sparkling off the rippled surface of the pool. Overhead, a faint breeze rustled the tops of the palms. Otherwise, all was silent. He lay down, stretching his great frame upon the rough blankets and yawning. Within minutes, he was asleep.

Two hours past midnight, something awoke him. For several minutes he lay listening, but there was nothing to be heard save the rustling of wind in the palm tops. He sat up and strained his eyes, but he saw nothing untoward. The moon bathed everything in a pale glow, leaving areas of deep shadow.

Puzzled, he rose to his feet. The air had cooled, but not enough for him to bother with blankets. He walked to the edge of the pool and crouched, scooping up water in his hands and bathing his face.

With water still dripping from his head, the Cimmerian heard again the faint splashing sound that had awakened him. He looked out over the water and saw something moving along its surface. For an instant, he almost made a run for his weapons, then he chided himself for the impulse. Surely, nothing menacing inhabited this little pool.

The thing drew closer and he saw that it was a human head atop a graceful neck that grew from shapely shoulders. All else was mysterious, hidden beneath the water. Conan relaxed. This was no enemy.

"Layla?" he said.

"It is I." Her voice was low and musical. Now he could see the shape of her features. Her hair lay slicked back against her delicate skull and gave her the aspect of a swimming seal. Like a seal, she was fluidly graceful in the water.

"Does your master know you are out here?"

"Volvolicus is deep in his nightly exercises. He cares not at all what I do when he is sequestered. I swim here nightly, for only during these hours of darkness is the air pleasant in this desolate place. The water is cool, and I have the moon and stars for company."

"But do the beasts of the desert not come here to drink of a night?" Conan asked.

"They will not harm me," she said. She made her leisurely way through the water to the place where Conan crouched and leaned her elbows upon the stone edging, her chin resting upon her hands.

"Not all the creatures out here walk on four legs," Conan rumbled.

She smiled, her teeth flashing white in the moonlight. "I know. I have nothing to fear from that sort, either."

"Say you so?" The Cimmerian was intrigued by the woman. She did not speak like a serving wench or slave, which he had assumed her to be. He wondered at her confidence, although the sorcerer's protective spells could account for that. Most of all, he wondered what delights lay concealed beneath the surface of the water. He had yet to see her in good light, but he had long experience in judging the forms of men and women by the subtleties of their movements. It was a matter of survival for a fighting man. What he had seen thus far proclaimed the woman to be as ripely formed as any in his wide experience.

"I say so," she said. Abruptly, she shot up from the water, wrapped her arms around his neck and kissed him, her lips warm and mobile upon his own. He sought to take her in his grasp but, slippery as an eel, she slid back into the water and swam away, laughing. He had seen little, but his brief feel of her said that she was as toothsome as he had imagined.

"Crom take her," he grumbled as he stood and made his way back to his blankets. "The woman knows how to ruin a man's sleep!"

In a dark chamber below his house, the mage Volvolicus prepared a seldom-used spell. He was long accustomed to his solitary studies, but this night he sought contact with his peers. He sat at a table of black marble, inlaid with mystic signs in threads of gold. The signs were connected by lines both straight and curved that radiated from a point at the center of the table, and above this spot lay a jagged green crystal, glowing softly. The mage made passes over the table with his hands, hesitating and stopping frequently, for he was out of practice.

Soon, though, his confidence returned and his movements became swift and sure. Points of light began crawling along the golden threads, slowly at first, then with greater speed. When the lights reached the symbols where the lines terminated, most of the symbols began to glow likewise, some of them at once, others after an interval of several minutes to an hour. A few did not respond at all.

Volvolicus lowered his hands, and the crystal began to glow more brightly. Slowly, human faces started to appear above the symbols inlaid in the black marble. Most of them were men's faces, although there were a few women. All were of middle to advanced years, and they represented a great many races and nations.

"Who are you, who disturb our labors with the Supreme Convocation?" asked one whose hairless head floated above a sigil in the shape of the constellation of the Scorpion. His features, those of an upper-caste Stygian, were terrible, his eyes as cold as a serpent's.

"I know this one, mighty Thoth-Amon," said an elderly man, also Stygian, with lower-caste features. "He is Volvolicus, a Turanian and a master of *Khelkhet-Pteth*. He came to me many years ago for instruction and was an apt pupil."

"A mere dabbler in the magicks of stone and crystal?" Thoth-Amon radiated contempt. "What business have you with sorcerers of the First Rank? All here are your masters many times over. To use the Supreme Convocation without just cause is to incur the eternal life that is more terrible than the foulest death."

"Speak quickly if you would not endure our curse," said a wizened Khitan whose eyelids and mouth were stitched shut. His voice seemed to come from all directions.

"He is back," Volvolicus said simply. "The evil more ancient than the serpent is back in the world of men."

"Absurd!" sneered Thoth-Amon. "Ahriman was driven from this very universe by the god-kings of Stygia with the power of Set! Spells more powerful than any now known were established to keep him away. You babble nonsense, fool! Prepare to endure the curse."

"Wait, Stygian," said a painted Pict who wore bones through his ears and a necklace of dried human fingers. "Ten moons ago, a strange man came to our shore from an island of the Western Sea. He was of no race known to us, but he spoke Pictish of a sort. It was not the tongue we know today, but that spoken to me in dreams by my ancestors of unthinkable ages past. He spoke fair words and he offered no harm, but there was that about him revolting to the senses of one attuned to the spirit world. He inquired of the land of Turan, and by what route he might make his way thither."

"Another such was seen in Belverus three moons ago!" said a Nemedian mage.

"What manner of men were these?" Thoth-Amon asked.

"Attend our thoughts," said the Nemedian. He and the Pict closed their eyes and all were silent. Then Thoth-Amon sucked in his breath, a remarkable demonstration for the reptilian mage.

"It is true! Men of the race long thought extinct have returned! How can this be? All the temples and sanctuaries of Ahriman were destroyed utterly, every gate through which the unspeakable god might return pulverized and then laid under dread curse!"

"Time is a great wheel, Westerner," said a rotund Vendhyan. "Nothing is ever wholly destroyed, nothing is exiled, never to return. All comes back in the circuit of time. A god cannot be annihilated. Far less can one be exiled."

"But how could this happen without my knowledge?" Thoth-Amon demanded.

"There speaks your vanity, Stygian," said a black wizard, his head painted white except for the eye sockets, so that he resembled a skull. His yellow teeth were filed to points. "You are a wizard like the rest of us. Are you so great that a god must ask your permission to return to the world of men?"

"No such thing, as you well know, Damboula!" the Stygian retorted. "But so epochal an event should have caused disturbances obvious to a first-year acolyte. Yet we, mages of the First Rank, felt nothing, and must be told by this learned stonemason!"

"Bridle your wrath, esteemed Thoth-Amon," said the aged Khitan. "As it happens, I agree with you. I believe this means that Ahriman has not yet returned. But his followers have somehow been resurrected, and it is they who prepare the way for their god to resume his place among the men, spirits and gods of this world."

"You speak wisely, Feng-Yoon," the Stygian acknowledged. "And whatever these lizard-men propose to accomplish, it is too great a work to bring about swiftly. I must consult my screeds and my spiritual advisors. Some of us serve bright gods, some of us the dark ones, and some deal with no gods at all, but Ahriman is the deadly enemy of everyone. If he cannot be destroyed, he must be contained. I charge you all to abandon your present labors until this threat is dealt with. Cease your feuds and work to contact all magicians of the First Rank who have not answered this convocation to enlist their aid. Are all in agreement?"

"Aye," they chorused.

"And you, crystal-gazer," Thoth-Amon said. "I charge you hie yourself to the lair of these Ahriman-worshipers and discover their secrets."

"As it occurs," said Volvolicus, "my steps take me thither

upon the morrow." He smiled thinly. "I am called there to render assistance in a most weighty matter."

"Then fear us and obey. Your reward will be great. Punishment for failure is unimaginable."

The images above the table faded, and Volvolicus pondered long before seeking his bed.

Four

The two men, accompanied by a woman, rode into the city amid preparations for the festival. They wore the robes of desert dwellers of the Geraut tribe; the men in black turbans, their faces tightly veiled to the eyes, the woman in a yellow head-scarf, her face exposed. All three wore long flowing capes of striped cloth, baggy trousers and soft, high-topped boots. The tall thin man wore the ornaments of a shaykh. His burlier companion was clearly a bodyguard.

"Lucky it is for you that blue eyes are not unknown among the Geraut," said Volvolicus. "Else those guards back there would have dragged that veil down and embarrassed us all."

"Aye, but this is a good time to evade the law," said Conan, in high good humor. "When a city is thronged by unwonted crowds, the guards have no attention to spare. They know that a festival such as this will draw every robber, cutpurse and burglar for a hundred leagues around. They will have their hands full for many days. At such a time, who will glance twice at a common desert nomad?"

"It does no harm that the Geraut have a reputation for cutting down any man who lays a hand upon them," said Layla. "A proud and touchy people, the Geraut."

Volvolicus, in his character as a desert shaykh, bore no weapon save a jeweled dagger in his sash. Conan wore a full panoply of arms: a long lance propped in a stirrup socket; sword and dagger at his belt; small, circular shield of steel thonged to his saddle pommel. He wore no armor, for the Geraut did not favor it.

The city through which they rode was crowded and noisy, with people occupying every available square foot. At nights the crowds slept in the streets and public gardens, protected by impromptu shelters of cloth, or by nothing at all. Everyone with something to sell had brought it to Shahpur in hope of finding buyers; established merchants and itinerants hawked food, drink or trinkets. All gawked at the entertainments and spectacles.

Dancers and tumblers performed on every corner. In circles scratched in the dirt, mountebank swordsmen challenged all comers, the purse to be awarded to the one who drew first blood, or, for the more resolute, the one who dealt two cuts out of three.

"A pity you cannot eat or drink through that veil, Cimmerian," said Layla. "A useful disguise it may be, but it prevents you from enjoying the festival."

"I do not carouse when I am working," Conan answered. "Celebration is best after you have done something worth celebrating." The woman had been darting sly digs toward him ever since they had left the wizard's desert lair. After her brazen demonstration in the pool, she had reversed herself and now treated him coolly.

Guardsmen were everywhere in evidence, but the Cimmerian saw no sign of Sagobal. Nor did Torgut Khan make an appearance, not that he expected the lofty viceroy to rub shoulders with the common herd. It was just as well because he was not certain that he would be able to control his temper should he see either of them. Hewing Sagobal or Torgut Khan asunder would be certain to upset his plans for stealing the treasure.

They reined in before the new temple. Recently completed, made of gleaming new stone, it looked uncannily like a building of great age, its facade pitted and streaked. They walked their mounts across the crowded public square and hitched them to a tree shading the courtyard of an inn facing the temple. As they sat at a low table, the innkeeper hurried over to serve them.

After ordering food and wine, Volvolicus questioned the innkeeper. "I was told that this festival was held to dedicate a new temple. Surely that old building cannot be the one?"

"Aye, it is hard to believe, and I like it not," said the man, making a gesture to ward off evil. "I saw the capstone set myself, back in the Month of Harvesting Wheat. Then it was new and gleaming, as you would expect. Now, only five months later, it looks as if it has been there a thousand years. Walk around the temple and you will see something passing strange: Three of the corners are sharp, but the southwest corner is rounded. All of the older buildings of this town are like that, for the desert wind blows from the southwest and the windborne sand eats away at the stone, but it takes many generations to do so."

Volvolicus made a hand-gesture used by the desert folk to ward off the demons of the southern winds. "What can this mean, my host?"

"I know not, but there is muttering in the town, and many declare that the temple should be destroyed. But," he amended, "not until after the festival, which is shaping up as a fine one."

"First things first," Conan said.

"Aye. I've not seen this many folk in the city since the great bandit Jemai the Cruel was executed when I was a child. A different torturer worked his arts upon Jemai every day. There was a great prize for the man who devised the most ingenious torment, but the one in whose care Jamai finally died was to forfeit his fee. The rogue lasted ten days."

The innkeeper smiled and sighed in fond remembrance of the good old days. "But we had governors then who knew what to do with criminals. This one just recently allowed the brigand Conan to escape, and we must be satisfied with the execution of a few dozen common thieves and murderers." He hurried off to fetch their orders.

"This does not look good," Conan said when their host was safely out of earshot. "I had planned a simple raid, thinking that building to be but an ordinary temple. I have plundered other such before and suffered no more than the attentions of the law. But this is no ordinary temple. Think you that violating it may bring some baleful curse upon our heads?"

"No longer so eager after the treasure, Cimmerian?" Layla taunted.

"I will have it!" Conan insisted. "But this situation may pose special dangers. Volvolicus, you are a master of wizardly arts. Do we incur terrible peril if we profane yon pile?"

"A good question," said the wizard, stroking his beard. "It may be that if the temple has not yet been dedicated, the god does not yet dwell within, in which case, we incur no untoward danger."

"But what of this uncanny aging?" the Cimmerian demanded.

"It is perplexing," Volvolicus allowed, "but it need signify nothing more than conniving quarrymen and masons passing off inferior, soft sandstone for stone of the first quality. By cunning arts, such stone may be given a finish to mock polished granite and last long enough for the swindlers to get away with their loot before it begins to crumble. It is a common ruse."

"Perhaps it is no more than that," Conan said, speaking as if he were trying to convince himself.

"I wonder if it may not be possible to go inside," Volvolicus speculated.

"It would be well if we could," said Conan, "little as I relish the idea of going within that place. I want to scout out the interior, so that we waste no time when we come back for the treasure."

"I shall make inquiries," said the mage.

They ate in silence, the men taking small mouthfuls, lifting their veils slightly for each bite. Their wine they sipped through decorated silver straws. As they did this, they watched the passing parade, which was colorful, cosmopolitan and polyglot. Most of the nations bordering the Vilayet, as well as the plains, hills and deserts surrounding, were represented.

At one end of the plaza, a large and imposing scaffold had been erected, and was the center of much attention. Besides a gallows, it sported many instruments of torture, readied for victims. Upon a tall white banner were painted the names of those to be executed, together with the crimes of each and the manner in which he was to be disposed of. For the benefit of the foreign and the illiterate, public criers read out the banner at regular intervals.

"That banner must have been made up in the last few days," Conan commented, "for my name is not upon it."

"Fame is fleeting," said Layla.

"You've a sharp tongue for a serving wench," the Cimmerian groused.

"She is not a servant," Volvolicus said. "She is my daughter."

Layla laughed at Conan's consternation. "I believe our barbarian companion blushes beneath his veil," she said.

"The girl gave me no cause to think she was your daughter," Conan said.

They were distracted by activity across the plaza. With a creak and rattle of metal, the fanged gate of the temple began to rise. Many onlookers gaped curiously, but others drew back, for the new temple inspired more dread than fascination.

"Come," Volvolicus said. "Let us see what is afoot."

They rose from their table and strolled across the public square toward the temple. A man in a russet robe emerged from the temple and stood upon the top step, his arms raised. His features were hairless and ascetic, strangely mottled with bluish shadows.

"Good people of Shahpur!" he announced in a loud voice. "Guests from abroad! Our honored viceroy, Torgut Khan, in his generosity has decreed that all who wish to gaze upon the splendors of the Temple of Ahriman may come within. I, Shosq, priest of Ahriman, will reveal its wonders and answer your questions." The man's thin lips curled as he spoke, as if the words left a foul taste in his mouth.

"There's a sour-faced rogue," said Conan. "I'll warrant he has no liking for this, guiding the common rabble through his holy of holies. Torgut Khan is forcing them to do it, to his own greater glory."

"And to our own greater fortune," said Layla.

"That is yet to be seen," grumbled Conan.

The priest had surprisingly few takers for his guided tour. The Cimmerian, the wizard, Layla, and perhaps a half-score of others trooped up the stair to follow the priest within. They were barely inside the vast, echoing interior when a sound from behind them made them turn. The fangs of the vertical gate lowered until they touched the floor.

"It is imperative that no unescorted persons enter," the priest explained. "The consequences could be terrible. For that reason, I must insist that none of you wander away from me. Now, if you will follow."

The group talked in subdued tones, for the atmosphere of the place was oppressive. The decorations were bizarre in the extreme, and they were rendered even more grotesque by the bloody light that flooded down from the clerestory.

Along the walls were rows of low-relief carvings depicting men, women, and creatures of indeterminate species engaged in improbable couplings. The priest explained that these symbolized the creation of nature. On another wall, the figures underwent torture and slaughter fit to sicken the strongest stomach, and these the priest explained as representing the necessary destruction that must precede the renewal of creation.

Layla paused at the base of one of the naked caryatids, admiring the lovely, agonized face and stroking a beautifully polished knee. She circled it and pointed out to her companions the marvelously detailed whip-marks that striped the buttocks and the bowed back, sculptured drops of blood flowing from them.

"Beauty in torment, an interesting concept," she commented. "What do these women represent, Revered Shosq?"

The priest shrugged. "Something must hold up the roof. Now, if you will come this way."

They followed him to an irregular, humped shape that was covered by a great silken cloth.

"This is the sacred altar of Ahriman," Shosq said. "Many of the local folk have been disturbed by its appearance, so we decided it best to cover it."

"Yet I would gaze upon this thing," said Volvolicus. "I have come far to see the wonders of this temple."

"As you wish, O shaykh," said the priest. He took the cloth and raised it, exposing about half of the altar. The onlookers muttered among themselves at its loathsome aspect, but the mage stared at it, rapt.

"Indeed, an unusual object," Volvolicus remarked as the priest let the cover fall back.

"It just looks like a pile of snakes to me," Conan muttered, attempting to hide his unease.

"These stairs—" Volvolicus said, pointing to the passage that led beneath the altar, "—do they lead to an inner chamber, where we may see an image of your god?"

"Great Ahriman has no form that human beings can descry or imagine," said Shosq. "This merely leads to the crypt. It is not properly a part of the holy precincts and is to be used as the district treasury."

They continued the tour, and the priest explained some of the practices of his religion. There was little else of note within the temple, which was more distinguished for its sheer strangeness than for its riches. He then led them back outside and announced to the crowd that the next tour would commence that evening.

The three collected their horses and rode from the town, attracting as little attention from the guards as when they had ridden in.

"Everything that priest said was a lie!" Volvolicus said when they were safely away from the town. "His explanations of the carvings were the rankest nonsense. What he calls his religion is nothing but a botched version of the Ormazd faith, with some elements of the more scabrous Vendhyan cults thrown in."

"What care I for that?" Conan demanded. "The blotch-faced villain may sacrifice daisies to a green toad for all I care! What did you think of the layout of the temple? That passage to the crypt looks cursed narrow to me."

"Oh, that," Volvolicus said distractedly. "It presents some problems, surely, but nothing insurmountable. The weight to be moved will have to be arranged in a long, narrow mass. I shall adapt the formula for moving an obelisk."

"And the gate or portcullis or whatever it is?" Conan asked.

"I shall have no attention to spare for it. You and your rogues must see to keeping it open yourselves. That is your specialty, is it not?"

"It is. I wish we had got a look at its mechanism," said the Cimmerian.

"I wish we had got a look into the crypt," the wizard said.

"Eh? Do you not think it is a mere hole in the ground?"

"It may be, but—" the mage hesitated "—this is difficult to express, for you know not the specialized language of *Khelkhet-Pteth*. From my many years of study, I have a feel for stone and crystal. Truly, all stone and metal are crystal, albeit in forms not visible to the unaided eye. I can feel masses and hollows as another may see them. Back in that temple, I could feel the crypt beneath us, but it was more than that."

"More?" said Layla. "How so?"

"It was as if there were more than a simple hollow carved into the stone. It was rather as if there were one regular hollow within a much larger one, far less regular."

"Like one box within another?" Conan asked.

"Something of the sort, but in this case, though both share the same space, one may be in another dimension."

Now the Cimmerian was thoroughly mystified. "Tell me this: Has it any bearing upon our going in and seizing the treasure?"

"That I have no way of knowing. That is why it would have been well for us to see inside the crypt first."

"Why must this be so complicated?" Conan groaned. "A man should be able to stage a simple robbery without involving disgusting gods and evil spirits!"

"What of that altar?" Layla asked. "It was surpassingly ugly, but it looked like mere carved stone. Did you find anything about it amiss, Father?"

"That was the uncanniest of all," said Volvolicus. "It was no natural stone, nor anything that had its origin upon this world. And the priest did not reveal all of it to us, just a part. I have told you that all stone and all metal is crystal. Each crystal has a vibration different from the others, and all of them are known to me. But this thing is different. It has no vibration detectable on this plane of being. It is inert, like a dead thing."

"Then perhaps it is not of stone, nor of metal," Layla hazarded.

"Nay, it is stone, but a stone unlike anything of this earth."

Conan disliked all such talk. "How does this have anything to do with the taking of the treasure?"

"I do not know, but it is a thing of great and terrible power."

"As I understood the gossip in the city," Layla said, "allowing their crypt to be used as a treasury is the price these priests had to pay before Torgut Khan would allow them to build their temple within the city. They may have no interest in guarding it. They might even be glad to see the treasure taken away."

"It is conceivable," the mage allowed.

"Saw you anything that must prevent us from taking the treasure?" Conan urged single-mindedly.

"Nay, I did not. If you and your men can get us in and hold the place open long enough, I can shift the treasure to your hideout."

"Good!" said the Cimmerian.

"But what of getting us out of the city?" Layla asked.

"That is entirely up to our barbarian friend. The concentration required to lift the metal will prevent me from accomplishing so much as the simplest spell of invisibility."

"And can you accomplish this?" she asked the Cimmerian.

"My course is set," Conan said grimly. "Any mortal man who stands between me and my revenge shall be cut down."

"How reassuring!" she cried with a mocking laugh.

Safely out of sight of the city, they turned from the road, taking a narrow goat-path that wound into the southern hills. An hour of riding brought them to a camp by a little stream, where the bulk of the band lounged around a low fire, drinking weak wine or brewing an herb tea much esteemed in the area. They looked up eagerly at the arrival of the riders.

"How went it, friends?" Osman asked.

"It can be done," the Cimmerian said. His words elicited a happy growl. "We must lay our plans carefully, for there is only one way in and out. One way for men, that is. The treasure will take a route we may not follow." He swung from the saddle and strode to the fire. "What of the camels?"

"Auda and the desert men have not yet returned, but I expect them by darkness," Osman said.

"Aye," Ubo reported. "There is a village called Telmak a day's ride from here. It holds a great camel-market thrice a year, and one such is going on right now. Auda and the rest said that it would be far easier to run off a few-score head of stock from one place than steal them by twos and threes from many caravans and villages."

"They must be right," said Chamik, "for those men are accomplished camel-thieves."

"Excellent," Conan said. "I must make some preparations, then I want all of you to gather and attend me."

For the next hour, the Cimmerian gathered sticks, rocks, leaves and other materials, arranging them in patterns upon the ground. The bandits watched for a while in wonderment, then wandered off about their own business, most of which consisted of loafing, tale-spinning and gambling for the loot they expected to win soon.

In late afternoon, Auda and two other desert men arrived, their horses tired, the men ebullient. "Ninety-three head of prime stock!" Auda announced to the cheers of his fellows. "They await us at the hideout."

"Where is Junis?" Conan asked.

"A camel-boy was a little too alert and Junis took a lance-point in his thigh. We have a camel-watcher at the spring, after all. He will probably live, if the flesh rot does not set in."

"And one less man for the raid," Conan said.

"One man is not much of a price for ninety-three camels," Ubo pointed out.

"I suppose not," said the Cimmerian. "Now, gather 'round, you rogues. You too, Volvolicus." The crew gathered around the strange assemblage of materials the Cimmerian had laid out on the ground. "You see before you the city of Shahpur."

"It's shrunk since I was last there," commented an Iranistani. Conan ignored him.

"These sticks are the walls of the city. The bits of vine outline the major streets and the squares. The large stones are the major buildings and the small ones are the lesser buildings."

With his dagger, he pointed out the features as he named them. "The little black stones are the places where the guardsmen are concentrated."

"What is that piece of camel-dung?" Auda asked.

"That is Torgut Khan," said Osman. "Do you not recognize him?" The others roared with merriment. Conan was gratified that the men were in such high spirits. Morale was as important in such a venture as it was in a military operation. He himself was not so sanguine. The temple and the wizard's reservations about it had depressed his spirits. Were it not for his burning need for revenge upon his tormentors, he might have abandoned the project. But he shook off the black mood and proceeded with his plan.

"Here is the main gate." His dagger indicated a gap in the sticks. "On the morn after tomorrow, you will enter singly or in small groups—more festival-goers come to gawk and carouse. You will behave like ordinary peasants and townsmen. Those who bear the marks of their offenses must cover them."

"But I am proud of these, Conan!" said a grinning Khorajan named Mamos, a man of noted degeneracy even among this company. His forehead had been branded with intricate designs, identifying him as the murderer of his parents. The rope scar around his neck proclaimed that he was one of those rare men lucky or evil enough to have survived a hanging. He always said that he had never been caught for his really serious crimes.

"Swallow your vanity and wear a head-scarf, Mamos," Conan advised. "It is only for a few hours. With the gold you shall win, you may have your scars gilded."

"Back to business, dogs," Osman said. "Our leader is going to tell us how we will all become rich men! Go on, Conan." He grinned, his eyes alight with greed.

"Volvolicus will go in when the gate is opened in the morning. Just before noon, when the crowd is the greatest, he will enter the temple with whatever sightseers are taken in at that time. The temple has only one entrance, and it is barred not by a common door or gate, but by a portcullis, such as a castle has. A team of you shall have the task of securing it open for the duration of our raid. We were not able to spy out the mechanism operating the thing, but I have a way to control it. This will take the finest timing, so we must rehearse the operation here, tonight and tomorrow, until every man knows his role by heart."

For the rest of the day, he drilled them. The men grumbled and groaned, protesting that they had not turned bandit in order to work for a living. But their banter was good-natured, for the prospect of incalculable wealth rendered even these men willing to work for a day or two. He broke them down into teams, each to have its own crucial mission: some to secure the temple portal, some to fight off the guards, some to assure that the city gates should not be closed behind them.

Stratagems were worked out and tested for practicability. Anything too elaborate, anything that left too much to chance, was ruthlessly vetoed by the Cimmerian.

"By the white thighs of Ishtar!" cried Mamos, wiping sweat from his scarified brow after a grueling run-through. "Why must we toil like slaves or peasants when this wizard," he gestured toward Volvolicus, "can accomplish the whole operation with a few muttered cantrips?"

"If he could do that," said Conan, "why would he need us at all?"

"I had not thought of that," the Khorajan admitted.

"Best leave the thinking to those equipped for it," jeered Osman. But a few minutes later, the small man went to Conan and said in a low voice: "My captain, just what *is* to keep the sorcerer from making off with all the treasure?"

"He says he does not care about wealth."

Osman placed a hand upon the Cimmerian's shoulder. "Conan, my friend, I must tell you that I have heard these words before, from many sources. Often the speakers were priests, or philosophers, or others who claimed that the things they valued were not of this world." He paused. "Conan, I am sorry to say that they all lied."

"I know that well enough," said Conan. "I've learned through sore experience that fair words often mask foul intentions, and that nothing is to be trusted less than pious protestations."

"Ah! You speak like a civilized man," Osman commended. "But here we have little choice. We cannot transport the treasure without his aid, so perforce we must trust him. At any rate," he added, "the treasure is secondary to me. What I want is the destruction of Torgut Khan and his dog, Sagobal!"

"Now you I trust," Osman assured him. "Revenge is always a more trustworthy motive than disinterested otherworldliness. And I am sure that you can be content without the spoils, but—" he looked around at the rehearsing band of outlaws "—what of these rogues? If they go to the hideout and find that the wizard has taken the treasure to his house instead, well . . ." He shrugged and smiled ruefully. "I would not wish to be the man from whom they demand answers."

"And you would be among those demanding such answers?" Conan asked, his voice low and dangerous.

"My friend, consider the position. I could protest my undying loyalty to you, and my belief in your utter innocence, but what would be the advantage of two of us roasting over a slow fire, instead of just one?"

"You are an honest man, within your limits. I do not feel that Volvolicus will betray us, but it only makes sense to be prepared for the worst. I have a new assignment for you. Upon the day of the raid, when the rest of us are securing the temple and the gates, I want you to go to Sagobal's stables and steal four of his best horses. The stables are hard by the temple, and the horses are the best in the district. In our escape, each of us shall ride one and lead one. Do not mount the spare until we are almost back at our hideout."

"And if the gold is not there, we just keep on riding, is that it, Conan?"

"At speed. Mounted upon fresh horses of such quality, the others will never catch us."

Osman sighed gustily. "Here I was, spending my wealth in my dreams, and already I make plans to be a penniless fugitive."

Conan clapped him on the shoulder. "Dreams are the wealth of any man, my friend! And you will not be poor even in that extremity. You will own at least one fine horse, and you will have your life, and that is not bad for a man who was destined to be part of the entertainment for the festival!"

That night, Conan was brooding over his plans when Layla came to sit by him. In his concentration upon the morrow, he had all but forgotten the woman.

"You seem to be a man of understanding for a barbarian," she began without preamble. "I wish to tell you of some things my father would rather not reveal to your scum."

"This being?" he asked suspiciously.

"The working of great magick is not the mere mumbling of cantrips, as your murderer would have it. It is a delicate and exacting task, and at the end of it, Volvolicus will be exhausted. He will need an excellent horse to bear him away. He cannot simply levitate himself along with the treasure. I must ride along beside him to assure that he stays in the saddle and on course."

"You!" Conan said. "Surely you do not intend to go along on the raid?"

"And why not? He will need my assistance throughout. I assure you, I can fight and ride better than most men. Have you the horses?"

"I will have such horses standing by for our escape," he said, knowing that this would reduce his own chances in the event of treachery. But he knew as well that the mage could scarcely contemplate betrayal, knowing that he would be within reach of the Cimmerian's blade. "But what of the mount he now has? It is a fine one."

"It will not be good enough if Sagobal presses us close. It is known that he and his troopers straddle the best horseflesh in the district."

"I have plans for their confusion," Conan said.

"And I know that plans usually go awry. Have two fine horses for us. Racehorses, if you can steal them." With that, she rose and walked away from him, swaying fetchingly.

"Crom!" Conan muttered to himself. "What am I, a leader of brigands or a horse merchant?"

Five

The clop of the horses' hooves was loud as the Cimmerian and his companions rode toward the great city gate. The guards at the gate nodded them through without even a perfunctory search. The tenements crowded against the city wall were nearly as deserted as was the tent-town without. Everyone in the city who was sound of body had crowded into the public square for the festival, which was to culminate with the mass execution of the criminals that afternoon.

Osman rode up to Conan. "It is like a ghost town."

"Only here, not in the square." Once again, the Cimmerian was attired as a Geraut warrior. He glanced with distaste at Osman's chosen disguise. The small man had elected to assume the character of a mendicant monk of Bes. These holy beggars attired themselves in a ragged loincloth, long strings of wooden beads and, most incongruously, a towering turban made of cloth-of-gold. "You look like a Shadizar harlot in that getup," he commented.

"And all the more invisible for it. What more natural place for a beggar than a festival like this?"

"What if a real monk of Bes shows up?" asked Auda, who rode behind them.

"No difficulty. There are always far more false holy beggars than real ones. I can impersonate a fraud far better than Conan can impersonate a real Geraut warrior."

"There is no besting this man in a trial of brazen impudence," said Auda.

"No more banter," Conan warned. "Our real business begins now."

They turned a corner, and the noise that had been muffled by the close-built structures of the city burst upon them in full force—clamors of the vendors, songs of the entertainers, howls of performing beasts, the general uproar of a crowd of people, each individual striving to be heard above the pervasive mutter.

The raiders nudged their horses to a slow walk, circling the periphery of the square, behaving like any other band of sightseers, anxious to view as much of the spectacle as possible. Casually, they rode past the temple steps, before which a pair of workmen wrestled with a wheelbarrow laden with seven-foot timbers, cursing each other as the unsteady vehicle almost overturned. Beyond them, Volvolicus and Layla watched with rapt attention as a Vendhyan woman, naked except for a coat of silver paint, writhed through a sensuous dance to the sound of flute and tambour, while a python as thick as her shapely thigh entwined her body.

They rode past the elaborate scaffold, where the torturers prepared their instruments, stoking their fires, sharpening evil-looking tools, and explaining to passersby the subtleties of their art. At one end of the scaffold was a huge wooden cage in which half a hundred condemned wretches awaited their fate in utmost misery, pelted with filth by the jeering crowd. The door of their cage was barred from without by a heavy timber resting in brackets, flanked by a pair of guardsmen with sword, spear and ax.

At Conan's nod, Osman turned his mount casually away and rode slowly toward the barracks stable. The full circuit took them the best part of half an hour, for the crowds were dense, forming open spaces only where mountebanks performed.

"Conan," Auda whispered. "I do not like this. These folk are packed together like dates in a leather bag. Making our way out of here will be like trudging through deep sand."

"I think not," Conan said. "When men gallop and shout and flourish their weapons, even such a mob as this fades before them like smoke. They will find a means to remove themselves from our path. It is like a working of magick."

"I hope you are right."

They dismounted near the temple steps and tethered their horses to stone bulls, passing their reins through the iron rings in the bulls' noses. A desert man named Izmil remained behind to mind the horses, his hand resting casually upon a strung bow cased at his saddle.

Conan and Auda sauntered up the steps as if to use the height to survey the crowd, not looking toward the temple itself. Many other people sat upon the steps, some of them laying out meals they had packed, claiming for themselves a good seat from which to view the coming executions.

Just before noon, a priest came to the entrance and intoned the invitation to come inside and see the temple. This time it was a man with strangely bumpy skin. Once again, only a few festival-goers showed an interest. Among them were Volvolicus and Layla. As if on a sudden impulse, Conan and Auda followed behind.

As the sightseers went into the temple, unnoticed by the crowd at large, the two workmen settled their argument and hoisted a pair of heavy timbers to their shoulders and began to trudge up the steps with them. No one in the crowd paid the slightest attention.

Equally unnoticed by the crowd, men were gathering upon the rooftops nearest the temple, overlooking the square. These men bore bows in their hands and kept themselves low, so that they would not be seen above the parapets. They ranged themselves along the edges of the roofs, fitted arrows to their strings, and waited.

Conan strode beneath the fanglike portcullis just as it began to creak downward. As he entered the temple, the two "workmen" went to the sides of the gate, just as if they had been commissioned to perform some task for the temple, and wedged their timbers against the sides of the passage. When the portcullis touched the timbers, it stopped, although the mechanical clatter from above continued for a few seconds.

The bumpy-faced priest turned at the alteration in sound. "What is amiss? Is the gate not working properly? We may not continue if—" Then he saw the two men standing by their timbers. "Who are you two? We ordered no work done on the gate!"

Conan pulled his veil down with one hand as he drew his sword with the other. "You are ordering nothing for the next few minutes, priest," he said. "On the contrary, you are taking mine. All of you, listen to me! We have business down in that crypt, and you are not to interfere. Do as you are told and none will be hurt. We are here for gold, not for blood. Fail to obey in any way and we will cut you down. Now, everybody into the crypt!"

The handful of sightseers gaped, then a woman began to wail in terror. A man, most probably her husband, clapped a hand over her mouth and pushed her toward the steps, grinning at Conan as if in apology for his mate's lack of decorum.

"That's better," Conan said, gesturing with his bare steel. "All of you down there, quickly." He looked at the gate, and the men there gave him the all-clear signal. Thus far, they had not been noticed.

"The curse of Ahriman will lie upon you for this, brigand!" cried the priest as he scurried down the steps, Conan's sword-point pricking his backbone.

"I take nothing from your god, priest," Conan said. "I

come to take Torgut Khan's treasure. Save for that, I will leave your temple as I found it."

"Lord Ahriman is not so easily mollified," the priest warned.

"Silence," Conan said.

Then they were in the crypt. It was not illuminated by torches set in sconces around the walls, but rather by fires burning in bowls held aloft by tripods taller than a man. The walls were not visible at all, and this disturbed Conan in a vague, formless fashion. He shook off the mood. Matters here required his full attention.

In the center of the chamber was a great stack of chests and bags of heavy leather. Already, Volvolicus was working over these, droning strange syllables in a stranger voice, sprinkling powders and striking the chests with a wand of ivory and crystal, while Layla prepared his instruments.

"Mitra!" Auda said. "I hope ninety-three camels will be enough to shift all this!"

"It is the sort of difficulty I can endure," Conan said.

"What you will endure for this outrage is beyond imagining," the priest said coldly.

"I warn you the last time, priest. Silence!" Conan pointed to the gaggle of onlookers with his sword. "You! Get back against the wall and stay there until we are well away, or you shall suffer. You too, priest."

"No!" the priest said. "You must not do that! It is—" Conan laid the flat of his blade against the priest's head, and the man fell like a sacrificial bull.

"Drag him back with you," Conan ordered the onlookers. "And not a sound out of you, if you would live!" Hastily, the people obeyed, grasping the priest by the robe and backing away until all were hidden in the gloom beyond the firelight.

The voice of Volvolicus deepened, and a creaking, shifting noise began. The tiny hairs on the back of the Cimmerian's neck stirred as the huge weight of metal in the chests and bags began to shake, then to rise. Within a few minutes, they were man-height from the floor, floating unsupported in defiance of all experience. Slowly the chests and bags began to shift like a crowded school of fish, forming themselves into a long, square-sided arrangement, pointed at one tip, flat at the other. It looked, Conan realized, remarkably like a Stygian obelisk.

He whirled at a sound from the darkness surrounding. The woman began to wail again, but the sound turned into a horrid, gobbling squawk, then was cut off abruptly. A man's voice screamed, but the sound seemed to come from a great distance.

"What goes on there?" Conan demanded, his usually steely nerves already stretched taut by the wizard's magick.

"Conan! You had better come quickly!"

He whirled again, to see one of the gate guards standing at the foot of the stair. The man's eyes widened at the sight of the mass of chests coming toward him, but he recovered and faced his chief.

"What is it?" the Cimmerian asked.

"Come! Come quickly!"

With a muttered curse, Conan bounded up the stairs behind the bandit. At the top, they ran the length of the temple, then paused as they neared the gate. The other man stood just within, in shadow. He gestured to Conan, then pointed. "Over there, Chief."

Staying carefully back in the shadow, Conan looked to where the man was pointing. For a moment, he saw nothing. Then there was a flash of sunlight gleaming from the spired tip of a helmet on the parapet of a nearby roof about two-score paces distant.

"And there!" said the man who had summoned him, pointing. On another rooftop, Conan saw the upper limb of a bow pass between two large, ornamental urns full of colorful flowers.

"Set take it!" he snapped. "Sagobal has got wind of us. It is an ambush!" How could this have happened? Were they betrayed, or just outmaneuvered? No matter. Conan of

Cimmeria was not one given to futile brooding. They were discovered, so they would just have to fight their way out. A scampering of footsteps behind them made him turn.

"All ready, Chief!" Auda reported. Volvolicus and Layla were close behind him.

"There has been a small change of plan," Conan announced.

Layla looked at him with an ironic smile. "What did I tell you about plans?"

"Quiet, daughter," Volvolicus said. "What has happened?"

"Archers on the rooftops nearby. Is your spell working properly?"

The magician pointed behind him. Slowly, majestically, the great shaft of treasure was emerging from the passageway. Conan shook off his revulsion at the sight.

"We were to walk out naturally and mount, and then ride off in the panic that is going to overwhelm that mob when the treasure floats out of the temple. So much for plans. What we shall do instead is let it go out first. We will go out beneath it and make our escape amid the confusion."

"It will be chancy riding through a mob that has lost its head, Chief," Auda said.

"Better than being skewered by a dozen shafts the second we step outside," Conan pointed out. "It will not be easy for the archers to find their targets in all the milling about."

"Let us hope the other men are having a better time of it than we," Layla said.

"They are good men," Conan avowed. "Let's worry about preserving our own hides and trust them to accomplish their missions."

"What is that?" Auda cried. From just beyond the square, a pillar of white smoke rose skyward. Soon flames shot up into the pillar. People in the square noticed, pointed, and an uneasy murmur spread through the crowd. Atop a roof, some archers stood to look, only to be yanked back down by their fellows.

"I do not know," Conan said, "but we can take advantage of it." He looked back and saw that the obelisk of treasure was upon them. "Get down and be ready to run!"

They lay flat, and the bizarre mass slid silently through the gate above them. Conan had to grit his teeth against the fear inspired by the huge weight suspended so unnaturally above them. Its base went by and the thing hung suspended over the steps.

"Go!" Conan shouted. They went out after the thing, and as it began to rise, they dashed beneath it to run down the steps. To his amazement, Layla was laughing with exhilaration. Arrows began to strike the steps near them and others thunked into the floating chests. Not only were they protected by the thing, he realized, but the incredible sight was throwing the archers off their aim.

They were not the only ones so upset. Someone in the crowd screamed, and people turned from viewing the more distant fire to see the looming mass of chests ascending toward the rooftops. A great turning of heads swept through the crowd. The result was instant pandemonium. A mass howl arose and, suddenly, people began to run in all directions.

Conan saw one of his bandits jump atop the scaffold, wrestle briefly with the timber securing the prisoner cage, then cast it from its brackets. "Scatter for your lives, rogues!" shouted the bandit, his voice cutting through the din. An instant later, the bandit plunged from the scaffold, an arrow in his spine. Howling in delight and fury, the condemned men stormed from the cage. One of them seized a headsman's ax and began to lay about him, hewing down the torturers with shrieks of demented glee.

Conan's own bowmen, stationed at various points around the square, began to shoot at those on the rooftops. The Cimmerian saw two fall from the roofs just as a gold turban cut through the crowd toward them. True to his trust, Osman led four splendid horses by a tether and reined up at the bottom of the steps.

"Mount up, Chief," Osman cried. "It is growing lively here!" An arrow narrowly missed his turban and skewered a fleeing citizen. Conan gauged that half the shafts aimed at him and his men were striking bystanders instead. The panic in the crowd redoubled as it seemed to the terrified masses that not only was the city afire with magick afoot, but they were under enemy attack as well. The casualties from arrows were as nothing compared to the trampling, which killed and injured the unfortunate without respect for age or sex.

Conan hauled himself onto a horse just as an arrow struck the cantle of its saddle and quivered there, humming venomously. Two of Sagobal's guardsmen ran up and sought to grasp his reins from right and left. Conan's sword whirled in a continuous figure-eight, taking a hand from each. Layla was helping her father to climb into his saddle when a guardsman grasped her around the waist, lifting her feet from the pavement. An instant later, Auda, remounted, galloped behind him and slashed him across the spine with a short, curved sword. The guardsman screamed, arching backward as he released the woman. Two seconds later, she was mounted.

"Ride!" the Cimmerian bellowed, looking wildly about him for a sign of Sagobal. Then he saw the man atop one of the roofs, directing the archers. He was pointing directly at Conan, his mouth open in a scream. Instantly, Conan dodged beneath the floating treasure and a half-dozen shafts struck wood or rattled from the pave. The great mass of wood, leather and metal was still rising, and soon it would be no protection.

"Follow me!" he shouted, making a dash for a side street, thanking whatever gods watched out for rogues that he had thought to steal Sagobal's horses—splendid war-beasts accustomed to the smell of blood and the chaos of battle. Ordinary mounts would be rearing and plunging by now, beyond all control. Followed by a virtual bee-swarm of arrows, Conan rode between two buildings and was out of the square. He looked behind to see a number of his companions following.

Osman's golden turban shone brilliant in the sunlight that made its way between the buildings, and he could see Layla as she sought to hold her father upright in the saddle. Auda had his bow out, and was shooting behind him as fast as he could fit arrow to string.

With startling suddenness they burst from the warren of tenements into the small square just within the main gate. There they found another battle in progress as a crew of bandits fought a larger knot of guardsmen. The bandits fought desperately to keep the gate open while the guardsmen fought as hard to shut it. The rogues fought with the fury of cornered rats that made up for their lack of numbers.

Conan's horse plunged into the crowd of guardsmen from behind and he began hewing at armored backs and heads. Quickly, he was joined by Osman and Auda, and many hard sword-strokes were exchanged before the guards broke, each man seeking safety however he could.

"Success!" the Cimmerian proclaimed to his surviving bandits. The exhausted men managed to cheer lustily, then all ran out the gate to seek their mounts.

Cheering and whooping, swinging his bloody blade overhead in a great silver-and-red circle, the bandit-chief thundered down the highway, closely followed by his companions.

Sagobal surveyed the chaos in the square with a look of grim furor. He crossed the pave, littered as it was with wreckage and the bodies of the slain. A half-score had been struck by ill-aimed arrows, many more were trampled. The cries of the wounded rose in the hot air, and the wails of the still-fearful could be heard from every direction. Stalls were overturned, spilling wares all over the square, and performing animals ran loose, confused by the uproar.

Slowly, the guard chief ascended the steps and looked over the scene of devastation. Slowly, with infinite slyness, an unwonted expression quirked Sagobal's lips. He smiled with satisfaction. The smile vanished as a burly form crossed the square, bellowing like a bullock being gelded.

"Sagobal!" Torgut Khan screamed. "Sagobal, what has happened? My festival is a catastrophe! There is fire and battle, and I hear madmen's tales of chests that soar through the sky like hawks ascending! What is all this? Upon your head, explain this to me!"

The obese governor labored up the steps, puffing and wheezing. His face was scarlet from an excess of wine and fury. His eyes were even redder than his complexion. He shook his fist in Sagobal's face.

"I should put you in my dungeon! I should place you on that scaffold to take the punishment that was coming to my escaped felons!" He pointed at the platform, now occupied only by dead executioners and torturers, victims of the prisoners' fury. The viceroy's hand trembled with wrath. "All of my carefully hoarded prisoners are gone! Half my city seems to be aflame! Answer me, you dog! How did this happen!"

"All was as I had planned, Excellency," Sagobal explained. "The bandits came into the town in a body, lured by the treasure. My men were stationed in ambush and the rogues had no clue that their every move was watched. But they did not try to flee with such of the treasure as they could carry, loading it onto horses for their escape. Instead, they employed a wizard to bear it away through the air, as if it were upon one of the flying carpets of ancient legend. I had no way of knowing they would engage in sorcery, Excellency."

The high color fled from Torgut Khan's face. "It flew? You mean these ravings I have heard of floating chests and bags are true? The bandits made the treasure fly from here?"

"That is so, Excellency."

"How—how much?"

"I was just going into the temple to find out. It looked like all of it."

"All? All of my treasure has fled?"

"Nay, Excellency," Sagobal corrected. "It was the king's treasure that fled."

"And I am a dead man if you do not get it back! Fool!" All but unhinged by rage and terror, Torgut Khan reared back and slapped his guard captain with a report that could be heard across the square.

Sagobal's face, emblazoned with a crimson handprint, went deathly. His eyes became pits of darkness as hatred blazed from his brow. Torgut Khan realized that he might have gone too far in provoking this supremely dangerous man. He pointed a finger at Sagobal's steel-sheathed breast.

"Find the treasure, Sagobal. Bring it back, and bring all the bandits back too, to die upon my scaffold." He whirled and stalked off, gathering his robes about him. "I must supervise the firefighting!"

Sagobal's face twisted with hatred, anger and contempt. "As if you cared whether your whole town burned down, you cowardly swine!" he muttered, chewing on an end of his mustache. "You flee to escape the reach of my sword! I will repay that blow, Torgut Khan. I will repay it in full!"

He saw another man crossing the square toward him, moving with a fighting man's easy swagger. "An amusing day, Chief," said Berytus of Aquilonia.

"Aye, it was even more devastating than I had expected," Sagobal acknowledged, his rage calming.

"Your superior gave you more than a tongue-lashing, eh?" Berytus said, grinning. "He left the five-fingered brand on your cheek."

"I shall settle with Torgut Khan, never fear. But I have lost many men and some of my horses, and the stables are aflame."

"Your men are second-rate," Berytus said. "We performed our part to your satisfaction, did we not?"

"Aye, your bowmen are as good as you claimed. Now your real task begins. You must track down the rogues."

"It is what we do best." Berytus looked up the steps with an expression of distaste, and Sagobal turned to see three rust-robed figures descending, fury writ upon their repulsively marked features. "Here's a set of maiden-faced beauties," the Aquilonian commented.

"Sagobal, I hold you personally responsible for this outrage," Tragthan hissed.

"Wherefore, priest?" Sagobal said. "It was a band of marauding bandits who wrought this slaughter."

"What care we for butchered townsmen?" sneered the one called Shosq. "The wretches profaned the sacred precincts of Ahriman! You boasted of the great concentration of treasure in the temple to lure them in so you could catch them easily, instead of doing your duty and running them down in their hills!"

Sagobal spat upon the step between the mottle-faced priest's feet. "That for you and your putrid god! I warn you not to provoke me, priest."

"There is more at stake here than worldly treasure and worthless blood!" cried purple-faced Nikas. "Those outlaws brought a wizard into the holy crypt! They herded their hostages and the priest Umos against the walls. Against the *walls*, Captain!" The man's eyes blazed with a sort of holy terror.

"And what of that, priest?" Sagobal demanded.

"It was more than mere sacrilege, you mortal fool!" Nikas cried, seizing Sagobal by the shoulder in rage and distress.

Snarling, Sagobal drew his ivory-hilted sword in a silver flash and struck downward, cleaving the priest from shoulder to waist. The carcass collapsed between Shosq and Tragthan, both of whom stood in stunned silence.

"Your friend did ill to lay hands upon me," Sagobal said to Tragthan. "He had no more substance than a jellyfish of the Vilayet. Take this boneless carrion back into your temple."

"Shall I kill these others for you, Chief?" Berytus inquired. "I'll not even charge you for the service. I hate all priests."

"No, we've more important matters afoot. Round up your men and the best horses you can find. Get on the track of those villains and stick to them. Do not let them get away."

Berytus saluted, striking knuckles to forehead. "They'll not escape me, Chief. No man has." With that, he turned and walked away.

Sagobal stalked down the steps, satisfied that all was going according to plan. The insolence of Torgut Khan was almost more than he could endure, but that would soon be at an end. He took a head-scarf from a dead woman and cleaned his blade, noting that the blood staining it was not properly red, but was rust-colored like the robes of the priests. Idly, he glanced up the temple stair and saw that priests and corpse were gone. He shrugged, sheathing his sword. There were more important matters afoot than foolish priests and their enigmatic mumblings.

"My chieftain," Osman said, his voice only loud enough to be heard above the clopping of the horses' hooves, "you said that these fine horses were for you and me to make our escape at need, not for carrying the wizard and his little wench." The smaller man had discarded his golden turban and his beads and rode dressed only in his ragged loincloth, sandals and weapon-belt.

"Plans change, Osman. He'll not try to betray us now, weakened and close at hand as he is." He looked back to see the wizard, upright at last but sagging wearily in his saddle. Layla rode close by with an expression of concern. "What of that fire back there? Was that your doing?"

Osman grinned. "Aye. I was alone there, everybody having gone to the festival. I had my horses picked out, saddled and hitched to my line, and I knew I had a little time before you would come out of the temple, so I put it to good use. I opened all the stalls and drove the guardsmen's beasts into the court. Then I struck a fire to the great hayrick by the ox-pen. I thought it might make a fine diversion."

"So it did," Conan said. "That was a clever thought."

"I am not a lunkhead like your other followers," Osman said, preening himself.

"Do not celebrate just now," the Cimmerian warned. "We are not away safely yet. How many of us are there now?" They rode at a steady trot through the hills, keeping off the skyline, taking hard, stony paths to leave as little trace of their passing as possible.

Osman looked back. "We are strung out and I cannot see everyone. Besides the two of us and the wizard and his wench, I can see Auda and Ubo, riding side by side. Aye, and there is Chamik—that one is too lazy to kill. I see no others."

"Surely that cannot be all," Conan said. "There is a small pool ahead. We will stop there and rest a short spell and let the laggards catch up."

"Is it not too soon to stop?" Osman asked worriedly. "Pursuit may be close behind."

"And they will catch us the quicker if we wear out our mounts," Conan insisted.

A quarter of an hour later, they reached the pool. At Conan's order, they dismounted and let their horses drink a little, checked girths and cinches, looked for wounds on men and beasts alike. While they waited, other men rode in, some of them wounded. Eventually, besides Conan and Osman, there were eight surviving bandits.

"By Set, we lost half our number back there!" said Chamik when it was clear there would be no more arrivals.

"That is not a great loss when one considers the size of the reward," said Osman, in high good spirits. "And each of us will have that much greater a share of the treasure."

"Aye," Mamos agreed. "I've been in many a band halved during a raid for a handful of horses or a small herd of cattle. None of us took up this profession in order to enjoy a long life."

"We lost good comrades in Shahpur," said Ubo as he poured blood from his boot. An arrow had struck him in the calf, causing a wound that was superficial, but which bled freely.

"That is right," said Izmil the desert man. "And there will be fewer of us to fight the battle should Sagobal catch up with us. What happened to your fine plan, Conan?"

The Cimmerian had his own reservations, but he was not about to show weakness before these volatile jackals. "Every man here and every man who died back there has lived with a rope around his neck. Death in a fight is quick and clean. We have all gambled with our lives. Some have won, some have lost. Come, we will gather our loot and pour out a draught of wine for our fallen friends. Let's have no mourning."

Ubo winced as he pulled on his soggy boot. "You have it aright, Chief. Let us ride."

There were some frowns and muttering as they mounted, but within the hour, the men were laughing and joking, making plans for their huge haul.

"Your men regain their good humor quickly, Cimmerian," said Volvolicus.

"Like children," said Layla, "who laugh and weep and laugh again within the space of a hundred heartbeats."

"They are men who have cut loose from their past and who have no future," the Cimmerian answered. "For them, nothing has great meaning save the present. And now, the prospect of much gold overrides all else."

They rode far into the night, beneath the gleaming stars. Many of them would have become lost amid the maze of hills, gullies and dry washes, but Conan guided them unerringly. As the light of morning paled the eastern horizon, they entered the defile leading to their hideout. When they came out by the pool, the men set up a happy growl for they could see the great file of chests. It had settled in its obelisk shape, then collapsed into a long, irregular heap as the wizard's spell dispersed. It was quick-witted Osman who first noticed that something was amiss.

"I like this not, Chief," he said to Conan.

"Crom!" Conan muttered in growing dismay. "Where are the camels?"

There were many tracks and other signs that camels had been there, but not a single such beast was anywhere in sight.

Six

Fresh sign!" cried Ambula of Punt. The lean brown man dismounted and ran through the canyon upon bare feet, his bow and arrows cased across his back, stooped over as if he were sniffing out the trail with his wide-flared nostrils. He bent, picked up something and ran back to Berytus, holding up a near-invisible few strands of glossy black hair.

"Horsehair?" said the Aquilonian.

"Hair from a clipped mane," Ambula said. "The guardsmen of Sagobal clip the manes of their horses. Smell them. It is ointment of the flowering tamarind, such as Sagobal uses to make glossy the hides of his mounts."

Berytus could smell nothing in such tiny quantity, but he knew he could trust the senses of his prize tracker. "This way!" he called. Ambula remounted and they rode off up the canyon.

"This is good," said Urdos of Koth. "For a while, I thought we had lost them."

"We never lose a man," said Berytus. "But I will allow

that this Conan is a canny prey. He chooses the best path to leave the smallest trace of his passing. If he were alone, on foot, it might take months to find him in this maze. But traveling with many men, all on horseback, there is no way he can avoid leaving some traces, and with such trackers as Ambula and Bahdur, we will not lose them."

Berytus spoke these words smiling, for he loved the chase. Even without the high pay he demanded of his employers, he relished the sport of matching wits and skill with his prey. Whether that prey was a terrified runaway slave, a band of ragged rebels or fleeing bandits, the pleasure was a matter of degree. Finest of all was the kind of sport he enjoyed this minute—chasing down a fierce, skillful fighting-man who might at any time turn and set a counter-ambush. He did not anticipate such an eventuality just yet, for the Cimmerian did not know what manner of men pursued him. But if Berytus and his followers could not bag the lot in a single ambush, the game would enter a new, and far more dangerous, phase.

For by now, Berytus knew that the man he pursued was one much like himself. Back on the rooftop over the city square, while the others were plying their bows, Berytus had taken no part in the fighting. Instead, he had watched Conan closely, weighing the man, judging his skills, his strengths and his weaknesses. Of the latter, he saw no trace save a certain reluctance on the man's part to run from his friends and save his own hide.

As a swordsman, he was very nearly the best Berytus had ever seen. The highest rating was one Berytus reserved for himself alone. As a planner and leader, the northerner was superb, carrying off the daring raid with wit and style. Only the intervention of the rooftop archers had spoiled what might have been a perfect robbery.

Yes, there could be no doubt of it. This was going to be one of his more memorable chases.

"Blood!" cried Bahdur as they rode from the little canyon into one slightly larger. He pointed to his find in passing and the others did not dismount to examine it, but only glanced as they rode by. A few drops glistened redly upon the top leaves of a desert weed that grew a bit above two feet high.

"Brushed from the foot of a mounted man," said Barca the Shemite as he passed it. "Probably a leg wound. It cannot be a serious wound, or we'd have seen more blood ere now."

"Aye, they had many killed, but they got away with remarkably few wounded," Berytus observed. "Such are the workings of fate."

By the time darkness overtook them, they knew they were only a few hours behind their prey. Whatever his precautions, there was nothing the Cimmerian could do about horse-droppings, and the condition of these gave the manhunters a fair estimate of the time since the robbers had passed.

"Shall we hunt on by torchlight?" Urdos asked Berytus.

"Nay, these are not runaway slaves. That keen-eyed mountaineer will see a single torch miles away and set an ambush for us before daylight. We'll camp here and continue at dawn. We'll have them by tomorrow afternoon, never fear."

They dismounted and unsaddled their mounts, curried them and secured them to a picket line. Then, without kindling a fire, they washed down preserved rations with water, rolled into their blankets and slept. When on the trail, these men did not pamper themselves. They became hunting beasts for the duration.

"Where are they?" Mamos screamed. He pointed at Conan with a grubby finger. "You! You said that the camels were to be here! Why are they not?"

Conan gripped his sheath with his left hand and pressed against his hilt with his thumb, loosening the sword. "You know where I have been these last few days, Mamos. If you think this is treachery on my part, you are as stupid as you are ugly, and that is stupid indeed."

"They were here!" Auda insisted. "You can all see the tracks and the dung they left behind. But where is Junis, whom we left to watch over the beasts and nurse his wounded leg?"

"That at least is plain," said Ubo. "Look." He raised an arm and pointed to the vultures circling over a spot a few hundred paces away, around a bend of the little canyon.

The men raced up the canyon and they found Junis in a stunted tree, although they had to drive away the flocking vultures in order to see him. Junis had been hewn into numerous pieces, and the various parts of him hung from the branches. Already he was well gnawed and substantial pieces of him were missing.

"They found him!" Auda wailed. "Those crawling, god-accursed camel-herders tracked their animals all the way here and they took them back! They butchered Junis and hung him here as a warning!"

"They must be demons in human form," Layla said ironically. "Who would think that men could be capable of such a deed?" She averted her face from the thing in the tree, repelled either by the sight or the smell.

"Do not mock us, woman," Chamik warned. "That is our comrade hanging there."

"Do not insult my intelligence, bandit," she said. "You rogues care no more for each other than do wolves in a pack. You fall upon the weaker with the savagery of beasts, so let us not prate about our poor, departed friends. The camels are gone. The problem is what to do with this great mass of metal."

The woman's cold-blooded words shocked even the hard-bitten brigands into reality.

"Aye, the wench is right," said Ubo. "What do we do now?"

"Great Volvolicus," said Osman, "can you not help us move the gold with your magickal arts? You brought it hither with such impressive power, surely you can so maneuver it again."

"I fear not," said the mage. "Moving the mass this far has nigh exhausted me. Even so, the spell cannot work again for a full turning of the moon."

"The moon?" cried Mamos, as if the very idea offended him. "What has the moon to do with anything?"

"A great deal," said the wizard. "I could explain to you about tidal forces and how they affect the crystalline structure of stone and metal, but you would not understand."

"You are probably right," said Mamos, drawing his dagger and thumbing its razor-keen edge. "I might think that you were spouting wizardly nonsense to conceal your true plans."

"Enough of that," said Conan. "If we are to fall to bickering among ourselves, we might as well make a gift of this treasure to Torgut Khan. We got the greatest heap of treasure any of us has seen this far, and is that not a splendid thing?"

All agreed that it was.

"Then," the Cimmerian went on, "we must simply work out a way to get it farther, so that it and we are beyond the grasp of Torgut Khan and his dog, Sagobal."

"Can we not steal more camels?" Osman asked.

"Nay," Auda said, "for every man in the district who owns a single beast will be guarding it now. Times will be hard for camel-thieves for months."

"More than that," Conan pointed out, "Sagobal's guards will be out searching. Soon they must stop at the village from whence the camels were taken, and they will need no great wit to figure out who needed so many camels and drove them to an obscure place. Those herdsmen could lead them right to this spot. We dare not tarry long."

"Say you that we must abandon the bulk of this treasure here?" Chamik bellowed. "Just ride off with such little of it as a man may bear on a single horse? I'll carve your liver ere I do such a thing!" The potbellied Corinthian put hand to hilt, and others did likewise. Osman and Auda drew closer to Conan.

Layla laughed musically. "Snarling dogs fighting over a dead horse! None can bear it away, and none can stand to see another get a piece of it. Never again shall I believe a tale about the fine, free life of the brigand. Such fools have I never beheld!"

"Be still, daughter," Volvolicus said in a low voice. "These are not servingmen to be upbraided."

But her words had stung the would-be rebels and caused them to think again.

"What's to be done, then?" asked one-eyed Ubo.

"We must conceal it here," Conan insisted, "until such time as we may come back and bear it off, taking only enough to pay our way until that time."

"Where?" Osman demanded, spreading his arms, indicating the bare landscape.

"There is a painted cave not far from where we stand," Auda said. "I discovered it once when I hid out here and another band hostile to my people occupied the oasis. I slept there many days and came down at night for water. They never suspected me."

"What is a painted cave?" Conan asked.

"They are much to be seen in the desert places," Auda explained. "Always, they are hard to find, their entrances small. I found this one when a hare I was pursuing darted into it. Within, their walls are painted with figures of men and animals. Hunting peoples must have sheltered there, and it must have been long, long ago, for many of the beasts are such as are not seen in this place."

"Show me this painted cave," Conan said.

They followed the desert warrior into a side canyon, and then into another, each of them so similar to all the others in the area that only experience could prevent a man from becoming lost among them. They mounted a shattered boulder that served them for a crude stair, and Auda indicated an irregular hole beneath a rock-slab overhang, all but invisible from just a few feet away. A grown man could enter only by crouching.

"There may be venomous serpents inside," Auda warned.

"Some of you go and make us torches," Conan instructed. "Take no brush from nearby, and take none from a living bush. Let's leave no sign of our doings."

Minutes later, two of the men returned with dry brush

bound into long torches. Osman, an able fire-raiser, sparked the brush to flame with flint and steel. Then, holding a torch before him, Conan ducked and squeezed his bulk through the opening. The others followed. Last of all came Volvolicus and Layla.

Within, they found a chamber of irregular shape, twenty paces long and eight or ten wide. There were no side passages, and the floor was littered only with the sort of refuse left by animals that had sheltered there: nesting materials, gnawed bones, feathers, eggshells and so forth. If human beings had kindled fires within, it had been so long ago that not even ashes or cinders remained.

"Set!" swore a man, raising his torch to examine the walls and ceiling. "What manner of creatures are these?"

The rough stone was covered with paintings of men and animals. The human figures were but crude stick-men such as children draw, but the beasts were splendid renderings, so detailed and subtle that the artists had captured not only the look but the movement, the very essence, of the creatures.

"That is an elephant, by Mitra!" said a bandit. "But look how its tusks curl, and it has long hair all over it!"

"I have seen a few of those in the far northern woods," Conan said, "although they are near hunted out now, and are rare."

"And here is a rhinoceros," said a man of Keshan. "And it, too, is hairy."

"Here are giraffes," Conan pointed out, "but their markings and horns are not such as I have seen. And these are aurochs or bison of some breed."

"Are these horses?" Osman asked, pointing to a group. "Yet they seem to be no larger than dogs, if the stick-men hunting them are represented truly. Wizard, what do these things mean?"

"First, that the world is an ancient and wonderful place. Go to the sandy desert and sift the sand through your fingers. Soon you will find shark teeth, for that desert was once sea bottom." The mage wandered among the paintings, admiring them. "Farmland was once jungle, a city on a flat plain is where a mountain once stood, before wind and water wore it away to nothing. A hillside in the icy northern waste reveals hot-water coral that once grew in a tropic sea. All is mutable.

"As for these," he gestured at the painted beasts, "I would hazard that the painters were a hunting folk who were also gifted artists. They did not create these images for the pleasure of it, but to make magick to aid them in their hunting. Look closely and you will see the marks where they shot the images with arrows or jabbed them with darts, hoping this would help them do the same with the living creatures. They went to great lengths to capture the essence of their prey, getting every gesture, color and contour in their renderings. Yet you see that they represent themselves only as stick figures, one indistinguishable from another? That was so that they would not fall victim to their own magick, for they knew that the image can capture the spirit of the model."

The bandits gaped in wonder at the strange, enigmatic paintings, until their chief's words brought them back to their situation.

"If the cave served those people then, it can serve us as well now," Conan announced. "We will carry the treasure here and erase all trace of our passage, then conceal the entrance even better than it is hidden by nature. It will be hard work, but there is plenty of room here and the chests will remain concealed for as long as need be. Let us be about it."

They left the cave and went back to their water pool. The rest of the day was a great toil as chest by chest and bag by bag, they carried the treasure to the cave. They cried out and grumbled, for they were opposed to hard labor on principle, but somehow knowing that the weight was gold and silver made it seem not so terrible. Often, two men would stagger under the weight of a single chest. Only Conan could hoist two of the chests to his brawny shoulders and carry them to the cave without having to pause for breath. At last, only a single leather bag remained.

"Auda," Conan ordered, "get rid of all the marks we left."

Auda and two other desert men prepared brooms of brush and carefully swept every inch of ground traversed by the bandits in their labors. When they were done, Conan inspected their work, piled some carefully chosen stones over the cave entrance, and at last pronounced himself to be satisfied.

The worn-out men lounged by the pool, drinking watered wine and rubbing the cramps from their sore limbs. The Cimmerian returned and walked to the final bag. This he grasped and raised one-handed, although it weighed better than a hundredweight. Only the knotted, vein-bulging muscle of his shoulder revealed the strain. The Cimmerian drew his dirk and drew its edge the length of the bag. The light of the setting sun glittered from the cascade of silver coin. A low moan arose from the bandits to greet the pretty sight.

"We divide this among ourselves," Conan said. "Then we ride. Pursuit may not be far off."

The men began to scoop up silver by handfuls. "Where do we go from here?" asked a desert man.

"I think we should split up," Osman said, "each to go his own way. That way, we will avoid pursuit the better. Then, when all alarm has died down, we can gather here once more, with pack animals to bear away our share."

"No!" Ubo shouted. "You say that because you want to sneak back here aforetime and take more than your fair share, you greedy cur! I say we all stay together until we return. I'll not trust a one of you out of my sight until our loot is divided fairly!" Many growled assent at these words.

"Well, it is not the safest, but perhaps it is the best," Conan allowed. "That leaves the problem of where to go. Torgut Khan will have patrols out in all directions, but they will be thinnest in the desert. I say we head for the Iranistan border. We can lie low there for a while, then come back. It should be no great wait. Before long, the king must learn of the theft of his treasure, and then heads shall roll, Torgut Khan's and Sagobal's first among them. A single moon should do it, then we can return from Iranistan with transport for the gold. Does that suit you rogues?" His lion gaze swept them all, taking in the whole group. They met his eyes, resignedly or truculently, but there was no rebellion.

"Iranistan it is, then," said Ubo.

"I shall return to my home," said Volvolicus, "there to await you. I shall claim no part of the treasure until you see to its division."

"No, you shall come with us!" Chamik said. "You are one of us for the nonce, wizard. You know where we have cached our treasure, wherefore should we trust you any more than one of our number?"

"Take care, bandit!" the mage said haughtily. "I may have played the outlaw these past days, but I am still a sorcerer of power. Do you doubt that I can smite you with fell curses for your insolence?"

Some of the bandits fell back, terrified by the power of magick, but not the more hard-bitten ones.

"Curse as you will, wizard," said Mamos. "I have survived worse than your spells." He indicated the rope scar encircling his neck. "You and the wench ride with us. You get your share when we do."

"Aye," said Ubo. "It's all together or none, and we settle it right here." Once again, hands went to hilts, swords were half-drawn.

"Do not trouble yourself with them, Father," Layla said. "Let us accompany them to Iranistan. Your guardian-spells will protect our house while we are away, and you may employ the time conferring with your colleagues in that land."

"Who knows?" said Osman with a grin. "You may find there a new rock, completely unknown to you!"

The bandits roared with mirth at what was, to them, penetrating wit. Swords were slammed home in their sheaths and good humor was restored all around. They mounted and rode from the canyon by way of the southernmost escape route. As they rode, they passed the wineskins from hand to hand and sang or told ancient tales. Out of immediate danger, they knew themselves to be rich men. What was the turning of a single moon, more or less? They even passed the wineskins to Volvolicus and Layla, regarding them now as a part of the band.

"Is it always thus with such men?" Layla asked Conan when the two of them rode a little ahead of the others. "Challenge and fight and rollicking good-fellowship all at once?"

"Aye, I have told you the sort of men they are. They lack the social graces, but all are good, reliable fighting-men when the blades are out. You saw how they acted back in Shahpur. Each man performed his task though his life were forfeit. It is only between operations that I must watch out for them."

"And you have always lived among such men?" she asked.

"Not always, but in many places I have known their like: pirates, *kozaki*, mercenaries between hires, outlaws of all sorts. They are much alike."

"You are not just an outlaw, then, but a professional adventurer?"

"Aye. I am a wandering man, and never can I abide in one place for long, but must always be up and seeking another land. For me, all sights, however wonderful, pall in time and I must search out new ones."

"A man who would live beyond all law must make his own," she said, musing. Near her, the wizard nodded in his saddle, asleep. She held his reins in her right hand.

"That is the way of it. Also, he must be strong and quick, or he does not live long." He turned and gazed to the northwest, as if his blue eyes could pierce thousands of miles and years of time. "My folk, the Cimmerians, are a people of clan and custom, and always have been so. I was near grown, and already a wanderer, before I ever heard of laws and judges, of courts, juries and prisons. These things seemed a great foolishness to me, so I enjoyed the hospitality of many a magistrate in whose jurisdiction I transgressed."

The Cimmerian smiled ruefully. "In time I came to understand why the common run of men need these things, so that dwellers in cities may do their work and go about their lives in peace, but always I have chafed beneath the yoke of law.

Most of all, I am enraged by foolish tyrants like Torgut Khan and their hyena lackeys, like Sagobal."

"So now you have put paid to those two?" she asked.

"That remains to be seen. Let us say that the task is well begun."

Two days of hard riding brought them to the River Ilbars. Turan claimed the land north of the river, and Iranistan claimed that to the south, although neither nation maintained any sort of significant military presence within several days' travel to either side. The claims were mere legal fictions, since all land had to be claimed by somebody, and no king was ever slow to claim land that did not have someone else's troops and forts upon it. The petty lords of the border usually acknowledged one king or the other as their sovereign, although generations might pass before they were required to render feudal service. The borderlands were more a haven for bandits, raiders and rebels than they were taxpaying provinces.

"Wizard!" cried Osman as he rode his mount down the gentle bank to the slow-flowing river. "Can you part these waters, so that we may cross without getting wet?"

Volvolicus was much recovered from his exertions now. "Water in its liquid state lacks a crystalline structure. If you will freeze it to ice, I will move it for you."

The bandits laughed in appreciation of this sally.

"It would be a crime offensive to all the gods to deny you men the chance for a bath," Layla said. The men roared even louder.

"Into the water, hounds!" Conan shouted as he galloped down the bank and into the stream, his horse's hooves raising a great spray. Whooping and cheering, the rest followed. The river was not deep, and the horses had to swim only a short distance. Upon the other side, they wrung the water from their clothes and dried their weapons.

"You wanted to see Iranistan, Chief," Osman said, oiling the blade of his dagger. "Well, here you are. What think you of it?"

"It looks like more of Turan, so far," Conan said, surveying the monotonous, green-brown landscape. The land along the river was verdant, but it grew arid just a few hundred paces from the water, and the low hills surrounding were cloaked in brown grass upon which occasional flocks of sheep and goats grazed, proclaiming that the land was not entirely uninhabited.

This borderland was a narrow, green strip of cultivation between near-deserts, capable of sustaining only scattered herdsmen and villages of subsistence farmers. The people of the land were mostly peasants who spoke a dialect of Turanian mixed with much Iranistani. They were short folk with the look of much inbreeding. They wore black robes despite the prevailing heat, and they wound coils of copper wire through the piercings in their noses. They looked upon the heavily armed strangers with suspicion, but Conan knew that to be the custom of peasants the world over.

"Are there any towns near here?" Conan asked the band at large.

"Aye," said Ubo. "We've time to pass and a little money to spend, so let us find a place where there is more than sour-faced dirt grubbers to take our silver from us!"

"Southeast of here," Auda said, "a day's ride from the river, there is an oasis town called Green Water. It is where several caravan roads cross. It is not large, but it has a fine bazaar and many taverns."

"That sounds a good destination," said Conan. "A town that earns its keep providing entertainment for travelers is just what we need. Lead on, Auda." With the desert man in the lead, the band rode off southeast, bright and cheerful at the prospect of some excitement and pleasure at last.

A few hours later, another band of men rode to the crossing point. First to arrive were a Hyrkanian and a man of Koth. Quickly, they were joined by others, among them an Aquilonian.

"They crossed here, Chief," said Urdos. "Shall we ride after?"

"No, we ride back to Shahpur," Berytus said.

"Why?" asked Barca the Shemite. "We can catch them in another day or two."

"Aye, and then what? They do not have the treasure with them, and that is what we truly need. We are low on supplies and our mounts are half-lame from this hard riding. We can resupply, remount and be back here within five days. Getting here was slow, because we were tracking. A straight ride by the shortest route will take but a fraction of the time." With that, he wheeled and rode back north. Casting glances in the direction of the fleeing prey, the others did likewise.

Beneath the altar of Ahriman, the priests met in conclave within the crypt. Tragthan and Shosq stood over a coffin-like sepulcher of stone. Within it lay purple-faced Nikas, his body nearly halved by Sagobal's sword blow, yet still alive. The huge wound oozed blood, along with less recognizable fluids, and the flesh at his waist, where the great slash ended, showed signs of healing.

"What is our situation?" Nikas asked, his lips barely moving, his voice as thin as a ghost's.

"Unknown and perilous," replied Tragthan. His cowl was pushed back, revealing a face more reptilian than human. His skin was yellowish, and scaly around the eyes and the lipless mouth. The eyes themselves were yellow, and his pupils were narrow rectangles with rounded ends. "At this time of all times, the men of the outer world have been playing their games of greed and lust. They have profaned our temple and brought worldly magick into our crypt, upsetting the delicate balance of our conjurations. We could face catastrophe."

"It was a grave error to allow the satrap to keep his foul gold in this holy place," Shosq hissed.

"What would you have me do?" Tragthan demanded. "It was necessary to allow this in order to get the corrupt swine's cooperation in building Ahriman's temple. I did not guess that Sagobal was using it as bait to catch the robbers, who would come hither amid bloodshed, before we were ready to summon our lord with blood and souls." He looked around them, his yellow eyes piercing the outer gloom.

"How fares Umos?" Nikas whispered.

"Between worlds," said Shosq. "Residing neither in our lord's world nor in this."

Tragthan and Shosq walked to one of the walls, the wall against which the bandits had forced their hostages to stand. It was utterly black, a black that was not merely absence of color, but that seemed to suck all color and light into itself. The surface was almost flat, but in several places it bore irregularities. Upon close examination, some of these resembled human faces writhing in agony and terror. A larger irregularity was in the shape of a man. At first glance, it seemed to be a human form carved in high relief, but closer examination revealed a more ghastly sight: It was as if a man were on the other side of a black membrane, striving to break through into the real world. His face was that of the priest Umos.

"Umos, can you hear us?" Tragthan called. For a long time, there was no answer, then came words as from a great distance.

"I hear you, Brother!" said the distant, wailing voice. "Our dark lord consumes his sacrifices, the wretched mortals cast in here with me. He hungers for more. Get me out, or find him others that he may sate his hunger upon their souls!"

"This is an ill thing," Shosq said. "It was not the time. We were to draw our lord closer to his worldly altar before feeding him the souls of his victims. He grows stronger and draws nigh in power before we have the time to assure the alignment of planets and stars, before we perform the rites and cast the spells to restore him to his proper self-knowledge." The priest spoke the words in a rapid, panic-stricken chatter, and he turned to Tragthan with terror shining from his eyes.

"Tragthan," he said, "we could draw into this world a thing that is both mindless and all-powerful!"

"And if we do that, is it so bad a thing?" said the reptilian priest.

"What can you mean?" asked Shosq.

"Are we children to perceive our god as a loving father? Great Ahriman is the lord of destruction, the shatterer of worlds. Even the contemptible cult of Ormazd recognizes that Ahriman must accomplish his act of annihilation, so that kindly Ormazd may rebuild the world, shining and bright. We know that destruction is an end in itself. Destruction is the glory of Ahriman!"

"But this is not the procedure of ages!" Shosq protested. "The magick-working of that wizard drew our lord's attention as a lodestone draws iron filings. He took the mortals pressed against his wall for sacrifices. This time . . ." The priest's voice trembled. "This time, *we* may be destroyed as well!"

"If that be the will and glory of Ahriman," said Tragthan, "then so be it!"

Seven

The bandits crested a line of low hills and rode along the dirt road toward the town that lay in the midst of orchards fringing a spring-fed lake. The place had low walls, now ruinous, but once grand. Obviously, it had been a town of some importance . . . long ago. Now it was simply a pleasant stop for caravans going from one place to another. Several caravans had their camels, horses, mules and oxen corralled near the trees, where they could benefit from the shade and the water while their owners did their business and their carousing in the town.

As they rode, the bandits sang, anticipating a fine time for themselves. One by one the voices faltered, and the song died out as each of them realized that something was wrong with the fine vista before them.

"What is that?" said Osman, pointing. "That is no caravan." The sight that gave them pause was an enclosure where more than a hundred horses were secured to picket ropes in straight lines. A number of men stood guard near the beasts, and sunlight gleamed from their burnished helmets, their lance-points and their round shields.

"An army patrol, by Set!" swore Ubo. "Has Sagobal got here ahead of us?"

"Even from here, I can see that those men do not wear his livery," Conan said, "nor any sort of Turanian uniform. This may be but a patrol of the Iranistani army, perhaps a governor's guard."

"An accursed strong patrol," Chamik said. "That is half a cavalry wing. And look there!" On the far side of the town, a line of horsemen approached, their banners flying. They passed out of sight behind the walls.

"There must be another such camp on the other side," Layla said. "This place is occupied by an army."

"What do we do now, Chief?" Osman asked.

"Are any of you wanted in this land?" Conan queried. The men looked at each other, shrugging and spreading their hands.

"It looks as if no ropes await us here, Conan," said Ubo.

"Then we ride on in like the innocent little lambs we are. We cannot pretend to be merchants, but if any ask, we will say we are mercenaries looking for work and I am your captain."

"What sort of mercenaries?" asked Osman.

"Irregular cavalry," Conan told him.

"They will believe you," Layla said. "You cannot ask for cavalry more irregular than this lot."

"If we are mercenaries," Ubo said, "then who is she?" He jerked his head in Layla's direction.

Conan grinned broadly. "Why, she is my mistress. Captains are permitted one." The men laughed and hooted as they rode toward the town.

"I'll play the part in public, but not in private, Cimmerian!" Layla announced, to yet more derision.

First they rode to the lake and dismounted, letting their horses drink, walking them, then letting them drink some more. Nearby, a stone enclosure had been built out into the lake. In it, women and young girls, dressed only in thin shifts, washed laundry, soaking and scrubbing it in stone tubs, then throwing it onto long, low stone tables and beating it with flat wooden paddles. Some of the bandits began sauntering toward the enclosure, but Conan called them back.

"Those are someone's wives and daughters," he said. "We want to rest here a long time, and we need no disputes with the townsmen. There will be professional ladies in the town to see to your wants. Come, let's find what this place has to offer."

They remounted and rode down a paved road lined with tall palms. At its end was a splendid stone gate that stood proudly, although the wall all around and above it was much dilapidated. As soon as they passed through it, they could hear loud music coming from somewhere near the center of the town.

"That is more like it!" Conan said. "Merriment is in progress. Let's go get a share of it!" They rode through the narrow streets and attracted only idle glances from the townsmen. Strangers, even heavily armed ones, were nothing new to them, for travelers were the town's lifeblood.

Everywhere they looked there were soldiers; men in pointed steel helms with spreading neck-guards of lacquered splints laced with silken cord, wearing short cuirasses of similar construction and steel-plated boots. They walked with the bowlegged lurch of born cavalrymen. Their garments were of padded silk dyed in bright colors, but they had fierce, predatory faces. Most of them appeared to be either drunk or working hard to get that way.

"These look a bad lot to pick a fight with," Osman said.

"Aye," Conan affirmed. "For once, I should have little trouble convincing my rogues to step lightly."

Like most cities of the arid lands, Green Water was built in the form of a rough square with an open plaza in its center that served as marketplace, center of government, and gathering and socializing area for the town, its inhabitants and visitors. As the bandits rode into the plaza of Green Water, they saw that it was far grander than they would have expected of so small a town.

Not only was it broad, but in its center was a fine fountain whose central spume rose high into the air, to fall back and fill a broad, circular bowl, from which in turn the water cascaded into a rectangular pond in which bright-colored fish frolicked. Several taverns fronted the plaza, each with an outdoor garden for eating and drinking, and before these were platforms whereon dancers performed to the music of skirling flutes and thumping tambours. Here and there, tall stately palms shaded the colorful tiles that paved the square.

"This looks to be a fair place to abide," said Conan, who had been expecting a squalid little caravan town like so many he had seen.

"Aye," said Ubo. "I would be happy with the prospect were it not for all these soldiers."

On the north side of the plaza, Conan espied a large public building above which flew the banner of the king of Iranistan, and beside it, on a lower pole, a flag with the figures of two scarlet lions upon a black background, facing one another in a rampant pose. Along the whole side of the building fronting upon the square was a broad portico shaded by a tiled roof supported by pillars carved with twining ivy, painted in realistic colors. Around a table on this veranda sat what appeared to be a score of officers in silvered or gilded armor.

"Let us find a place as far as possible from that lot," Osman advised.

"My very thought," said Conan. They rode around the plaza until they came to a tavern on the side farthest from the officers' headquarters. They hitched their horses and found places at a long table. From a serving woman Conan ordered food and wine for all hands. Upon a nearby platform a number of women danced, whirling through intricate patterns amid many flying veils. They wore bright, voluminous dresses, and their arms clattered with bangles. Their veils and head-scarves framed dark faces and black eyes, noses ablaze with jeweled studs connected to elaborate earrings by tiny, golden chains.

"These women wear too many clothes for proper dancing," one of the bandits groused.

"Doubtless entertainment more to your taste is available in some of the establishments to be found down the alleys," Conan said.

"Aye," said Auda. "I saw shrines to the god of harlots before some houses near here."

"Perhaps you should call at a bathhouse first," Layla suggested. "There are some things to which even the lowest of women should not be subjected."

"Aye," said one-eyed Ubo, twirling the ends of his mustache. "I should find a barber as well, to help restore me to my accustomed beauty."

"That would be beyond the powers of the finest barber," Chamik told him. "Perhaps our wizard could help."

"By striking everyone blind, all else failing," said Osman. The table roared with laughter.

Conan had more serious matters on his mind. He leaned aside to speak to a substantial-looking man seated among companions at a table adjacent.

"Your pardon, sir, but we are strangers just arrived. Are you a resident of this fine city?"

"That I am," the man said. "I am Ushor the spice merchant, and these are the resident freemen of my guild." He indicated the others at his table, all of them substantial men, who inclined their heads courteously.

"Then perhaps you could tell me who all these soldiers are. Is there war here in the border country?"

"Ah, these are the cavalry of General Katchka, commander of the Army of the North. They are here protecting us from the rebels who have come to infest these lands in recent years."

"And do you require protection from these rebels?" Conan asked.

"Of a certainty! Their defiance is intolerable, and we here

are all loyal subjects of the king." Ushor said this loudly, then he and his companions smiled with infinite cynicism.

"I understand," Conan assured him.

"What does this mean?" Layla asked as their pitchers and platters were delivered.

"It may mean that we are in luck," said Conan. "If this general is just chasing rebels, he will have little interest in a few foreigners. From a king's point of view, a handful of homegrown malcontents is more of a problem than a whole foreign army. These troops are probably reasserting royal authority in a place where it hasn't been seen much lately, and no doubt their general is collecting several years' worth of unpaid taxes."

"You are better acquainted with the doings of kings and generals than I would have credited," she said, picking up a skewer of spicy meat and nibbling daintily.

"I am not always a bandit," he explained. "I have served as an officer in many armies."

"I must make enquiries," Volvolicus said, "to find whether there are any practitioners of my craft in this place."

"Can you not, well . . ." Osman cast about for words ". . . can you not *feel* the presence of another magician?"

Volvolicus looked at him quizzically. "Where do you get your ideas of sorcerers' abilities? Of course I cannot feel the presence of such a one. If I were in the midst of a spell, with my wards in place, I might well detect the aura of another mage engaged in his own works nearby, but only then."

"Say you so?" Osman said, looking disappointed.

"What will you do if you find one?" Conan asked.

"It is always pleasant to converse with a colleague," said Volvolicus.

This seemed strange to Conan, for in his experience, wizards were a solitary lot, much given to mutual suspicions and jealousies. If this one was sociable, why did he live deep in the desert with only his daughter for company? In his younger and more impetuous days, the Cimmerian might have asked for an explanation, but time and experience had taught him that it was often best to keep his suspicions to himself until more evidence came his way.

They were allowed to finish their meal in peace, and the serious drinking began. As the pitcher was passed around, a man in officer's garb appeared at their table. He was tall and thin, with a slightly more refined version of the predatory look common to the soldiery.

"I am Captain Mahac," the man announced, bowing slightly. "May I be permitted the honor of addressing the spokesman of this group?" The tongue of Iranistan was closely related to that of Turan, and Conan had no trouble following the man's words.

"I am the captain of this band," he stated.

"My leader, the illustrious General Katchka, would greatly esteem the pleasure of your company at his table, sir." The formality of the captain's words in no way decreased the deadliness of his manner.

"I am honored," Conan said, standing. Then, to his men: "Stay out of trouble."

"In luck, eh?" Layla said.

"It is no cause for alarm," Conan assured her. "It is natural for a military commander to be suspicious of a band of armed men in his territory. I would think it unusual if he did not summon me sooner or later. It seems that this General Katchka is a man who wastes no time."

The Cimmerian strode along behind Captain Mahac. As they crossed the square, the desert wind blew a cooling spray from the fountain in their path. Whoever had designed and placed the fountain, he thought, had done the town a favor beyond reward. No wonder the general had chosen the spot for his headquarters.

They mounted the stair and found the table full of officers already far gone in drink, but they appeared to be the sort of hard-bitten professionals who were as dangerous and efficient drunk as they were when sober. At the head of the table sat a man who appeared at first glance to be fat, but a closer look revealed that he was as burly as a wine cask, with heavy muscle beneath a deceptive padding of flesh. He wore a sleeveless vest of mail, the flat rings plated with gold and carved with protective charms. He gestured to a stool next to his chair.

"Be seated, stranger. Have something to drink." His voice was low and hoarse.

Conan sat and took a cup of hammered silver, raising it. "To your Excellency's health."

Katchka raised his own cup. "And yours." The two drank, then the general went on. "You and your little band caught my eye as you rode in. I desired to speak with you, but you showed the signs of a long ride and I thought it best to let you refresh yourselves first." The blast of winy breath was fit to shrivel hair, but his words were clear enough.

"Your courtesy is deeply appreciated," Conan said. "How may I be of service?"

On Conan's other side sat a tall, hatchet-faced man dressed in fine clothes. This one spoke. "I am the Vizier Akhba, his majesty's military commissioner for the northern district. The general and I had some discussion concerning your band. May we know your name?"

"I am Conan of Cimmeria."

"Cimmeria?" Katchka said. "Where is that?"

"It is a nation of the far north," the vizier said, "beyond even Aquilonia. I have never encountered a man of your nation. How do you come to be so far south?"

"I am a captain of mercenaries. Wars are few in the north just now. My men and I came looking for a quiet, peaceful spot in which to spend our pay and wait for opportunity to come our way."

"May an old soldier observe," said Katchka, "that your men display little of the discipline customary among professional soldiers?"

"They are irregulars," Conan said.

"Irregulars. I see," said the vizier, smiling as if they all shared a joke.

"So long as you cause no trouble here," Katchka said,

"you may stay as long as you like, as far as I am concerned. As for the townsmen, they will make you welcome as long as your money lasts."

"I am accustomed to that," Conan said.

"I trust you have had no dealings with the rebels in these parts," said Akhba.

"Nor even heard of them until this very hour," Conan assured him. "I take no interest in other people's wars unless I am hired to. In my experience, rebels rarely have the money to pay professional troops."

"It is good that you think that way," said Katchka, refilling Conan's cup. "Keep thinking thus and you and I shall remain friends."

"Who are these rebels?" Conan asked. "I want nothing to do with their cause, for we crossed the Ilbars only yesterday and ere we saw this town, we saw only villages and sour-faced peasants. But if there is war here, I would know who is fighting whom."

"That is wise," said the vizier. "Know then that His Serene Majesty, Xarxas the Ninth, has occupied the Phoenix Throne by grace of Lord Mitra for seventeen years." The court official pronounced these words rollingly, as if this were a formula that prefaced all pronouncements concerning the king. "Upon his accession, in accordance with the custom laid down six centuries ago by the founder of the Dynasty, Djaris the Supreme, he had all his brothers strangled that there should be no disputes over the succession and thus peace should reign in the land. This is a harsh law, but a wise and just one. Better that a few supernumerary princes should die than the nation be devastated by civil war."

"It is a custom widely practiced," Conan averred, "although I never ere now visited a nation where it was part of the code of law."

"Djaris the Supreme was a man of clear vision," said the vizier, "and he maintained that nothing was more superfluous than a superfluity of royalty."

"He'll get no disagreement from me," Conan said.

"Sometimes a prince gets overlooked," Katchka said. "This time, a concubine concealed the fact that she was with child. She whelped the brat in secret and had him raised by her kindred here in the north. Now that the stripling is old enough to ride at their head, his mother's family has proclaimed him the true heir and raised a rebellion."

Conan paused with his cup halfway to his lips. "The son of a concubine? Is he taken seriously?"

"Perhaps our law differs from those with which you are familiar," said the vizier. "To inherit, one must be a son of the former king by a lawful wife or concubine. That is all. All of the royal princes are educated in war and administration, as if each were to be the sole heir. At the king's inevitable death . . ." He shrugged as if the results were self-evident.

"Then the winner of the squabble takes all, and the most ruthless inherits the throne," Conan finished for him. "Djaris the Supreme again?"

"Just so," said Akhba. "But I must point out that Djaris the Supreme prized cleverness as highly as courage, and the winner most often is the son who can first lay hands upon the royal treasury. There is a good deal of art to this accomplishment."

"Aye, it is the loyalty of the soldiers that decides who is to be king," Conan said. "And it is not only among we mercenaries that their first loyalty is to their paymaster."

"All too true," the vizier agreed. "In any case, be warned that there are rebels in this district. The rebellion is petty, and we shall put it down handily. But the land is vast, and the rebellious dogs have many hiding places and strongholds and we must winkle them out of all of them in order to crush this thing. Do not make the mistake of getting involved with them."

Conan knew better than to protest friendship or loyalty. He merely shrugged. "If they be poor, I'll have nothing to do with them."

"Very good," said Katchka. He pushed a tray of honeyed

sweets toward the Cimmerian. "Have some. They are a specialty here."

Conan took one and bit into it. It was indeed delicious. Beneath the layer of honey were chopped dates and nuts in a thin pastry shell. He knew that the two were leaving much unsaid about this rebellion, and he knew as well that it would be far safer to question someone else about these lapses.

"Who knows?" said the vizier. "It might well be that we ourselves could use your services."

Something in his tone made Conan extremely cautious. "I have seen His Excellency's camps outside the town, and his soldiers within. The horses are splendid and kept in the finest military order. The men have the look of hawks. What use could he have for my little band, much depleted by our last campaign? We do not even know this area."

"What is destined to transpire shall transpire," said Akhba with the air of a man quoting an old proverb. "We may find more to do up here in the north than chase rebels, and it may be that the services of a specialist are required."

"My men are happy spending their pay just now," Conan said, uncomfortable with the implications.

"Let them enjoy themselves," Katchka said. "Their gold will not last long here, if they spend it the way my riders spend theirs." The general stroked his mustache. "You had a comely woman with you when you rode in. Surely she is not a part of your band."

"She is my mistress. Among us, men of the rank of captain or higher are permitted to carry one along on campaign." This could get tricky, should the general wish to claim the woman for himself.

"You've good taste, if the rest of her matches her face." His interest, to Conan's relief, seemed slight. "Who was the older man who rode beside her? He looks more the scholar than the soldier." The general was crude and unpolished compared with the vizier, but he also seemed shrewd.

"That man is a wizard named Volvolicus," Conan said, seeing little advantage in prevarication.

"A wizard!" said Akhba. "How comes such a one to ride with ban . . . that is to say, with mercenaries?"

Conan was sure that the slip had been deliberate. "A certain operation during our last hire called for his skills. He chose to stay with us for a little while before he returns home."

"You have an interesting band, Cimmerian," said Akhba. "Enjoy your stay in Green Water. Be sure, before setting out upon any journeys, to report to us beforehand. This is a province under military government, and one may not travel about freely as in ordinary times."

Taking this for dismissal, Conan stood. "I shall be sure to do so. However, I think that most of my energies will be spent in dragging my tosspots out of taverns and brothels and breaking up their brawls."

"See that they do not brawl with my men," Katchka warned. "My discipline is severe, but when my men fight with civilians, I always find in their favor unless they stab someone high-born."

"I shall impress it upon them," Conan said. "A good evening to you, my lords."

The Cimmerian walked back across the square amid serving boys who were setting up torches, for the sun was already low and darkness would fall with startling swiftness when the orb dipped below the horizon. Music of drum and harp began to replace that of flute and tambour, and the new dancers were less sedate. The merchants were folding up their awnings and packing away their goods for the evening, when the public bazaar would be devoted wholly to entertainment.

The bulk of those visiting the town were desert caravaneers, but Conan saw a sprinkling of merchants from faraway lands: dusky tradesmen of the Black Kingdoms dressed in white robes and bearing long spears of steel; short, pudgy Vendhyans in bright turbans; even a small group of men from far Khitai, with long, plaited hair and robes of colorful silk. Their leader was a white-haired man whose four-inch fingernails were encased in sheaths of jewel-studded gold.

"Are you all sober enough to hear my words?" Conan asked as he reseated himself at the table.

"By Set, Chief, we've but had time to take the edge off our thirst," Ubo protested. "Give us at least until midnight to grow truly drunk."

"Then attend me closely. Our lives may depend upon your behavior from here on." Briefly, he sketched the situation, describing General Katchka, Vizier Akhba, and the rebellion in the north, along with the instructions of those redoubtable men.

"By Asura!" groused Mamos the Khorajan. "We but wanted a peaceful spot wherein to revel. Have these people no regard for the good of their fellow men?"

"What is all this about wanting our services?" Osman asked uneasily.

"That I do not know," Conan admitted. "But I intend to do my best to keep us out of their business. On the other hand, it could be suicide to refuse. Then we must decide whether we can run for the border faster than they can pursue."

"These are well-mounted cavalry," said Auda. "Those of us on Sagobal's stolen horses might make it, but even that is doubtful, for we have no surplus racers for remounts."

"Then we must be very cautious," Conan stressed. "Give them no cause for offense, and try not to attract their attention."

"We shall be as innocent baby birds, Chief," Mamos avowed.

"Aye," muttered Layla in a low voice. "Forever lolling about, waiting for somebody else to gather worms and poke them down your gullet."

"See that it is so," said Conan. "If the soldiers are insolent, smile meekly and put a good face upon it. You cannot win, for they have their general's protection."

"Not even if they insult my mother," said Osman, "who begat me and then picked the very finest, the softest and most fragrant dung heap in Shagara whereon to abandon me. Even if I hear their lips question her virtue, I shall smile and bow and walk on by."

All the others expressed similar intentions of good behavior. Conan knew the futility of it. These men had less self-control than so many squalling infants. He would be lucky not to lose some of them before the night was out.

"I'm for livelier entertainment!" said Chamik, standing. "Who goes with me?" Most of the others growled eagerness and rose to accompany him. He turned to Conan. "What about you, Chief?"

"Nay, I'll abide here. With that general's eye upon us, I must keep my wits about me. The rest of you go on. Go easy on your money. That bag of silver may not last us all a moon in this place. Prices are always high in a caravan town."

"What of it?" said Mamos. "When money runs out, you steal more."

"Not here," Conan growled. They roared with mirth and strode off in search of the town's more disreputable alleys.

"Surely," Layla said when they were gone, "you do not think that general gave you the whole story of this rebellion?"

"Of course he did not," Conan said. "Do you take me for a fool?"

"I shall reserve judgment on that. I wonder how it is that this royal bastard can hope to take the throne from one who has held it for seventeen years?"

"He may just want to set himself up in an independent province," Conan hazarded. "That is often the way of it with rebellious nobles. Rather, since he is so young, it is probably his older male relatives who want to place him on a petty throne and rule through him."

"You are a man of the world, Conan," Volvolicus commended. "And you are wise to avoid burning your fingers on this business."

"If I had a real mercenary troop," Conan said, "I might well choose a side, for there is often wealth to be had in such a situation. But I would want at least a hundred seasoned professionals, all well mounted and well armed. I can do nothing with this band of jackals."

Volvolicus seemed distracted. "I think I should go and seek my colleagues in this town, if indeed there be any such. Daughter, I shall arrange for accommodations here. Perhaps a fellow wizard will share his house. Will you put up at an inn, Conan?"

"No, a place that caters to caravaneers is likely to be verminous. I shall camp in the oasis near the horses. The night bids to be a fair one."

"I shall keep our brave captain company and seek you out later," Layla assured her father.

"Good evening, then." Volvolicus wandered off, leaving them alone.

"He is a trusting man, to leave his daughter with the likes of me," Conan observed.

"Perhaps he has faith in your sense of chivalry," she said, laughing at the absurdity of it. "Nay, barbarian, he knows that I am safe. No man can lay a hand upon me save I wish it."

"And what if you should not wish it?"

"That man would spend perhaps a score of heartbeats dying in terrible agony. Not for nothing am I a wizard's daughter."

"Magick gives you an unfair advantage," Conan grumbled, pouring himself a cup of wine.

"Oh, and your great size and bulging muscles do not?" She took another cup for herself. "Tell me, barbarian, how comes it that a soldier like you lives as a starveling bandit in southern Turan, or rather, Iranistan?"

"Soldiering is ever a chancy trade," Conan said. "Sometimes you pick the wrong side and lose everything in a single battle, or your paymaster decides to avoid paying you by treacherously attacking his mercenaries the minute the war ends. But most often it is peace that ruins us. This past year and more, all the western kings and their nobles have been at peace, recovering from the last string of wars. An out-of-work soldier, if he has no land to return to, is a brigand. So, looking for a good war, I fell in among a band of professional bandits and decided to abide with them for a while."

"As you say, a chancy trade."

"Aye. But there is one comfort in this situation."

"What might that be?"

"Peace never lasts for long," he said, grinning. "When the kings are recovering from the last wars, that just means that they are preparing for the next. My services shall be in demand again, and soon. How comes it that you dwell in the desert, with only your father for company?"

"I have asked you about your past, so I suppose it is fair that you should ask about mine. I am the only child of Volvolicus, and it is customary in Turan that a daughter remain with her widowed father until he should decide she is to be wed."

Conan snorted. "When did wizards ever feel bound by the custom of the land?"

"You have seen enough of my father to know him a little. Does he seem like a dread practitioner of the black arts?"

"I'll own that he seems more the scholar than the wizard," Conan admitted.

"Do not underestimate him. But it is true, he has no interest in summoning fell spirits or wreaking terrible spells, although like all mages of the higher ranks, he has studied these things. Most fathers marry off their daughters for wealth or advantage. My father has no need of these things. And I have no desire to wed. I have yet much to learn from my father."

"He is training you to be a wizard?" Conan asked, liking the idea very little.

"I learn from him. He is too tradition-bound to give me the full training I need, for in all of history, female mages have been few, but in the fullness of time, he will see that he must yield to my demands. There are more important things than marrying some troublesome lout and raising brats."

"And yet," Conan said, "that night by the pool of your

father's oasis, you did not seem so averse to male company."

"I did not say that I had no use for men," she said. "I just have no desire to become the wife of one."

They sat for a while, enjoying the cool of the evening. As the torches were lit, the dancers changed to slower, more languid dances, and wore far fewer clothes.

Just before midnight a rider galloped into the square, scattering late strollers from before his horse's hooves. The man jumped from his saddle in front of the government house and ran up its steps, shouting something to General Katchka. The commander screamed and a trumpeter began a series of shrill, snarling blasts upon his instrument. Officers ran for their horses, and troopers boiled out of the various houses of entertainment, running for the town gates and the camps where their mounts were picketed. As they ran, they cursed and many of them were still pulling on their clothes, but they moved with the smartness of men who knew that a brutal flogging was the best they could hope for should they fail in their duty.

For a few minutes the square thundered with shouting officers and prancing, excited horses. Then they were off, riding toward the main gate with General Katchka at their head. A great silence fell over the town. The dancers and musicians resumed their activities, and the caravaneers laughed and spoke more loudly. The whole mood lightened, as if a great, oppressive weight had been lifted. Only the tavern-keepers and harlots looked downcast, for they had enjoyed the free-spending habits of the soldiers.

"I never saw so many drunks on horseback in my life," Layla said. "It is a wonder they all got out of here with no broken necks or tramplings."

"That is what real professionals look like," Conan told her. "They will ride and fight in worse condition than that."

"What do you suppose happened?"

"That rider brought an alarm from someplace. The rebels must have attacked one of their outposts and the royal troopers have set off to catch them." He leaned back and stretched. "At least now I can relax. There will be no fights between my men and the troopers this night. With luck, the soldiers will be away for a few days, running down rebels."

"But you think they will be back?" she asked.

"Assuredly." He pointed to the banner that flew above the government house, with the smaller flag beside it. "There flies the royal arms, with General Katchka's personal colors beside it. This is his headquarters, and he'll not find a better town for many a day's ride. They will be back."

Eight

Volvolicus rapped upon a door of heavy timbers, strapped with iron wrought into curious designs. The house was on a narrow street in the northwestern quarter of the town. Like others in the district, it was two-storied, but unlike any other, it had a narrow tower rising a further four stories above its flat roof. It was flanked by small shops selling oil and candles. A nearby perfumer's made the air fragrant, and from somewhere nearby, the mage could hear the music of a lute. At his third knock, an ancient crone opened a small viewing-port in the upper part of the door.

"Who calls at such an hour?"

"I am Volvolicus," he said. "The name is known to your master. Please fetch him." The old woman grumbled and closed the little port. A few minutes later the massive door creaked open and a slightly less aged man stood in the opening, beckoning the Turanian wizard in.

"Volvolicus? Are you truly the one who called the Supreme Convocation?"

"I am that one," said the wizard, entering. "Peace unto this house and all who dwell therein."

"And unto you," the old man muttered quickly. Then: "Only yesterday did I learn of your action. As it happens, I was deep within my wizardly meditations when the summons came, and I missed the first gathering." Volvolicus knew that the man was far from the highest rank of his craft, and that was why he had not been drawn by the Convocation. "Forgive my lapse of manners, but I never expected to see you here. I am Elma, wizard of Green Water."

"I knew I would find a fellow of the craft here when I espied your tower."

"Aye, I practice the Way of Stars and Water. But surely you are a long distance from your own home."

"I live but a few days' ride from here," Volvolicus said, "and certain business has drawn me hither."

"You honor my house," Elma said. "Have you eaten?" Even wizards had to obey the sacred laws of hospitality in this land.

"I have just come from a caravanserai and with the rest of my party, partook of its fare. However, I may be in this town for some days and I would crave lodging for myself and my daughter."

Elma bowed. "You do me further honor."

"Then I would ask one thing more, and this a matter of far graver import: This night I must call the Supreme Convocation again."

Elma gasped. "Of course you may use my poor facilities for this purpose. To my knowledge, never has such a summoning emanated from this part of the world."

"Not for millennia have there been times such as these," Volvolicus said. "And now, if you please, time is of the essence."

"Please come with me." Elma gave the crone orders to secure the house and wait by the door for the arrival of the daughter of his guest. Then the two went to a stairway and began to climb. Two flights took them to a broad roof-garden.

It was a cool, pleasant place in the desert night. Many of the flat-roofed houses had such gardens, where the inhabitants were accustomed to meet and socialize after the sun had set.

Elma went to the tower and unlocked its sole door with a key belted to his side. Within, a cramped stairway spiraled upward. This the two mages ascended, coming out upon a much smaller terrace overlooking the town and the oasis and desert beyond. Its parapet bore instruments of bronze, and there were numerous images of metal, wood and stone here and there. In its center was a stone basin of clear water. The lip of the basin was curiously carved with human and animal figures.

Volvolicus went to the parapet and examined a bronze standard that supported a flat, polished crystal the size of a dinner plate. With the eye of a connoisseur, he judged both the crystal and its intricately wrought setting. It was mounted in a gimballed bezel that allowed it to be manipulated to any angle.

"A fine star-crystal," he commended.

"And we shall have need of it this night," said Elma, adjusting its angle. "See, the Dog Star rises, and with it rises the Great Wanderer, a most powerful conjunction."

"Let us begin," said Volvolicus. The two men sat cross-legged by the basin, gazing into the water. Its surface reflected the stars overhead, and the crystal focused the light of the Dog Star upon its center. In time, the water disappeared from their consciousness, and they seemed to be floating among those stars, which in turn shifted and drifted into unfamiliar juxtapositions, finally forming a pattern of strange geometry. Then, above each star, there formed the head of a wizard. There were far more at this summoning than upon the earlier night in the house of Volvolicus. Over a star that, uncannily, seemed to gleam black, there formed the face of Thoth-Amon. He was first to speak.

"I see that this time you have brought a wizard of as little account as yourself," he said. "Times have come to an ill turn when great events devolve upon such petty mages."

"Hold your tongue, Stygian," Volvolicus said coldly.

"Yes, be still," said Feng-Yoon of Khitai. "The gods do not choose their instruments capriciously, and because a student of the arts has not chosen to wallow in black evil as you have, it does not mean that he is not qualified for the highest ranks among us."

At the great Khitain mages's rebuke, the Stygian blazed with fury, but he said nothing more.

"What has happened since your last communication, Volvolicus?" asked the Khitain. "Did you enter this Temple of Ahriman? Did you behold its crypt?"

"I did. Allow me to describe for you the events of the last few days." Using the secret language of wizards, in which far more can be conveyed than in ordinary speech, he laid out his story, to which the others rendered rapt attention.

"How outrageous!" said a Nemedian when the recitation was done. "This great cosmic event takes the form of a bandit's adventure!"

"Even the immortal gods," said a Vendhyan, "have been known to display a sense of humor."

"That crypt was no ordinary gap in stone," said the Pictish wizard. "It is the very maw of the god. If those fools touched the walls, not only are they condemned to an unthinkable death, but it was like giving tiny scraps of meat to a starving tiger. By now, it is roaring for more."

"This leader of your band sounds a bold fellow," said a wizard of Kush. "Who might he be?"

"He is a great northerner, a barbarian and an adventurer," Volvolicus said. "I will convey to you his likeness." Slowly, the head and powerful shoulders of the Cimmerian appeared amid the assemblage.

"That rogue!" cried a black wizard in feathers and paint. "I knew him years ago when he was Amra the Pirate!"

Others exclaimed that they, too, had encountered the barbarian.

"Ah, this is most interesting," said Feng-Yoon, his stitched-together eyes and mouth unmoving but his countenance mysteriously growing brighter. "This must be one of those singular men who trample over the world, driven by a destiny they but dimly perceive, setting at naught the vaunting plans of kings and wizards. Such men have even been known to challenge the gods and live to tell of it."

"Like Rustam the God-Slayer!" said an awed Zingaran.

"Exactly," said the Khitain. "Such a one was Ma-Tsu, in the reign of Emperor Lin, two thousand years ago. This one we must watch closely, for he can be our instrument of salvation, but he can wreak great mischief as well."

"What is your will, my masters?" Volvolicus asked.

"You must keep close to the barbarian," said the Khitain, "but you must also go back to that temple. Some of us wend our way thither even now, but all takes time. Many obstacles have fallen in our paths, and I believe this to be the dire working of Ahriman. I myself could be there in a day, could I but summon a dragon to fly me thither, yet for the first time in three hundred years, none heeds my call."

"As it happens, we must go back soon," said Volvolicus. "The outlaws want to stay in this little town for a full turn of the moon, but I know this cannot be."

"Very good," said Feng-Yoon. "The others are not of great importance, but it is imperative that you go back. I think it would also be well if this Cimmerian were to go back too. As for the rest, they are common mortals and mean little."

"It shall be as you wish, Master," said Volvolicus.

"Succeed," said the Khitain, "and you shall ascend to the First Rank. Fail, and you need not concern yourself with your standing among your colleagues. It may then be the end of the world for us all."

"Into Iranistan, eh?" Sagobal said, stroking his beard. "It was a wise move, whether they knew it or not. There is some sort of rebellion in the northern province, and we are strictly forbidden to cross the river." The guard captain and his men were encamped near a village to the south of Shahpur. They had been making a sweep of the countryside, ostensibly in pursuit of the fleeing bandits. Here Berytus had found his employer and rendered his report.

"There are no more than a dozen of them left," Berytus said.

"But they did not have the treasure?"

"Not any great part of it, certainly. They had only the tired horses they were riding."

"The question, then, is this: Have they made contact with the treasure and hidden it? Or are they yet to find it? How far could that wizard have flown such a weight?"

Berytus shrugged his bare shoulders. "That is a question I cannot answer. I've had no experience of flying treasures, and little enough of the earthbound sort."

Sagobal pondered. "Could the wizard have sent it to a hiding place in Iranistan? That would be a problem."

"You say that the mage has his house near here?" Berytus asked.

"Aye, that he has."

"Might he not have sent the treasure there? The flight into Iranistan might be a ruse to throw off pursuit. They might have recrossed the river at another point and returned to the wizard's house to divide up the loot."

"That makes sense," said Sagobal. "I will give you a guide. Fare you to the house of Volvolicus and search the place, then report your findings to me. But if you find the treasure, be sure that you say nothing about it to anyone save me."

"As you wish, Chief. We need fresh horses."

"Take them from among our remounts. Apply to my quartermaster for such other supplies as you need. Anything he does not have," he pointed at the cluster of buildings nearby, "take from the village."

"What if the villagers protest?" Berytus asked.

"Kill any that hinder you. I am concerned with matters more important than wretched villagers."

Two hours later, Berytus and his manhunters rode from the village on fresh horses, fully supplied. Behind them they left a few slain villagers, for some had not wished to give up their belongings and others had been unwilling to supply their daughters for the amusement of the murderous band.

Leading them was a Turanian trooper, a small man on a fast horse who carried the stripped-down gear of a scout. They rode tirelessly over the arid landscape, pausing only occasionally to rest their horses. Just before nightfall, they came within sight of the house of Volvolicus.

"There is the place you seek," the guide said, pointing. "My captain has given me orders that I am not to accompany you there. I shall abide here until you return."

"Let's go," Berytus said, reining his horse into the small valley where the house sat by its pond. No smoke rose from its roof, and there were no signs of men or beasts nearby. They knew this could be deceptive, for all of them were well versed in the art of occupying a hideout while leaving no external signs of their presence. Accordingly, they proceeded with caution.

Barca the Shemite rode a little ahead of the others, arrow fitted to string. He rode barefoot, with toe-loops depending from his saddle in lieu of stirrups. Carefully, he scanned the ground before him, his gaze searching out all nearby rocks and brush where danger might lie. The ground closest to the pool was littered with dry twigs fallen from the brush nearby. As he approached, these twigs seemed to shimmer and vibrate; then his horse reared as they transformed into a nest of writhing, hissing serpents.

"Bel and Marduk!" the Shemite swore as he fought his mount back under control.

"The sorcerer's home is protected by spells!" said Urdos of Koth, superstitious dread in his voice.

"There is no danger," said Ambula. "See, they writhe like real snakes, but they leave no marks in the sand. Watch me." The man from Punt dismounted and gathered up a handful of small stones. Armed with these, he walked fearlessly to the nest of vipers and began to throw rocks at them. When struck, each reverted to an inoffensive twig. "It is just an illusion. The wizard of my home village knew this trick."

"I am convinced," said Bahdur the Hyrkanian. "Persuading my horse is another matter."

"We will leave the horses here," Berytus instructed. "Even if we take the time to destroy all these false snakes, they would just be frightened by the next illusion."

"Go ahead on foot?" asked Urdos. "There could be enemies here."

"I doubt it," Berytus said. "Would he have bothered with these feeble safeguards if he were in residence, with his bandits to protect his home? Be cautious, though. Some of his wards may be more than illusion. The snakes might just be there to discourage the local camel-herders from using his water. The house could be better protected."

Weapons at the ready, the men walked toward the house. The men armed with bows scanned the tops of the palms overhead, while others watched the house and the nearby terrain. None neglected to look behind from time to time. These men knew more about ambushes, both setting them and avoiding them, than most professional soldiers ever learned. Berytus called a halt twenty paces from the site.

"Ambula, Bahdur, circle the house." The men set off at a fast walk, their eyes on the structure, their weapons balanced for instant use. Two minutes later, they were back.

"No sign of life from inside," Bahdur reported. "There is a window on each end, two more in back, all shuttered. No door save this one." He pointed at the symbol-carved wooden portal in the center of the front of the house, which faced the pool. The roof was flat, with a slightly raised parapet.

"Do we go in, Chief?" Urdos asked.

"Not yet. Ambula, climb a tree and get a look at the roof."

The brown man selected a stately palm that grew a dozen paces from the house. Jamming his slender spear into the ground by its butt-spike, he unwrapped his turban and looped the broad band of cloth around the trunk. With the horny soles of his bare feet gripping the ridges of the trunk, he shinnied to the top as nimbly as a squirrel. From this point of vantage, he scanned the flat roof. It was made of woven withies, waterproofed with bitumen.

"No men or other creatures," Ambula reported.

"Now we go in," Berytus said. They walked toward the house. "Uglak, take your mace and smash in the door."

The man so named, a burly Argossian, readied the weapon he had been carrying across his shoulder. The mace had a three-foot shaft of steel, topped with a circle of thick, triangular flanges. It was a weapon for smashing armor and the bones beneath armor, but was equally handy for smashing in doors. Uglak swung a mighty blow against the portal.

Instead of smashing the wood to splinters, the mace stopped as if it had struck a slab of steel. It did not rebound, but stayed fast, the tip of a flange touching a jagged design that abruptly flamed with red light. The light shot along the haft of the weapon, and in an instant, Uglak was caught in a net of crackling, writhing red lightning. He screamed as his clothing flashed away in a puff of flame and smoke and his flesh seared, blackened and bubbled. The last of the scream came out as a stream of foul black vapour from his burning lungs.

After the space of thirty or forty heartbeats, the unnatural red fire vanished and the blackened skeleton of Uglak fell to the ground before the door. Beside it, the steel mace glowed bright orange, darkening to sullen red as it slowly cooled. The manhunters stood gaping, silenced by horror. Berytus was first to recover his power of speech.

"Well, it looks as if we'll not get in that way," he said.

"Surely you don't propose to go in now," said Urdos. "This is no illusion of phantom serpents—the sorcerer commands real power! Let us be away from here!" The others chattered their agreement.

"Nay, it galls my pride to let some—" His words broke off short as, abruptly, the door slammed open and something huge and hairy shot out, foam flying from its yellow-white fangs. Before any of them could move, its unbelievably long arms reached out and misshapen hands grasped the neck of a man, pulling him close. The grotesque, snapping jaws closed on his face, shearing away flesh and bone, exposing the quivering brain with one eyeball still horridly attached by a stringy nerve. In his death-spasm, the man thrust his shortsword into the thing's belly, spilling blood and entrails.

At the sight of blood, the manhunters threw off their paralysis. This was no uncanny fire, but a living creature, of sorts. And they knew how to deal with things that lived. The bowmen shot arrows feather-deep into the thing's hide even as Ambula and other spearmen thrust their points into it. An axman brought his weapon crashing down on the thing's skull and it dropped, its tiny brain split by the keen edge.

For a few heartbeats, they stared at the repulsive corpse. The creature's apelike body, coupled with a long, wolflike snout, identified it as some sort of baboon, but it was five times the size of any natural monkey of that breed. A loud slam jerked their heads around to stare at the house. The door was shut once more.

"No more of this, Chief," Urdos said.

"I agree," Berytus answered him. "Back to the horses, all of you. Do not run, walk. Keep your guard up. This wizard is both more powerful and more clever than I had thought. He may have set traps for fleeing men."

From long habit, the men spread out, close enough for mutual support but far enough apart to avoid making the mass of them an easy target. As they passed near the pool, the water in its center began to roil and churn to white foam. Thin tentacles broke the surface and snapped in the air like long whips. At first they groped blindly, then they shot toward the men. At this apparition, the nerve of the manhunters finally broke and they ran toward their horses, screaming in terror.

Most of them made it, but getting mounted on the terrified, plunging beasts was no easy task and one man took too long about it. Just as he managed to get a foot into his stirrup, a tentacle wrapped around his body and dragged him back. Swiftly, other tentacles wrapped his limbs and he was raised from the ground. Some of the thin wand-shapes were lined with suckers, others with short, back-curving teeth. Each was tipped with a jewellike green eye. Screaming in agony and horror, he was dragged back to the foaming water. The bulk of the creature was still hidden from view.

The men did not wait to see what the rest of the thing looked like, but rather, spurred their horses to the greatest speed they could manage. The spurring was unnecessary, for the horses were even more terrified than the men. The screaming died out behind them and they put many miles between themselves and the wizard's house before they at last slowed down.

"Father?" Layla said, seeing Volvolicus stagger. "Is something wrong?" She rushed to his side and took his arm, guiding him to a stool of camel-hide stretched over a wicker frame. They were in a bazaar of Green Water, on a side street where awnings stretched between facing buildings, shading the stands and carpets of the petty merchants whose wares were on display, leaving only a narrow strip in the center of the street for walking. Light fell softly, tinted by the colorful awnings through which it filtered, or brightly in narrow bars, through gaps between the awnings.

Conan, who had been trying on a new desert burnous, turned at the woman's words. "What ails you, mage?"

"It is nothing, it will pass," Volvolicus said, sinking onto the stool. At Layla's signal, Conan approached.

"It is not the heat that weakens thee, Father," she said.

"Nay," he said in a low voice so that none could overhear. "The wards I set to guard our house have been activated. When this happens, it draws upon my magickal energies and drains me for a while."

"What means this?" Conan asked.

"It means that someone has tried to enter our house," Layla said.

"Aye, I set harmless illusions to frighten away casual interlopers and they are nothing. But any who seek to break into the house awaken the deadly guardians."

"Might it have been raiders from the desert?" Conan hazarded.

"Raiders are not so persistent. These were vigorous enough to rouse no fewer than three of my guardians. Desert raiders would have run screaming from the first."

"Sagobal, then," Conan said. "Or one of his search parties. You must have been recognized in the city."

"Perhaps, but it will have taken no great powers of deduction to light upon me as the one most likely to have removed the treasure. My powers are not unknown in the district, although I have always sought obscurity. They did not get in, nor shall they."

Conan pondered for a minute. "If Sagobal thinks the treasure is in your house, he will be back with siege-engines. Can your home resist such an attack?"

"Aye, if necessary. Should he make such an attempt, fire elementals will burn his engines, and venomous flies from the desert will swarm in to drive his men and horses mad. All this will happen long before he is even within bowshot of the house."

Conan held his own counsel. Unless the man was boasting, he was a far more powerful mage than the Cimmerian had at first thought him to be. Somehow, he doubted that the man's words were mere windy braggadocio. He had yet to catch Volvolicus in a claim that the mage could not back up with deeds.

"Torgut Khan will be desperate, for the king must know soon that his treasure has been taken, if he does not know already. Is it possible that he could summon a sorcerer more powerful than yourself to set your protective spells at naught?"

Volvolicus laughed dryly. "As it happens, all the truly powerful magicians are otherwise occupied. Torgut Khan may be enjoying their company soon, but he will have no service from them."

For this enigmatic utterance, Conan had no comment to make.

"We had best return to Elma's house," Layla said. "Rest for a while. Then you may wish to fare out again."

"I am well recovered, I tell you," Volvolicus protested, but he allowed his daughter to tug him to his feet and lead him back toward their lodgings, while he leaned heavily upon her shoulders.

Conan watched them go, then shrugged and returned his attention to the burnous he had been inspecting. A clatter of hooves drew his attention toward the mouth of the street, which intersected the town's main thoroughfare, running from the oasis gate to the square. He saw horses rush by amid a jingle of arms and accoutrements, ridden by men in armor. He muttered a curse. General Katchka and his troopers were back. For three days he and his bandits had enjoyed a carefree carouse. The only potentially serious incident, when one of his men and a caravaneer had drawn daggers on each other, he had resolved by laying both men out senseless. Now it looked as if the carefree times were over.

To make matters worse, his men were drinking, wenching and, especially, gambling their money at an alarming rate. It had never been Conan's habit to hoard his wealth, and ordinarily he spent as freely as any of them, but this time he knew it would pay to be cautious. Not so his men. Their silver would run out in a few days, and then there might be trouble. Either they would try to steal more, which was bad, or they would want to return to the treasure before time, which could prove much worse.

That evening he met with a number of the others at the tavern in the square. At this hour, most of his men were just rising from whatever harlot's den, flea-infested caravanserai or oasis camp in which they had slept the day away. Ubo and Chamik, older than the rest, were more moderate, preferring to stay perpetually half-drunk in the less uproarious taverns. In this company, Conan was a virtual ascetic, never drinking enough to lose his sobriety, gambling only for small stakes and sleeping mostly at night. This was a matter of necessity rather than inclination.

"The soldiers are back," Ubo said. "I knew it was too good to last long."

"I wish I could find something for the men to do," Conan said.

"Do?" asked Chamik, as if he had never heard the word before. "What mean you, 'do'? While we have silver, we've no need to do anything save spend it."

"That is our problem," Conan told him. "If we could get out of this town, perhaps go on a little raid, it would keep the men out of trouble and help pass the time. I expect a run-in with these troopers before much longer, and then it could fare ill for us."

"Many caravans come and go here," Ubo pointed out. "We could pick one with good booty and few guards and when it leaves, follow after."

"Aye," said Auda, who had joined them, yawning and scratching. "We could tail them for a few days, so that we be far from town and witnesses, strike the caravan, kill the witnesses, and be off."

"We could not bring the camels back here," said Ubo. "They might be recognized."

"Sell them in nearby villages," Auda advised. "If the price be right, no one will inquire as to where we came by them."

"It's a thought," Conan said. "It well may come to that, though I dislike the idea of petty thieving when we have that great heap of treasure waiting for us at the hideout." He looked up to see a familiar form approaching. The others followed the direction of his gaze.

"It is that popinjay Captain Mahac," Ubo said, spitting a pomegranate seed onto the tessellated pavement. "What does the general's little dog want this time?"

"He's no little dog," Conan said. "More like a wolf, so be polite."

"A good evening to you, Captain Conan," said Mahac, pronouncing the military title with the slightest of sneers. "His

Excellency and the Vizier Akhba crave the pleasure of your company at their table."

"Once again I am honored beyond my merits." Conan rose and picked up his sword, attaching its hanger to his belt. He followed the captain across the square and found Katchka seated in his accustomed place. This time he greeted Conan jovially.

"Greetings, my captain! Welcome to my table. I trust you have not yet eaten?"

"I have not," Conan replied, bowing.

"Then partake of our dinner," said the vizier.

Without hesitation, the Cimmerian seized the leg of a roast fowl and tore it from the steaming bird, then dipped it in a savory, pungent sauce. "I trust Your Excellency's recent foray was a success?" He bit into the leg, then washed the mouthful down with a draught of sweet date-wine. He did not fear poison from a man who could have him cut down with an idle gesture and need explain the deed to no man.

"It was agreeable enough," Katchka said, his hoarse voice seeming to come from somewhere deep within his paunch. "We chased the rebels and caught a few of them and crucified them as an example. The bulk of them fled across the river into a stronghold of theirs."

"Across the river?" Conan said. "You mean the Ilbars?"

"It is the only river of any consequence in this district," said the vizier.

"Can your king not petition the king of Turan to drive them out?" Conan asked.

"As it happens," the vizier explained, "the land into which they fled is disputed territory."

"How is that? I thought the Ilbars was the boundary between Turan and Iranistan."

"It is," said the vizier, "but boundaries defined by rivers sometimes change." He dipped his finger in the wine and drew a wavy line on the table. "Here is the Ilbars. And here," he made a wide loop, "is the land where the rebel stronghold lies. It used to be entirely south of the river, in Iranistani territory, enclosed in this loop of the river. Then, some years ago, the river flooded. Its increased flow cut through the narrow neck of land, leaving this territory north of the main current, although still enclosed in its loop. The king of Turan maintains that the main current is the border and that this land is now his. Our king, naturally, maintains the opposite: that the northern loop is the effective border and the land is still his.

"While the land remained uninhabited save for sheep and goats, this bickering could have gone on for generations. As it is, the matter is troublesome. His Majesty, who is a cautious monarch, has ordered us not to cross the river even here, because he does not wish to provoke a war with Turan."

"Is the king of Turan in sympathy with the rebels?" Conan asked.

"Naturally, he protests he is not," Akhba said. "Just as naturally, he is, although we do not think he gives them any meaningful support."

Conan wondered why they were telling him all this, but he did not have to wonder long.

"His Excellency has a proposition for you," said the vizier.

"Aye," said Katchka. "Since you and your men are strangers here, and have no connection to the throne of Iranistan, you could go to the island and enter the fort without causing trouble between the nations."

"I am pleased that you think us fit for such duty," Conan said, "but my band is much depleted. Surely we could not overcome a force that was sufficient to cause you so much difficulty."

"It was their swift flight that troubled us, not their numbers," Katchka growled.

"Indeed, they are but a handful," said the Vizier Akhba. "But, truthfully, we do not ask you to go and fight them."

"Then what service do you wish?"

"We want you to join them!" said Katchka, breaking into laughter. It sounded like a tiger coughing.

"I see," Conan said, feeling the words as a noose around

his neck. "I presume that you wish intelligence of these rebels, their numbers and disposition, the weaknesses of their fort?"

"No, all that is of little use to us," said the general. "I want you to kill this rebel 'leader,' this pretender to the throne. Bring me his head and I will pay you three thousand ounces of purest gold, enough to keep you and your rogues drunk for a year!" Again he released the tiger-cough laugh.

The Cimmerian's mind had been working swiftly while the general spoke, so he did not betray himself with any hesitation.

"Done!" he cried. "For three thousand ounces of gold, I would go and assassinate the king of Turan himself!"

At these words, general and vizier laughed heartily and pounded their guest upon the back. The general refilled Conan's cup with his own hand.

"Have you a name and a description of the pretender?" Conan asked.

"His name is Idris. None of us have laid eyes upon the stripling, but he is sixteen years of age. If he is truly the king's son, he will be rather small, with fine features. His mother was a great beauty, else she would not have been a royal concubine. You may assume therefore that he is a handsome lad. If they display some hulking, ugly boy as Idris, you will know that this is an imposter with whom they wish to deceive assassins. Look for a comely youth to whom all defer, even though he be dressed like a beggar and called by some other name."

"They'll not gull me," Conan assured them. "I have done this sort of thing before."

"Excellent!" said the vizier, beaming. He heaped Conan's platter with sweetmeats and called for wine from the general's private stock.

An hour later, Conan returned to his table outside the tavern. Layla and her father had joined Ubo, Chamik and Auda. He unhooked his sword and resumed his seat, his face grim.

"You and the general seemed to be getting along famously," Layla said. "I am surprised you can still walk."

"There is an art to keeping your wits when men ply you with strong wine," he said. "Now listen to me, all of you. We are in mortal danger."

"Say on, Chief," said Ubo.

Quickly, Conan sketched out the offer Katchka and Akhba had made him. The eyes of the bandits lit up when he mentioned the gold.

"Not just a mercenary and a bandit," Layla said, "but an assassin as well! I did not know you for a man of so many talents."

"I do not see the problem, Chief," said Chamik. "The job may be a little risky, but no more so than riding into Shapur. For three thousand ounces, the risk is worth it."

"Aye," said Auda. "Not to mention the danger of trying to back out."

Conan spat on the pavement. "Do you fools really think that armored pig is going to pay us three thousand ounces of gold? Even if we succeed, he will merely take the boy's head and kill us all to conceal their cowardice and treachery. Then he and that scheming courtier will go back to the king and show him the head and tell him of the great battle with the rebels in which they won their trophy. They will reap rewards and titles while we feed the jackals in the desert."

"Oh," Ubo said. "I see."

"Then what are we to do?" Chamik asked.

"We ride out as if to undertake this mission," Conan said. "We will have to ride at least as far as the island, for Katchka will have his hounds following us every step of the way. I propose we ride right on past the rebel fort and cross the river-loop on the far side."

"Into Turanian territory?" asked Volvolicus. He seemed to be fully recovered from his weakness earlier in the day. "Do we not then run the risk of meeting with Torgut Khan's patrols?"

"Aye," Conan said, "but just now I adjudge that to be the lesser risk."

"Then it seems that we must do as the general wishes," said Volvolicus.

The next morning, Conan rounded up the rest of his little band, dragging some of them from the floors of low taverns, forcing them with cuffs and curses to find their horses and gear, saddle up and mount. Glum of expression, some of them reeling in the saddle, they rode from the town. At the edge of the oasis, they found a party of mounted troopers waiting for them.

"Captain Mahac," Conan said, saluting, "what brings you here? A formal military farewell is scarcely necessary."

"But my general insists that you be honored with an escort for the first part of your heroic mission." He favored them with an evil grin as he surveyed the bleary-eyed group. Then his gaze fastened upon Layla. He pointed at the woman. "All except for her. She stays here."

Conan's hand went to his hilt. Then it paused there as a hundred troopers drew their bows against him. "Explain yourself, Captain!" he hissed.

"I need not explain myself to you, barbarian, nor does my general. However, he graciously consents to tell you that this lady is to remain here as his guest. She will receive the finest accommodation, and she will not be molested in any way. But she stays here."

Conan fumed, but Layla placed a hand upon his arm. "It seems I am to be the general's guest. It will be foolish to resist. Go on and accomplish your mission. I will be here when you return." She looked at her father. "I will be safe."

Mahac snapped his fingers and a trooper took her reins. He led her horse back into the town, and Layla did not look back. The captain inspected the band of outlaws once more and burst into raucous laughter.

"Surely there is no sight more stirring than the warriors of an elite unit setting off on a mission!" The rest of his troop roared with mirth, while the bandits sat their horses in frustrated anger.

"Lead on, Captain Conan," Mahac said. "My soldiers and I shall be following behind, but not too close. Even the common troopers have noses too sensitive for that!"

Almost choking on his rage, Conan spurred his horse to a trot and rode past the sneering officer, vowing revenge. Behind him rode his little band of outlaws.

Nine

I do not understand it," Osman said, still reeling in his saddle, his head throbbing from the previous night's debauch. "Why can the wizard not spirit his daughter hither with his magick arts? Has she no spell of invisibility whereby she may simply walk from the town and steal herself a horse?"

"Once again," said Volvolicus, "you reveal your ignorance of magick. Mine are not the arts of petty conjurers, such as entertain the masses at fairs! Great magick is not a matter merely of knowledge and spoken words. I am far from my books and instruments, my objects of power. The swinish general has me in a vise like the rest of you."

"He and that vizier must have guessed that Layla was not my mistress, for they would know that she would be a hostage of little worth if that were true," Conan said.

"I do not see how she is so valuable a hostage as it is," Mamos said. "I, for one, have no aversion to riding away and leaving her back there."

Conan rounded upon the scarred man, snarling. "I'll not

abandon her and neither will you. If you wish to ride off now, you'll not get far." He jerked a thumb back over his shoulder. Behind them rode Mahac's troop.

Ubo thumbed the edge of his curved knife. "And should you try to ride on into Turan without the rest of us, what are we to think except that you intend to go back and grab the treasure for yourself? We stay with the chief, Mamos."

"I am not disloyal," Mamos said sullenly, "but I think it foolish for good men to risk their necks for a single wench. The wizard was not a part of our band."

"We are all together now," Conan said. "And we stay together until this business is done with and the treasure divided among us. I will find a way to satisfy Katchka and get the woman back safely."

"How?" Osman asked.

"All in good time," Conan told him. They rode on toward the river.

"You mean to say that Volvolicus's demons drove you away?" asked Sagobal with an expression of utmost scorn. "I thought you made of sterner stuff. I could almost suspect that you found the treasure and think to frighten me away from it."

"Do not speak like a fool," said Berytus coldly. "If I had found that treasure and wanted to keep it for myself, do you think I would have come back here?" The men sat in Sagobal's chambers in Shahpur. "Instead, I have lost three good men and now I have to listen to your insults. If you think you can do better without my services, I will gladly go elsewhere."

Sagobal bridled his anger. "Nay, I spoke hastily. The way these base rogues have eluded me gives me great annoyance. Torgut Khan is almost mad with fear, for the king's revenue officers will be here any day. Daily, I must listen to his ravings and blubberings." He went on in a calmer tone. "So, my friend, this wizard has protected his property with terrible spells? I suppose such may be overcome with counterspells, if a mage of sufficient power were to be found."

"I wouldn't waste my time," Berytus told him. "I think there to be very little chance that the treasure is in the wizard's house."

"Why say you so?"

"The mage was with the bandits when they crossed into Iranistan. Why would he stay with them if the treasure were in his own home? I think it is because he is now a part of the band and the treasure has yet to be shared out. At most times, bandits will fly apart like thistledown in the wind, each man going where he pleases. But they stick together like rings in a shirt of mail when the loot is yet to be divided, each man jealous and suspicious of the others."

"You speak wisely," Sagobal said. "I believe you have the truth of the matter."

"We must watch for them," Berytus went on. "I think it likely that the treasure was stashed in one of the bandit hideouts. They wait for pursuit to die down to come back and share it out."

"Then you and your men go back south and ride the river. When you find them, follow but do not let them know they are detected. Send a messenger to inform me that they have been found and stick close."

Berytus rose. "It shall be as you wish." He turned and strode from Sagobal's quarters.

The river-crossing was easy, the water shallow and the current slow. The Cimmerian stopped near the middle, bent from his saddle and scooped water over his face and head with cupped palms. The day was hot and the weedy banks of the river buzzed and clicked with the noises of insects.

"Our friend Captain Mahac is no longer behind us," Osman reported, turning in his saddle to look back along the path they had taken.

"He is not in sight, you mean," Conan corrected. "No, it would not help our mission were the rebels to see that we have an escort of Iranistani regular cavalry." He kicked his horse into a trot and the animal rushed up the opposite bank in a spray of water, mud and reeds.

"Where do we ride, Chief?" Ubo asked.

"North. The island is a small one. We should see the fort before we have gone far. More likely, the rebels will intercept us before we see it."

"If they are any sort of real rebels," Chamik said, "they will have spies in Green Water. They may already know who we are."

"Just leave the talking to me," Conan instructed.

They rode for less than an hour before they saw the first rebel lookout. He was a single man on horseback, stationed atop a low hill. A long red pennant fluttered from the tip of his slender lance, and sunlight flashed from the polished steel of his small, round shield.

"There's a bold devil," said Volvolicus. "He cares not who sees him."

"Aye, that bespeaks confidence," Conan said. "That is good for us."

"How so?" asked the wizard.

"Frightened men are more likely to attack than those who are secure in their strength."

Another quarter-hour of riding brought them within sight of the fort. It was a rude structure of earth and logs, with a crude facing of undressed stone. From its open gate rode a file of horsemen in armor.

"Reception party," said Ubo, spitting on the ground.

"Smile and be friendly," Conan warned them. "Remember, we have come to join them. If they are weak, they will not scorn the aid of armed adventurers, even if we care nothing for their cause and only want to fight for loot."

The riders drew closer and the Cimmerian saw that their armor was in the same style as that of Katchka's troopers, but much of it was old and dingy. Upon the breast of each cuirass had been crudely painted a blue dragon against a black background. There were about forty of them, and they reined in, forming a semicircle between the bandits and the fort.

"I am Hosta," announced a man in worn but serviceable armor, "troop leader in the army of His Majesty, King Idris the Seventh of Iranistan. Who might you be, and what is your business here?"

"I am Conan, captain of free-lances. We have ridden from Turan, and word reached us that your king might want the services of professional fighting-men in his war against the usurper, Xarxas. Hence, we rode hither." The Cimmerian smiled broadly, as did all his men. The rebels remained grim, with leveled lances.

"His Majesty is served by loyal retainers," said Hosta. "However, I cannot presume to speak for him and I will take you into the stronghold for an interview. You will all surrender your weapons now." At this, the bandits bridled, but Conan held up a hand for quiet.

"By all means. We wish only to display our goodwill toward your king, and we willfully entrust ourselves to his." Conan unbuckled his weapon-belt and handed it over to Hosta. Slowly, reluctantly, the bandits did likewise. There was a perceptible relaxation among their escort when they were disarmed.

In silence they rode within the confines of the fort. It had no true gate. Instead, heavy timbers were piled behind them, wedged between others buried deep in the ground. Warriors patrolled the earthen parapet, which was topped with a timber palisade. Conan had long experience of war, and he knew this place would not last a day against a determined enemy with sappers, siege-engineers and determined infantry. It was barely adequate against a cavalry force such as Katchka's.

Within the crude walls were a half-score of buildings and many tents, among which perhaps four hundred men drilled and practiced combat while women washed, cooked and tended the sick and wounded. There was a significant number of the latter. Many of the men drilling in the open areas wore bandages. Others hobbled between the tents upon crutches. These men had seen some hard fighting and they seemed to be determined.

Conan and his men were escorted to an open area in the center of the fort, where a wooden dais was set up beneath a tall staff from which depended a long black banner bearing the figure of the blue dragon. A small crowd stood upon the dais, surrounding a single, seated figure.

"Wait here," commanded Hosta. While the bandits sat their horses in silence, the captain rode to the dais and dismounted. He said something to the men assembled there in a voice too low for Conan to hear. Their escort now formed a line behind them, spears leveled at their backs.

"Come forward, the one of you named Conan," called a man with a stentorian voice. The Cimmerian rode forward and halted at the dais. There he dismounted and stood before the platform. Its sole piece of furniture was a massive chair of wood, richly carved. Upon this field-throne sat a youth in blue robes. He was burly, with curly red hair and a sullen look. Around him stood a number of men in their middle to elder years, better dressed than the bulk of the rebels. Conan guessed these to be the family chiefs who had raised the pretender in a bid for power.

"Foreigner," said a white-bearded man, "you stand before King Idris the Seventh, rightful ruler of Iranistan. What is your business before His Majesty?"

Conan looked at the youth upon the throne; then his gaze slid beyond, past the older men and down the line to where a slight, dark-haired boy stood between towering guardsmen. The Cimmerian looked back to the one on the throne.

"Get off the chair, boy," Conan said. The men upon the dais bristled, some of them grasping weapons. With an insolent smile, Conan strode until he stood before the slim, fine-featured youth. "Your Majesty, I would like to offer you my services and those of my men."

The youth laughed delightedly and turned to the older men. "I told you it wouldn't work! No real soldier would take a foot-slogger for a true prince."

"As to his status," said the white-bearded man, "that we have yet to determine." He snapped his fingers at the youth on the throne. "Back to your pike drill, boy." Hastily, the lad got up and stripped off his blue robe. The smaller youth slipped on the robe and took his seat.

"Wherefore should we wish your services, foreigner?" the white-bearded man demanded coldly.

"Just a moment, Grandfather," said the boy. "What sort of outlander are you, Captain Conan?" he asked eagerly. "I have never beheld your like before."

"I am a man of Cimmeria," Conan said. "My clan's hearth-fires burn far to the north, amid mists and rocky crags. We are a warrior people, fighting with our neighbors and each other year in and year out. In fact, we are the greatest warriors on earth. Years ago, when I was about your age or even younger, I took part in the sack of Venarium, when the warriors of Cimmeria drove the Aquilonians from our land, slaying the Gundermen and the Bossonians with whom the Aquilonians thought to colonize our ancestral territory."

"Venarium!" the boy said. "I have heard of that battle!"

"A northern skirmish is little qualification for one who would serve the rightful king of Iranistan," said the man Idris had addressed as his grandfather. The boy ignored him.

"Who are your gods, Conan?"

"Our god is Crom, who dwells in a sacred mountain deep within Cimmeria. Crom is just like us, caring only for battle. For untold centuries he has fought Ymir, the god of the Aesir and Vanir. When we are born, he gives us strength and courage and a fighting heart. Beyond that, he cares little for us."

"A harsh god. Do you pray to him and make sacrifices?"

"We do not pray, for he would not listen. Crom has little use for any who would beg a higher power for favor. He is pleased with the blood we shed in battle, both our own and that of our enemies."

"That sounds like a true fighting-man's god," the boy said, sending a disdainful look at a man who wore the robes of a priest of Mitra.

"This is the deity of a primitive people, Majesty," said the priest with a sniff. "A civilized sovereign honors the gods of order and justice, the gods who are pleased by the arts and industries of civilization. When a king rears a magnificent temple to his god, all the world has to acknowledge his splendor."

"Aye," said Conan, "and the priests get a fine new house in the bargain." He noted that some on the dais were secretly pleased with his insolent words. Others were scandalized. "My lord, I am ready to answer all your questions about myself, my god and my people, but I would like to know whether you wish to accept my services."

Idris looked over Conan's band with an extremely dubious expression. "Surely the rest of these are not Cimmerians. One has the aspect of a priest or scholar. The rest have the aspect of a pack of brigands."

"Your Majesty has a good eye for men," Conan admitted. "Yes, they are a crude lot, with none of the spit and polish of a guards regiment, but one does not hire warriors for their fine looks. These are irregular cavalry of the finest stamp, scouts and raiders beyond compare."

"I can well believe they know how to raid," said a man in armor with curling lip. "No doubt many a caravan and band of pilgrims have learned that to their cost. As for scouting, it is true that such men often spy out their prey from hiding, carefully noting that such as they would attack are weak, unsuspecting and as nearly helpless as possible."

"Perhaps, Cousin Dunas, you are too hard on them," chided the putative king.

"Nay, Your Majesty, he is quite right," Conan said, "but what of that? Do we speak here of holding polite balls for the court ladies and foreign ambassadors? Nay, we speak here of manslaying! It is a hard business, best left to hard men, and these are masters of the craft. If they are such men as you would not see in your kingdom in times of peace, have no concern on that point. Let peace come, give them their pay and they will be off forthwith, riding across your borders to seek excitement elsewhere, for these are men who cannot abide a land at rest."

Idris laughed again. "I like him, my councilors! I want to hire him and his men. He amuses me, and perhaps they will serve me well."

"Your Majesty," the white-bearded man protested, "this is intolerable! The rightful ruler of Iranistan cannot be served by lowly brigands! It would make you unpopular with the common people, and the foreign kings around your border would claim that you are no true king, but rather, an imposter supported by criminal hirelings!"

The youth turned in his chair and stared at the older man. "Grandfather, am I, or am I not, the rightful king of Iranistan?"

"Of course you are king, my grandson," the old man said, his face coloring.

"Then my will is law here, and it is my will that this Conan and his men serve me."

The old man bowed. "It shall be as you wish, Your Majesty."

"Excellent!" said Conan. "And, Majesty, you need not concern yourself with what the neighbor kings think of us. A king like the usurper Xarxas, who is served by the likes of General Katchka and the Vizier Akhba, is nonetheless regarded as a sovereign like any other."

The man called Dunas strode to the front of the dais. "How comes it that you know the character of those men, outlander?"

"Why, until just yesterday we were in the town of Green Water, which is Katchka's headquarters." He saw that Dunas looked somewhat crestfallen, as if this were intelligence he had planned to spring by surprise.

"And did you offer him your services as well?" asked a bleak-faced man who stood behind the throne.

"I had no need to," Conan said. "Katchka and Akhba sought me out personally."

The old man laughed disbelievingly. "What use had those men, served as they are by first-class cavalry, for a barbarian sellsword like you, with your band of ragged ruffians?"

Conan looked at the man as if his sanity were in doubt. "Why, they wanted me to kill your king. What else?" He heard a sharp indrawing of breath from his men behind him. "They promised me three thousand ounces of fine gold to bring them the head of Idris, whom they hold to be a pretender."

There was stunned silence from the dais. Then the man who stood behind the throne spoke again. "But you were not fool enough to think they would honor the bargain, is that it?"

"Aye. Of course, I agreed to do it. We rode hither with a band led by one Captain Mahac dogging our heels, so we had little choice. If your sovereign does not offer me an absurd reward and a suicide mission, I think he will be a better master to serve than his usurping half-brother."

The man behind the throne nodded. "For the first time, Your Majesty, I begin to believe this rogue. He looks as if he knows his trade. I will reserve judgment on his men until I have seen them in action."

"Splendid, Uncle," the boy said enthusiastically. Then, to Conan: "This is my mother's eldest brother, General Eltis, commander of my forces. His father and my grandfather is the Vizier Jemak." The white-bearded man nodded slightly.

Eltis beckoned, and Hosta, the leader of Conan's escort, ran up and saluted. "My lord?"

"Find a tent for these men and enroll them among the scouts. You are to keep them under close observation and report to me."

"As you command, my lord," Hosta said, bowing.

"I will speak with you later, Captain Conan," said the young pretender.

"At Your Majesty's pleasure," Conan said, bowing. He turned and remounted his horse. The little band followed Hosta to the warren of dingy tents.

"What is the name of this village?" Sagobal asked.

"Telmak, my commander," said the troop commander. His

was one of many such cavalry detachments scouring the countryside. "It is an insignificant place, with nothing of note save a camel market. They know naught of the men who struck the temple." The young captain wiped sweat from his brow, for the day was scorching. "Nothing of importance has happened here in years, save that a few days ago, ninety-three of their camels were stolen, but the villagers tracked the beasts down and recovered them."

"This is a waste of—" Then the captain's words tickled something in Sagobal's memory. What was it? Suddenly he remembered. Berytus had told him that he and his men had tracked the outlaws to a small gorge wherein lay a good water supply. There were signs that a great many camels had been there recently, but the camels had gone off in one direction, unladen. The bandits had arrived later, for their tracks all lay atop those of the camels', and they had ridden off in another direction. This was something to look into.

"Summon the head men of the village."

The men arrived, looking suitably fearful. "Tell me about this theft," Sagobal said brusquely.

"Excellency," said a man whose forked beard was dyed yellow, "some few days ago, just before the full moon, bandits came here and ran off ninety-three head of our best stock. The next day, our best men armed themselves and set out to track them."

"Aye," said a younger man. "It was not so difficult, for there were a great many animals and the thieves did not break them up into smaller herds, taking different routes, as camel-thieves usually do. The tracks led to a small canyon deep in the hills, a watering place on the old caravan road. Few use it save shepherds now, for in past years it has served as a lair for bandits."

"We found all the camels there," said the yellow-bearded man, "guarded by a single bandit, who had been wounded in stealing them. Him we slew, and we butchered his body and hung him in pieces from the branches of a bush, as a warning to the others. Then we drove our stock back home."

"But you saw no sign of the rest?" Sagobal asked.

"No, Excellency. The camels had trampled over any other tracks."

"Some of you lead me to this place," Sagobal directed. "I want to see it."

A few hours later, Sagobal walked up and down the little canyon. The winds had carried away most of whatever tracks the thieves had left behind. It was a perfect outlaw's lair, no question of it. But what had happened here? His mind began to fit the pieces together.

The big herd of camels had been stolen and kept together because someone had a great deal of cargo to carry. A single, wounded bandit had been left behind to watch the camels while the rest had gone on to gather that cargo. But then the villagers had come to reclaim their stock. The bandits returned and found their transportation fled. What then?

The crucial question was: Had the treasure, so magickally transported from Shahpur, been here? Or had they planned to take the camels elsewhere to load them? If the former, then they must have concealed the treasure someplace nearby.

"What are your orders, Excellency?" the young officer asked, breaking into Sagobal's thoughts.

"Eh? Oh, we ride back to Shahpur now." It was tempting to order the men to search the area, but the last thing he wanted was for someone other than himself to find the treasure. If it was here, the bandits would be back for it soon. And he had Berytus and his matchless manhunters to track them to their fate, here or wherever else the treasure might be hidden.

He mounted his fiery horse and rode back toward Shahpur, his men following behind.

"What do you think of the young pretender, Conan?" Volvolicus asked.

"The lad has spirit," said the Cimmerian, "but he is too young yet to be fairly judged. It is good that he does not let his older kin control him as they would like, but such willfulness in a youth can easily turn to cruelty." He shrugged. "He may become a strong king, but he has the makings of a tyrant as well. It's naught to me, for I do not plan to keep him for my sovereign. Not that there is any great danger of that in any case. The kingdoms of the world are littered with the bones of pretenders, most of them nothing but imposters put forth by conniving relatives."

"You think the boy has little chance of winning the Phoenix Throne?"

"Next to none," Conan said. They sat in the hot tent, conversing by the light of a single candle while the other men snored the night away. "This fort is scarcely strong enough for a robber-baron to set up in to plunder his neighbors. Idris's soldiers seem devoted, but that could be because up here in the borderland, they consider the true Iranistanis to be foreigners. I suspect that Xarxas is a weakling or he is distracted by a war elsewhere on his borders or within his kingdom, else he'd long ago have put down this little insurrection. He's left Katchka up here to fight a war with few men and much territory to cover, then further hampered him by not letting him invade this little island for fear of offending Turan. It is no wonder the swine was looking for a cheap, quick way to end the trouble here and sought to hire my services as assassin."

"I see what you mean," Volvolicus said. "But I still do not understand what you intend to do about it. If I were back in my home, I could employ my powers to rescue my daughter from Green Water. As it is, the time and distance factors are too great. By the time I made the journey and returned here, it could be too late. How long will she be safe in the hands of those villains?"

"Not for a minute," Conan replied. "But she told me that she was proof against the unwanted attentions of any man. Is this true?"

"Her small powers give her unwarranted confidence," the mage replied. "She is safe enough from the pawings of most men, but here she is not dealing with men of the ordinary sort. A man with an army at his beck can accomplish what he will."

"You lack your books and instruments," Conan said. "But surely you have some small enchantments at your command that require no elaborate preparations?"

"Some, yes. Have you a plan?"

"Aye. Listen to me, and tell me what you think." The two men spoke on late into the night.

The next day, Captain Hosta took them along on patrol with his own men. They rode to the river to watch for signs of intrusion. Each of Conan's men wore a sleeveless surcoat with the figure of the dragon worked upon it.

"Do you see much action on these patrols?" Conan asked.

"Nay, curse it!" Hosta said. "We are in strength sufficient only to spot the enemy and run back with our report. I long for a good fight."

Conan smiled. This was working out better than he had hoped. "How would you like a little skirmish with a certain small force of cavalry near here?"

"How small?" Hosta asked suspiciously.

"With my men reinforcing you, the odds will be on our side. I will bait them, then you may ride in and catch the lot."

"You have but just joined us," the man said doubtfully. "It is soon to allow you to plan an action against the enemy."

"If you do not like my plan, you can ride away and leave us to die," Conan said. "Come now; the risk is little and you have said you long for action."

Hosta glared at him, then nodded. "Agreed."

"Good," said Conan, scanning the grassy land near the river. "Now we need just one more thing."

"What is that?"

Conan pointed to a flock being driven to pasture by a man with a crooked staff. "One of those sheep."

The bandits rode single file through the draw, its stony sides forty feet high, the way narrow. As they rode, a man spied upon them from the rim, then ran off to the south. The Cimmerian's keen eyes caught the flicker of movement and knew it for what it was.

"Be ready," he said quietly. Down the line of riders there was a faint click of swords being loosened in their sheaths, of bows being taken from cases of oiled leather.

Abruptly, the draw widened until they were in an oval enclosure perhaps two hundred feet wide, its sides still sheer. When all the riders were within the oval, they saw men run to the rim overlooking them, bows in hand. With a thunder of hooves, a file of horsemen galloped into the oval and spread out until they drew rein, facing the bandits in a broad crescent. One man rode a little forward.

"Greetings, my friends!" Captain Mahac crowed. "How good to see your lovely faces again. You were not on the island for long. Did you lose your nerve?" He stared at them with an eager, bloodthirsty look.

Conan rode forward. "It was not much of a task," he said. "I accomplished what I had agreed to do last night and we rode thither forthwith." He pulled up knee-to-knee with the Iranistani officer and grinned into his face. "I believe I now have business with the mighty General Katchka, and his esteemed friend, the distinguished Vizier Akhba."

Mahac's cruel face was nonplussed. "Truly? You have slain the pretender? Let me see."

Conan took a bloodstained bag of homespun cloth from his saddlebag. "I give this to General Katchka and no other."

Mahac smiled again. "A splendid feat! You are an extraordinary warrior. Now, be so good as to let me confirm your kill. Show me the head."

"Did you bring the woman, Layla?" Conan asked.

"She is with His Excellency, enjoying the finest of hospitality, and she will be released to your care upon delivery of the usurper's head. Now show me!" The last words came out in a shrill scream.

Conan shrugged. "Oh, very well." He opened the bag and held it before Mahac. "Here, look."

The officer stared down into the bag. Staring back up at him was the foul-smelling, woolly head of a white sheep. He made a strangled sound and grasped his sword-hilt. "Kill them!" Then a sound made him look up. Riders rode wildly along the rim, whooping and pushing his archers off to tumble onto the canyon floor and lie there unmoving. At the same time, a bellowing squadron of armored men stormed in from behind the bandits, swords out. In an instant, all was a confusion of struggling, slashing, slaying men.

Conan smashed Mahac alongside the jaw with his bagged sheep's head. The man reeled in his saddle but still managed to draw his sword and hew at the Cimmerian. The blow was clumsy and ill-timed and Conan managed to duck it even as he drew his own sword. For ten heartbeats, the two swords licked out and chimed musically together as the horses circled one another and the men sought each other's life. Finally, Conan spurred his mount against Mahac's, bowling the smaller animal over and throwing its rider to the ground.

The Cimmerian flung himself from the saddle, landing upon the fallen man as he tried to rise. Mahac managed a single curse, then Conan drew his dirk and sheathed it in the captain's throat. Mahac fell back gurgling, blood spraying from the gash, spurting from his mouth and nostrils. He thrashed for several seconds, drumming his spurs on the sandy ground, then lay still.

A great quiet had fallen over the canyon, broken only by the shuffling of horses with the smell of fresh-spilled blood in their nostrils and the occasional moan of a wounded man. Coming after the brief but furious clash of arms, it was like a dead silence. Captain Hosta rode up to the Cimmerian, smiling happily.

"All of them slain," he said, "and I have only three wounded. There is nothing like the advantage of surprise in warfare." He wiped blood from his long, curved sword. "Your rogues did not fare so well, but they were fighting regulars."

Conan saw that he was down to five men besides the wizard and himself: potbellied Chamik, one-eyed Ubo, Auda the desert man, the unregenerate Osman, and the evil and seemingly unkillable Mamos. Already they were looting the bodies of the slain.

"I have an errand to perform, and the scholar will go with me," Conan said. "The rest of my men will ride back with you."

Hosta shrugged. "As you wish. You have earned the right to do as you will. We shall cut off the right hands of all these traitors. His Majesty will be most pleased with the trophies I shall bring him."

Conan led his horse to where his men were efficiently stripping the bodies of valuables. "Gather 'round," he said. They joined him, stuffing coins, rings and jewels into their sashes and boot tops.

"Volvolicus and I go now to Green Water to fetch the woman back." He spoke in a low voice, so that only they could hear. "Tonight, when all are asleep save for the sentries, I want you all to desert. Ride across the bight of the old river channel into Turan and ride northwest toward our hideout. Stop at the first village and abide there until we come to join you."

Ubo grinned and nodded. "Aye, that's an order I'll not hesitate to obey! These farm-boy recruits will never hear us pass by them in the night." The others nodded happily. Pleased by their loot, they were not at all bothered by the death of several comrades.

Conan found Volvolicus brooding over the scene of slaughter. He had taken no part in the fighting, but had ridden his horse to one side and whiled away the time avoiding the flying weapons and seeking to keep the gouting blood from his clothing.

"You are an efficient killer, my friend," the mage said to him.

"Often it is a matter of necessity," Conan told him. "With Captain Mahac, it was also a pleasure."

"If all evil men were slain," the wizard pointed out, "the world would soon be depopulated."

"Aye, I'd not want that to happen," Conan concurred. "Besides being numerous, it is the bad ones that make life interesting."

The two men made their preparations, then rode off toward the oasis town of Green Water.

The gatekeeper of Shahpur shook his head as another strange man entered the city. He had thought most of the colorful characters had departed with the end of the catastrophic festival, but lately a strange assortment had arrived, men of nations seldom seen in these parts and some of them bizarre of appearance even for strangers from remote parts of the world.

The day before, there had been the fat Vendhyan whose turban seemed to glow. Then there was the Nemedian so thin he might have been suffering from a plague, but whose movements were unnaturally swift. Now there was this man from Khitai, whose robes were rich but whose face was covered with a veil.

It was all most puzzling, but he was shaken from his reverie when Sagobal came riding toward the gate, returned from one of his unending patrols and looking to be in a killing mood. At such times, a man did his best not to attract the guard commander's attention. The gate guard stiffened to attention, his face blank of expression as Sagobal rode past, the weird foreigners forgotten.

Ten

The Cimmerian and the Turanian wizard rode back to the caravan town of Green Water. All appeared much as it had upon their first arrival at the oasis. Camels and horses drank from the lake among the palms. Other animals were picketed in areas all around the greenery, and men had set up camp, cooking and brewing at small fires, some having erected tents, others preferring to take their chances with the weather. Few paid any attention to the two riders. Cavalry horses were still tethered in their orderly picket lines.

When the two rode through the gateway, they once again heard the strains of exotic music coming from the square. This time they made a small detour down a side street. In a lot between two shops in a food market, they bought a large bundle of well-seasoned firewood tied with twisted withies. With this balanced across the pommel of the mage's saddle, they rode on into the public square of the town.

Music played there, and the dancers gyrated. The riders ignored them and proceeded on toward the government building, above which still towered the royal banner and the personal banner of General Katchka. They drew to a halt at the base of the wide stairs leading up to the portico.

As the officers seated at the long table noted who had ridden up, their talk fell off and then there was silence. General Katchka was still seated in his accustomed place, and when he noticed that his men had gone silent, he looked to see what was wrong. His eyes were red and bleary and he moved slowly as he turned to face the riders. Next to him, the Vizier Akhba looked up, his eyes going wide with surprise at sight of the Cimmerian and the wizard.

"What is this?" Katchka demanded, his voice even more hoarse than usual. "Cimmerian! You were not away for long!"

"I do not waste time, General," Conan said.

"Where is Captain Mahac?" Akhba inquired. "He was to meet you on your way back and escort you here, lest you be pursued by the rebels." He was recovering from his surprise, and his customary look of smooth slyness reclaimed his features.

"Doubtless the captain is in a suitable place," Conan said. "Where is the woman, Layla?"

"Where is the head of the pretender, Idris?" Katchka countered.

"Bring the woman to me and you shall have the head," Conan replied.

"We do not believe you, barbarian," Akhba said.

"Then behold." Once again Conan took the bloody sack from his saddlebag. He reached into it. When his hand emerged, his fingers gripped a head by its long black hair. The face was that of a handsome youth.

"It is he!" cried Akhba. "This is the spit of the old king."

"Aye," Katchka rumbled. "It can be no other."

"The woman," Conan urged.

"A moment," said Akhba. He turned and shouted a few words into the building. Minutes later, two women servants came out with Layla between them. Her face was sullen and apprehensive, but her expression brightened when she saw her father and the big barbarian.

"Now," Akhba said, "the head." He held his hands out like a boy waiting to catch a ball.

"Let the woman come over here first," Conan demanded.

"We waste time," said Akhba. He began to call orders to the guards nearby, but at that moment the wizard cast the bundle of firewood to the pavement between the horses. He pointed at the wood with a long finger and called out a string of words that rang through the square with uncanny resonance. Instantly, the wood burst into intense blue flame. The horses sidled in fright, but Conan forced his own mount to stand still and he held the head dangling by its long hair above the flame.

"If I drop it, it will be consumed instantly," he said. "You'll have no trophy to bear to your king with your stories of danger and heroism. Give us the woman."

Katchka could not take his eyes off the ghastly head, his piglike eyes glittering with greed. "The woman is nothing," he said. "Let her go!"

Akhba nodded to the servants, and Layla began to move forward. She descended the steps and walked to her father's horse. Gracefully, she placed a foot in a stirrup and mounted behind him. For once, she had no taunting words for the Cimmerian, who held the head rigidly over the fire.

"Go," he said to Volvolicus. The mage wheeled and galloped from the now-silent square.

"Very well, you have her," said Akhba. "Fulfill your part of the bargain."

"How about my three thousand ounces of gold?" Conan smiled at their expressions of consternation, but not for long. The magickal fire was dying down, leaving only crackling, blackened twigs.

Katchka was about to shout something to his guards, but his jaw snapped shut when the Cimmerian tossed the head toward him. Forgetting all else, the general reached out and caught the bundle, laughing with glee. The barbarian wheeled and set spurs to his horse. The magnificent beast bounded for the nearest exit.

"Kill him!" Akhba shouted. Then he, too, was caressing the youthful head.

Conan had almost reached one of the side streets before two of the soldiers grabbed for his reins. He drew his sword and halved the skull of one, then kicked the other back. He ducked a spear that whistled viciously over his head, and then he was off down the street, heading for the gate.

The general and the vizier ignored the bustle around them as their half-drunken officers scrambled to mount their horses and give chase.

"So, Idris!" Katchka said. "You thought to put yourself on the throne?" He spat into the face and laughed.

"This repays you for dragging me here," said Akhba. "Making me leave the court and come to this bleak province to chase a stripling and his primitive kin!" Then he, too, spat.

As the spittle struck the face, its skin began to writhe and shift, roiling like liquid in a boiling kettle. Katchka cried out in shock and surprise and dropped the head as if it had suddenly grown red-hot. The glossy black hair became lank and brown, and the pale, aristocratic complexion darkened. The general and the vizier cried out in rage and horror. Staring up at them from the top step was the familiar face of Captain Mahac.

Conan roared with laughter as he thundered down the main street of the town. People stared at him, doubtless wondering at the cause of this reckless horsemanship. The mage and the woman had ridden that way minutes before in a similar hurry. He heard the snarling of trumpets from behind him and knew that now the chase would begin. He had left some angry men back there.

He passed through the gate and rode between the rows of palms, past the oasis and into the desert beyond. Minutes later, he caught up with Volvolicus and Layla. The woman was now astride the mount they had brought with them and tethered outside the oasis. It was another of Sagobal's stolen horses.

"Now we must ride, my friends," Conan said. "Men thirst for our blood!" Still he whooped with laughter, like a boy who has just gotten away with a particularly naughty trick.

Layla rode alongside him, smiling broadly and, for once, without malice. "Accept my apologies, Conan," she said, shouting to be heard above the drumming of their horses' hooves on the soft desert ground. "It is true. You are very nearly the hero you make yourself out to be."

"It was a pleasure to do those swine a bad turn," he said, grinning. "Had you any hurt from them?" He looked back but saw nothing save his billowing cloak and the desert beyond. Pursuit was not yet in sight.

"I would have, but both Katchka and Akhba drank themselves into a stupor each night. I do not know how long that would have lasted, though. It was well you came when you did."

"Men behind us!" Volvolicus announced. Conan turned once more. A broad line of horsemen came over a rise of ground far behind them, the men and their mounts little more than black dots in the distance.

"Can they catch us?" Layla asked, her face now worried.

"It will be close," Conan admitted. "Our horses are better, and while they are fresh, we'll have the advantage of them. But you can safely wager that each of those troopers has two or three remounts. They can keep up the pressure, with some of them riding full speed to make us do the same, others of them hanging back and hoarding their strength. It is the chase of the wolf."

"That has an ill sound," she said dubiously.

"Wizard!" Conan called. "Can you whistle us up a sandstorm?"

"One does not summon wind elementals by whistling, northerner. I have told you of the difficulties of working magick under these circumstances."

"Deeds, magician!" Conan called impatiently. "We need deeds, not words!"

"I will try," Volvolicus said.

For hours they traveled, the horses growing lathered, breathing hard. Conan and Layla rode in silence, saving their breath. Volvolicus mumbled loudly, trying to work his magick. He seemed to have little success. When the sun was below the horizon and the first stars gleaming overhead, a sudden great wind began, raising clouds of sand and dust.

"It will not last," said the mage. "We must take advantage of it now."

"An hour out of their view will help greatly," said Conan. The men behind them had drawn much closer during the evening. Now, in the shrouding curtain of dust, the three were able to take some evasive action unseen: riding down side draws, turning onto stony paths where they had to slow down, but where they left no tracks. In time, Conan called a halt and they rested the horses. Beasts and riders were covered with dust, and the Cimmerian used the rest-time to rub the animals down and inspect their hooves.

"This cannot last," said Layla. "We will ride these horses to death keeping up this pace."

"Aye, it grieves me to abuse the beasts," said Conan. "But if we must ride them to death, we shall, lacking any other choice." With his dagger-point, he dug a tiny rock from between a horse's shoe and hoof. "I hope Katchka is leading the pursuit personally."

"Why do you wish that?" she asked.

"For one thing, should they catch us, it would give me great pleasure to have a chance to hew him down. For another," he released the animal's hoof and straightened, "no horse can make its best speed with that great hulk in its saddle. He will slow down the whole chase if he is with them."

The wind died down and they rode on beneath the stars, traveling cautiously, with Conan in the lead. To his fiercely trained senses, the stars and the pale crescent of the moon supplied sufficient light for them to maintain a swift trot.

Even so, there was never true safety to riding at night. Even eyes as keen as Conan's could miss an animal's burrow large enough to admit a horse's hoof, and it was beneath the stars that the bigger desert predators hunted. Lynxes and foxes were numerous. Harmless in themselves, their sudden appearance could cause a horse to shy. Once, in the distance, the Cimmerian descried a pair of lionesses out hunting, seeking the gazelles and oryx that frequented the desert fringe and the land near the river.

"Have we lost them?" Layla asked as the eastern horizon began to turn gray.

"No chance of that," Conan said. "They can spread wide and sweep the riverland like a great net. But if we are far enough ahead when they see us again, we may make it."

The gray turned to pale rose; then the sun broke ferociously over the horizon, and the fleeing trio cast long shadows as they rode their weary horses into the cultivated fields near the river, where for centuries the dour peasants of the area had dug irrigation ditches to bring water to the parched land.

"Men coming!" Volvolicus shouted. The wizard was far more worn down than his daughter or the Cimmerian, for he lacked the youth of the one and the iron strength and endurance of the other. He reeled in the saddle as he pointed to their left, where a line of riders in glittering armor bore down upon them. In their van, Conan recognized the brutish figure of General Katchka. Roaring with triumph, the Iranistani drew his sword and whirled it overhead, urging his men on. Riders on fresher horses, carrying less bulk, began to draw ahead.

"To the river!" Conan shouted. "Kill your horses if you must!" He dug in his spurs, and Layla tore the belt from her slender waist, using it to flog her mount to greater speed. But the horses were capable of no final burst of effort. They were near the end of their strength.

"Men to the right, now," Volvolicus said wearily.

Conan looked and cursed. An even larger group of horsemen bore down from that side. "Caught in a vise!" He drew his sword. "You two go on to the river. I am going to kill that swine!" Layla cried out for him to stop as he wrenched his horse's head around and faced the oncoming general, trying to calculate his chances of getting in a killing blow before he was inevitably cut down by the others.

"Conan!" the wizard shouted. "These are not Katchka's!"

But the Cimmerian had no attention to spare for the mage's enigmatic words. His mind and will had focused narrowly upon the oncoming general and the sword in his own hand. Then, abruptly, something happened. The men riding toward him slowed. The outriders rejoined the main body and the whole formed a compact mass, with the general in the middle.

Conan risked a brief look behind him and saw that the men bearing down from that direction were not clad in glittering armor, but rather, in the dingy, battered gear of the rebels. In their forefront rode Hosta and Eltis, and behind them he could see the youthful figure of Idris, riding between two hulking guards.

With a howl of pure joy, the Cimmerian charged straight for the enemy line. The men opposite snarled and cursed, but they behaved like the hardened professionals they were. The first to block Conan's advance was hewn from shoulder to saddle, his lighter horse bowled over on its back by Conan's larger mount. Vaulting the sprawling animal and its halved rider, Conan swung his great sword with both hands, taking out a trooper with each glittering arc of steel.

Then the two battle lines collided and were instantly intermixed. It was a slashing, hewing, spearing chaos, without sense or order as each man sought to kill as many of the enemy as he could before eating steel. Horses and men screamed alike as weapons made music against other weapons, with a bass undertone: the sickening smack of sharp steel into yielding flesh, the staccato snap of bone.

Then Conan saw the raging, roaring figure of General Katchka before him. A rebel rider rode in and sought to thrust his lance through the big belly, but Katchka contemptuously batted the vicious point aside with his sword, and with his return blow, flicked the sharp edge across the man's neck. The rebel rode on headless, a column of scarlet blood fountaining three feet into the air from his severed neck.

"Barbarian!" the general screamed. "You tricked me! You insulted me before my men! Dog!" He seemed to run out of words with which to express his rage. With an inarticulate howl, he charged toward Conan. Gleefully, the Cimmerian rode to meet him. Steel rang against steel in a swift exchange of blows, each man swinging his weapon with both hands. With a dextrous twist of his sword, Conan caught Katchka's blade between his own blade and its long crossguard, locking the two weapons in place. As the horses circled, the men twisted at their hilts, each seeking to wrench the weapon from his enemy's hand.

Feeling his grip weaken, Katchka did not seek to prolong the struggle but released his sword. In the instant that the Cimmerian was off balance from the sudden lack of resistance, the Iranistani butted him in the face with his steel helmet, throwing one massive arm around Conan and with the other, drawing his dagger.

The blow to his face caused white light to flash in Conan's head, almost blinding him. Instinct, though, was swifter than thought. He released his own weapon and grabbed the general by the upper edge of his cuirass even as his other hand shot out and found the hand that held the dagger, gripping the thick wrist in fingers like steel. Katchka tried to drag Conan closer to his own blade. Conan held him at arm's length as he twisted the heavy arm, bending it inward, slowly bringing the knife closer to Katchka's own body.

It was a titanic struggle of main strength, but it could not last. Katchka's face twisted with rage, then his eyes bulged with horror as, by inches, his dagger drew ever closer to his own neck. He tried to release the weapon, but Conan's relentless grip held his hand paralyzed.

The general began to scream as the tip of the curved, razor-edged blade touched the flesh beneath his jaw. The trickle of blood became a stream as the blade slowly penetrated. Then the scream rose in pitch as the point rose upward through his tongue. Blood mixed with foam bubbled from his lips as the point pierced the roof of his mouth. Still he tried to hold Conan's arm back, and did not relent until the knife pierced through his brain. Then all his muscles relaxed at once and General Katchka toppled from his saddle like a huge sack of animal guts in a slaughterhouse.

Suddenly, Conan became aware that he had been struggling amid a great silence. He shook the stars from before his eyes and looked around him, discovering that he was in the center of a great circle of rebel riders who sat their horses, gaping at him. Volvolicus was among them, looking tired but happy. Layla was enraged.

"I tried to get them to put some arrows in that pig, but they would not listen!" she cried.

"Arrows?" Idris said, scandalized. "I'd not have missed a spectacle like that had it meant giving up my throne!"

"If only Akhba had been with them," said Dunas, the pretender's cousin.

"His king will give him what he deserves," said Eltis with satisfaction. "When he reports that not only did he fail to destroy us, but he lost his general and half a wing of cavalry to boot—" he paused to smile with satisfaction, savoring the image "—well, he had better hope that Xarxas is in a good mood and merely crucifies him."

"How came you here so timely?" Conan asked, blotting up the blood that ran from his nose.

"We rode out last night on a patrol in strength," said Eltis. "The men were elated with bagging Mahac's troop, and we were hoping to catch another. We found two troopers who got separated from this lot yesterday in a sandstorm. They said that they had been chasing you and that Katchka was in personal command of a small force."

"We calculated that you would try to lose them in the badlands near here," Hosta said, "and that if we rode hard, we might catch them somewhere near this spot, for their horses had to be tired. Lucky for you we got here before they caught the three of you."

"You will notice that your men are not here with us," said Eltis. "They seem to have deserted our cause."

"They are probably just drunk in a tavern someplace," Conan said. "Good, loyal soldiers like them do not desert."

"If they found a tavern," said the commander, "then I suspect it must be many miles north of the river."

"Who cares about them?" said Idris, smiling as one of his soldiers tied General Katchka's head to the pommel of his saddle. "The people of the north will flock to my cause now, for I have defeated one of Xarxas's generals in open battle. I have the proof right here!" He patted the ugly head. "Conan, ride with me and I will make you commander over all my cavalry."

Conan saw the glowering expressions the senior officers bent in his direction. "I fear I must decline, Your Majesty. Urgent business calls me to Turan."

"This northerner is a mighty warrior, my king," said Eltis. "But I fear he would be a most uncomfortable man to have around when you assume your rightful throne. His men deserted, but he has done you good service, and we saved his neck just now. Let us call it even and allow him to depart. To keep him would be dangerous, and to slay him would be the act of an ingrate."

The boy looked sullen, unhappy at losing his new hero. "Oh, very well. Conan, ride on with my thanks. In the future, should your path lead to Iranistan, know that the king of this nation holds himself in debt to you."

They were kingly words to come from a boy surrounded by ragged soldiers, but Conan knew better than to laugh. Instead, he bowed from his saddle.

"Your Majesty does me great honor. And now, I take my leave of you. Good fortune in your struggle to regain your rightful throne."

The pretender inclined his head graciously and the Cimmerian rode from the circle of rebels, closely followed by his two companions.

The river-crossing was an easy one, and Conan paused almost in mid-stream. Hanging his weapon-belt on his pommel, he took off his boots and dismounted, plunging beneath the water to rinse the blood, dust and sweat from his body and his clothes. He stood up and began to wring the water from his thick black hair. As he did this, he noticed that Layla had followed suit. She stood wringing out her own tresses, and the water caused her dress to cling to her like a coat of dye, revealing not only that her body was as beautiful as her face, but that she wore nothing beneath the silken shift.

"You should join us, Father," she said.

"I shall wait until we reach proper bathing facilities," he replied with dignity.

Already, Conan felt like a new man. He was recovering quickly from the fatigue of the previous day and night, and of the morning's brief but furious combat. His nose did not seem to be broken, although it and his face would pain him for days to come. His only regret was that Volvolicus was present, for he had a great urge to seize Layla and carry her to an inviting, shady spot on the riverbank.

Lacking the opportunity at the moment, he resolved to seek one out in the near future. He remounted and rode dripping from the river. The others rode with him.

"Considering what you did for him," Layla said, "the young pretender should have rewarded you richly." She reveled in the coolness of her damp gown as the morning breeze dried it upon her body.

Conan could only laugh. "That stripling will be doing well if he can provide breeches for his riders in the years to come. He is a penniless claimant, raising a rebellion in the poorest part of Iranistan. Barring lucky accident, he'll be nothing but a defiant baron, prospering only because he pays no taxes to his king. If some courtiers close to the seat of power think that they can better themselves by doing away with Xarxas and elevating this royal bastard to the throne—" he shrugged

"—then things will be very different. I think the life of a king can be as chancy as that of a wandering warrior."

They rode to the edge of the grassy land, and there Conan ordered a halt.

"We need sleep," he announced. "More important, these fine beasts need rest. Let them crop grass peacefully for the remainder of the day. We will ride on tonight when it is cool."

"That suits me well," Layla said, dismounting. "There is shade here, and I am too tired even to be hungry."

Conan unsaddled and curried the horses while Layla spread a blanket upon the grass beneath a tree, to which her father lowered himself stiffly. Soon he was snoring and his daughter lay curled up next to him.

Satisfied that the animals had plenty of forage and were soundly hobbled, the Cimmerian walked off to find a promising shade-tree beneath which to sleep. They enjoyed a good view in all directions. He would wake in plenty of time should strangers approach. Finding a likely spot, he spread his cloak upon a cushion of shaded grass and tugged off his boots. With weapons laid close to his hand, he drew the light material of his desert cloak over himself and allowed his weary muscles to relax.

He was almost asleep when something tugged at his cloak. Layla slipped beneath it, and it was clear that she had left her gown elsewhere. "My father is a very sound sleeper," was all that she said before rolling into the circle of his waiting arms.

The next day they rode into a small town of some prosperity, not the usual market village, but a mining community where men toiled to wrest tin ore from a great open pit. The town had no gate or guard, so Conan addressed a fruit-seller whose stall, a flimsy shelter of cloth supported by thin poles, was set up at the outskirts of the village.

"Where is the lowest tavern in town?" he asked. "The one where all the rogues gather."

"You want the Craven Warrior," the old man said. "It is

down this street, near the public latrine. The smell will tell you when you are near. Would you like to buy some oranges? They were picked fresh this morning."

Layla bargained for fruit while Conan and Volvolicus rode on. They went past the center of town until they found a low, mud-walled building. Its facade had been whitewashed and upon it was crudely painted in garish colors the figure of an armed man sprinting for safety, closely pursued by a cloud of arrows, spears, axes and other missiles. As predicted, the smell from the public facility fouled the air chokingly.

"If I know my rogues," Conan said, "they'll be in this place."

Leaving their horses tethered to a stone trough, they entered the dive through a curtain of hanging beads, which did little to keep out the swarms of flies that buzzed busily all over the area.

"Chief!" Ubo cried happily. "You are back! And I see you have the wizard as well. Come join us." The one-eyed Turanian was dicing with Chamik, while Auda snored on the floor. Between them was a pot of ale in which floated several drowned flies.

Conan took a seat. "Where are the rest?"

"Mamos is in the back room with a harlot desperate enough even for him," Chamik reported. "As for Osman, we've not seen him since the night before last."

"He's probably taken up with some woman whose husband spends his days in the mine," Ubo said. "He is a smooth talker, that one." He slammed the leather cup on the table and lifted it to reveal a disastrous lineup of images. Crowing, Chamik scooped up the silver coins. "Did you get the wench as well?"

"She is with us," Conan said. "Has all been quiet?"

"None have molested us," said Chamik, "since we have money to spend. But a story has come to our ears that we find disturbing."

"What is this tale?" Conan asked.

"There has been a party of men riding the river," Ubo told

him, "men of many nations. The townsmen say they do not look like soldiers, but they are well armed and fierce. Their leader is a hulking brute of an Aquilonian, and they were asking questions."

Conan felt a tingle of alarm. "What sort of questions?"

"They were asking about a band of men that sounded very much like ours," Chamik said, "save that the band they seek is more numerous, and is led by a big, black-haired northerner. Since we were only five men with no such foreigner among us, we were not to be confused with this band."

"I can easily believe that men are looking for us," Volvolicus put forth. "But why a mixed group of foreigners? Why not Sagobal's guardsmen, or constables in the livery of Torgut Khan?"

"This Aquilonian leader," Conan said. "Had he a name?"

"He did not noise it about," said Ubo, "but a camel-seller told me he heard one of the men address him as Berytus."

Conan hissed a curse, his hand slapping the tabletop.

"Do you know him?" asked the wizard.

"By reputation only. He is a manhunter. It is his living and his sport. He hunts down wanted men and runaway slaves for the reward. What ill luck brought him here just when Sagobal had need of such?"

"You think him more dangerous than Sagobal himself?" Volvolicus asked.

"I'll warrant he and his men are far more dangerous than any Sagobal has. Manhunting is a duty and a task for soldiers and constables. Some are good at it, most are not. But Berytus's band will be made up of picked men, each of them an expert. How many of them are there?"

"The first time they came through here, not long after we left Shahpur," said Ubo, "there were a score of them. The second time, just two days before our arrival, there were seventeen."

The wizard looked at Conan. "My house! A few days ago, I sensed it when my wards were roused. I would wager that was when this Berytus lost his men. And they must truly be formidable, if only three of them were killed."

"Seventeen are too many for us, Chief," Chamik said quietly, "even if they were just ordinary soldiers."

"Aye, we are in no condition for a stand-up fight with them. And this is not a good place for us."

"Where shall we go?" Ubo asked.

"I counsel we ride back to our loot," said Chamik. "Each man to take as much as he can carry and all of us to flee in different directions."

"That might just lead them straight to the treasure," Conan warned. "No, we need a few more days, during which time Torgut Khan will be recalled by the king, and Sagobal executed in disgrace. Then the land will be unsettled enough to allow us to go back and get it all. I will also need time to spy out this band of manhunters and decide how to deal with them."

"Where to, then?" asked Chamik.

"To the wizard's house," Conan said. "They have already been there. He has wards and ways of knowing when any approach. What think you, Volvolicus? Can you conceal us safely for but a few days?"

"I can," he agreed with some reluctance. "It will not be convenient, but it can be done." In truth, he had a pressing need to get back to his books, his instruments and his place of power.

Conan stood. "Then round up the rest and let's be away. Some townsman could be leading those manhunters back here right now."

An hour later, Conan, the wizard, Layla and four of the bandits were gathered and ready to ride, but Osman was still nowhere to be found.

"I knew it!" said Mamos, his scarred and branded face twisted into an expression of surpassing ugliness. "That little schemer has fled back to the treasure!"

"What of it?" Ubo said. "How much can he take? Will he lead his own caravan thither?"

"I am more concerned that he will lead the hunters there," Conan said. "I will ride after him. The rest of you go to the wizard's house."

"Wait!" said Mamos. "How do we know you do not plan to take it for yourself? The agreement was that we were to stay together until the sharing-out!"

"Be still, fool," said Ubo. "As for staying together, Osman has taken care of that. And for all we know, he is down a dry well with his throat slit or his head bashed in. It is a common fate for thieves and men who trifle with other men's wives. I trust our chief, although I'll warrant that I'd trust none of the rest of you."

"I cannot say that I like the idea of having them live near me for days without you to keep them in line," Layla said, "but if it must be, it must be."

"Woman," Chamik said, "we know better than to mistreat a wizard's daughter in the wizard's own house. He could turn us into scorpions."

"In that case, your disposition would not change," she said, "although you would be prettier to look upon." At this sally, the men laughed heartily, their good humor restored.

"I will be with you in a few days," Conan said. He wheeled and rode away to the west. The others took a more northerly direction, toward the house of Volvolicus.

Eleven

"Three of them crossed the river here, Chief," said Bahdur. The squat, slant-eyed man leaned from his saddle and studied the marks left in the soft ground of the bank.

"Is it certain?" Berytus asked.

"They were all shod by the same smith who shoes Sagobal's horses," the Hyrkanian reported.

"But only three?" Berytus said, perplexed.

"Only three," Bahdur affirmed.

The Aquilonian saw two of his men riding across the shallow water of the river bight. Urdos and Ambula rode up the bank and across to their leader.

"There was a good-sized fight over there yesterday," the huge Kothian told him. "Plenty of blood on the ground, but no smallest bit of armor, weapons or horses. Whoever won left nothing behind but marks."

"Perhaps that is why there were only three," Bahdur speculated. "Maybe the rest were killed in that fight."

"It is possible," Berytus mused. He longed to be after the

three fleeing northward, but he knew that he had to learn something of the situation across the river.

"Ambula, Barca, you two ride after the three who left their prints here. Find them, but keep your distance. They may be the ones we seek, or they may all be dead in Iranistan, and three others on the horses they stole from Sagobal. I am riding over there to ask some questions."

Followed by fourteen men, Berytus of Aquilonia rode into the water. The two detached men rode northward.

Conan rode westward, making broad zigzags, seeking to pick up Osman's trail. But the desert in this area was stony, and even a tracker of Conan's skill was put to the test trying to find a single man's spoor. Eventually, he decided that he was wasting time. He rode straight for the hideout, timing his approach so that he would arrive there after dark.

He hobbled his horse a half-mile from the canyon and went the rest of the way on foot. Just before sunrise, he was crouching outside the cave wherein the treasure was hidden. All the way there, he had heard nothing but the sounds of night animals and insects. He smelled no hint of smoke upon the air. This was puzzling. The city-bred Osman had no special skills of elusiveness in the wild. More than likely, the Cimmerian thought, the man had simply gotten lost trying to find the place.

The sun rose and Conan, satisfied that he was alone, moved some rocks aside and went into the cave. The light streaming through the entrance revealed that the treasure was exactly as they had left it. He went back out and reclosed the cave.

Next he went to the water, where he startled a pair of desert oryx drinking. The beautiful creatures bounded away and he looked over the ground. Instantly, he saw that a number of horsemen had ridden through the canyon several days previously. They were not Sagobal's men, for their horses were not shod in the Turanian fashion. These, he knew, must be the manhunters.

A quick examination of the various side-canyons proved that the hunters had not conducted a systematic search of the area, but had ridden off in the same direction the fleeing bandits had taken. So they had been here looking for the bandits, not for the treasure. But where was Osman?

The Cimmerian all but groaned at the thought of the task that lay before him, but it was necessary. He began walking back toward the cave.

"Where is it?" Torgut Khan screamed. "Where is my treasure?"

"My men are combing the countryside for it," Sagobal said. "I have a score of search parties turning over every rock between here and the Iranistan border."

"Your men are worthless!" Torgut Khan bellowed. "As you are worthless, scum!"

Sagobal had had enough. He strode up to his superior and Torgut Khan fell back a pace, knowing he had gone too far.

"Do not take such a tone with me, you toad!" Sagobal thundered. "The king's silken noose lies around your neck, and nothing will happen to me that will not fall upon you a thousandfold. I have stood your insolence and insults and even your blows for long enough! I am your only hope, Torgut Khan. Only I can save you from a hideous death in deepest disgrace. So you can cease your bombastic ravings now!"

The viceroy's face went scarlet; then he seemed to deflate, like the toad Sagobal had named him. "You are right, my friend. The king's treasury officers are on their way hither and we must now help one another to escape the royal wrath. Find the treasure, and all will be well with the throne."

Sagobal smiled and bowed. "As you say, my commander." He turned and walked away, knowing that now he was the master here.

In the Temple of Ahriman, the priests met in solemn conclave. Standing around the hideous altar were Tragthan. Shosq and Nikas, the latter's near-halved body now almost healed by their magical arts and the nearness of his god. The priest Umos was still embedded in the wall of the crypt, horridly alive and sentient, in a state best described as half-digested.

"All is in turmoil," Tragthan told the others. "Not only does our dread lord arrive untimely, but I sense a great power of hostile force drawing nigh, like a vast army come to besiege a city."

"I have felt this as well," said Shosq. "What can it portend? Have the enemy gods sensed the return of our lord? Do they come hither to keep him from coming into this world?"

"It is not a gathering of such power as that," said Nikas. "As I lay near death, I was vouchsafed visions, and in these visions I beheld many flames, flames of many colors, and some of them had the aspect of darkness burning, and these flames were drawing close to this place."

"Priests of the gods who are our lord's enemies?" Shosq asked him.

"Nay, I think these to be the wizards, the mages and sorcerers of this age."

"Wizards!" Shosq exclaimed with a humorless laugh. "The petty practitioners of sorcery in this age have no such power! Even the great ones of past ages could not contend with a god!"

"The sorcerers of ancient Stygia could," Tragthan intoned. "The wizard-kings drove our lord from this plane and kept him away for untold ages."

"They had the aid of Set," said Shosq. "The sacrifices they made to gain that power were almost beyond belief. No mage of this era has such power."

"But so many together, with our lord so weakened . . ." Tragthan paused. "We must do something about this."

"What action should we take?" Nikas asked.

"First, we must search." Tragthan told them. They all looked down and contemplated the nest of serpents that was the altar of Ahriman. Slowly, beneath the bloody light streaming in so unnaturally through the windows overhead, the serpents began to writhe.

Sagobal sat brooding in his quarters, gnawing at his mustache. Things had been quiet for too long. This matter should have been settled to his satisfaction long before now. Could it be possible that a half-savage northern barbarian had outwitted him? Impossible! Accident and unforeseen circumstances must have taken a hand. From outside his door, the butt of a spear beat three times upon the floor.

"Enter," Sagobal said. The door opened and the guardsman stepped through.

"A man has come to crave audience with you, sir. He said to show you this." The guard handed him a small, folded sheet of paper. Sagobal opened it and studied the single sigil it bore.

"Show him in, and then leave us."

The guard left. A few minutes later, a man in a hooded robe entered the chambers. The door closed behind him and he pushed the cowl back. The face thus exposed was that of Osman the Shangaran. He bowed ceremoniously.

"I greet you, most valorous Commander Sagobal."

Sagobal glared at him. "What has taken you so long, villain?" he asked coldly." You should have reported to me many days ago . . . unless you truly do not know that which I must know. If that is the case, your death will be dreadful."

Osman's face took on a look of mock-hurt. "I am shocked that you should speak to me so, to poor Osman, who has borne such hardship and degradation in your loyal service." His eye lit upon the pitcher standing upon Sagobal's table. "Who, indeed, has grown most shockingly thirsty in his loyalty to you."

"Go ahead," Sagobal said, fuming. Osman filled a goblet, drank deep and smacked his lips.

"Ah, my lord, you would not credit the terrible swill your poor servant has had to choke down these many days past."

"You would not credit how unpleasant my dungeons can

be, when you occupy a cell as a true prisoner rather than as a ruse."

"No need to be threatening," Osman protested. "Has not all fallen out as planned? Have I not fulfilled all my instructions as charged?"

"With one exception," Sagobal said, his voice dangerously silky. "The bandits and the treasure have eluded me. Where are they?"

Osman went to a chair and seated himself. "You do not trust me, Sagobal."

The guard commander's eyes went wide with amazement. "Wherefore should I trust you, villain?"

"Nonetheless, you assured me that I would have free rein to bring matters to a satisfactory conclusion, that I was to be allowed to operate free from interference." The small man leaned forward and spoke intently. "And yet I have learned that you hired foreign manhunters to comb the district for me and my erstwhile companions."

"I conduct my affairs as I see fit," Sagobal said. "You are a hireling. Do not presume to comment upon my arrangements."

"You had done better had you trusted me. By now, Conan knows about your jackals and he may be taking further precautions. Ere now, he thought that time was all he needed, that before much longer, you and Torgut Khan would be dragged away in chains for punishment, leaving him free to make off with the treasure. Now he is alerted, and he is a man who has his own way of dealing with things."

"My patience is—" Sagobal stopped speaking when the spear-butt struck the floor without the door three times. Once again the guard opened the door, this time to only lean in.

"The Aquilonian is here, Commander."

"Send him in," Sagobal instructed.

The hulking man entered, the spiked plates covering the backs of his hands scraping the door frame as he passed through. He flexed his fingers slightly and the leather straps encasing his forearms creaked. His blue eyes took in Osman with a cool, idle glance.

"Your little dog has returned, I see," said Berytus.

"Somewhat in advance of his big jackal," Osman said. "You have never seen me from so close. How did you know me?"

Berytus smiled contemptuously. "You think I need to see you in a golden turban to know you? Once I have a look at a man, from however far away, I will know him at midnight in the bottom of a pit."

"That arrow came damnably close," Osman complained.

"Bahdur does not make mistakes with his bow. I would have told him to nick your ear, but I feared you would faint with terror and ruin my employer's plan."

"What have you to report?" Sagobal broke in.

"There is civil war across the Iranistan border," Berytus said, "and the Cimmerian is mixed up in it. That rogue makes himself known wherever he goes. But he and his men had no treasure when they crossed the border, nor had they any when they came back."

"I could have told you all that, my lord," said Osman. "You did not need this foreign brute."

"But I feel much better hearing these things from two sources," said Sagobal.

"Some four or five of the bandits stopped not far from here in a tin-mining village—" Berytus began.

"I know the place," Sagobal interrupted. "Was the Cimmerian with them? Or the wizard?"

"Nay. That was how they were able to escape suspicion, for all were asking about the big Cimmerian and the mage. Then, a few days later, three more crossed the river, right after a fight on the southern side between a party of royal troops and a band of insurgents. The three were mounted on your horses. We tracked them back to the mining town." He jerked a thumb toward Osman. "He was with them, ere they fled again."

"Aye," said Osman. "With Conan gone and the others

drunk, I saw my opportunity to make my escape and report to you, my lord."

"Was the Cimmerian among the three who rode from Iranistan?" Sagobal demanded.

"Aye," Berytus affirmed. "It was he, and the sorcerer, and a woman."

"Woman?" Sagobal said. "We saw a woman when they made their way from the temple, but I had thought her a hostage."

"She is the wizard's daughter, Commander," said Osman.

Sagobal snorted through his predatory, beak-like nose. "This is a strange band to have running loose in my territory!"

"There are only four bandits now, besides Conan," Berytus pointed out. "And the wizard and his daughter. Seven against my band portend favorable odds."

"Conan is more than one man in a fight," Osman pointed out.

"Who cares that there be seven or seven hundred?" said Sagobal. "What matters is the location of the treasure. Osman, can you tell me that?"

"Aye, my lord, I can," the Shangaran said languidly.

Sagobal leaned forward across the table, his fingers laced before him. "Then tell me swiftly, else I will have Berytus begin cropping your fingers until you have yielded all your knowledge to me."

"But of course. It is no great mystery, after all. I am surprised you have not deduced it already."

"Speak!" Sagobal barked.

"The treasure is in the house of the wizard Volvolicus."

Sagobal raised his face and glared at Berytus. "Heard you that, dog? Yet you claimed that it was not there!"

Osman turned and looked up at the Aquilonian who towered above him. "Say you so, Commander? Allow me to guess what happened. This hulking brute and his minions went to the wizard's house and tiptoed daintily to his door. Then they were frightened by the spectres he left behind to scare off fearful, superstitious tribesmen. Did he say to you that he had searched the house?"

"Nay," said Sagobal, "he did not claim even that."

Berytus grasped Osman by the neck and lifted him bodily from his chair as he drew a broad, curved knife from his belt. He laid the razor-edge beneath the Shangaran's nose.

"I can occupy a pleasant hour just whittling a man's nose away," he said, almost crooning. "And a noseless man can make his living as a beggar, claiming he lost the appendage to some loathsome disease. True, it makes life difficult for him if he has been in the habit of seducing women to support himself in comfort."

"Master!" Osman squawked. "Would you let this evil man mistreat your servant thus?"

"Silence, both of you!" Sagobal ordered. "Osman, are you certain of this? Have you seen it with your own eyes?"

Berytus slowly lowered Osman into his chair, and the smaller man massaged his neck, which bore the marks of the Aquilonian's thick fingers.

"Well, Master, I have not actually *seen* it, so to speak, since it went soaring away so majestically from the temple."

"I'd have sheared your head from your bony shoulders had you claimed so," said Berytus. "For I know that none of you have been to the mage's house since you fled Shahpur."

"Peace, Berytus," said Sagobal. "Go on, Osman."

"But I have keen ears, and in the nights I have heard the Cimmerian and the mage plotting. From the first, they planned to send the treasure to the wizard's house, but none of the other bandits were to know this. They believed that the treasure was to go to their hideout in the hills at the edge of the desert, and they stole many camels, taking them to their hideout to await the arrival of the treasure, so that each man could load his share upon one of the beasts and go where he wished.

"But when we got there, the camels were gone! The Cimmerian and the wizard pretended to be surprised, though in truth, Volvolicus had used his magickal arts to guide the villagers to their stolen animals. They assured the men that the treasure had been transported to a nearby cave, and that we would return to fetch it with more beasts after the pursuit had died down."

"And those outlaws believed this?" Berytus said skeptically, "Without being taken to this cave to behold the treasure for themselves?"

"Naturally, there was some murmuring," Osman said. "But the wizard claimed that pursuit was close behind us. We even saw the plume of dust rising above the nearby hills, coming our way. We could even hear the sound of hooves and the clink of arms." Osman shrugged and spread his hands. "Of course, I now realize that it was but another of the wizard's illusions, but at the time, I was convinced. Conan urged upon us that we must flee forthwith into Iranistan, and not return until Torgut Khan was replaced with another viceroy and yourself executed. Then, while the new officers were still learning their territory, we would have opportunity to return and bear away our loot. We were confused and afraid, so we took his words to heart and fled."

"I would not have credited that crude barbarian with such cleverness," Sagobal said.

"He is not as simple as he sometimes seems," said Osman. "He has traveled widely and served in many armies. And he has the wizard to advise him. Doubtless it was Volvolicus who suggested to him that there was no need to split the treasure with his confederates. And I daresay the plot would have worked, except for two factors unknown to them: There was civil war in Iranistan, and you had an agent in their midst. I think I can flatter myself that they never suspected me."

"I think this one lies, Commander," Berytus said, his cold gaze steady upon the Shangaran. "He has the tongue of a serpent. I still do not believe the mage would have fled with them if the treasure were in his own house."

"But the outlaws would have it no other way," Osman protested. "They said that all must stay together until the share-out."

"You said yourself that they would think thus, Berytus," Sagobal pointed out.

"Why then did the Cimmerian and the magician not kill the others?" Berytus asked.

"You will notice that there are far fewer of the bandits now than when they rode into Shahpur," Osman observed. "Their numbers were halved in the fighting here in the city, then halved again in the fighting and fleeing since. They will have no trouble taking care of the rest. Probably the mage intends to do away with Conan, unless his daughter fancies the barbarian too warmly."

"Then we must strike at the wizard's house," Sagobal said.

"I do not like this, Commander," Berytus protested.

Sagobal regarded him contemptuously. "Are you just a hunter, then? Have you no stomach for a fight?"

"I do not fear the Cimmerian or his friends," said the Aquilonian. "I would welcome a tussle with them. But the wizard is powerful, that I saw for myself. His wards are no mere illusions, whatever this wretched parasite claims."

"Perhaps there is a way out of this quandary," Osman put in smoothly.

"If so, I fain would hear it," Sagobal said, "even from a source so polluted."

"To combat magick," Osman pointed out, "the best weapon is greater magick, is that not so?"

"Aye, it is," the commander answered. "But this Volvolicus is the only wizard of any power to be found in this district. I have none to call upon."

"Not so, Master," said Osman.

"What do you mean?"

"You must go and solicit the aid of the priests of Ahriman, in the new temple."

Sagobal stared at him as if he suspected the man's sanity. "What? Those wretched mountebanks of an unclean god? Away with you! In the first place, they were helpless to prevent the violation of their crypt. In the second, upon the day of the raid, I hewed down one of them, the purple-faced priest called Nikas."

"And yet I heard Volvolicus tell his daughter that he had a great dread of these priests. When he was in the crypt, working his spell to raise the treasure deposited therein, he understood that these are not the mere parasitic priests of a filthy deity, but sorcerers of great might. They will be furious over the profanation of their temple, burning for revenge. They might well lend a sympathetic ear to your request for aid. In their lust to destroy Volvolicus, they just may be willing to overlook your understandable fit of temper."

"I do not like this, Chief," said Berytus. "Do not listen to him."

Sagobal jabbed an accusing finger at the Aquilonian. "Be still. You do not stand high in my favor just now. You have done little more thus far than keep track of the movements of these wretched outlaws, while Osman has infiltrated their ranks. If he is right, you were wholly mistaken in dismissing the wizard's house as the most likely hiding place of the treasure."

"I still hold that I am right, and even if these priests give you aid, it would put you in their debt, and I've no doubt but that they have unpleasant means of extracting recompense."

"Allow me to worry about that," Sagobal said. He rose and began to belt on his weapons. "Come, both of you. We shall make a call upon the Temple of Ahriman."

Osman smiling, Berytus grumbling, the three left the chambers of the commander and walked through the nighted streets of Shahpur to the great temple. As they crossed the square, flooded with the light of the moon that seemed to be impaled upon the spire of an ancient tower, they were watched by evaluating eyes.

Atop the steps, they found the iron grate lowered. Berytus hammered upon it with the spiked knuckles of his half-gauntlet. The metal rang hollowly, the clashing notes reverberating through the cavernous, unnaturally red interior.

Minutes later, a tall, skeletal figure appeared on the other side.

"What would you have?" asked the priest named Shosq, the red light flowing repellently over the mottled skin of his face.

"I wish to speak with Tragthan," Sagobal said. "Let us in!"

"You are bold to come here so," said the priest. "Yet I will allow you entrance." He neither spoke nor moved, but the portcullis began to creak upward until it was high enough for the three to pass beneath. They stepped through and it began to lower once more.

"Follow me," said Shosq. They passed the beautiful, tortured caryatids, which Osman examined appreciatively. In the back, near the ghastly altar, two more figures stood.

A shudder went through Sagobal when he realized that one of the priests was Nikas. "You!" he said involuntarily. "I had thought you dead!"

The priest's cold, reptilian eyes regarded him unblinking. "You thought that your puny sword could slay a priest of Ahriman?" His laugh had nothing human about it. Through the open mouth they could just see a tongue that seemed to have more than a single tip and glistened blackly in the horrid light.

"What would you have?" Tragthan demanded.

"Your aid, priest," Sagobal answered.

"After what you did to this temple and to us, you would come begging our help?"

"I do not come begging, priest," Sagobal spat, angered but still shaken at the sight of Nikas whole again. "I come to offer you a chance to revenge yourselves upon the wizard who profaned your crypt."

"Speak on," said Tragthan.

"In an oasis not far from here, the sorcerer Volvolicus has his house. It is there that he has stored the treasure stolen from your crypt."

"Then why do you not hie yourself thither and fetch it?"

Shosq demanded. "Why do you come to us, whom you have most grievously wronged?"

"The wizard has guardian-spells of power. Additionally, he may well be back in residence, and the remains of the scummy robber-band with him. I want counterspells to neutralize the mage, so that I may enter that house and reclaim the treasure for my king."

They stared at him for long minutes. "Why do you think priests of a great god want something so petty as revenge?"

At this, Berytus laughed. "What man of spirit does not crave revenge? Granted, you are not precisely men, but you have all the markings of great pride. The bandits and their wizard insulted you, and they likewise insulted your god! You must burn for vengeance, for all your pose of superiority. Your god will not thank you for letting such a deed go unpunished."

"What say you to that?" Sagobal demanded.

Once again, minutes passed while the priests were silent, seeming to communicate on a level impenetrable to ordinary humans. Finally, Tragthan spoke.

"Very well, we will help you. One of us will accompany you to this wizard's house and will combat his spells while your men invade."

"One?" Sagobal said indignantly. "Why not all three?"

"Certain matters detain us here in Shahpur. Our dread lord was most unsettled by the sacrilege committed within the sacred precincts of his temple. He must be propitiated."

"Does he require sacrifice?" Sagobal asked. "If so, we have apprehended most of the felons who escaped in the chaos on the day of the festival. You may have them."

"That is not the sort of propitiation our lord requires," Tragthan said. "But it will take great effort to settle the unrest on the supernatural plane. One of us accompanying you shall suffice for your purposes."

"Excellent. We ride at first light. Have your representative ready for the journey." Seeing no need for further pleasantries, the commander whirled and stalked away, closely followed by Osman and Berytus. At their approach, the gate raised like an opening mouth, and it lowered behind them, seemingly without any human effort.

As they strode across the square, the eyes still watched them, but they were not followed, for it was the temple that occupied their observers' attention. As the three men left the square, a short, round figure swathed in robes approached a taller, more austere man whose face was covered with a veil.

"What think you this portends, venerable one?" asked the Vendhyan, his turban glowing subtly in the flower-scented night.

"More evil afoot, I've no doubt," said the Khitain master. "Those three had nothing of the magickal about them, but if they had business with those within, it probably portends another stage in their efforts to bring Ahriman back into this world. We must watch them and stay alert."

"Aye, Master," said the Vendhyan, who was himself a sorcerer of the First Rank.

As dawn light stained the horizon, a line of horsemen rode to the gate of the city. At their head was Sagobal, and behind him rode Berytus and the manhunters. Last of all was the priest Shosq, awkward in his unaccustomed saddle.

An hour after their passing, a tall man swathed in desert robes strode from the caravan campground nearest the gate. He was veiled to the eyes, which were unusually blue for a desert tribesman. At the gate, he paused beside a guard.

"I have dispatches for Sagobal, commander of the guard," announced the desert dweller. "Do you know if he is in the city?"

"You just missed him," said the guard. "He rode out but an hour ago, with that pack of foreign scavengers and some others."

"Scavengers? Mean you the Aquilonian of whom I have heard? The manhunter?"

"Aye. They have been combing the territory since the festival, seeking the bandits. I suppose it was a good thing they were on hand when the trouble happened, for our own men have done little good."

"You mean they were in the city *before* the great festival?"

"Aye," said the guard. "And that was passing strange." The man was clearly bored with his duty and wished to talk. "For some days before the festival, those hard-looking men rode into town through this gate. That same day, they rode out again. But rumor has it that late that same night, an officer came and took charge of the gate for an hour, and someone claims to have seen those same men ride back in. After that, there was no sign of them in the city until the robbers came to steal the king's revenues, when those same men were upon the roofs, lying in ambush along with the viceroy's guards."

"That is indeed passing strange. Have you any word of whither they rode?"

"Nay, but wherever it was, Sagobal does not trust his own men to go there, for there was not a man of the viceroy's guard in his company, just the foreigners. And, although I can hardly credit this, I could swear that I saw one of the priests of the accursed temple riding with them, attempting to conceal himself in a swathing desert robe like your own. But it was no desert man, for he rode wretchedly, and those unholy priests do not move like natural men. The city would be well rid of them, aye, and their disgusting temple as well."

Conan bade the talkative guard farewell and walked back toward the oasis. He had known that his desert garb would probably keep him safe from detection, but he had not dared to ride one of Sagobal's stolen horses into the city. He had thought to carry out a discreet assassination, perhaps to catch Berytus and his employer together and eliminate them both at once. Such, it seemed, was not to be. Now his mind spun with the implications of what he had just heard.

The manhunters had been in the town for days prior to the assault upon the temple! That had to mean that Sagobal had planned the operation far in advance. It strained credulity that the foreign band should just happen to be in the city exactly when they were needed. So Sagobal had used him to bring all the bandits into the city!

By the pool of the oasis, he sat to think, unmindful of the shouting caravaneers and their complaining, foul-smelling camels. Since the frenzied action of the raid, he had been continuously fighting or fleeing and he had not paused to think things through. All this just to bag the bandits? It could not be. Sagobal and Berytus between them, with so much preparation, should have been able to catch them all, not just half, permitting the others to flee.

"Crom curse me for a fool!" he said aloud, startling a desert boy who held the reins of a drinking horse. The Cimmerian leapt to his feet. Sagobal had no intention of bringing that treasure back to Torgut Khan and the king. He was out to take it for himself! Now many small events of the past days began to fall into place, making sense where there had been none before.

Those guards who had stood outside the window of his cell, so conveniently discussing the upcoming festival and the depositing there of the district's royal revenues—that conversation had been part of Sagobal's plan, the men probably hired actors.

Then the greatest piece of the puzzle fell into place. "Osman!" he shouted, further alarming the boy who was watering the horse. Of course! That sneaking little thief had just happened to have the cell next to his own, whence he could speak to the Cimmerian through the hole in the wall. He had been certain that he could lift the heavy anvil. And the anvil, with its hammer and chisel, had been left at the top of the stair instead of in the guardroom, where such things were usually kept.

The guard commander had gone to such lengths to arrest and secure Conan, the one felon he knew could fight his way out of the dungeon to go back to the outlaw band and plan the temple crypt robbery. But how had he been so certain that the Cimmerian would find a way to get the treasure safely away?

He remembered the evening at the hideout, when they had discussed the plan. The problem of moving the great weight had come up and then . . . Osman again! It had been he who had suggested Volvolicus as a solution to their quandary. Not only had Sagobal had an agent in Conan's own camp, the guard commander had masterminded the whole plan! Almost in spite of himself, Conan found himself admiring the man's brazen cunning. He must have spent years plotting this, planning to make himself fabulously wealthy at Torgut Khan's expense. The new temple with its crypt and the presence of the formidable Cimmerian bandit in the district had provided the perfect foils.

The one thing Sagobal could not control was the exact route the treasure would take. For that, he needed Osman to tell him. But the bandits had been watching each other like hawks since the theft and Osman had had little opportunity to escape. He was trusted even less than the others, because he had not been a part of the band prior to the raid on the temple.

Even as these thoughts passed through his mind, the Cimmerian was in the saddle and riding. No wonder Osman had worn that conspicuous golden turban! He had been worried that he might be killed by mistake in the confusion, so he had made himself unmistakable. Conan remembered the arrow that had passed so close by the turban. That must have been to make it look realistic. He remembered the one that had thunked into his own saddle. Had that been a ruse as well? Had Sagobal wanted him to get away alive, so that he could get the rest of the band, including Osman, to the place where the treasure was hidden?

That was the past. For now, there was an even more pressing question: Where had Sagobal gone? Was Osman with him? If so, was the little thief even now leading him to the cave where the gold was concealed? It was all too likely, for the guard commander was riding without any of his guard, only his hirelings. Naturally, he would not risk any man loyal to Torgut Khan learning of the treasure's whereabouts.

But why the priest from the new temple? Conan could make nothing of that. Perhaps the gate guard had been mistaken. He knew one thing clearly: He had to get to the wizard's house and find his surviving men, as well as the wizard, and ride with them to the hideout. There was a chance they would catch Sagobal and his men as they were removing the treasure.

He was certain it would be a desperate fight, for his band was greatly outnumbered and the men of Berytus were undoubtedly better fighters than his own men. On the other hand, he knew without undue modesty that he himself could make up for a sizable part of the enemy's numerical advantage. If the wizard could assist them with his deadly spells, it would tip the balance. Using sorcery to win was a repellent maneuver to the Cimmerian, but matters had grown too serious to allow his personal scruples to weaken their position in any way.

He rode on long into the evening; near the site of the house of Volvolicus, he beheld an uncanny spectacle.

Twelve

"Stop here," Berytus said. They were in a draw below a high, rocky ridge of ground. Just beyond the ridge lay the house of Volvolicus.

"Why so far away?" Osman demanded. "We can ride much closer yet than this."

"We must leave the horses here," said Berytus. "The wizard's wards are terrifying enough to men. For horses, they are even worse. When we made our retreat from this place some days ago, many of us were nigh unable to mount, so panicked were the beasts."

"He exaggerates," Osman said.

"Nonetheless," said Sagobal, "his advice is sound. I have lost too many of my own horses of late, and would as lief lose no more. If we should be left without horses in this place, it would mean a long, long walk back to Shahpur."

The men dismounted and Berytus detailed a lean, predatory-looking Poitainian to stay with the beasts. They continued on foot. With Berytus in the lead, they climbed the ridge, all of them moving swiftly and silently, even the reptilian priest, who was far more agile on his own feet than on horseback. At the crest, they lay against the slope and peered over the ridge.

Below them lay the tree-fringed pool of water, shimmering in the light of the rising moon. From the small windows of the house shone lights of shifting color. There were horses tethered near the water, and from the roof of the house drifted a plume of white smoke.

"It seems they are back," said Sagobal, satisfaction oozing from his words.

"Aye," said Berytus. "Before, we contended only with wards the mage left behind to guard the place in his absence. Now he is in residence, and who knows what sort of demons he can call up."

"We accomplish nothing here," Sagobal said. "Aquilonian, you know how best to employ your men. Make us a way into that house."

"Aye, I know how to use them, and your other dogs as well." He turned to Shosq. "Priest, can you tell whether the wizard has detected us, or has spells ready to receive us?"

"Think you that these things shine through the air, to be descried like signal fires burning upon hilltops?"

"I care not, but you are supposed to be with us for some reason. Thus far all you have done is slow our progress with your wretched horsemanship. We should have been here an hour ago."

"When Volvolicus seeks to use his spells, fool, then you shall be joyful that I am with you."

"See that you are of service then, priest," Berytus warned.

"It appears that you must lead this assault," Osman said to the Aquilonian. "For such a swordsman as you, it should prove no great task."

"No, that I shall not. You shall go in first, Shangaran."

"I?" Osman said, alarmed. "I make no claim to be a great fighter or a hero!"

"And well should you not. No, you shall approach the door openly, calling out the names of your companions, for you have been lost in the wilderness. One as treacherous as you should have no difficulty with betraying the same companions twice."

"But they will kill me!" Osman protested.

"Then it will be a test of your smooth, lying tongue. In years to come, you will preen yourself upon such a performance."

Osman turned to Sagobal. "Master, I accepted your service in the capacity of spy and secret agent. It is this foreign thug who undertook to serve you as swordsman and hired bravo! Tell him to cease his cowardly prating and get on with the attack."

"It will do no harm if we can persuade them to lower their guard. Go in, Osman. We shall be close behind you, keeping out of sight just within the trees."

"But—"

"Go!" Sagobal growled.

Fearfully, the small man rose and went over the crest of the hill. The others did likewise, following a few steps behind him. They descended the slope on the oasis side, the scree loose beneath their feet. Berytus and his men walked over this unstable footing in perfect silence, with the skill of hunters. The priest Shosq was likewise silent, not with the appearance of great skill but as if from his own nature, for he seemed more serpent than man. Osman's progress was a loud shuffle by comparison. Last came Sagobal, his keen eyes keeping them all under observation, his ears picking up every faintest sound. As near as he could tell, they had achieved complete surprise.

"Conan!" Osman called out as he neared the house. "Ubo! Auda! Are you in there, my friends?" A few paces from the door, he halted. "Revered Volvolicus! Beauteous Layla! Are you in your home?"

The portal opened and a bulky form appeared in the door, naked steel in hand. It was Chamik, his great belly bulging over his scarlet sash, his eyes squinting into the darkness. "What man is that? Osman, is it you?"

"Chamik, my friend! I have been wandering for days in the desert, suffering as one damned. Is our chief here?" He took a few tentative steps toward the house.

"Not so fast," the bandit cautioned. "Why did you disappear from the village while we were carousing?" Ubo appeared behind Chamik and peered over his shoulder with a single, suspicious eye.

"Ah, my friends, you know my habit of getting into trouble over women. The wife of the overseer of the mine was comely and found me likewise attractive. Her husband spent his days at the mine, leaving us free for dalliance. But he came home untimely, and I was forced to flee through a back window. He chased me for many miles through the wilderness. When finally I lost him, I found that I had lost myself as well. By the time I had found a nomad camp and stolen a horse and regained my bearings, I dared not return to the village, so I made my way hither, knowing that you would rendezvous at the wizard's house."

"Here?" said Ubo. "We deemed it more likely a sneaking jackal like you would go to—"

Osman's hand had been inching toward the breast of his tunic. Now it darted inside and emerged as swiftly, coming up over his shoulder, snapping forward and down. Even as something spun glittering through the air, Chamik, swift as a cat for all his bulk, bounded back and swung the door shut. Osman's dagger struck the door and hung there quivering for a moment, then glowed red. It brightened from sullen crimson to searing orange, then erupted in a shower of white sparks.

In the trees, someone screamed. Sagobal jerked around to see one of the manhunters enveloped by a huge serpent, thick as a man's thigh. Something manlike and hairy dropped from a palm onto another man, tearing with teeth and claws.

"They are in the trees!" Berytus shouted. "Get out from under them!"

"Do something, priest!" Sagobal commanded. But Shosq was already chanting, his voice pitched so low that the men in the suddenly chaotic oasis could barely hear it, yet it caused the very stones and trees to vibrate. The designs on the door began to glow and shimmer, and the edges of it began to smoke.

The shutters of the windows opened violently, slamming back against the walls, causing chips of mud plaster to fly. Brilliant beams of light shot forth from the apertures, luridly colored in hues that shifted rapidly, even as the beams darted from place to place with a speed that had nothing in it of human operation. Blue light changed to yellow with no gradations of shading, while green transformed to scarlet and then to violet, rapidly yet subtly. Some took on hues that were not natural, colors that confused the eye and made the scene even more surreal than it already was.

Sagobal saw a man caught in a beam of pure white light. Thus imprisoned, he froze in place, screaming. Then the flesh flew from his bones in bloody, smoking clots. Within three heartbeats, only his blackening skeleton stood there; then it collapsed into a steaming black heap.

"Arrows into the windows!" Berytus shouted. Immediately, his archers plied their weapons, and the beams seemed not to affect the flight of the shafts, for they sped through the openings undeflected and unharmed. From within came a scream.

"At least someone is doing us some good," Sagobal said. A glowing, unstable shape arose from the ground at his feet, its arms outspread. Quick as a thought, his sword flicked through it. He felt the slightest of resistance, then the thing dispersed in fading dots of dim light. "Some of the wizard's defenses are naught but illusion," he said.

"Where is Osman?" Berytus asked, enraged. "He acted too quickly and gave us away! I will slit his gullet!" Just then one of the ape-monsters attacked the Aquilonian, and Sagobal saw the quickness, coolness and skill that had kept the manhunter alive in the fighting-pits. Berytus did not waste a motion, nor did he allow fear to affect him in the slightest.

His left hand shot out and he buried his fingers in the thing's throat, holding it stiff-armed, ignoring its snapping jaws and clawing hands as he plied the short, heavy blade of his curved sword. He jammed the blade into its belly and twisted it about, eviscerating the animal in seconds. Then he withdrew the reeking steel and brought it down on the sloping skull, splitting bone and scattering teeth. The beast thrashed with unnatural life for a few seconds, then was still. Berytus dropped the carcass and looked about for his next foe. Sagobal knew that an ordinary swordsman would have lopped off his own hand with that last blow.

Shosq took something that looked like a ball of herbs from a pouch at his waist and cast it at the house, where it expanded, fastened and threw out tendrils that spread to envelop all the walls, red sparks crawling along the network of lines until the whole structure was covered with moving, blinking points of red. The beams of light from the windows faltered and faded.

"This is too much," Berytus announced calmly as he watched three of his men struggling with something that looked like a crab the size of a bull. With a huge pincer, it snipped an arm from one of them even as the other two sent their axes crashing through its brittle shell, hewing away legs and spilling its entrails. "We must go back to the horses!"

"I shall have all his defenses neutralized within minutes!" hissed the priest.

"Many of us can die within minutes," Berytus countered.

Sagobal was shaken by the supernatural apparitions, but he lusted for the treasure. In any case, it was not his men who were being slaughtered. Even as the thought struck him, a manhunter trod upon something unseen and was enveloped in green flames that licked over his body. He screamed and fell to the ground and thrashed even as the green fire faded away to nothing. The burned man continued to howl until a comrade put him from his pain by drawing a dagger swiftly across his throat. The blood fountained for a moment before subsiding.

"We stay," Sagobal said grimly. Then he looked around. "Osman!" he shouted. "Where are you, jackal?"

* * *

Above the ridge, flashes lit the sky like distant lightning, but in colors no natural lightning ever boasted. Conan heard thunderous noises, and faint screams. Something bat-winged arose with a struggling human form clamped in toothy jaws and flapped away to the north. Just ahead of him, the Cimmerian heard the pounding of hooves, then a score or so of horses came pounding down the draw. He reined aside and as they passed, he saw that a single human figure rode among the saddled but riderless mounts, hunched over and flogging his horse's rump as if he could never run fast enough. Then they were past and Conan rode on.

Lying on the ground surrounded by hoofprints lay a human body. Conan halted by it and dismounted. He squatted and examined the corpse. He did not know the man, but his belt and dagger were Poitainian, as was the way his hair was dressed, although he wore the voluminous desert robe common to the district. He had been stabbed from behind, the thrust passing neatly between the ribs, piercing the heart. If this was one of the manhunters, Conan mused, then he had been slain by someone he knew, for such a one would not be ambushed in this spot.

He rode to the top of the ridge and gazed down upon the spectacle below. The lights from the house were fading and the structure seemed to be wrapped in glowing embers. A few of the men still surrounding it were struggling with uncanny creatures, but these brutal fights were soon ended and there was near silence. He saw a small group of men standing before the door. One was Sagobal. Another looked like one of the temple priests. The third was a hulking, dangerous-looking man. The way he moved told the Cimmerian that this was a formidable swordsman. The attackers seemed to have gained the upper hand.

A faint nickering sound drew his attention. A number of horses were picketed at the end of the pool farthest from the house. The vicious fighting, with its unaccustomed sights, sounds and smells, had upset them, but they were securely tethered and they were now calming. He began to make his way toward them.

"Can you make that door safe for us to assault?" Sagobal asked the priest.

"The web of Ahriman sucks the power from it even now," replied the priest. "When the last of the red fires extinguishes, all magickal power will have been drawn from the house and you may go in."

"What sort of traps might he have waiting for us inside?" Berytus demanded.

"All magickal power is drained from the place," said Shosq. "If you cannot deal with the men inside, that is your problem and one with which I decline to aid you. The wizard's power is exhausted."

"Men I can deal with," Berytus said.

"Then do so," Sagobal commanded.

Berytus began to station his men, with the bulk of them before the door. Others took up station near the windows with arrows nocked to their bowstrings. Two of them hewed down a palm tree and began fashioning it into a crude battering ram.

"We are ready," Berytus announced.

"Wait," Sagobal commanded as a few sparks of red crawled listlessly over the fragile-looking web, like dying fireflies. Then the last of them winked out and the web fell to pieces, as if it were made of ashes.

"Now!" Sagobal commanded. Berytus waved his arm and the men with the ram rushed forward. The soft, pulpy wood of the palm trunk was not as effective as that of a hardwood tree, but gradually the stout door began to bend inward, straining against its hinges and locking-bar. The men stood nervously, fingering their weapons. The archers sent an occasional shaft inside, but were reluctant to waste too many arrows when they could not see their targets.

"It will break in soon," Sagobal said, gloating. "Then the treasure is mine."

* * *

Conan led the horses around to the back of the house. He moved carefully, but the men surrounding the place were so preoccupied that none even glanced in his direction. Picketing the beasts at a safe distance, he made his stealthy way on foot to the rear. This wall had but a single window, and a few paces from it stood a pair of archers, poised to shoot.

They never heard the Cimmerian come up behind them. His dagger was in the throat of one before the other could even turn his head. Conan jerked his knife from the first man's neck and slashed it viciously across the larynx of the other, severing flesh and cartilage all the way down to the spinal cord. The two men dropped almost as one, their blood spraying onto the sandy ground. He wiped his blade on the tunic of one and stepped silently to the window.

"Ubo! Chamik! Volvolicus! Are you alive?" His voice was a loud whisper. He jerked aside as a long, curved sword thrust out on the end of a silver-braceleted arm. With a blow of his fist, he knocked the weapon to the ground.

"It's me, fool! Conan!"

"How did you get here?" Ubo asked, rubbing his stinging wrist.

"Never mind that. The rear is unguarded and I have horses nearby." The sound of loud thumping came from the front of the house. "How many of you are alive?"

"Auda took an arrow in his leg, but we can all ride."

"Then come with me quickly. They will be through the front door soon."

The four bandits piled out the window without delay and made their way toward the horses, guided by Conan's pointing finger. Auda limped heavily, but he was no slower than the rest. Layla pushed her father through the aperture, burdened as he was by a sack of books and instruments.

"Leave those," said Conan in an urgent whisper.

"I cannot," the mage declared. "They are my whole life."

"They are apt to prove your whole death," Conan said. "Woman, hurry up!"

"I have something to leave for them," she said. "It will be but a moment."

The Cimmerian fumed while he waited; then she all but dove through the window and he caught her. She kissed him soundly, squirmed from his arms and began to run. He was close behind her.

"What did you leave them?" he asked.

"Just some things we no longer needed . . . some tow, old oil, and a bit of fire."

They ran on into the night to where the others, already mounted, awaited them.

Berytus called a halt. "It will go down within the next three or four blows. Be ready." The men were already alert and tense.

"What is that smell?" Sagobal asked, sniffing. There was a tinge of smoke upon the night air.

"Probably one of my men burning," Berytus said.

"Light from inside!" cried an archer stationed at one of the windows. "A flame!"

"They've fired the place," Berytus muttered. "Resume!"

Three times more the improvised ram struck the door as smoke began to pour from the windows. With the fourth, the thick portal smashed inward. At the inrush of air, flames leapt high and the foremost ram-handler jumped back, beating at the flaming cuff of his sleeve.

"Bring water!" Sagobal shouted. "Use whatever you have! Helmets, purses, anything that will hold water! Someone search for buckets or jars!"

From their proposed man-slaying, the hunters turned to fire-fighting. Their attempts to quench the blaze were futile, for the little water they could dash upon the burning material did naught more than spread the burning oil. The flames reached the dry wood and palm thatch of the roof and roared fifty feet into the air.

"Get back," Berytus ordered. "This is futile!" The men

pulled back and sat on the ground, some of them bandaging their wounds. The heat from the house grew intense.

"Why did they do this?" Sagobal wondered, tugging at his mustache.

"Perhaps they did not wish to face your dungeon and instruments of torture," said Berytus.

"Rogues and bandits? I never yet saw one take his own life. Always, they try to preserve their wretched existence one more day, one more hour."

"It might have been the wizard, or the woman," the Aquilonian pointed out. "The bandits may all have been killed by the arrows we shot in. Whatever the case, you have little to worry about. If the treasure is in there, such a fire as this will not damage it much."

"Aye," said Sagobal with some satisfaction.

"I must see to my men." Berytus went off to count his dead and evaluate his wounded.

"Well, priest," said Sagobal. "Are you content with your night's work?"

"That I shall tell you when I have been within the house and have seen what lies therein. If the wizard be dead, and if I see no sign that he has wrought us greater hurt, then perhaps I shall be satisfied."

"These are strange words," Sagobal said. "His house is destroyed and the wizard himself almost certainly dead. What more can you wish? And what do you mean by 'greater hurt'?"

"That is a matter that concerns only myself and my brethren," the priest answered. Then the mottled face resumed its expressionless contemplation of the burning house.

Berytus returned to them as the flames were dying down. "I have had six killed and four so wounded as to be useless for months to come! I am down to seven men, counting myself!"

"What is that to me?" Sagobal said coldly. "Men are cheap. Come, let us see what is in there."

"Two of my men are out back with their throats slit,"

Berytus told him. "They were watching the single window in the rear wall. Somebody must have come upon them from behind. That means that side of the house was unattended, probably from before the time we noticed the fire." He watched rage fill Sagobal's face. "*Now* let us go see what is in there."

The rising sun of morning revealed the devastation in the little oasis. Dead men and the carcasses of uncanny creatures lay everywhere. The palms had been ravaged and the house was a gutted hulk. Only the pool was untouched, its waters shimmering placidly.

Berytus in the lead, they walked into the now roofless house, the hard, hot cinders crunching beneath their boots and sandals.

"Ambula," Berytus said, "this is no place for a barefoot man. Go over the ridge. You and the Poitainian fetch our horses back." The dark man saluted with his spear and trotted off to do his commander's bidding.

They searched the main room, then the small rooms opening off it. They found nothing save ashes. There were no human remains.

"Where are they?" Sagobal asked.

"Stairway here," said Barca the Shemite, tugging up a charred trapdoor. "A cellar lies below."

"If any took refuge down there, they must be suffocated," Berytus said. "But be cautious anyway. Urdos, go you first."

The huge Kothian drew his short-handled ax and descended the stair, his steps light for one of his bulk. A minute later he called up through the trap. "No one down here, but it is a strange place."

"They got away!" Sagobal raged. "Those fools of yours in the back allowed themselves to be killed and let them escape!"

"Calm yourself, Turanian," Berytus said contemptuously. "They cannot have carried much with them."

Reminded of his true reason for being in this place, Sagobal rushed down the stair and stood within the wizard's chamber. It seemed empty except for the strange table of stone, but the light flooding down from the open roof above revealed that walls and ceiling were covered with close-set carvings of exotic and wondrous design. Otherwise, it was even emptier than the rooms above.

"Where is my treasure?" Sagobal shouted at the top of his lungs. "I want you men to tear this place apart until you find it!"

"It is not here," Berytus said, coming down the steps. "And it has never been here, just as I told you. All this was for nothing, because you chose to listen to that lying, sneaking villain, Osman. Who, by the way, is nowhere to be found. It is too much to hope that one of those monsters carried him off."

"Go after them!"

"I intend to," Berytus said, "for once I have undertaken to hunt a man down, I always catch him. But that is the only reason, for this commission has already cost me more than your pay will recompense."

"I care not for your problems, manhunter," said the guard commander. "Just carry out your orders."

The Aquilonian went up the stair and the priest came down. Shosq ignored the fuming Turanian soldier and went to the table, running his repellently long, flexible fingers over its intricately marked surface. It seemed to Sagobal that the fingers of those hands had far more joints than was natural for human hands to possess.

The priest left the table and examined the walls and ceiling, emitting a low, whistling sound as he walked along the lines of carving. Disgusted by Shosq and by the night's fiasco, Sagobal went back up the steps. He found Berytus just as Ambula returned.

"Where are the horses?" the Aquilonian asked.

"They are gone," said the man of Punt. "And the Poitainian is dead, stabbed through the back."

"Now there are six of us," Berytus said. "Six of us, and we are afoot."

"More of your bungling," Sagobal said. "There are some

horses at the other end of the pool. Fetch them and we may ride to Shahpur. More can be sent back for the others."

"Those horses are gone," said Berytus, his conversational tone masking his deadly anger. "What do you think the bandits and the wizard escaped on? Bahdur found the place where they mounted and rode away. One man rode in and took those horses, led them around behind the house, and killed my men. Perhaps he killed the Poitainian and ran off our horses, perhaps it was Osman. But it must have been the Cimmerian. Among them, only he has the skill to accomplish such a thing undetected."

"Conan!" Sagobal bit out, beside himself with rage. "Will that barbarian plague me to the end of my days?"

"I should add that he was riding one of your horses. Some of those tied down at the other end of the pool were yours as well. We could tell by the way they were shod."

Sagobal saw red and almost began to draw his sword. The Aquilonian's fearless gaze and steady voice made him pause.

"Do not mistake me for an unarmed priest, Sagobal," he warned. "You are a dead man if you draw your steel on me. We must be away while the day is still cool. Pull yourself together and let us go. If we retrace our steps, perhaps we will come across some of our runaway horses."

Sagobal whirled and stalked off toward the ruined house. He needed to calm himself, knowing that he needed this man if he was ever to see the treasure and kill the Cimmerian. He went down the stairs and found the priest still examining the wizard's inner sanctum.

"We must go," said Sagobal.

"Go, then," said Shosq, not looking at him.

"The horses are gone. We have to walk. We must leave now."

This time the priest turned and regarded him with snakelike eyes. "Take whatever way you can to get back to your city, Turanian. I shall remain here. There is work for me to accomplish. I will make my own way back. Have no concern on my account."

"Be assured I shall not," said Sagobal. He went back up the stairs and out of the ruins. His thoughts were black.

Ubo, Chamik and Mamos laughed for a long time, joyous with their escape when all had seemed lost. Auda was happy, but in too much pain to laugh about it. The wizard was grim, and Conan was silent. Layla seemed content to be riding through the night, apparently undisturbed by the destruction of her home.

"What happened back there?" Conan asked when he was satisfied that they were safe. He called for a slackening of pace and they trotted along beneath the desert stars.

"The mage told us they were near almost an hour before Osman called to us from without . . ."

"Osman?" Conan said. "He came there?"

"Aye, and he led them!" Ubo said. "He called from outside the door and we would have killed him then, but the wizard needed more time to complete his spells, so we spoke with him a while. Then he cast a dagger at Chamik and the fun began!"

"I wish we could have seen more of what happened outside," Mamos said, "but arrows came in through the windows and it was unsafe to look out. It sounded as if they were being fed into a grinding mill!" At this, the others burst into renewed laughter. Even Auda managed a weak chuckle.

"We will have to stop soon to see to Auda's leg," Layla said.

"A man of my tribe can ride day and night hurt worse than this," the desert man protested.

"As soon as it is light enough, we will pause," Conan told them. "Their horses were driven off, so it will be a long time before they can mount a serious pursuit. By that time, we shall be past their finding."

"Where to now, Chief?" Ubo asked.

"Into the trackless waste," Conan said. "We will keep to the stony places so as to leave little trace behind us. We will camp at the smallest water holes and avoid inhabited places. This way, we will make our way back to our old hideout."

"Is it time now to divide the loot, Chief?" asked Mamos, his evil face lighting up like a happy child's.

"Aye. And we must protect it as well, for the secret of its location is no longer safe. Osman has turned traitor and who knows what the rogue may be up to?" They rode on into the night.

Thirteen

Just before midday, Conan called a halt. They were far into the trackless country and had seen no sign of the passage of men for many hours. They dismounted and stretched the soreness from their muscles. Layla examined the bandage she had placed on Auda's leg that morning. The country was brushy semi-desert. They saw no sheep or other domestic animals, only the occasional desert gazelle, or the stately oryx—wary beasts who studied these strange, intruding creatures alertly, ready to spring away at first sign of danger.

"The wound could be worse," Layla said, "but it will not heal well while he has to ride. There are some herbs I know of that will help, if they grow around here. Have I time to go look for them?"

"Aye," said Conan. "We can wait out the heat of the day here and press on this evening. Just now, we are short of rations. If I had a bow, I would go out and bring us back a gazelle."

"That sounds a good idea," said Ubo, rubbing his sore

backside. "All this fighting and fleeing gives a man an appetite. I don't suppose the wizard could magick you up a bow and some arrows?"

Volvolicus sighed. "No, but now that we are still for a few hours, I will study my books. When we go on, I think I can produce a few small whirlwinds to erase any signs of our passage."

"That will be time well spent," Conan approved. He bent and picked up a few fist-sized stones, placing them in the pouch at his belt. "I will go with Layla as she hunts herbs. Perhaps I can knock over a few hares with stones. In Cimmeria, a ten-year-old boy is accounted a poor prospect if he cannot fetch his own dinner with a rock or two."

"That is better than nothing, I suppose," Chamik said as he spread his blanket and took his ease upon the ground. "Woman, while you look for healing herbs, see if you can find some savory ones to season our dinner with."

"It is well that you are so good at stealing," Layla observed, "for the lot of you are too lazy to live otherwise. I should not be surprised upon our return to find you all dead, having forgotten to breathe."

"A sharp-tongued woman is an abomination before the gods," said Mamos as he rigged a cloth shelter to shade his head. "But I will forgive you this time."

"Auda," said Conan, "lend me your lance. If I come upon a larger beast unawares, I'll hazard a cast."

"Take it," said the desert man. "I'll not be using it for a while."

Conan and Layla left the camp. They walked for half a mile, the woman stopping from time to time to examine some plant. Each time she rejected it as the wrong variety or else at the wrong stage of its growth. Conan hurled a rock at a hare, but he missed by inches and struck a larger stone. With a loud crack, rock chips went humming through the air and the swift animal sped away unharmed.

"There must be some hungry boys in Cimmeria," Layla

observed, "if you are any example. You have alerted that hare's relatives for miles around."

"I am out of practice," Conan said, nettled. "I . . . Crom! What is that?" He pointed toward the northwest. From that direction, a lone, tiny figure was striding straight toward them.

"At a guess," Layla said, "I would say it is a man."

"Aye, but . . . but what is a lone man doing out here? He is walking straight toward us, as if he knew we were here."

"Why not? We know *he* is here. It may be a hermit, or a wandering holy man. Such are not uncommon in the wastelands. They seek the vast solitudes in order to meditate far from the distractions of their fellow men."

"I do not know," Conan said, scratching at his bristly chin. "There is something about him that I find disturbing."

"We shall know soon enough," she said. "He will be here in a short while."

They watched as the man drew closer. Something about the way he moved seemed wrong to the Cimmerian. He walked exactly as if there were perfectly level pavement beneath his feet, making no allowance for the unevenness of the ground, with its dips, mounds and shifting rocks. He wore robes Conan recognized as Khitain, and despite the fierce sun overhead, he wore no head covering other than his long, snow-white hair.

As the figure drew nearer, Conan realized with a start that the man walked with his eyes shut. Surely, he thought, a blind man could not walk with such assurance, without even a staff to feel ahead of himself. His wonderment turned to horror when he saw that the man's eyelids were sewn together with tiny stitches. The same silken thread stitched his lips tightly shut.

"Crom and Llyr!" Conan said, raising the lance for a cast. The man gestured with his fingers, and a jolt of some powerful, nameless force shot from the steel lance through Conan's hand and arm, inducing a pain that was not like fire, but that sent his muscles into instant convulsion. With an involuntary cry, he dropped the spear to the ground.

"My apologies," said the man, "but you were about to make a serious error." His face was utterly immobile, but his words were perfectly audible and sounded like a natural voice. "My name is Feng-Yoon. I am a magician of Khitai, a senior master of the First Rank and Jade Personage of the Order of the White Phoenix. I come to confer with the Turanian wizard Volvolicus."

"I am the daughter of Volvolicus," Layla said, as if this sort of thing happened often to her. "I will take you to see him, but I seek some well-dried Moon of Ashtaroth. We have a wounded man in our camp and I must dress his injury."

"Ah, you need what we call Flower of the Red Sunrise. I passed some but a little way back. I will take you to it."

"That would be a great kindness, venerable sir."

Conan massaged the cramps from his tight arm, then picked up the lance and followed the two. "What business have you with Volvolicus?" he asked. "How did you find us?"

"It is nothing with which you need concern yourself," the Khitain told him. "You are the barbarian from the north, are you not?"

"I am the only such for some distance around," Conan acknowledged.

"You are a man of destiny. If I had the leisure, I should like to speak with you at some length concerning matters of historical import. But time presses and I must confer with my colleague, the esteemed Volvolicus, instead."

"What is so urgent?" Conan asked, thoroughly mystified.

"Matters of such weight that should we not be successful in our endeavors, there may *be* no further history, and therefore no reason for me to speak with you."

To the Cimmerian, this made no sense at all. "All I wanted to do was to commit a great robbery and get my revenge," he said. "How did matters get so complicated?"

"Estimable goals," Feng-Yoon said approvingly. "I myself

have accomplished some splendid robberies in my career, although I suspect that the things I stole would not strike you as valuable, and I have been known to take such vengeance as has excited broad admiration even in Khitai, where vengeance is esteemed as an art form. Ah, here we are."

With a long, pointed and jeweled fingernail, the wizard pointed at the ground, not inclining his head as if he were looking with his eyes. Layla stooped and began to pull up the herb he indicated, carefully, so as to keep the roots intact.

"This is perfect!" she said. "It died and began to dry just after the last full moon, at the height of its potency. I might not have found such a specimen by searching all day. I thank you, Master Feng-Yoon."

"After three or four centuries, my child," he said, "one acquires a knack for these things. And now, I must go and speak with your honored parent."

"I will accompany you," she said.

"I'll keep hunting," said Conan. He had been hoping for a bit of dalliance with the woman while they were away from the others, but the advent of this bizarre foreigner drove all lustful thoughts from his mind.

The two walked back toward the camp and Conan resumed his hunt. His senses stayed attuned to his surroundings, but his mind roamed elsewhere. Things had taken a supernatural turn he did not like. He was half-minded to keep on roaming and not return to the camp at all. It was not as if he needed the others. With his sword, he could make his way anywhere in the world. He could live off the land and wander aimlessly until he came to a place far away from these repellent doings.

But he knew that he would carry the venture through. It was not as if he needed the treasure. In truth, it meant little to him. And his vengeance was as good as accomplished, for the king of Turan would soon punish Torgut Khan and Sagobal for failing him. The wizard he had only needed to move the treasure, and the woman . . . well, the world was full of women.

No, he thought, he would see it to the finish, foolish

though the undertaking might be, because it was not his nature to desert comrades and leave a job half done. True, the bandits were as worthless a lot as he had ever thrown in with, but when Conan of Cimmeria sided with a man, he remained true . . . unless he was betrayed.

Thinking of betrayal caused him to think of Osman. What was the vicious little thief up to now? Since he first spoke to Conan through the wall between their cells, he had performed nothing but treacheries so complex that the Cimmerian grew dizzy in their contemplation. What would he try next? He could have ridden straight for the treasure, but if so, he could hope to carry away only a tiny portion of the hoard before he was caught. Even if he believed that the outlaws were all slain in the house of Volvolicus, he knew that Conan was still at large and would soon return to the painted cave.

Would he seek to enlist the aid of others? He would need a sizable caravan to bear it all off, and that would mean a sharing-out. He would get no more than his rightful share had he remained faithful to his companions, assuming that his new confederates did not cut his throat and keep it all for themselves. As Conan knew to his sore cost, few men can be trusted around great wealth.

He was jarred from his musings when he came upon a lone gazelle. At his approach, the creature started from behind a bush and ran away in swift bounds. Conan was even quicker. His right arm, balancing the slim spear, shot back behind his shoulder and came forward in the same motion. The gleaming spear flew out in a graceful arc, aimed at a spot far in front of the leaping gazelle. The animal took one more bound. In mid-flight, the paths of gazelle and spear intersected. The spear caught the animal behind the shoulder and the beast went over on its side, kicking spasmodically for a few moments. Then it was still.

The Cimmerian smiled. At least a few things were still simple and satisfying.

He carried the small carcass back to the camp, where he found Volvolicus and the Khitain in deep conversation, employing a language he had never heard. Layla tended a small fire, and the rest were asleep. He walked over to Ubo and nudged him with a toe. The one-eyed Turanian rolled over and looked up at him, blinking blearily.

"Ah! Dinner!" Ubo said.

Conan dropped the carcass upon Ubo's capacious belly. "You can clean it."

Ubo sat up, grumbling. "The things a man has to do to keep his chieftain happy." He got up and began to draw his knife.

'Take it away from the camp to do that," Layla said. "The offal will have every fly in the district plaguing us."

"As you command, my mistress," Ubo muttered. With the gazelle over his shoulder, he trudged off into the desert.

Conan found a spot that seemed no stonier than anyplace else nearby and lay down, covering himself from the sun with his burnous. Within minutes, he was asleep.

With no flicker of emotion showing in his snakelike eyes, Tragthan heard the report rendered by Shosq. Together with Nikas, they stood in the crypt beneath the temple. From the walls around them came groaning sounds, and the uncanny, unstable walls themselves seemed to move, rippling and contracting like the inside of a huge stomach. The sight, coupled with the unnatural geometry of the place, would have driven an ordinary mortal insane. But the priests of Ahriman took no notice, except to register any truly perceptible changes.

"This is disturbing," Tragthan said at last. "But are you certain that you read the hieroglyphs aright?"

"There can be no doubt of it," Shosq reiterated. "The wizard called Volvolicus is a master of the Stygian art of *Khelkhet-Pteth*. It is the most ancient and the most powerful of all the Stygian arts, even though the Stygians of this age have forgotten the fact. For many centuries it has been employed mainly to move great stones in their endless, vain building projects. They think of it as little more than a magickal refinement of the stonemason's craft!"

"The fools!" Nikas said. "Do they not understand that this most ancient of magickal arts involves the manipulation of crystal, the very substance of which most of the solid matter of this plane is formed?"

"No, and fortunate for us they do not," said Tragthan. "A master of *Khelkhet-Pteth*, were he powerful enough and had the inclination, could rend this world asunder by disrupting its crystalline structure. I suspect the ancient Stygians never understood this. Instead, they chased after the disciplines of bending demons to their will and seeking the favor of the lesser gods."

"Does this mean a change in our plans?" Shosq asked.

"Nay, it does not," Tragthan said. "In the first place, things have moved beyond our powers to halt them." He gestured with a spidery hand, indicating the repulsive crypt in which they conferred. The groaning coming from the walls sounded like a gigantic monster feeling the pangs of hunger. The three winced, even their immobile faces registering alarm. "You see? You hear? We cannot stop it from happening. But I think we have little to fear from this Volvolicus. Surely he understands no more of his art than do the Stygians, for they trained him, and he has been content to dwell in obscurity in this remote corner of the degenerate nation of Turan. Surely, if he understood the power that is his to command, he could reign as do the priest-kings of Stygia."

"Let us hope you are right," Nikas affirmed. "In the meantime, what is to be our course?"

"We must aid our dread lord in his rebirth into this world in the best way we can. It cannot be the perfect advent we had anticipated for so long, but I think now, with the heroic spell-making we have performed in recent days, despite the thinning of our numbers, that it need not be as catastrophic as we had feared."

"How do you mean?" Shosq asked. "This undue hastening of his return almost assures that not only will our lord be unwontedly weak, but he will be almost mindless, not even knowing himself."

"Aye, but not for long," Tragthan assured them. "With our labors on his behalf, and with the aid of the powers we shall invoke, he will quickly assume his full capabilities. The destruction will be terrible, of course, but that is ever the way of Lord Ahriman. What matters the annihilation of millions of mortals, the rearranging of terrain and atmosphere? What counts is that we, his loyal slaves, shall live to serve him in his new reign, and he will make us lords over his new creation."

"Praise the dread Lord Ahriman," the other two intoned.

"Excellent," Chamik pronounced, tearing strips of broiled gazelle from the bone with his gapped teeth. "Our chief is a mighty hunter, and the Lady Layla is a splendid cook."

"Spare me your praise," Layla said. "Auda, can you eat?"

"A little," he said. The desert man was feverish, his thigh swollen to almost double its normal girth. Layla had pronounced these things normal and warranted that the wound would heal well now that it was poulticed with her herbs. She sliced some thin strips of meat from a joint and took them to Auda.

Conan brooded as he ate. The bandits, even Auda, ate as if they had not a care. They took the steaming joints in their teeth and slashed off oversized mouthfuls with their daggers, nearly slicing their noses away in the process. They chewed with abandon, smacking their lips mightily, grease and blood running over their chins and onto their tunics and vests.

At another time, the barbarian could as easily have lost himself in the moment, with no thought for the future. But now he had to think for all of them. As he ripped at the tough but savory meat with strong white teeth, he watched the two wizards. They had not paused in their conversation and neither of them showed the slightest interest in the meal.

Ubo tossed a stripped bone into the brush and a moment later, a lurking jackal ran away with it clutched tightly in its jaws. Three of its fellows raced along after it, trying to seize the prize for themselves. Ubo laughed. "These are creatures after my own heart! Have at it, brothers!"

"I noticed the resemblance," Layla said.

"Chief," Mamos said, taking his attention from his food for a moment, "this seems to me a good place. It is far from Sagobal and the manhunters. There is no one to observe us. If we can find water nearby, why not abide here a while and give the king a few more days to flay and burn Torgut Khan and his dog?"

"There is wisdom in that," Conan said, "but I cannot rest while I know Osman is out there someplace, plotting. Either he is already at the hideout or he is headed to it. If it is the former, we must catch him there and kill him. If the latter, we must be waiting there when he arrives."

"What if he is not alone when he shows up?" Chamik asked.

"That is something to think about," Conan conceded. "It seems to me that he must want to take the whole treasure for himself, but he has proven too clever too many times. He may think all of you dead, leaving only me and himself alive to know where the treasure is hidden. He may think he can kill me."

"That little rat?" Ubo said. "He has seen you in action. Surely he knows better."

"There are more ways of killing a man than in open fight," Layla said. "A poisoned arrow in the back is as deadly as any sword. A dozen hirelings can bring down the greatest warrior. But then, such men as you do not need me to lecture you upon the techniques of murder."

"You are right about that." Conan said. "But something now occurs to me: Last night he led Sagobal and the manhunters to the wizard's house to see to it that you should all be slain. Might he not have hoped that the wards of Volvolicus would kill all of them as well?"

"Aye, and many were killed, you may lay wager to that!" said Chamik.

"I wish I knew how many of them were left alive," said

Conan, "for now I believe that they are all we have to contend with. Sagobal wants that gold for himself, so he will not come with his guards, or risk in any way Torgut Khan's learning of its location."

The wizards finished their conversation. The Khitain stood and faced them. "You are all to come to Shahpur," he announced.

The bandits looked at one another, on their faces expressions of stunned incredulity. Then they laughed.

"You are mad, old one," said Chamik. "We have seen all of Shahpur that we wish. Never again shall I grace that city, for I am not welcome there, and if the inhabitants there are feeling well-disposed toward me, they will merely hang me."

"Nonetheless," said Feng-Yoon, "you must come to Shahpur."

Mamos got up lazily and drew the dagger from his sash. Its ten-inch blade was curved, its edges cruelly keen. "I think it is time to put this one from his confusion. A disordered mind is an offense to the gods." He approached the Khitain with an evil leer, waving the knife before him. Feng-Yoon gestured and the bandit's arm jerked spastically. The knife flew from his nerveless fingers, narrowly missing Ubo, who had to scramble from its path.

"Mitra!" Mamos cried. "What was that? Vipers have burrowed into my arm!" He rubbed the muscles that rose into knots from wrist to shoulder.

"I could have told you not to do that," Conan said. "But I thought you ought to learn it for yourself." Then, to Feng-Yoon: "Why must we go to Shahpur, Khitain? We all have excellent reasons to wish never to see the place again. Ubo is right."

"There are matters afoot that are far more important than your petty treasure. Certain things must be accomplished in Shahpur, and you will help us bring them to fruition. Disguise will be provided you that is far more effective than the deceptive clothing you wore upon your last visit. Volvolicus will bring you to the place where you are needed. Heed my words. I assure you that you do not wish to incur my curse."

"By no means do we wish that," Ubo said disgustedly. "What is mere fabulous wealth when instead I may be of service to an outlandish wizard from Khitai?"

The irony was lost on Feng-Yoon. He turned without another word and began walking across the desert, in the direction of Shahpur.

"I am glad to have that one gone," Chamik said when the Khitain was out of earshot. "The sight of those eyes and that mouth makes my flesh creep. And to hear him speak makes it even worse." He turned to Conan. "Chief, are we truly going to do his bidding?"

"You must," said Volvolicus. "As my power of magick is superior to that of a street-corner mountebank, so his power is superior to mine. Even among wizards of the First Rank, Feng-Yoon is a being of awesome power. He may be even greater than Thoth-Amon."

That was a name familiar to Conan. "Then it is true that we must not risk incurring his curse. Volvolicus, will this disguise of his truly protect us?"

"It will. He wishes you no ill, but terrible matters lie before us and he must have helpers. When you stole the treasure from the crypt, you altered the pace of certain sorcerous practices taking place there. That makes you—this is difficult to put in mundane language—but it makes you uniquely suited to go back into that crypt and further disrupt an operation that must not be allowed to come to fruition."

Ubo gaped at him. "Go *back* to that crypt?"

"Hear him out," said Auda. "Perhaps there is another treasure there."

"Aye," said Mamos, grimacing and flexing the fingers of his right hand. "Perhaps this new wizard will summon one of the famous dragons of Khitai to fly our gold away." He walked off muttering, looking for his dagger.

"You have no choice," Volvolicus said. "Neither have I.

My daughter must go as well, and you know I have no liking for that idea."

"Well, if we must ride, then we must ride," said Conan. "But we need not ride in the heat of the day. When you finish eating, I want each of you to see to your horse. I will take care of Auda's myself. Then all of you get some sleep, for you'll have none tonight. We can be outside Shahpur by dawn. This wizard's ability to disguise us may be great, but I would as lief not go through that gate in the full light of day. We will go in early, while the light is still uncertain."

"Your disguise will be provided by the Vendhyan mage Asoka," Volvolicus told him. "He is the master of illusion."

"Khitai, now Vendhya?" said Conan. "What means this gathering of magicians, Volvolicus?"

"It is something you do not wish to know," the mage said. "But all will be made clear to you upon the morrow."

"Why not now?" Chamik said, suspicious.

"Do not ask," Layla said, smiling. "For I suspect that if we were to know the truth, none of us would get any sleep."

With that, they had to be satisfied.

Fourteen

At gray dawn, Volvolicus called for a halt. They were still within a range of small hills just off the Shahpur road. They started when a form detached itself from a rock a mere few paces before them. He had been sitting cross-legged atop it, so still that even keen-eyed Conan had thought him a part of the boulder. He proved to be a small, round man, dressed in simple garments with a large turban upon his head. He steepled his hands before his chest and bowed deeply from the waist.

"Greetings, my friends. I am Asoka, a humble magician of Kaleekhat, in Vendhya." As he spoke, his turban glowed faintly. "I am here to provide you each with a new likeness, for I am accounted knowledgeable in the art of *Maia*, which in the Vendhyan tongue means 'illusion'."

"I hope you are accounted more than just knowledgeable," Conan said, "for all our lives are in your hands."

The Vendhyan smiled. "Indeed, some have been so kind as to characterize me as more than knowledgeable."

The sun was still below the horizon when they came to the great gate of Shahpur. The portal was just creaking open, and the farmers, peddlers, and caravaneers who had camped without the night before now crowded to get in. The Cimmerian and his companions waited patiently, for it would no longer be in character for them to push to the front. They led their mounts by the reins as they dawdled at the back of the crowd.

"Names and business?" asked the official at the gate. He glanced at the new arrivals and saw a little band of Turanian villagers. Volvolicus was their elder, with a long, snowy beard sweeping his breast. Conan was a sturdy, black-bearded smith. Layla was a boy of about sixteen. The others were artisans and farmers. The illusion was complete. Even the horses had become village nags, and when Conan spoke, a hearer would detect only the accents of the Turanian backcountry.

"We are from the village of Uhvas," said Volvolicus. He gave the assumed name of each of them. "We have come to petition Torgut Khan for a lessening of our taxes. The harvest has been scanty this year, and there has been disease among the sheep and cattle."

"You may petition as you wish," said the official. "But I might as well warn you that this is a bad time to speak to the viceroy about taxes. That will be one-quarter dinar for each man and one-quarter dinar for each horse. Three and one-half dinars in all." Volvolicus dug around in his purse and came up with a few coins. He counted among these carefully and handed over the sum demanded. "Next!" shouted the official.

"That was easy," Auda said. He limped heavily, but he could walk, leaning upon Chamik's shoulder.

"I hope it is all as easy," said Conan. "Now we must find a stable. Auda, you will stay with the horses. I do not know what this wizard wants us to do, but if our leave-taking of this town is as hurried as it was the last time, a man with a wounded leg cannot run. But you can have the horses ready for instant action."

"You can rely on me, Chief," Auda said, relief in his voice.

Like the rest, he had no wish to take part in whatever the wizards had in mind. As with many towns that relied upon an extensive caravan trade, Shahpur had a district devoted to the care and sale of horses, camels, donkeys and mules. It was near the main gate and here they found a small stable that met their needs.

"I will take your money and let you have stable space," the stableman said, looking the horses over contemptuously. "But I do not understand why you want to waste money thus. These bone-sacks ought to be picketed out on the common." One of the animals reared and lashed out in protest at being penned, breaking a heavy rail with one forehoof.

"They have some spirit in them yet," Conan said to the gaping stableman. "You need not deal with them. Our companion will see to their care."

"Whatever you wish," said the man, dropping their coins into his purse.

They went from the stable district toward the center of the city. It was a busy, bustling place, but after the overcrowding of the festival day, it seemed half empty. For a while they wandered among the stalls, pretending to examine wares, satisfying themselves that their disguises were reliable. Nowhere did they attract the slightest suspicion.

"Think you," Ubo said at one point, "that this Vendhyan mage would like to throw in with us? I believe that this art of his could come in very handy for men in our line of work."

"Ubo," said Mamos, "in your new guise, you have two good eyes. Can you see out of both now?"

Ubo picked up a tiny figurine of the dwarf-bodied, lion-headed god Bes, holding it close to his left eye, turning it this way and that. He closed his right eye. "No. Blind as a stone."

Mamos shrugged. "Then his magick is not so great."

"What should we be doing?" Conan asked Volvolicus.

"We must wait. I do not think anything of importance is planned for the day. Midnight is a more likely hour. In the meantime, we play the role of bumpkins visiting the great city. Gape at the splendid buildings, admire the entertainers in the market, but do not drink yourselves into insensibility."

"The man thinks we are drunkards," Chamik said, offended. "We are gentlemen of the horse and the sword, but at need we can play mere workers in wood and grubbers in the earth."

"Your condescension is a marvel to us all," said Layla.

Conan nudged her. "Be careful how you speak. Village boys do not show insolence toward their elders."

"I can see that this is going to be a trial," she sighed.

They found a shady spot in the public square and sat, keeping mainly to themselves, talking with townsmen and visitors from time to time. It was instantly evident that the populace shunned the Temple of Ahriman. There was a broad, open area before it, for people upon entering the plaza walked in a wide circle to avoid straying too close. Trees planted near the temple were withering, whereas all others in the square flourished. The facade of the temple was even more decrepit than before. The building appeared to be a thousand years old.

"Look!" said Mamos as the shadows of late afternoon stretched long across the square. Seven men rode in single file on dusty horses. In the lead was Sagobal, his face as bleak as a desert sandstorm. Behind him rode the big Aquilonian, likewise grim. The others were dangerous-looking men of various nations.

"Can that be all that is left of them?" murmured Ubo. "Surely, we are great warriors to have reduced their numbers so!" The others chuckled quietly.

"They managed to round up a few horses," said Layla. "Conan, what sort of men are those? I have seen Hyrkanians ere now, but the others are strange to me."

"That big man behind Sagobal is an Aquilonian," Conan said, "and he bears the marks of a pit-fighter. The next is a man of Koth. The one in the white robe is from Shem, a nation of great bowmen. The brown man who rides barefoot has the aspect of Keshan or Punt. You see how his eyes keep sweeping the ground, even here in the city? He is a tracker. The other is a Zamoran."

Conan studied Berytus carefully, seeing him at close range for the first time. The man looked as formidable as any opponent the Cimmerian had ever encountered. All his weapons were of the highest quality, and his minimal armor proclaimed that he depended upon his speed and skill in a fight, rather than on passive protection. His steel-and-leather-covered hands and forearms meant that he used these as primary weapons, an undoubted legacy of his pit-fighting days.

The others were specialists and probably excellent fighters. Conan had no illusions about the fighting qualities of his own men, who were more accustomed to ambush and murder than to open combat. Even with their sharply reduced numbers, these manhunters had a decided advantage, should it come to a fight.

"They do not look so terrible," said Mamos.

"Think you so?" said Layla. "Last time they were nigh, you spent your time lying on your belly on the floor, cowering."

"Layla," Conan said warningly.

"My apologies," she murmured without repentance.

"You know," Ubo said idly, "now might be a good time to eliminate them. Consider: They will have no suspicion of us, for we are but lowly villagers, beneath their notice. We could wait until they alight, walk around behind them as if we were on some other errand, and each of us plant a dagger in a back."

"One of us would have to be very quick," Mamos said. "There are seven of them and only six of us. Chief, why do you not take Sagobal and the Aquilonian?" His leer was even more evil than usual.

"I forbid it!" Volvolicus said. "We are here on business far more important than your fight with Sagobal."

"Say you so?" said Mamos, his humor turning vicious. "Pray tell me, wizard: Just what sort of business is more important than killing an enemy? These swine will track us until all of us are dead, or we kill them first! Ubo is right. Why not deal with them now, when this change of appearance gives us the upper hand?"

"Peace, the lot of you," said Conan. "I would like to slay them all as well, but this is an enemy we know. Do you want to make enemies of the wizards? Mamos, you remember what happened when you drew steel upon the Khitain. You think he cannot kill as easily? There are things here we do not want to trifle with."

"The chief is right," said Chamik. "One enemy at a time. A man really needs no more than that."

Evening drew on, and Layla went among the stalls of the vendors, returning with bread, fruit, cheese and thin beer for their dinner. They sat and ate and waited for something to happen.

"This is weak fare," said Mamos, wrinkling his nose in distaste at the dry food and sour beer. "What I crave is some plump roast-fowl and strong wine! Let us go and find a tavern."

"Is this a holiday?" Conan asked him. "Remember, you are a poor villager, who must live on his hard-earned money. You are no longer a bandit who can make free with the earnings of others."

"It is dark," Mamos groused. "Who is going to notice?" The complaining subsided and the men dozed where they sat. They attracted no attention, for in the sun-washed cities of the south, it was not unusual for those having business before the courts and magistrates to spend many days in waiting to be heard. In front of every public building were to be found people sitting upon benches or on the ground, simply waiting. In this case, the wait was not a lengthy one. Shortly before midnight, the Khitain came to them.

Conan stirred to wakefulness just as the moon seemed to be impaled upon the spire of a tower, the stars behind it like a huge treasure of diamonds, sapphires and rubies scattered across a curtain of black silk. From the positions of those stars, Conan knew the hour to be near midnight.

Before him stood the strange Khitain mage and the Vendhyan. There were others: a Turanian much like the local people except for his skeletal thinness, others of nations even Conan could not recognize.

"It is time," said the Khitain. The rest snapped awake and looked upon the newcomers.

"Time for what?" asked Conan.

"Attend me," said Feng-Yoon. He seemed to float to a sitting position and his companions did likewise, until the whole company formed a tight circle facing inward. "Asoka, work your art."

The Vendhyan chanted and gestured briefly, and seemingly without effect.

"Now we cannot be seen or heard," said Feng-Yoon. "Should any stray near, they will see nothing."

"What if they trip over us?" Mamos asked, unimpressed.

"One who comes near will simply walk around us," said Asoka, "without understanding why. Just as all avoid the space before that accursed temple."

"I thought people simply deemed it an evil-looking place," Conan said.

"You and your men like to wallow in evil places," Layla pointed out.

"That is the simple and understandable evil of mortal men," Ubo explained to her. "We enjoy that sort of evil."

"If we may keep to the point," Volvolicus said patiently. "Midnight draws nigh."

"Yes," said Feng-Yoon. "To business. Know, then, that the priests of that temple seek to bring the god Ahriman back into this world."

"A moment," said Conan. "I have seen temples of Ahriman and Ormazd in many places. How does this one differ?"

"The Ahriman of the Ormazd cult is no more than a memory of the true god," Feng-Yoon explained. "The struggle between the gods of light and dark is cosmic, ongoing and eternal. Forever, the creators battle the destroyers. Greatest of the destroyers was Ahriman, who was so evil that even the gods of Stygia contended against him. In time, so long ago that few legends survive, the priest-kings of Stygia, aided by their god Set, drove Ahriman from the world, destroying his temples, killing his worshipers and his priesthood. He was thought to be banished forever and his priests eliminated."

"But nothing is forever," said the Vendhyan. "Nothing is truly eliminated from the world. Some things only wait."

"Just so," said Feng-Yoon. "This year some unknown force, perhaps some alignment of the stars and planets of which even we are ignorant, roused several of the priests of Ahriman, long entombed beneath their ancient shrines, to wakefulness. Even the most learned of the Stygian mages were astounded to learn that this had happened. These unclean priests, who are of an unholy race long thought extinct, half reptile and half human, homed unerringly upon this town of Shahpur."

"What brought them here?" Conan asked.

"I have studied this place since my arrival two days ago," said the Nemedian. "I am Pyatar of Aghrapur, and like all my countrymen, I had thought Shahpur to be a mere caravan town and district capital like a half-score of other cities in Nemedia. Now I know it to be an unthinkably ancient city. That which most of us see is but the topmost layer of settlement, no more than a thousand years old, built upon the ruins of ages past. And the most ancient part of it is that temple." He pointed at the sinister house of Ahriman.

"Rather," Pyatar went on, "the foundation is unbelievably old. And at its center is an altar and a crypt, and to these things no words of age apply, for they do not truly exist in this world."

Conan did not like the sound of this. "Do not exist? But we beheld the altar! We went into the crypt and stole from it Torgut Khan's treasure!"

"I said they do not exist *in this world*. They belong to another plane entirely, and it is most uncanny that the altar is visible at all. Is it not hard to look upon?"

"It twists the gaze and the mind," Conan acknowledged.

"And," said Feng-Yoon, "did you truly *see* the crypt, or did you just behold the treasure you sought?"

"We went down the stair," Conan said. "We held the priest and the others at sword's-point while Volvolicus raised the gold. Chamik, did you not force them back to stand against the wall?"

"I did, Chief! I brandished my blade in their faces and they backed away, carrying that priest you laid out with the flat of your sword."

"Then you saw the wall?" Pyatar asked.

The bandit pondered. "Well . . . I cannot say I actually saw it. It was naught but a great darkness down there. The candles were set only around the treasure. The hostages began to make sounds of terror, but I was soon distracted by all the excitement when we made our escape."

"Ah!" said Feng-Yoon. "This explains much! If mortals actually touched the walls of that crypt . . ." He let his words trail off as if he were in a reverie. "My friends, that crypt is the belly of Ahriman!"

"So I suspected when I descended therein," said Volvolicus. "It is no natural place of true stone, and the altar is something totally other. It is not a natural substance."

"The belly of Ahriman!" Conan exclaimed.

"Aye," said Feng-Yoon. "When the Stygians sought to eliminate the god from this world, he left himself a means to return. In order to do so, he must have a way to absorb strength, as a man must eat to live. In a manner of speaking, that crypt is his stomach in this world, wherein sacrifices are to be made to Ahriman that he may gain the power to reenter this world from which he was driven so long ago."

The Khitain slapped his long-nailed hands upon his knees. "Now much becomes clear. Volvolicus, when you practiced your art within the crypt, you stimulated the god and aroused him from his slumber of eons. This much you described to me yesterday. But so absorbed were you in your magicks that you did not notice the hostages being herded against the walls! That was like throwing scraps to a famished lion. Now the god rages with hunger!"

"It was just a robbery like any other," Chamik protested. "How were we to know?"

"These priests had planned their ritual carefully," the Khitain continued. "They waited for the correct alignment of the stars, the planets, and probably of other forces unknown to the scholars of this age. When all was ready, they would have worked their dread sacrifices, performed their rites, and brought their lord triumphantly back. But when you wrought your magick within the crypt and gave Ahriman his untimely sacrifice, you destroyed the delicate balance of their schedule. This means there is an opportunity to frustrate their plans utterly."

For the first time, the Khitain's face showed expression. His sewn-together lips bent into a ghastly parody of a smile and he seemingly looked around at them. "My companions, I had thought that tonight's actions would be undertaken in the direst desperation. Now I feel that there is cause for genuine hope!"

"You wanted us to throw our lives away out of your own desperation?" Conan said hotly.

"That was not even to be considered," said the mage. "Either we succeed, or all die. I wish to devise the best way out of this, the one cheapest in lives and in expenditure of wizardly power. Count yourselves fortunate that it is I who am in charge here. Thoth-Amon wanted to undertake this, and he would not hesitate to sacrifice whole populations for a slight advantage."

"Learned Feng-Yoon," Volvolicus said, "you have spoken of the crypt. What have you now deduced about that hellish altar? Even the dullest of the workmen who toiled on this temple could not bear to look upon it."

"It is a thing of awesome power," said Feng-Yoon, "as well it should be, for as the crypt is the belly of Ahriman, so the altar is his head."

"His *head*?" Conan said. "I will warrant you the thing is disgusting, but it is only a great bundle of stone snakes!"

"It is not stone," said Volvolicus. "I have told you that."

"I use the word 'head' in the most symbolic sense," said the Khitain. "But as the crypt was left behind to receive the sacrifices to restore the god's strength in this world, so the altar stands ready to receive his intelligence, that he may work his will upon the world of mortals."

"This much is clear, after a fashion," Conan said. "What is not clear is this: Just what is it that you expect us to do?" He gestured toward his men, all of whom leaned forward attentively, with expressions of fear and dismay. "We are but ordinary bandits. We are not wizards, to contend with the very gods. We are men who use our wits and our skill and our weapons to earn a living. Judges and the soft folk of the cities think our ways evil, and the peasants of the countryside and the caravaneers consider us a sore plague, but none thinks us unnatural. Who are we to undertake such work?"

"Having violated the sanctuary of the god," said the Vendhyan, "the dreadful sacrificial maw, so to speak, you men have acquired a certain power superior to that of others. It is a principle well known in the study of magick that contact with things sorcerous bestows upon one a certain affinity for the supernatural."

"Perhaps that explains," Conan said ruefully, "why I always seem to fall afoul of wizardry, as hard as I try to avoid it."

"That may well be," said the Vendhyan, nodding happily.

"You are to enter the temple," Feng-Yoon said, answering Conan's question at last. "And you are to slay the priests."

There was silence for a moment, then Conan spoke. "I see. We are to walk in there," he pointed at the portal, its portcullis less inviting than the mouth of a dragon, and shut as tightly. "We are to slay creatures that are not true men at all, that all the sorcery of the Stygian priest-kings could not kill. These creatures have lain alive in their tombs for thousands of years and you expect us to kill them?" Conan's voice rose through this recitation until he was shouting the last words.

"Tell him, Chief," Ubo said approvingly.

"Aye, I want none of this," Chamik agreed.

"In truth," Asoka said, "nothing can truly slay these evil priests save their own god. It follows, therefore, that you must induce their god to kill them."

"How is that to be done?" Layla asked. Alone among them, she seemed to be taking this in her stride.

"There were four of these priests until the day of the festival," Feng-Yoon said. "Since then, only three have been seen. The one called Umos has disappeared, and that is the one you forced into contact with the wall of the crypt. His god has eaten him. That is how you must destroy the others."

"You are the wizards," said Ubo. "Why do you not do these things?"

"We could," said Pyatar of Aghrapur. "But they would know us the instant we set foot within the temple, and they would have opportunity to prepare. It is imperative that you, experts that you are, break into the temple and slay the priests before they can begin to work their sorcery."

"And what will you be doing, wizard?" Mamos asked bitterly.

"We will be dealing with their god," said Feng-Yoon.

"And if we refuse?" Conan asked.

"You cannot," Feng-Yoon replied. "You will go willingly or you will go under compulsion, but go you will. You will perform better if you have full command of your limbs and your wits."

"You leave us no choice, then?" Conan said.

"None."

"You have heard them," the Cimmerian said to his followers. "You know that they make no idle threats."

"It looks as if we must go, then," said Ubo indignantly. "But it vexes me sorely that we must pull a dangerous break-in with no prospect of gold to steal!"

"Can you raise the portcullis for us?" Conan asked.

"Easily," said Asoka, "but that would tip our hand untimely."

"I have looked the place over," Conan said, "and I could find no other access."

"There is a way in," said Pyatar. "You must enter through the roof. There are portals in the clerestory."

"What is a clerestory?" Mamos asked.

"In large buildings," Volvolicus explained, "light is often admitted through a row of windows running around the building just under the roof. That is the clerestory."

"Oh," Mamos said. "I have broken in through many of those. I never knew what they were called."

"In this temple," said Feng-Yoon, "the clerestory consists of a series of circular windows, made of a thick substance that is not true glass. These windows flood the interior with a scarlet radiance, but it is not the natural light of this world. The magickal glass brings light from a faraway red star, which may be the place where the race of the priests of Ahriman had their origin."

"You men would never be able to shift one of these windows," Asoka said. "But the esteemed Volvolicus, master of all things composed of crystal, can accomplish this. He shall accompany you to the roof and he shall extract one of the windows from its setting. Then you shall descend and carry out your task."

"We will need rope," Conan said. Now that the decision had been reached, he wasted no time with complaint and recrimination. "We will need a very long rope."

"I happen to have such a rope," said the Vendhyan, his turban glowing gently in the dark night.

"Then let us be about it," Conan said, standing.

"A man of firm purpose," said Feng-Yoon. "This is something of which I approve."

"Just be ready to deal with Ahriman," said the Cimmerian. "If we are to descend into the belly of the god of darkness, I want you standing by to lop off his head."

Conan, Volvolicus, Layla and the three bandits walked in the direction of the temple. The wizards faded into the surrounding darkness except for Asoka, who accompanied them.

"There is little light upon the western side," Conan said. "We will go up there." They walked around to that side, which was faced only by the blank, windowless wall of a law court, and halted midway along its length. "Where is your rope, Asoka?"

"Here," said the Vendhyan. He reached within his robe and withdrew a huge coil of rope, far too large to have been so concealed. This he dropped upon the ground.

"I will not ask you how you did that," said Conan. "I will ask you if you can produce a grapple."

"No need," Asoka said, smiling. "This is an old Vendhyan specialty." He bowed his head over steepled hands and sang in a quiet voice, his song a succession of sour, quavering whines fit to set the teeth on edge. Slowly, an end of the rope rose from the center of the coil and began to ascend.

"I saw this trick once," Ubo said, striving to sound unimpressed. "It was in the bazaar of Shadizar."

"Silence!" Layla hissed. With deadly action imminent, even she seemed nervous.

When the Vendhyan's song ceased, Conan stepped to the rope and tugged at it. It felt not so much like a tight-stretched rope as it did a bar of iron.

"Volvolicus," said the Cimmerian, "when the rest of us are up, we will hold the rope and Asoka can return it to its natural state. Tie an end around your waist and we will haul you up."

"I was about to suggest as much," said the wizard. "I am no young athlete and will need all my energy when I attack that portal."

"What about you?" Conan asked Layla. "I know you can ride. Can you climb as well?"

In lieu of an answer, she kicked off her boots and jumped at the rope. With the rope grasped in her hands and between her toes, she swarmed up it as nimbly as a monkey. A minute later she scrambled over the parapet and disappeared. Then she reappeared, waving.

"All clear up there," Conan said. He took the rope and began to pull himself up. When his feet were clear of the ground, he braced them against the wall and half-climbed, half-walked up to the roof. Once over the parapet, he surveyed their prospect while Mamos began his ascent. The roof was flat, made of white stone dotted here and there with statues of strange creatures. A few paces from the parapet, the clerestory rose a further seven or eight feet, with the round windows set into its surface. The roof suffered from the same strange malady as the facade, for the sculptures were worn down as if by the rains and winters of centuries.

Within ten minutes the three bandits lay on the roof, puffing and wheezing from their exertions. Since they were going to be useless for a while, Conan took hold of the rope and waved to Asoka. The rope went limp and Volvolicus fastened it about his waist, then signaled that he was ready. With one foot on the roof and the other braced against the parapet, Conan began hauling the wizard up, the great muscles of his arms, back and shoulders rolling powerfully beneath his bronzed skin. Layla watched him admiringly.

When the wizard was on the roof and freed from the rope, they crossed to the clerestory and crouched by one of the windows. From this side, it appeared to be an opaque, black disk. Volvolicus ran his fingers over its surface while Ubo recoiled the rope. Conan pointed to a nearby sculpture, and the bandit made one end of the rope fast to it.

"Secure your weapons," Conan cautioned in a low voice. "One dagger dropping to that floor as we climb down might as well be an alarm gong."

The wizard chanted slowly, his eyes closed, his fingertips tracing invisible designs upon the surface of the glass. There came a faint grating noise, and gritty dust fell from around the edges of the window. Then, very slowly, like a cork being withdrawn reluctantly from the neck of a bottle, the window began to back out of its setting.

As it slowly came out, a thin circle of red light defined its periphery. The red line transformed into a definite band, and beams of red light shot from the interior. The glass proved to be as thick as a man's forearm was long. Its outer edge was inky black, its center a sullen red. From the rim that pointed inward to the interior of the temple there flared a beam of lurid scarlet.

"Mitra!" said Ubo. "What kind of unholy thing is this?"

Torgut Khan sat sleepless in his chambers. He was frantic with fear and frustration. The officials of the royal treasury had been due for two days, and his continued existence was probably owing only to contrary winds on the Vilayet causing them delay. His luck could not hold. As he brooded, he tore frantically at his hair, knowing that the king's torturers would not be far behind the treasury officials. Where was his treasure? How could it happen that a pack of scruffy bandits could elude his forces for so long?

Looking up through his window as if for inspiration, something caught his eye. It was a trifling thing, a mere flash of color, but so desperate was Torgut Khan for distraction from his troubles that his attention fastened upon it. What could it be? Then he saw it again, like a flash of summer heat-lightning, but coming from the wrong direction, and red instead of white. He got up and went out onto his terrace for a better look.

Amid the silence and the fragrance of flowering plants, he walked to the balustrade surrounding the terrace and leaned upon it. There! The flash came again, brightening steadily, until a great beam of red light shot into the sky. He shivered involuntarily at the uncanny sight. What could it be? What was its source? Then he saw that it came from the roof of the accursed Temple of Ahriman.

He had never been satisfied with the tale of how a wizard had gone within the crypt, accompanied by the most flea-bitten pack of unhung rogues ever to plague the territory, and simply levitated the treasure out into the open air. Flown it away, like a hawk from the wrist of a falconer! A suspicion formed in his mind. Suppose the treasure had never left the temple? Suppose the whole spectacle of the flying chests and sacks had been mere illusion?

Once the idea was in his brain, it fastened there as tenaciously as a leech, strengthened by his desperate need. Yes! He was sure of it now. The priests had stolen his treasure! His salvation lay in the Temple of Ahriman!

The red light was no longer visible, and he knew that he must act immediately. He ran from the terrace, grasped the handle of his door and swung it wide.

"Guards!" he bellowed. "Sagobal! Come to me! We must invade the Temple of Ahriman!"

"Cover it!" Volvolicus said urgently. The thick window rested on the roof upon its black side, casting a brilliant beam straight overhead. Had there been any clouds above, it would have made a bloody spot upon their undersides. Ubo cast his black cloak over the pane. The light came through weakly, so that it glowed sullenly as a low-burning coal. At least it no longer shot its rays abroad for all to see.

Conan leaned in through the round hole and looked downward. The interior was flooded with unnatural red light from the remaining windows. They were almost directly above one of the naked female caryatids.

"Is anyone down there?" Chamik asked. "Are we discovered?"

"No sign of life," Conan said. "And no sense in waiting. Give me the rope." He pulled back from the portal, grasped the coil of rope in his arms and heaved it through the opening. Instantly, he followed after it. The rope fell, uncoiling to its full length, and snapped wildly about for a few seconds. Then it swung lazily, just a few inches short of the floor.

With a Cimmerian's practiced skill in all forms of climbing, Conan lowered himself hand under hand, kicking away from the caryatid from time to time when he swung too close, and in less than a minute dropped soundlessly to the floor. He stepped away from the rope and drew his sword, the blade making a faint hiss as it cleared his sheath.

All senses alert, Conan looked around. A great silence reigned over the vast interior. There was no movement. The place might have been deserted.

Quickly, Ubo, Chamik and Mamos came down the rope. Each stood blowing upon his stinging palms for a few seconds, then drew his weapon and stood by his chief. Layla swarmed down with agility and held the end of the rope while her father descended. By the time he reached the floor, his palms were bleeding, but he took no notice. He stood by Conan and surveyed the temple as if his eyes could pierce through its stone walls and floor. He signaled and began to walk slowly toward the far end of the building.

Just as cautiously, the others followed him. They crouched, sliding their feet so as to make little noise, holding weapons well clear of their bodies to avoid steel clashing against a buckle or the pommel of a sheathed dagger. They drew closer and closer to the awful, repellent altar.

In some indefinable fashion, the hideous knot of serpents seemed to have changed. When last they had seen it, the thing had been half covered by a heavy cloth. Now fully exposed, it appeared somehow larger, with the serpent-heads protruding farther than they had before. The viper-heads were subtly altered, having no eyes but with their mouths gaping open. The usually impassive Volvolicus seemed to be shaken by the sight, and a line of sweat beads appeared along his hairline. Somehow Conan did not think that this was caused by the mage's strenuous descent down the rope. He leaned close, so that his lips were near Volvolicus's ear.

"Where are they?" he whispered.

Slowly the wizard pointed, a long, thin finger extended. It was directed straight down the stairway to the crypt.

"That solves one part of our problem," Layla whispered. "How to get them down there."

The bandits rolled their eyes in terror. Even the curse of the wizards seemed a little thing in comparison with returning to that crypt. Conan brandished his blade at them and pointed. His fierce eyes told them that no amount of danger was more certain than the death he would inflict instantly. Gulping, their fingers flexing nervously around the hilts of their swords and daggers, they began to tiptoe down the stairs.

Layla followed after the bandits, and after her went her father. Conan had a final look around the temple before he started down the steps. Then something about the altar made him pause. It was one of the serpent heads, one that protruded yet farther than the others. It was also somewhat larger, and its sketchy features different from theirs. It had something like the aspect of a human face, but these features were fading and the substance seemed to move, smoothing out to blankness. A thrill of horror went up the Cimmerian's spine as a thin line appeared horizontally across its surface. The line widened into a definite split, then the two edges began to pull back. What they exposed looked horribly like an eye.

Not waiting to see more, Conan rushed down the stair. At the bottom he found his companions and he heard a loud chanting in a language that was not merely incomprehensible, but was made entirely of syllables unpronounceable by human tongue and palate. The three priests of Ahriman stood bathed in an ugly green light, and that light also revealed that the walls of the chamber were angled in a fashion that was not possible in the natural world, so twisting the human eye that one could not even count how many walls there were. Not only that, but they were in constant, agitated motion, rippling like a vat of sea anemones. It resembled nothing so much as being within the stomach of a giant.

"What do we do now, Chief?" Mamos cried, terror raising the pitch of his voice to a shriek. All of the bandits seemed paralyzed with the horror of their situation.

"You must do as Feng-Yoon commanded!" Volvolicus said, having to shout to make his voice heard above the rumbling chant and the even more horrid sounds coming from around them. Conan could not understand how they had not heard any of this ghastly cacophony while they were above.

"To the wall with them!" Layla cried.

For the first time, the priests seemed to take notice of them. Their faces looked less human than ever. They continued their chant, but their visages altered into a parody of terror. Conan leapt before the one named Shosq and thrust his sword at the priest's belly.

"Back!" Conan commanded. "Get back against the wall!"

At this, Tragthan ceased his chant. "No! You must not do this! It will be—"

But the Cimmerian was beyond hearing him. He wanted to be away from this place as he had desired few things in his life. He pushed at his hilt, forcing the priest backward a slow, reluctant step at a time.

"It cannot be!" screamed the priest. "The Lord Ahriman will take—" Then the priest's back touched the repulsively rippling wall and his face was transfigured by pain and horror. His voice rose into a prolonged howl, smoke and vile fluids shot from his mouth. The shapeless, crawling stuff of the wall began to ooze over him. Still the priest howled and bubbled.

The bandits snapped from their paralysis and rushed forward. Ubo and Chamik seized Nikas, one to each arm, and thrust him toward the wall, hurling him face-first into the unearthly, half-organic substance. It erupted into fingerlike tendrils that grasped Nikas and oozed an acidic fluid over him. As the bandits gaped, Nikas began to smoke and liquefy.

Mamos took Tragthan by the throat and shoved him back, digging at the priest's belly with the point of his dagger. "Back!" Mamos screamed with an hysterical laugh. "Back into the wall!" He pushed and Tragthan fought, resisting with the reptilian strength of a desperate python.

Layla ran to Tragthan and added her weight to that of Mamos's. Fighting at every step, the archpriest staggered back. "No! Lord Ahriman wakes! We must control his advent, else—" Then his inhuman eyes began to start from their sockets, for his back had touched the wall and he was sinking into it like a man falling into thick mud. Layla jumped back, but Tragthan's clawlike hand sank its talons deeper into the shoulder of Mamos, convulsively drawing him closer. The black substance of the wall wrapped them in thin tendrils, and Mamos's high-pitched laugh rose to a keening wail as the two figures, human and semi-human, began to melt together.

"Out!" Conan shouted. "Get out of here now!" He could take no more. Shifting his sword to his left hand, he drew his dirk with his right and hurled it, splitting the back of Mamos's skull and the brain beneath. He hoped that sudden death would spare the bandit from being absorbed into the unthinkable being of Ahriman.

Ubo and Chamik needed no urging. They rushed to the stair. Even as they bounded upward, the walls and ceiling, which had been of natural stone, began to alter, to lose their clear definition as cut stone and become something hideously other, and to glow an unhealthy green.

"Go!" Conan shouted, shoving at Volvolicus, who stood transfixed. His daughter seized an arm and began to drag him toward the metamorphosing stairway. The wizard seemed to shake off his paralysis and stumbled toward relative safety. The Cimmerian was close behind them, pushing at Volvolicus's back.

Conan's flesh crawled as he felt the steps shift and soften beneath his feet. From behind them came rushing, liquid sounds, as if the crypt were filling with thick, viscous fluids. The shrieking of the priests could still be heard above the horrid uproar; then it trailed away in choking gurgles. The walls of the stair began to ripple and contract.

Just as Conan thought he could bear no more, he and his companions burst from the stairway into the temple. Even as the Cimmerian dived head foremost through the opening, it shut behind him with a disgusting, smacking sound. He scrambled to his feet and saw that Ubo and Chamik were backing away, pointing behind him and looking even more terrified than they had down in the crypt. Behind them some sort of commotion was stirring, but Conan had no attention to spare for it. Sword still in hand, he whirled and was frozen to the spot by the horror that was rising before him.

The former altar was now in a grotesque writhing motion, the snakes transformed into squirming tentacles tipped with wetly flexing, toothless mouths, each rimmed with waving scarlet tendrils. A thicker central tentacle bore a huge, glowing eye that shone yellow and swarmed with tiny pupils. The monstrous object rose from the floor on a thick neck ridged and grooved like the rough bark of a tree. A sickening, acidic stench filled the air as an opening gaped in the forepart of the neck and belched forth glowing steam. With growing dismay, Conan realized that the disgusting mouth had been the door to the crypt. The stairway was the grotesque creature's gullet.

The Cimmerian was shaken from his horrified reverie when he understood that he was surrounded by foreign sorcerers and that they were all ignoring him, engaged as they were in casting their complex spells with strange gestures and songs and incomprehensible apparatus. Foremost among them stood Volvolicus, his arms raised and spread, eyes wild as he screamed out a powerful spell. Above them, the very stones of the temple began to shift. A round, glowing window fell from the clerestory and shattered, exploding into a mighty scarlet glare. Another huge stone fell upon the unnatural head of Ahriman, pulping several of its tentacles.

Around the lower rim of the chaotic head of the god, some of the tentacles grew and thickened, transforming into reaching arms. They groped toward the rushing figures on the temple floor. A Zamoran's spell proved inadequate protection and he was snatched up screaming and thrust into the thing's gaping maw.

Volvolicus turned and directed his spell toward one of the caryatids. Slowly, a change came over the stone woman and she began to move. Creaking, her head turned toward the god who was struggling to be born into the world of men. Her leg stretched out and she descended from her base, tearing loose the massive, blocky capital she had been supporting. A large piece of the ceiling above the capital collapsed and shattered into fragments on the floor.

The magnificent, naked giantess of marble strode toward

the monster, the floor of the temple trembling beneath her feet. She raised the heavy block of stone overhead, and the carved muscles of her back rolled powerfully as she hurled the capital into the midst of the writhing tentacles. The awful head reeled under the blow, and foul fluids gushed from the crushed tentacles. The stone woman rushed forward and grappled with the creature, the two of them swaying in an obscene embrace.

"Chief!" Ubo pleaded, tugging at Conan's tunic. "Come! This is no place for us!" A great crash made them turn. Another caryatid was stepping down from her base amid a shower of masonry.

"The whole place must come down soon!" Chamik said. "If the god does not eat us first!"

"Aye," Conan agreed. "We've no work in this place. Let us be gone." He looked around for Layla and saw her backed against a stone pedestal beneath one of the still stationary caryatids. With her arms pressed against the unyielding stone, she stared upward at the rising head of the god, the horror of the events before her finally destroying her iron nerve. Conan rushed to her side and pulled her away even as the naked stone woman above her began to move.

"Get away from there!" Conan shouted, snatching her from beneath the descending foot of the colossus. They ran from the falling blocks as the caryatid strode toward the struggling mass, the chains of marble with which she had been bound clattering against her naked thighs.

"Oh, no!" shouted Ubo. "Have we not troubles enough?" He halted in his mad race for the portal, for armed soldiers were pouring in through the now open gateway, the fanglike bars of the portcullis looming above them.

"Over here!" Conan said, punching and dragging his companions behind the vacated base of a stone giantess. "They'll pay us no notice once they see what lies before them."

Indeed, the soldiers came to a skidding halt when they saw the struggle going on at the far end of the nave. Four of the stone caryatids now grappled with the god, their glossy stone skin slimed with the sickening fluids as they tore tentacles from the unnatural thing with their hands and bit at it with teeth of marble.

"What is all this?" shouted a near-hysterical voice. "I will not have it! I must have my treasure back!" Someone pushed through the gaping mass of soldiers and strode out before them.

"What is—" Torgut Khan's jaw dropped as his eyes took in the spectacle. He scanned the gigantic room, the frantically struggling forms, the wildly gyrating figures of the magicians, who made the temple flash with the power of their spells. More of the windows fell from above, causing the light of a distant star to explode throughout the nave even as chunks of stone rained down. Unable to comprehend all he saw, Torgut Khan's eyes fastened upon Conan, still crouching behind the pedestal with his companions.

"You!" the viceroy shrieked. "You brought all this about!" He snatched a spear from a guardsman. "Die, barbarian!" With all his might, he hurled the weapon at the Cimmerian.

Even as the spear hurtled toward him, Conan was in motion not away or to one side of the weapon's path, but directly toward it. When the cruel, flesh-piercing point was only three feet from his body, Conan leaned easily aside and caught it as it passed, catching the shaft precisely at the balance-point.

"Thanks," he said as he made a half-turn and faced toward Ahriman and the stone women. His arm came up and back, balancing the ash shaft in his palm, the steel point pausing for a moment by his right ear. Then he cast the weapon with a mighty surge of his whole body, every muscle putting its force behind the weapon, every bone adding its own power of leverage.

The onlookers gazed in stupefaction as the spear flew in a high arc for the entire length of the nave, soaring for a distance no ordinary man could ever achieve. The spear reached the top of its trajectory and began to descend, seeming to pick up speed in the process. It passed over the beautiful, glossy shoulder of a marble woman and sank its full length into the evil, staring eye.

A terrible, unearthly moan resounded through the temple, its high pitch rending to the ears, its low tones shaking yet more masonry from the ravaged temple. The twisting tentacles began to change color, and thin streamers of yellow and blue lightning crawled over the monster's surface, glowing green where they crossed. A stone woman thrust one entire arm and shoulder into the thing's gaping mouth and tore out a great handful of something that resembled grayish brain tissue. She dropped the nauseating mass to the floor and reached inside for more.

Regaining control of their limbs, the soldiers whirled and fled screaming, dropping weapons and shields, knocking over and trampling upon one another, forgetting everything in their terrible, driving need to get out. They crowded into the gateway, filling it to choking. Torgut Khan was in their midst, hacking at his own men with his sword to carve himself a faster means of exit.

"Now is our chance!" Conan said. "All will be chaos outside and we can escape unnoticed."

"My father!" Layla cried, tugging at him.

"There is nothing we can do to help him," Conan said. "He will survive or he will not. We must be away."

She tried to pull back. "I will not leave him!"

With a muttered curse, Conan grasped both her wrists in one hand, stooped, and gathered her ankles in the other. He hoisted her over his shoulders and began to trot toward the gate like a shepherd returning a lost sheep to his flock.

"Women sometimes have strange moods," Ubo commiserated, running alongside the barbarian. They reached the gate just as the last of the soldiers passed through and paused outside.

"Let them spread the panic," Conan cautioned.

"Aye," said Chamik. "That is wise."

The square had filled, the townspeople awakened from

sleep and drawn to the site of the commotion. Fire-gongs were ringing all over the town, for the light flaring through the great holes in the temple roof had caused distant watchmen to think the town center was afire. The outrush of the terrified soldiers spread the panic to the gawkers as well, and the soldiers even plied their weapons against the townsfolk, stabbing and cutting down many in their frantic need to escape. Soon the uproar was general.

"There's a cool one," Ubo commented. He pointed to a tall man who was walking calmly toward the temple, ignoring the chaos around him. He began to mount the steps as if he were in his own house. Conan recognized the long black robe as Stygian, and the cadaverous features and shaven skull as belonging to the priestly caste. The man crossed the stone pave and did not glance at them as he passed within. Thoth-Amon had arrived.

"This way," Conan said. Still carrying the thrashing woman across his shoulders, he ran along the edge of the square and ducked into an alley between two buildings. With his unerring sense of direction, he led them through a warren of narrow streets, where the inhabitants were thrusting their sleep-tousled heads from windows and doorways to ask each other what was happening.

Soon they were back at the stable, where they found Auda awake, their horses saddled and ready. Conan set Layla down. "Are you prepared to act sensibly now?" She nodded silently.

"What goes on?" Auda asked. "There is uproar all over the city!"

"Heroic doings," Ubo told him. "We slew a god, but the folk are confused, so we must not tarry to await their thanks." He swung into his saddle and the others did the same.

They rode from the stable to the nearby gate, where the guards accosted them.

"Who are you? You must wait until we open the gates in the morning to leave the city! There is an emergency, do you not hear the gongs and see the fires?" The officer of the guards raised his lantern and studied them while the two sentries kept their poleaxes leveled at the riders. "I do not like the look of you. I'll warrant you are part of whatever is happening in the city. I arrest you. Dismount now or be slain!"

"Not likely," Conan growled. He drew his sword and cut the officer down. Auda thrust his lance through a sentry's throat, and Chamik swung toward the other with his axe, but the blow missed and the man ran off into the city screaming.

Ubo and Chamik scrambled from their saddles and hastened to the gate. They tried to manhandle the bar from its brackets, but their strength was not great enough to move the massive door. Conan jumped down and put his shoulder against the heavy timber, and with his powerful legs driving, they were able to open it wide enough for their horses to pass through. They remounted and rode into the night.

As they rode, Ubo and Chamik roared with laughter. "Those townsmen should be sorry to see us gone for good!" Ubo cried, wiping tears from his face with the back of his hand. "We always bring such excitement into their tedious lives! Shahpur will be but a dull place without us."

Sagobal and Berytus walked through the square, now as littered with bodies—some inert, others moving and groaning—as on the day of the disastrous festival. Gradually, townspeople were venturing back into the square, but timidly, for all was not quiet just yet. Though the temple of Ahriman was a heap of rubble, from it there still came unearthly groans and less-describable noises; flashes of strange-colored light continued to stream from between the toppled stones.

"Is there any idea what happened here?" the Aquilonian asked.

"Everyone I have spoken with is a gibbering wreck," Sagobal said. He had been deep in exhausted sleep when Torgut Khan raised his alarm, and then had taken his time about answering the summons. He decided it might be best to let someone else do the fighting for a change. By the time he and Berytus reached the scene of the night's uproar, all was long over.

"Men speak of a hideous god," Sagobal went on, "and giant women of stone wrestling with this god, and wizards by the chanting score putting on a show, and a rain of stone and flaring, flaming stars fallen from the ceiling like pots of fiery naphtha thrown down from the walls of a besieged city. It is as if half the guard had chewed black lotus and suffered a collective hallucination."

"It would not be the first time odd things have come from that temple," Berytus pointed out. Even as he spoke, a piece of red-glaring glass popped up from the wreckage and fell back to shatter into a thousand tiny, winking fragments. The crowd roundabout murmured at the show.

Sagobal saw a man seated at the edge of the square, chin on fist, gazing at the ruined temple and pondering. For some reason, the spectators kept their distance from him. Then Sagobal understood why. It was Torgut Khan.

"I must go and speak with our swine of a viceroy. Come with me. He will rail at me for tardiness and cowardice, and I will certainly lose my temper and draw my sword. Be so good as to restrain me, for I would far rather he die at the hands of the king's torturers."

"You will be fortunate to escape those hands yourself," Berytus said.

"My horses are swifter than his, and I am not as fat."

The two walked over to where Torgut Khan sat upon the lip of a fountain, his booted feet crossed in front of him, resting on the body of a dead woman. He looked up at their approach, and to Sagobal's surprise, he showed no anger or hostility.

"Ah, Commander, it is good that you have arrived. We must talk together." The viceroy heaved his bulk to his feet and placed a hand upon Sagobal's shoulder. "An eventful night, eh?"

"Most eventful, Excellency," Sagobal concurred. "And

most uncanny, if I can credit a single word of what I have heard."

"It was strange beyond imagining," Torgut Khan told him. "and you shall hear all from me by and by. But we must keep one thing in the forefront of our thoughts. With the temple collapsed, and its crypt buried beneath tons of rubble, and the very ruins now a palpably evil and unholy place, ridden with blackest sorcery, it will be impossible to get at the king's treasure, eh?" His voice was low and conspiratorial, and it carried a throaty chuckle.

"Are you well, Excellency? Surely half the town and a thousand or more visitors saw—"

"Saw *what*?" Torgut Khan barked, still keeping his voice down. "Will they say that they saw a great Stygian obelisk of chests and bags come floating from the doorway of the temple and fly off into the air? An obvious illusion! No, the treasure was safe in the crypt of the temple until this night, when it became the focus of forces beyond our ken and collapsed, torn asunder by its own evil. When the king's treasury officials arrive, this is what they must hear from us. We shall show them the ruins, and deplore our inability to secure the king's revenues."

"I understand, Excellency," Sagobal said.

"Good, good," Torgut Khan chuckled. "Now we need not be so keen in our pursuit of those wretched bandits, eh? But you must trail them anyway. Take only your hired manhunters. No need for the royal officials to wonder what has become of my personal guard."

"As you wish, Excellency," Sagobal said, seeing an even finer opportunity for himself in this new turn of events.

"You can start immediately," Torgut Khan said. "I saw the rogues here tonight."

"Is this possible. Excellency?" Sagobal said, astonished.

"Of course it is possible. Anything is possible these days!" He gestured wildly toward the rubble, from which twin beams of yellow-green shot skyward in a gigantic V. "Would you call me a liar?" Then, in a more normal voice, "When I led my guardsmen in there, I saw the black-haired barbarian, your prize trophy. He was with some three or four others. I was not so unsettled by the terrors within that temple that I would not hazard my body to avenge my honor. I cast a spear at the rogue, but some sorcerer's spell caused it to miss. After that, I was too occupied with supernatural matters to take further note of him. But I think he and his companions may have escaped."

"How so, Excellency?" Sagobal asked.

"They were near the door when I espied them, and I think they would not have tarried long in so deadly a place."

And neither did you, Sagobal thought. I'll wager you were out the door well ahead of them. He bowed. "All shall be as you wish, Excellency. I shall go to every gate of the city and find out if any such persons have sought exit. If they are still within the walls, they shall not escape. If they took advantage of the confusion to make their getaway, I shall track them down. They shall not elude me again, Excellency."

Torgut Khan smiled and clapped his guard commander's shoulder heartily. He was a reprieved man. "Good! Good! And, Sagobal . . . " his voice went low and conspiratorial again " . . . when you find them, bring them to me, eh? Only to me. To none other. We shall interrogate them personally. No need to bother the king's officials with this little matter, eh?"

"None at all, Excellency," Sagobal concurred.

"Then go, my friend, go. Catch these outlaws and bring them to me. I have some questions to ask them. Nothing concerning treasure, of course, since it never left the city."

"As you say, Excellency." Sagobal bowed and took his leave. Berytus, who had been standing at a discreet distance, rejoined him.

"There is nothing more wretched than a stupid fool who thinks himself subtle," the guard commander said.

"I'll not argue with that," answered the Aquilonian.

"The swine thinks he is playing a deep game. He would

have the treasure for himself, sharing nothing with the king, and he hopes to keep his titles and honors while doing so."

"That is an ambitious plan," said Berytus.

"Aye, and he is not the man to carry it off. Come, Aquilonian, rouse your men and mount fresh horses. We shall have the curs' trail again, and this time we will not let them go until they are dead and the treasure is in my hands!"

Fifteen

When Ubo and Chamik awoke, they found Conan already up, a brace of hares at his feet, for he had been hunting in the early light of dawn. The two bandits yawned and scratched as their chief built up their small fire, feeding it with well-dried wood and old camel-dung that burned almost without smoke. He tossed the hares to each of his companions.

"Here is breakfast," the Cimmerian said, "if you've the inclination to prepare it."

Chamik raised a beast by its long hind leg. "I think it will hold me until afternoon. We ride to the old hideout?"

"Aye, but we go the long way, taking a winding route."

"And why do we do that?" Ubo asked, making a slit with his knife in his hare's leg. He began efficiently peeling the hide away.

"Sagobal and the manhunters were not in the temple last night, nor did I see them in the throng out in the square."

"That pack of rabbit-livered townsmen were so panicked that I would scarce have noticed the king of Turan, had he been there with all his entourage," Chamik said, quartering the small carcass and spitting it on sticks of green wood.

"I would have seen them," Conan assured them. "So we may be certain that they are on our trail even now. We shall lead them a fine chase, and in these hills we know so much better than they, we shall lose them. Then we go get our treasure."

"That makes sense," Ubo said. "We can carry off plenty of gold in our bags and fare away to some place where we are not known and lie low for a while, perhaps for as much as a year. Then we can return with a whole caravan and fetch the rest. It will be easy to do, now that there are only three of us . . ." His words trailed away as he realized that something was wrong. "*Three* of us?" He looked all around. "Where is that woman? Where is Auda?"

Chamik sprang to his feet. "They have taken their horses and gone! The wench and that desert rascal have deserted! They go to take the treasure for themselves! Chief, how did you allow this to happen?"

"Sit down and get breakfast ready," Conan told them. "I hunger and we must ride soon. Layla is on an errand and it is by my orders. If you will examine her tracks, you will see that she did not ride off in the direction of our hideout. Auda has ridden back along our trail, not to erase all our signs but to ride off far to the west. With his wound, he cannot ride as swiftly as we, so he will take a shorter route and reach the hideout at about the same time."

Slowly the tension left the suspicious bandits. "Are you laying a false trail for the manhunters to follow?" Chamik asked, grinning. "That is wise, Chief. And if they catch her, that is no loss. Neither is Auda, although he has been a faithful companion. His wound has slowed our escape."

When the hares were roasted, they ate them with flat bread, hard cheese and dried dates. Thus fortified, they remounted and continued their flight, riding deeper into the maze of arid hills, unseen by any but wild ibex and other beasts of the hot land.

* * *

Torgut Khan mopped the sweat from his brow. He did not yet feel truly safe, but the examiners seemed to be satisfied for now. They had arrived in the afternoon, while the city still buzzed with the tale of the previous night's spectacular catastrophe. Contrary winds on the Vilayet had indeed delayed their voyage from the capital to Khawarism, and only this had preserved him. They inquired of the king's revenues, and he showed them the destroyed temple and told them the harrowing tale of the uncanny events that had begun with the great festival and culminated with the unholy struggle of the previous night.

He wept and tore at his hair as he related his tale, for not only was the royal revenue buried beneath accursed rubble, but he had suffered a catastrophic personal loss, having sunk so much of his own fortune into rebuilding the ancient temple to be a stronghold to guard the wealth of His Majesty whom he, Torgut Khan, had served with such splendid loyalty for his entire life.

The treasury officials might have proven suspicious, but the ruined temple was a most impressive argument in his favor. Like a great volcano that erupts mightily, then for months afterward belches occasional smoke and lava, the wreckage of the temple continued to manifest the echoes of its sorcerous demise. Hideous sounds came from within at intervals. Uncanny lights, visible even in daylight, shone out from time to time. Bits of masonry flew upward as high as the surrounding rooftops, to fall back and shatter.

Clearly, Torgut Khan explained, it would be many years before anyone could be induced to excavate for the treasure that, he assured them, still lay beneath the rubble. They seemed to be satisfied for the moment.

Torgut Khan snapped his fingers and a slave girl poured wine into a jeweled cup. He sipped at it and pondered. Now that his immediate danger was past, he could think clearly again. He realized that his conviction of the night before had been a delusion of his overwrought mind. The treasure had indeed been spirited away on the day of the festival. So where was it? Sagobal was undoubtedly upon the trail of the outlaws, but should he track them to the treasure, would he report back to Torgut Khan?

Ere now, the viceroy had depended desperately upon his guard commander. Should he do so now? But what else could he do? He had no trackers to match the ones employed by Sagobal. It was most frustrating.

He was startled when something flew through his window and landed clinking on the floor. His first sensation was rage. Was some townsman expressing contempt in this crude fashion? He was about to call for the guards when he saw what it was: a flat, roughly circular pellet of lead about three fingers in width, stamped with his personal seal. Each of the chests and bags stored within the crypt had borne such a seal.

"Leave me," he said to the slave woman. She bowed and left quickly. Torgut Khan rose and walked to the center of the room, where he bent and picked up the seal. It was still fastened to bits of leather thong. Obviously, it had been used to secure one of the leather sacks of silver.

"Whoever you are out there on the terrace," he said, "come in here. I wish to talk to you."

A man walked in through the long window. He placed spread fingers against his breast and bowed. "Greetings, most mighty Viceroy Torgut Khan. The one you see before you is your obedient servant, Osman of Shangara."

"Speak very quickly, Osman of Shangara, for I am a man of little patience." He held up the seal. "How came you by this? Are you a member of the outlaw band who stole my treasure?"

"More accurately, Master, I was the agent of Sagobal. He placed me within the prison to aid in the barbarian's escape and lead him and all the others back to Shahpur so, he explained, he might bag the lot. I assure you, I believed him to be serving you faithfully."

"I am sure. And so you took part in the raid?"

"I did."

"And you know where the treasure is concealed?"

"I do."

"Then tell me."

"That would be useless. It is deep within the warren of hills to the south of the city. Words describing the location and route would mean nothing. But I can lead you there."

"Splendid!" Torgut Khan said, his elation rising. "You will do so immediately."

"Ah, well, my lord, there are certain matters we must discuss first. Sagobal promised to reward me richly for my faithful and most hazardous service. However, I no longer deem him to be a man of honor and I deeply suspect him to be plotting against you, seeking to seize the whole treasure for himself."

"Never mind that," Torgut Khan said. "It is not for one such as you to judge your betters. But I am not ungenerous. Lead me to the treasure and I will reward you with the fiftieth part of it."

"My lord is kind," Osman said. "But even as a bandit, I would have had the twentieth part of it."

"The tenth part of the treasure then, damn you!" Torgut Khan said, sorely vexed. "That is more than you would ever be able to steal in your entire villainous life!"

Osman smiled and bowed deeply. "I am my lord's obedient servant."

"They have split up," Berytus reported. "They have made some attempt to cover their tracks, but not sufficient to fool my trackers."

"Does that not itself make you suspicious?" Sagobal asked. "Perhaps they lead us to ambush."

"Perhaps, but they have lost all but one of their desert men, and that one is wounded. Several times we have found bloodstains near tracks of the horse shod desert-fashion. It is not the horse's blood. Ambula can tell the difference by the taste. The desert men were the ones sweeping their tracks before, and they made our task difficult. There are no more than five of them left, one of them a woman."

"So," Sagobal said. "Four men left, one of them wounded."

"Aye. We are six, all of us fighting-men of the first order. Let them try an ambush. Of the lot, only the Cimmerian could give us an amusing fight."

"Very well. Will you split your men and follow all of them?"

"No. The woman went south. The wounded desert man went west. The barbarian and the other two rode on together. We follow the barbarian."

"Then let us ride," Sagobal said, setting his spurs to his horse's flanks.

Conan and his two companions spent three days riding among the hills, taking a dizzying path that crossed and recrossed itself many times. In some places, they were at pains to cover their tracks. At others, they made no such attempt. There were places where the Cimmerian led them over broad stretches of stone, leaving no marks discernible to the eye of an ordinary man. In others, they rode heedlessly over sandy ground, leaving behind them deep, plain hoofprints. By the morning of the fourth day, his comrades had had enough.

"By Set!" Chamik said over their breakfast fire. "We have laid a trail a desert tracker aided by hounds could not follow! Let us go to our hideout, Chief!"

"Aye," Ubo agreed, rubbing his sore backside. "I did not become a bandit in order to toil like this."

"As you will," Conan said. "We go. Mount up." Grinning and rubbing their palms in greedy glee, the bandits did as they were bidden.

They rode for the rest of the day and as evening descended, they came to the small canyon with its cool, spring-fed pool. As they approached, they saw a robed figure seated by the pool, his horse cropping grass behind him.

"There is Auda!" Chamik said. He kicked his horse into a trot.

"Hold!" Conan called. "I do not like—"

But Chamik seemed not to hear him. "Auda!" he called. His mouth was still open when a steel-barbed shaft entered it and pierced the roof of his mouth to stand out the breadth of a palm from the back of his skull.

Even as the bandit toppled from his saddle, the Cimmerian was in motion. He dove from his horse and rolled into the brush. Arrows pursued him, but he was gone as swiftly and silently as a desert snake.

Ubo, who rode fifty paces behind the Cimmerian, wheeled his mount and spurred away, leaning low over the horse's back. An arrow struck the rear of his saddle, but then he was around a bend of the canyon and out of sight.

"Forget the bandit!" called a voice with an Aquilonian accent. "He'll run until he gets to Khawarism or farther. It is the barbarian we want. Secure his horse."

Conan's body worked like an oiled machine as he crawled among the bushes and rocks. Had any been able to see him, he would have resembled a serpent crawling upon its belly, but this would have been deceptive, for only his fingertips and the sides of his feet touched the ground. Thus he kept low and made no sound. He knew the men after him were exceptional trackers, but Conan of Cimmeria had evaded Pictish trackers in their own forests. Even this semi-desert furnished cover for such a man as he.

"You may as well surrender, Cimmerian," Berytus shouted. "Your desert man furnished us some amusement, but he was weakened by his wound and did not last long. Come and tell us where you hid the treasure and spare yourself much suffering."

Conan did not allow himself to be distracted. If the man wanted to boast, let him. Darkness was coming on, and darkness would be of more aid to Conan than an army.

"You did not fool me with your stupid maneuvers and false trails, Cimmerian," Berytus called. "Once I saw what you were doing, we rode here and waited. I was here on our first pursuit, when you ran into Iranistan. I could see even then that this was where you planned to load the treasure on camels, but the villagers took their camels back, so you hid your illegal gains here and rode on. When your desert man rode in, I knew it had to be true. So come in, Conan. The sport is over and this grows tedious."

The man might be given to bragging, Conan knew, but more likely he was trying to hold the Cimmerian's attention while his minions sought to encircle him. He crawled to an overhanging ledge of rock concealed behind a clump of brush. This might be a good spot to wait for darkness. He crawled within and as his eyes adjusted to the dimness, he saw that he was not alone in favoring the spot. An evil-eyed viper lay coiled in the shade, regarding him without favor. The reptile struck, but Conan's teeth snapped down upon its head, crushing it. He remained still while the ropy body thrashed about. After many minutes, the dead snake stopped its struggles and Conan let it fall from his mouth.

The ledge was just broad enough to accommodate his body. With arms pulled in tightly and feet drawn up as much as was feasible, he was hidden from view, and the heavy brush completed his concealment. Once he heard stealthy feet pass near by, but he could tell from the sound that the tracker had not noticed his lair. He was certain that he had left no mark of his passing from the instant he had dived from his saddle. No horse could travel without leaving some slight traces behind, and very few men could do better, but Conan could traverse even soft ground and leave no more sign of it than a moonbeam.

"I like this not," Sagobal said. "It grows fully dark, and your supposed experts have not found a single blundering barbarian who has to be concealed no more than a hundred paces from this spot." The two men stood by their fire while Berytus's four remaining trackers hunted for the Cimmerian.

"He is as well-schooled in the hunting arts as any man I have ever encountered," Berytus admitted. "I myself examined where he threw himself from his saddle into the brush.

Not a mark where he landed." The manhunter shook his head. "He must have been taught by Picts. But how can that be? The Cimmerians and the Picts are deadly enemies."

"Ordinary Cimmerians also do not fare to Turan and steal treasure," Sagobal said. "But this one did."

They turned to see Urdos of Koth approaching. The huge man had a scowl upon his black-bearded face. "Not a sign of him, Chief. It is as if he—" The Kothian had no opportunity to finish what he had to say. A pale shape rushed up behind him and on into the outer darkness. There was a flash and a smacking crunch, and a great look of surprise came over the face of Urdos. He stood still for a moment, then toppled stiffly and lay on his face, unmoving. His spine had been halved.

"Barca! Ambula! Bahdur!" shouted Berytus. "To me! The Cimmerian dog has killed Urdos!"

Conan crouched behind a rock, waiting. He had heard the Shemite, and he knew from the sound of the sandaled feet where the man had to be heading . . . clearly, he hastened to rejoin his chief, but his steps were cautious. The Shemites were at their best when mounted, but this one had no choice save to dismount when he pursued the wily Cimmerian.

Conan saw a trousered leg pass in front of him and he sprang. The Shemite tried to bring his arrow to bear, but he was far too late. The Cimmerian's brawny arm pinned his arms to his sides while with his other hand, Conan rammed his sword through the man's body from side to side. The Shemite made a strangled cry, and Conan lowered him to the ground, wrenching his sword from the body with a wet sound.

He was straightening from his crouch when Ambula of Punt fell upon him. Even as he jerked around to evade the first thrust of the spear, Conan was forced to admire the stealth with which the brown man had come upon him. The keen ears of the northerner had never detected a sound. The second thrust would have spitted him, but Conan batted it aside with his sword. It was a desperation move, for it made noise the Cimmerian had wished to avoid.

"Berytus!" Ambula shouted, "He is here!" The cry distracted the man of Punt and caused him to lose the coordination of his attack. Conan feinted high at his head, and Ambula raised his spear to deflect the blow. The blade made a lightning change of direction, flashing beneath the Punt's spear, slicing off both arms just below the elbows. Before the man could even scream his dismay, another blow took his head off.

Conan did not have time to feel satisfaction, for a scraping sound made him whirl about. In the dimness he saw the Hyrkanian fifteen paces away, drawing his bow. Before Conan could move, something bulked up behind the Hyrkanian and a knife flashed, severing the bowstring and the archer's windpipe and jugular in a single sweep of razor-edged steel.

"I do not understand," Ubo said, wiping his blade on the man's coat, "why these hunting dogs think they are the only ones who know how to handle themselves in the dark." He resheathed the knife.

"By Crom, I never thought I would be glad to see *your* ugly face!"

"Ambula!" Berytus shouted. "Barca! Bahdur!" There was no sound from the surrounding darkness. He turned to Sagobal. "I heard steel. I heard Ambula call. Now I hear nothing. They are dead."

Sagobal spat in disgust. "So much for your great band of manhunters! How does it feel, knowing yourself bested by a barbarian outlaw chief?"

"He has yet to slay me," Berytus said coldly. "As for the men, I can always find more. Meanwhile, I will slay him with my own hand." He turned and began to stride away.

"Where are you going, coward?" Sagobal called.

Berytus did not turn around. "Out of the firelight. He has two bows now."

Sagobal almost fell in his haste to get away from the light.

* * *

"There they are!" Ubo whispered. The two lay on the reverse slope of a small ridge, peering over into the little canyon. Their faces were smeared with dust, and with the sun rising behind them, the pair in the canyon below could not descry them. "Will you hazard a cast? I was no bowman even when I had two good eyes."

"No," said Conan. "I can shoot, but no man can use an unfamiliar bow effectively. I've not had the leisure to practice with this one."

"Then what do we do?" Ubo said. "We could just go down and fight them, but a man could get hurt that way."

"We wait," said Conan.

"Wait for what?"

"I think I hear someone now," Conan said. In the distance they could hear a drumming of hooves.

"Who could this be?" Ubo said.

"Watch."

The men below them whirled at the sound, clearly alarmed. Then the first riders came into the canyon. They wore the heavy equipment of Torgut Khan's guardsmen. Among them was Torgut Khan himself. Beside the viceroy rode a smaller man.

"By Set!" Ubo swore. "It's that rogue, Osman!"

"Aye," said Conan. "I knew he would be along soon, trying to play all sides against all others, as usual. We are fortunate they did not get here earlier. But that fat swine Torgut Khan cannot ride fast, and I'll warrant Osman got lost a time or two leading him here. He does not know this country well. Come, this should be enjoyable." With that, the Cimmerian slid down the reverse slope. Confused, Ubo followed.

"Viceroy," Sagobal cried, enraged but under control. "How came you here?"

"This man led me," Torgut Khan said. "Now explain yourself!"

"You listened to Osman, eh? The treacherous little swine

led us into an ambush at the home of the wizard. What game does he play now? We tracked the bandits to this place and have fought them all night. At least one of them is still alive, although he will not be for long. I believe that the—" An abrupt gesture from Torgut Khan silenced him. The viceroy dismounted and walked up to him.

"Osman says he knows where the treasure is hidden," Torgut Khan whispered. "Let us determine if he is telling the truth, then we will discuss this further."

Sagobal saluted. "Very well." He turned to Berytus. "Aquilonian, stay you here with the guards. Osman, come with us."

Berytus shrugged, as if washing his hands of the matter. Grinning and bowing, Osman stepped out before them. "If you will follow me, gentlemen."

As they walked, Sagobal kept his eyes sweeping the heights. He knew that he could easily dodge an arrow shot from a distance. It was only when arrows fell in storms, or came from the dark or from behind, that they were truly dangerous. Should one be shot at Torgut Khan, that was no concern of his.

But none attacked them, and they came to a tiny side-canyon where Osman scrambled up the slope and tore at some stones. His labors revealed a natural cave well concealed by nature, and he gestured grandly toward its entrance. "Behold! Within is a painted cave, wherein resides the stolen treasure, of which you, Viceroy, have promised me a tenth part."

Sagobal drew his sword and held its point beneath Osman's chin. "You go in first, jackal! I remember the last place you led me to."

Osman held out a hand for calm. "Of a certainty, Master, but remember . . . I am under Torgut Khan's protection now, and he has many armed men with him."

"Go in," Sagobal said coldly.

Osman scrambled in through the gap and all was still. Then they heard a great cry from within.

"What is it?" Torgut Khan shouted.

"It is gone!" Osman wailed. "Every chest and sack of it, every last coin—gone!"

"What?" Sagobal exclaimed. The two pushed their way through the opening and stood inside. The morning sunlight flooding in revealed a cave with strangely painted walls and ceiling, but no treasure.

"You see the marks on the floor!" Osman cried desperately. "That is where we stacked it all! But it is gone! Believe me, Masters! I do not lie to you!" He began to back toward the entrance as Sagobal came toward him, sword in hand. Osman turned and rushed out, the guard commander close behind him. Before he was ten paces down the slope, Sagobal bounded upon him like a tiger.

"You have tricked me for the last time!" Sagobal shouted, slashing Osman across the back of both knees so that he could not run. "I curse the day I took you from prison!" He slashed a hand off. "I curse the mother that bore you!" Off came the other hand. "Here is the reward you asked for!" A huge vertical slash opened Osman's body from neck to belly, exposing bone and viscera, but inflicting no mortal wound. Osman screamed and gibbered, beyond coherent speech.

A great laugh erupted behind them. Sagobal turned. Torgut Khan, just emerging from the painted cave, did likewise. Upon the slope above them stood Conan of Cimmeria. His sword was bare in his hand and he regarded them with supreme mockery.

"Are these the mighty ones who sent me to prison and wanted to make a show of me in their festival?" He laughed uproariously. "These are but fools whom I have toyed with these many days!"

Sagobal could stand no more. With a howl of inchoate rage, he charged up the slope at the Cimmerian who had made such a shambles of his careful plan. Curved blade and straight clashed, rang, clashed again. Both men were fine swordsmen, but Conan's was the greater weight and reach of arm. He began to inflict small wounds, then greater ones, while remaining himself unharmed. At last a low cut brought Sagobal to the ground, then another made him drop his sword from his nerveless hand. The guard commander squalled in rage, but Conan placed a foot against him and rolled him down the slope. He came to rest atop the body of Osman, who was still conscious and howled at this new assault.

"I wish you two the joy of one another's company," Conan said. "You both may last until midnight, if the hyenas do not get you first."

"Asura, Conan!" said Ubo, gaping. "But you are a man who takes his revenge seriously!"

"Aye. Where is Torgut Khan?"

"He ran off that way." Ubo pointed in the direction of the pond. "Well, what *did* happen to the treasure?"

"When we rode from that mining village and the rest of you traveled on to the wizard's house," Conan explained, "I rode back here to make sure Osman had not come hither to try to make off with the treasure. He had not, but I knew that he might do so at any time. So I moved it all."

"Moved it?" Ubo said. "Where?"

"To the pond. It is all there, under the water. It took me a day and a night to shift it all, then cover up my tracks."

Ubo scratched his shaven head in wonder. "I have never liked the idea of hard labor, but I suppose such treasure is worth it. What do we do now, Chief?"

"We see what happens next," Conan said. "Come on."

The two rushed to another vantage point, this one overlooking the pond. Torgut Khan, still puffing from his run, was bawling at his troops to search the area for a dangerous Cimmerian. The men milled about, confused by his half-coherent orders.

"More riders coming," said Ubo, his face a study in puzzlement. "Who might this be?"

From the southern defile, another pack of horsemen rode into the canyon. They were a tough, ragged lot, utterly unlike the polished troopers of the viceroy's guard.

"Wait!" Ubo cried. "Is that not the officer who thought he could give me orders?"

"Aye," Conan said. "Captain Hosta, of the Iranistani rebels. And there is Idris, the young claimant to the throne."

"How did *they* get here?" Ubo asked. Then he saw Layla riding among them. "Oh. I see."

"I sent her to fetch them," said Conan. "I knew we would soon have more of a fight on our hands than we could readily deal with, since Osman was still at large. Torgut Khan was the only one left for him to use. Give me the bow."

Ubo handed him the weapon and Conan sighted on a trooper. Unused to the bow and its arrows, he missed his first shot, came closer with the second, and with the third, he brought a man down from his saddle. By this time all below was a whirling melee. Troopers and rebels cut and thrust at one another, sword and lance licking out with deadly effect. The rebels had greater numbers, the troopers superior armor and weapons.

"It is too much to hope that they will all slay each other," Ubo said. "Why are you helping the rebels?"

"Because it is Torgut Khan I want to destroy," Conan said. When he had shot his last arrow, he rushed down the hill and joined the fight. A blow from his sword emptied a saddle and he replaced the rider.

Hewing his way into the mass of struggling men, he bellowed, "Torgut Khan! Show yourself, you swine!" Then he saw the man, frantically trying to keep his guards between himself and these unexpected strangers. Conan bulled his way through and forced Torgut Khan's horse back into the water.

"Barbarian!" Torgut Khan cried. "Are you immortal?"

"Nay," said Conan, batting aside the viceroy's ineffectual defense. "And neither are you!" His sword swept across Torgut Khan's fat body, shearing armor, flesh and bone alike. With a scream, the viceroy fell from his saddle and floated facedown upon the water of the pond, which was growing crowded with corpses. The last sight Torgut Khan's eyes beheld, filtered through the billowing red stain of his own blood, was a great heap of chests and bags resting upon the bottom of the pond.

The crashing and the shouting died down. The forces of the rebels were depleted, but the troopers of Torgut Khan were annihilated. Bodies were strewn everywhere, and wounded men lay on the ground or sagged in their saddles, groaning.

"Be sure that none have escaped!" said General Eltis, the pretender's cousin.

"Yes!" cried young Idris. "We cannot risk bad relations with Turan. As far as the king is concerned, Torgut Khan and his guards disappeared!" Then he noticed Conan and smiled. "Greetings, Captain! This woman tells me that you have something for us."

"That I have," said Conan. "You shall have to dredge the pond for it, but it is all down there."

"Hey!" Ubo ran up behind Conan. "You are not going to let them take it all, are you? By Set, but we deserve our share!"

Idris looked at his cousin. "General, did this man not desert my service, and does he not deserve hanging?"

"That is the proper punishment, my liege," Eltis said, nodding.

"What!" Ubo said indignantly. "You would call yourself a king and treat me thus, when I have brought you all this great treasure?"

Idris smiled. "Nay, you are safe enough as long as you stay out of my kingdom, but a bandit like you should be grateful he is allowed to breathe, and not trouble kings for further reward." He looked at Conan. "But if the treasure is what this woman claims, I will give you one chest of the gold."

"Majesty," Eltis protested, "you are too generous. A handful of dinars should suffice such rogues as these."

"Nay, I would not have men deem me unkingly. A chest of gold."

"As you wish," Eltis said, looking pained.

"My liege!" called Captain Hosta. "What shall I do with this one?" He pointed to a circle of horsemen who held lances lowered at Berytus of Aquilonia. "He took no part in the fighting, and he is not Turanian."

"Is he one of yours?" Idris asked.

"He is the hired dog of Sagobal," said Layla, reining up. "He led his pack of jackals to attack my father's house and he has dogged our trail since we seized the treasure."

"Kill him, then," Idris said.

"Wait!" Berytus shouted. "I claim right of vengeance!"

"Vengeance for what, dog?" Conan said contemptuously. "I never sought a fight with you. It was you who accepted Sagobal's pay to track me down. I slew your men because they hunted me, and no man can do that and live!"

"You think I care about them? I want vengeance for Venarium!"

"Venarium?" Idris said. "I have heard that name. Was it not a great battle in the far north, many years ago?"

"Not so many years," Berytus said bitterly. "The king of Aquilonia founded a colony upon land north of the Bossonian marshes and my kin were among the settlers. The wild tribesmen of the Cimmerian hills fell upon us and wrought a great slaughter. All my family were slain."

"Your king planted his colony on the ancestral lands of our clans!" Conan said. "It was our right to throw the trespassers out. It was my first battle. Though I had seen only fifteen winters, I slew many—Aquilonians, Bossonians and Gundermen. But it was battle, not ambush or treacherous assault. No man can claim vengeance for defeat in a fair and open fight."

"I was a boy as well," Berytus said. "And when the fighting was over, I was sold as a slave."

"That is a lie!" Conan shouted. "Cimmerians do not keep slaves, nor do they sell prisoners to traders. When the slaying was over, we went back to our hills and took naught with us but our dead and wounded."

"All was not over with the fighting," Berytus said. "For months after the battle, slavers rode through the countryside, rounding up refugees and driving them to the slave markets. Most were women and children, for few men escaped death at the hands of the black-haired wolves from the north. I toiled as a slave, but I had too much spirit to work the land. I earned my freedom as a pit-fighter, and ever since, I have made my way as a fighting-man and hunter. And never have I ceased to thirst for vengeance upon the Cimmerians. I was quick to take Sagobal's offer when I learned that the leader of the bandits was one such. I have hunted many men in my time, but never a member of that accursed race."

"Aye, and you hunted me to your sore cost."

"This is foolish, this talk of old battles and vengeance," Layla said. "Slay him."

"No!" Conan said. "He is an evil jackal who hunts down fleeing slaves and desperate men, but I'll not say he lacks courage. And he has some justice in his claim. Draw your steel, Aquilonian. You and I shall fight Venarium all over again."

"This is insane!" Layla said. "You have already won!"

"This is extraordinary!" exclaimed Idris.

"Aye," said Eltis. "Perhaps they will slay one another. That will save us a chest of gold."

The rebels drew back in a wide semicircle facing the pond. Within this cleared space the two northerners drew their swords and cast away their sheaths. Then they circled one another slowly, each seeking an advantage before hazarding a blow. They were well matched in size and weight. Berytus was somewhat bulkier, Conan a bit longer of arm and leg. Except for the Aquilonian's steel cap and the plating on his hands and forearms, neither was armored.

The two feinted a few times, feeling each other out. Then Berytus shuffled in, his feet flat, sending a flurry of cuts at the Cimmerian's head and body. Conan was forced to give ground, defending himself without opportunity to counterattack. The manhunter wielded his broad, curved sword in a quick series of short, powerful chops, keeping his armored forearms close to his body. Conan recognized the style. It had been perfected in the fighting-pits and was ideal for combat within confined quarters.

Conan jumped back a pace and sent a flurry of blows toward the head of his opponent, forcing the man to cease his own attack. Berytus fended the blows with his sword or batted them aside with his hand-plates.

Simultaneously, the two men sprang apart. Both were breathing heavily and sweating profusely. They had taken one another's measure, and the next exchange would be the final one. The spectators maintained utter silence as the two deadly combatants paused. Berytus was tense, every muscle coiled. Conan was almost relaxed.

Then the two sprang together and the blows rained too fast for those watching to follow. Steel rang on steel in a continuous clatter that sounded like all the armorers in a workshop hammering at once. They advanced and retreated until they were in the pond, fighting in water almost to their knees. The clashing of steel silenced for long seconds as the two hilts locked and the men pushed at one another, muscles straining, the breath wheezing from their lungs as from a cracked bellows.

Then there was a convulsive spasm of flesh and steel. Conan's sword twisted down, the plated hand of Berytus flashed out. There were meaty smacks of metal on flesh. Then Conan staggered back, blood streaming from four long, parallel furrows in his face where the spikes over Berytus's knuckles had ripped the skin bone-deep.

The Aquilonian lurched forward, trying to follow up the terrible blow with more of the same, but his arms and his feet would not obey his will. Conan had released the hilt of his sword, and the blade remained thrust through the Aquilonian's body, the crossguard tight against his belly, two feet of bloody steel protruding from his back.

"Curse you for a Cimmerian swine," Berytus said. Then he toppled and splashed his full length into the bloody water. Conan walked over to the corpse and tore his sword free. He dipped the shining steel into the water to cleanse it of blood and flesh.

"Crom," Conan said, "but that one was a worthy enemy!

Had he not been an evil, murdering hyena, I would send him off with a fine funeral."

"Splendid!" Idris cried. Eltis looked less pleased, for now he was out a chest of gold.

For the rest of the day, the rebels toiled to bring up the treasure. Men dived into the blood-fouled water and secured ropes to the chests; then the ropes were snubbed to saddle pommels and the heavy treasure was dragged ashore. Other men waded out with leather bags of silver upon their shoulders.

"It is even greater than the woman described," Idris said, full of elation. "With such treasure at my disposal, all of northern Iranistan will flock to my cause. I will drive the usurper from the throne!" His men cheered lustily.

"Conan," Idris continued, "you have been of good service to me, although I would not truly care to see you within my borders again. Choose a chest and take it. It is yours."

Conan selected a chest, and hoisted it to his shoulder and carried it to the place where his horse was picketed. Ubo had ridden out and rounded up the beast after the fight with Berytus. Now the bandit sat on the ground, disconsolate.

"So we have a single chest and the rebels have everything else. What is the good of that?"

"We could have nothing," Conan said. The blood had dried on his face, but his cheek looked as if a tiger had swiped a paw across it. "Have you ever stolen as much as lies in this chest?"

"Nay, not in my whole career."

"Then do not complain. The world is full of gold, and a man of spirit can help himself to it."

An hour later the treasure was packed up and the rebels were gone, riding back toward Iranistan. They had taken their own dead, but the manhunters and Torgut Khan's troopers lay where they had fallen. Jackals and hyenas prowled the heights, and even a rare desert lion made an appearance. The air was thick with vultures.

"Let us go," Conan said. The two strapped their chest to a

trooper's horse that Idris had allowed them and they mounted. They rode to the other side of the lake, where Layla was speaking with a new arrival.

"I rejoice to see you alive, Volvolicus," Conan said. "Ordinarily I do not like wizards, but you have been a faithful companion, even though you were carrying out your own scheme with that accursed temple and all those foreign mages. Is the thing dead?"

"It never dies," replied the wizard, who had no horse, yet had arrived dressed in spotless white robes. Conan was not inclined to ask him how he had accomplished the feat. "But it will not try to be reborn for another thousand years, or perhaps ten thousand, or a hundred thousand."

"Then I'll not concern myself further," said the Cimmerian. "You were one of our band. The gold is not as much as we took, but you are welcome to your share of it."

The wizard shook his head. "I need no gold. I have been elevated to the First Rank, and such a one need never concern himself with worldly matters."

"Farewell to you then," Conan said and turned to Layla. "You were more than capable in the doings of these past days. Will you ride on with us?"

She smiled. "Nay, this has been a glorious adventure, but I stay with my father. He has much yet to teach me and I think your wild life would pall on me before long. Goodbye, Cimmerian."

"Farewell to you both then." Conan saluted, wheeled his mount and trotted away, followed closely by Ubo, who led their packhorse.

The two men rode for a number of hours until they were out of the hills and upon the edge of the great desert, laced with its caravan trails linking the rare water holes.

"Where to now, Chief?" Ubo asked.

Conan pointed a finger due west. "Over there lies a city called Zamboula. It is a wicked place, and it welcomes men with gold and does not ask how they got it. If the water holes are full, we can be there in ten or twelve days."

Ubo scratched his chin. "That sounds a congenial place. This chest of gold holds a year's income for a good-sized town. In such a city as you describe, it might last us for a month or more! And then we can round up another band of robbers, for wicked cities are always full of men who want gold and know better than to toil for it."

"Aye," Conan said. "To Zamboula!" Laughing, the two men rode away from the hills of Turan. Behind them, the vultures circled.